THE

Kaleidoscope Season

THE

Kaleidoscope Season

A NOVEL

Sharon Downing Jarvis

DESERET
BOOK

SALT LAKE CITY, UTAH

Visit us at deseretbook.com

Library of Congress Cataloging-in-Publication Data

Jarvis, Sharon Downing, 1940–
    The kaleidoscope season/Sharon Downing Jarvis.
        p.   cm.
    ISBN 0-87579-568-4
    I. Title.

PS3560.A64K35   1992
813'.54—dc20   91-43131
                                                               CIP

Printed in the United States of America   72076-7120
Publishers Printing, Salt Lake City, UT

10   9   8   7   6   5   4

To all my dear ones, past and present,
especially my parents,
John and Maggie Downing,
who taught me to read
and encouraged me to write.

W hen I look back, it seems to me that everything began to change the summer before I turned twelve. People, places, and events all kaleidoscoped into a whirl of changing colors and patterns, brilliant but precarious. And just when I thought I had everything in focus, someone would tap the kaleidoscope again, ever so gently, and with a faint tinkle the colored bits would readjust themselves into a new pattern. I tried to do the same.

I spent a lot of time listening that summer — to friends, family, and the words in books. Mostly I listened to Granna, who somehow seemed to take on a lot of substance in those three months, as did Star and Miss Mary Afton and Uncle Bob and a few other people. It was as if all my life I had been looking at one of those old 3-D movies and had finally thought to put on the flimsy magic glasses that turn the blurry screen images into real, breathing people, ready to step down and touch you.

Maybe it was all due to the fact that I was nearly twelve. Granna seemed to think that being nearly twelve made a lot of difference — or ought to, anyway. "Emily Jean," she would say, "now that you're nearly twelve, I certainly think you'd be able to keep your hair combed." Or, "Now that you're nearly twelve, it's not wise to play out after dark or walk home alone. After all, you never know." Just what it was I never knew, I never knew. I wondered sometimes, when the kaleidoscope had shifted again, that if being nearly twelve was this confusing, what would the real thing be like? I had until October thirty-first, that year of 1948, to find out, and I was in no hurry.

By then, I would have been in seventh grade—junior high school—for two whole months, and that thought conjured up whole flocks of butterflies in my stomach. Junior high girls were known to be interested in wearing heels and lipstick and foundation undergarments and such, and they haunted the corner Rexall store for interests other than ice cream and comic books, and they chattered about clothes and movies and boys. Well, movies were fine, although I couldn't see much point in collecting shoe boxes full of movie-star pictures as Star's older sisters had done. I felt clothes ought to be comfortable more than anything else, and as for boys—well, all the ones I knew would have to undergo some whopping changes before I'd get all giggly and excited about them! I knew them too well—Arnie Blalock, Fred Silver, Junior Bailey, and their ilk. There'd been too many spitball fights through the years, too many warm summer evenings of hide-and-seek and softball and any-eye-over, and too much teasing and tattling and hair pulling for me to get all quivery over them. So obviously I wasn't ready for junior high.

I had been quite happy in the sixth grade at J. J. Audubon School in Tatum, Georgia, and had no desire to leave, although the closing exercises that year were nearly enough to give me that desire. At Granna's insistence, I had sat through two hours of ruffled-organdy torment, listening to the presentation of awards. I nearly got the language arts award, but Sally Ann Compton had turned in ten extra book reports. I could have doubled that if I'd known, and they'd have been better books too!

Our principal, Mrs. Spearman, then made her farewell remarks to departing sixth graders, telling us moistly what wonderful "buoys and gulls" we were (she'd never said that before!), and how we must always remember and appreciate what our dear teachers had tried to do for us (that was more like it), and that we must take every opportunity to learn and reach higher and higher, setting our sights on the stars, building on the firm foundation of these, our formative years, but never being content with the present, and realizing that the past can never return, going ever forward and upward. She practically inspired us out of our seats. In fact, I did see one paper airplane soaring higher and ever higher.

Finally, after Arnie Blalock read his poem, "Thanks to Our Teachers Dear" (which I knew for a fact his mother had written), and Starlett Hargrave played "Meditation" on the piano, and the Reverend Mr. Blackthorn from the Presbyterian Church said a prayer, we were free to soar.

I couldn't even take off. I hadn't remembered to sit down carefully with my dress tucked under, as Granna had taught me, and the backs of my sweaty legs had stuck to the tacky varnish of the auditorium seat.

"Move, Knowles," growled Bobby Joe Pruitt.

"Yeah, Red, what's holdin' up the train?" added Junior Bailey.

"Y'all go on by," I mumbled, tucking my feet under the chair. "I'm waiting for Star." I didn't much mind Junior calling me "Red" because his hair was twice as red as mine, and he was freckled as a bullfrog. But I didn't take it from anyone else.

Carefully I detached my skin from the seat and edged toward the aisle, trailing my fingers along the hand-carved graffiti on the chair backs: "Gus loves Gail," "Marilyn and Tommy, 1939," "I hate sch —," and one spot where some well-meaning citizen had recently added an "O" to a rudely scratched "Hell." I looked around. The place had cleared of both students and faculty in nothing flat. Star gathered her music at the old baby grand with its cracked finish, as I waited in the aisle, watching the afternoon sun filter through the bent green Venetian blinds and play upon the dust motes trying to settle after the exodus.

Star came down from the stage, her kitten face serious under brown bangs. Her dress was white — bouffant nylon with puffed sleeves and a tie sash — and like everything else she wore, it seemed two sizes too large for her, making her look younger and smaller than she was. Actually, she was thirteen months older than I was, but an earlier bout with rheumatic fever had kept her out of school for a year. She was considered frail, and this, along with her big green eyes and serious expression, made nearly everyone feel pro-

. . . . 3 . . . .

tective toward her. Even the boys didn't chase and tease her quite as much as they did the rest of us, so being her best friend sometimes afforded me a degree of protection too.

And Granna encouraged our friendship. "Well-bred," she said of Star. "All the Hargrave girls are well-bred. You could take a leaf out of her book, Emily Jean."

"Did it sound all right?" Star asked anxiously as she approached. "Could you tell all the mistakes I made?"

"It was really good," I told her. "I wish I could play like that." The truth was, I was still thumping out "Lily Pad Waltz" and the simplified version of "What a Friend We Have in Jesus" while she was playing all the hymns for our Sunday School Department with appropriate trills and flourishes.

"Oh, Emily Jean, why do you say that? You play good too."

"Well, if you think so." I laughed, knowing she was trying to make me feel good. "Come on, I have to go out to the classroom to get the rest of my stuff."

"I'll go with you. Maybe Miss Mary Afton's still there, and we can say good-bye again, just us."

Our sixth-grade classroom was located in a temporary wooden structure adjacent to the main brick building. There were three such classrooms, fading into shabby permanence as funds for a real addition to the school continued to be channeled elsewhere.

"I hope she's here," Star whispered, as we mounted the worn steps. Miss Mary Afton MacDougal wasn't our real teacher. She served as a teacher's aide to the fifth- and sixth-grade teachers, taking over such duties as supervising recess and lunch, grading some of the papers, putting up bulletin boards, tutoring, and doing whatever else either teacher would rather not do. To say that we loved her was far below the truth; she was patient and friendly, and she managed to give us, without undue praise, a sense of our personal worth. What's more, she was beautiful. Even the boys, who scorned female charms as unworthy of their sixth-grade attention, would roll their eyes at each other as she passed their desks. Our real teacher, Mrs. Chapman, was a fine person who somehow saw to it that we could identify the countries on the globe, use fractions, and diagram complicated sentences. But Miss Mary Afton was the one who tutored our souls.

She looked up from packing a box of books as we entered, perspiration dampening the hair around her face. "Well, Starlett, Emily—I thought you two would have headed for the wide open spaces by now."

"I came to get the rest of my things," I said shyly. Star, hovering beside me like a hummingbird, added, "I came to tell you good-bye again," and she rushed into Miss Mary Afton's arms, sobbing. I stared in disbelief and envy. How could she! And why couldn't I?

Miss Mary Afton held Star and patted her shoulder, but she lifted her head and gave me a smile so warm that I felt as if I had been held and comforted too. Thus reassured, I moved to my desk by the window and began collecting my belongings. The playground outside was already so empty that I had the sense of having come to school on a Sunday by mistake. The early June sun bore down without pity, and not even a breeze moved the heavy tire suspended by a rope from the branch of a huge oak tree. Cicadas buzzed somewhere nearby, and the Spanish moss in the upper quarters of the tree hung motionless. There wasn't any moss on the lower limbs; the boys had snatched hundreds of handsful to chase the girls with, crying, "Witches' hair!" or "Dead men's beards!" We knew, of course, that it wasn't witches' hair, but we ran and squealed anyway, partly for the fun of the game and partly because we knew the moss was full of chiggers—a worse affliction than witches any day.

Star settled into occasional sniffs, and Miss Mary Afton tactfully supplied her with a tissue and set her to packing books. "I'll soon be through here, so why don't we all walk along together as far as your streets?" she suggested, and we happily agreed.

It was a rare treat to be allowed to walk the streets of Tatum with our golden idol. And golden she was: honey-tan skin; rich, syrupy, amber-colored hair; and laughing, golden-hazel eyes fringed with dark lashes.

Walking proudly on either side of her like young attendants to a queen, we left the shady schoolyard and headed for the business district, where she turned in at the Rexall and bought three chocolate ice-cream cones. "To celebrate," she explained, setting her books on the counter to present our cones in person.

"M-mm, thank you, ma'am," Star said, and I echoed, "Yes, thanks a lot," wondering why I could never get ahead of Star in the niceties of life. We lingered under the ceiling fan to finish our treat, then drank cold water from little paper cones before braving the sun-baked sidewalk again. At Star's corner we paused. A magnificent magnolia tree, much larger than any other along the street, shaded the entire corner, and Star and I had chatted and said good-bye under it almost every day.

"Uh . . . well," Star faltered. "Reckon maybe I'll walk on to your house, Emily Jean. Mama's not home, anyway."

"Oh, I think Granna wants me to go shopping with her soon's I get home," I fibbed, eager for the next two blocks alone with Miss Mary Afton.

Star looked at me curiously. "Emily Jean Knowles, you know as good as I do that your Granna's the same place as Mama. Today's Joanna Circle."

Oh, drat Joanna Circle! How could I have forgotten? "Well, anyway, I'd better clean my room before she gets home. I left an awful mess."

"I could help you."

"Oh, no, that's okay. Look, call me after supper, okay? Or just come on over."

"If I can," she agreed with a dubious frown.

Miss Mary Afton, who had been gazing noncommittally over our heads during this exchange, smiled at Star. "Keep in touch this summer, won't you, Star?"

"Yes, ma'am, I will. And I'll—I'll read some books this summer too. I promise."

"Good girl. Have a nice summer, now."

" 'S'ma'am. Thank you. Bye." Her voice squeaked, breaking again as she turned down the side street. After a few steps she began to run, her too-thin elbows flapping above her flounced skirt. Guiltily, I realized she was crying again.

Miss Mary Afton and I walked on in quiet companionship, not needing to say anything to prove we were together. I had a calm trust in her that no other adult except Uncle Bob had ever inspired in me. At my corner we paused again, and she looked at me thoughtfully.

"Remember that bulletin board we did, Emily? The one about the snake?"

"Yes'm. 'A Narrow Fellow in the Grass.' I liked that poem."

"Well, that was written by another Emily—Emily Dickinson. I wondered—would you like to have a book of her poems?" She handed me a thin brown volume, the edges frayed. "I kept hoping it would be you who won the language arts prize," she explained with a smile.

Reverently I opened the book to its frontispiece. In fading ink but boldly written was "John David MacDougal, his book. 1923." And under that, written in her own script in blue ink, "Mary A. Mac-Dougal."

"But," I said, "it was—your father's?"

"Yes. But I have others of his and another more complete book of Dickinson. And besides, I know you'll take good care of it."

"I will," I promised. "But... sometimes I underline things I like—in my Bible, or in poems and stuff—and once I colored all the pictures in *Tom Sawyer*."

"Well, that's not mistreating books—that's making friends with them. You wouldn't tear pages out of old Tom, though, or toss your Bible under your bed with some muddy old shoes, would you?"

I shook my head.

"There, you see? It's different. I've watched you handle books all year, and I'm not a bit worried about the health of this one. Now, some of the poems you'll like right away, but most of them are for you to grow up to. Later on, you'll understand them better."

I nodded. Lots of books were like that.

She smiled. "This Emily had red hair too, and she was shy."

I stared at the sidewalk, basking in the realization that I must be at least a little special to Miss Mary Afton. To my knowledge, even Star had never been given a book!

"You have a good summer too, Emily Jean. Come see me."

"Yes'm, I will. I sure will. Bye."

"Bye-bye."

I walked slowly toward home, then turned and ran panting to catch up with her. "Miss Mary Afton! I didn't even say thank you!"

"Yes, you did, Emmy," she said gently.

. . . . 2 . . . . .

I rounded the corner on Trenton Avenue in time to see two dark-suited men with briefcases turn away from our front door. Salesmen, I decided, and I met them at the gate, prepared to send them away unless they were from Fuller Brush, whose products Granna trusted.

"Hi, there," the taller of the two greeted me, holding the gate open to let me pass. "Do you think your folks will be home soon? We'd like a word with them."

His smile was nice, and green eyes twinkled from a tanned face topped by blond hair.

"I live with my grandmother," I explained. "She should be here in just a few minutes, if y'all'd like to come back. What are you selling?"

"Oh, we're not salesmen. We represent The Church of Jesus Christ of Latter-day Saints, and we'd appreciate the chance to talk with her for a few minutes."

My eyes widened. "Are y'all both ministers, then?" They seemed so young.

"Yes—or missionaries, to be more exact," answered the shorter man, who had slicked-down black hair and wore glasses. "We travel around and teach people about the gospel of Jesus Christ." His voice was low and friendly.

Well, I knew what to do with ministers; all of Granna's teachings hadn't been in vain! "Y'all come right on up and rest on the front porch, and let me get you some cold lemonade. It's just real hot out today."

They looked at each other, hesitating.

"Granna'll be right home, honest. She's real interested in missionary work. In fact, she's at a missionary circle meeting right now, and I just know she'll want to meet y'all."

The tall one shrugged. "Sounds good to me," he said, and they followed me up the front steps to sit in Granna's glider swing.

I set my books in a wicker chair by the door. "Is lemonade all right, or would y'all rather have iced tea?"

"Lemonade's fine with me," said the taller one. "How about you, Elder?"

The one called Elder looked a little startled, then laughed. "Lemonade sounds just great."

I hurried, measuring the boiled lemon syrup Granna kept in a mason jar in the icebox for use as tea flavoring or lemonade base, and adding ice cubes and tap water. I debated using Granna's best glasses, but they were in the china cabinet behind the blue glass pitcher that had been her mother's, and I didn't dare. I compromised by filching a couple of maraschino cherries and floating them on top.

"Say, this really hits the spot," said the tall, blond man.

"I agree, Elder," said the one called Elder. I looked from one to the other, confused. Meeting two such young ministers was curious enough—they looked even younger than Uncle Bob, who was still studying to become a preacher—but for both of them to have the peculiar name of "Elder," which I couldn't recall ever having heard, was too much. Of course, they obviously weren't from Tatum. They talked a little different, but not like the tourists from New York who had asked directions of me a while back.

"Where y'all from?" I asked, settling my organdy ruffles in a wicker rocker.

"Elder Taylor here is from Salt Lake City, and I'm from Wyoming—a ranch outside of Thayne. I'm Elder Jensen," explained the one with blond hair.

Salt Lake City! Wyoming! They might as well have said Russia or Tibet for all I knew of those regions, although I could locate them well enough on a map, thanks to Mrs. Chapman. But a ranch—yes, that explained the look he had of many days spent in the sun and wind, squinting into distant spaces. I had read enough Westerns and horse stories to know that.

"You know," he continued, "I have a sister at home just turned eleven. Her name's LaRae. How old are you—about twelve?"

"My name's Emily Jean Knowles, and I'll be twelve in October. LaRae—does she live on the ranch too?"

"Oh, you bet! LaRae and two boys, and another little sister just three."

"Then you're the oldest. That's why your name is Elder!"

He laughed then, showing strong white teeth. Elder Taylor laughed too and explained, "No. You see, Elder is a title in our church, referring to our calling in the Priesthood. Just like you might say 'Deacon Jones' or 'Pastor Evans.' "

I giggled, not even embarrassed to have made such a silly mistake. They didn't seem to mind at all.

"Do y'all have horses on your ranch?" I asked Elder Jensen.

"Sure do—lots of horses and cattle. As a matter of fact, LaRae has a horse of her own—a pretty little Appaloosa called Stormy. She's probably riding Stormy right now, glad to be out of school for a while. Wouldn't mind joining her myself, to tell the truth." He grinned.

It surprised me to hear a minister say such a thing. But then he was such a young one, and more like Uncle Bob than like Pastor Welch, who had been our minister for all of my life and longer. I became even more curious, but I swallowed my envious interest in LaRae to ask, "Where have y'all been as missionaries? We heard a man speak last month who had been in the Philippine Islands, and he came through here to give talks and collect enough money to go back. I reckon that's the kind of thing y'all are doing?"

"Well, not exactly," said Elder Taylor. "This is our mission field, right here in the South."

"Here? But we don't have any heathens! At least," I amended, recalling some of Granna's comments about various townspeople, "not as many as you'd find in China or Africa."

"No, I'm sure not," Elder Taylor agreed, smiling. "But still we're here, paying our own way, to explain more to folks about the gospel of Christ than they may already know."

"But don't you mean that your church pays you to come?"

"No, my family is helping to support me, and I plan to pay them back. Elder Jensen here raised and sold several prize-winning cattle to finance his mission."

"But—that seems mean to make y'all pay your own way."

Elder Jensen shook his head. "Nobody's making us do it. All our lives, we wanted to and planned to. Besides, it's only for two years, and then we go home again, back to our regular lives."

I frowned. "You mean . . . you're only ministers for two years?"

"That's as long as our mission lasts," Elder Taylor agreed. "But we'll be the Lord's servants forever in other ways."

"But it takes longer than two years just to study to *be* a minister," I protested. "My Uncle Bob's in his third year at seminary."

"We don't have that kind of formal training," Elder Jensen explained. "We teach what we've learned while growing up in the Church, and we get up really early every morning to study the scriptures and prepare ourselves."

"Oh. Well, do you . . . do very many people around here let you teach them?"

They exchanged wry smiles. "Not as many as we'd like," Elder Taylor admitted.

"Well, I know Granna'll want to meet y'all." I peered down the street. "Here she comes."

I was proud of Granna as she stepped quickly along the sidewalk, looking as if the heat of day couldn't touch her. She had had Emma Tully put a blue rinse on her gray hair, and with her blue eyes, powdery pink cheeks, and lavender and blue print dress, she looked cool as an April morning.

I was proud, too, to have Granna see how well I had entertained these special guests, seating them in the glider where the trumpet vine shaded them from the sun and serving them a cool drink while they waited. Reaching the front gate, she frowned delicately and shaded her eyes with her lace-edged hanky, trying to see who they were.

"Emily Jean?" she queried, not recognizing them.

"Granna, these are missionaries who've been waiting to talk to you. This is my grandmother, Mrs. Markham."

"Mrs. Markham, how are you today?" the tall, blond missionary inquired with a smile as they both rose politely. "I'm Elder Jensen and this is Elder Taylor. We represent The Church of Jesus Christ of Latter-day Saints, and we've come to—"

"Mormons?" Granna demanded, her stance suddenly rigid. She looked the two up and down, her glance resting suspiciously on the briefcases as if she thought they harbored serpents.

"Yes, ma'am," Elder Jensen replied. " 'Mormon' is a nickname sometimes applied to our church, but—"

"*We are Christians*," she was saying, "and we are totally satisfied with our faith. I'm sorry if my granddaughter has led you to think otherwise. Now if you'll excuse me, I'm very busy. Emily Jean, come inside *at once*."

I couldn't believe that Granna was being so rude as to interrupt him again, after all the scoldings she'd given me for interrupting people. She stepped between us and went into the house, her heels clicking decisively on the hardwood floor of the hall. There was a moment of complete silence. It seemed the kaleidoscope had shifted again, this time into Granna's lavender-blue pattern.

Elder Jensen and Elder Taylor set down their glasses and picked up their briefcases. I saw them do that, but a big lump had risen in my throat that made it impossible for me to raise my eyes to look at their faces.

"I'm awful sorry," I whispered.

"So are we," Elder Taylor said. "But thanks anyway for that good lemonade and the chance to rest. I hope you won't get in trouble for it."

I shook my head dumbly, staring at their shoes, which showed some shine even through the reddish dust. Elder Jensen tilted my chin up with his finger. "Goodbye, Miss Emily Jean. I'll remember you to LaRae and Stormy."

I tried to return his smile, but felt my mouth quiver. They went quickly down the walk and out the gate, turning toward Silvers'. I saw Elder Taylor clap Elder Jensen on the shoulder and lean over to say something to him as they walked. Elder Jensen shook his head. I felt sorry for them. The Silvers wouldn't listen, either, I felt sure. Granna said they were Jewish and didn't even believe in Jesus.

"Emily *Jean!*"

"Coming, Granna."

I picked up the empty glasses and gave the elders one last glance as they turned in at the Silvers' gate. I didn't expect ever to see them again, and, perversely, I was sorry.

. . . . 3 . . . . .

Granna was tying a fresh apron over her dress. I tiptoed behind her and set the glasses in the sink, wishing at that moment to be anywhere else in the world. I filled the glasses slowly with water, hoping to escape the inevitable. Granna had disjointed a chicken and was holding each piece in turn over the flame of a gas burner on the range to singe away any remaining pinfeathers. She held her head tilted up and away, her mouth pursed against the smell.

"Well, reckon I'd best change my clothes," I remarked, hearing the pitch of my voice go half an octave too high as I edged toward the door. I nearly made it.

"Emily Jean."

" 'S'ma'am?"

"I would have thought, being as you're nearly twelve, that some of my teachings would have begun to take root by now. The good Lord knows I have tried to instill in you certain principles of conduct, but . . . I see I have failed."

She sighed wearily and began to dredge the chicken in seasoned flour. It didn't seem safe to agree or disagree with her last statement, so I stood and waited, knowing more was to come.

"The very idea of coming home to find you had allowed two strange men—*Mormons*—in my house, with me gone. I just can't credit it."

"They weren't *in* the house," I pointed out hopefully.

"Oh, no. They were sprawled on my front porch for all the world to see!"

That was worse? "They said they were ministers, Granna — missionaries."

"Well, yes, they'll *say* anything to get a foothold, especially with an innocent young girl. Now you listen to me, Emily Jean, and remember this: they always come in pairs, like those two today — all smiles and dressed fit to kill. Usually all you have to do to get rid of them is just stand firm, like I did. As James said in the Bible, 'Resist the devil, and he will flee from you.'"

" 'S'ma'am." I looked down, ashamed to have been tricked.

"Now once in a while around here, we'll get one of those Jehovah's Witnesses — might be a man, woman, or even a child. Mind you don't let them get started talking. They go on and on with a memorized spiel. Just say you're not interested and shut the door. But if somebody comes from the Seventh-Day Adventists, they want money. They do a right good work with their medical missions, so I generally give them a dime or quarter, and they're on their way. You know that little blue jar where I keep the paperboy's money?"

I nodded dumbly.

"Well, there's usually a little extra change in that. Not for ice cream, mind you. Do you understand?"

" 'S'ma'am."

"Well, I should hope. Now run and change, and come back and help me."

I escaped to my room at last, going out to the front porch first to retrieve my books. The missionaries were nowhere in sight. Mormons! They had been Mormons! And I had made them welcome. As I climbed the stairs, I tried to remember all I knew about Mormons, but the only thing I could recall was something from last year's social studies book — an illustration of a wagon train heading West. I couldn't remember why they were so bad; I wasn't even sure I had realized any of them still existed. But apparently they did, at least out in Utah and Wyoming. And to think they looked like ordinary people!

My room was on the front of the house, and in summer, all I could see from my window was a tossing cloud of bright green chinaberry leaves and a corner of the front porch. I put my books on the closet shelf, except for the volume of Dickinson, which I laid carefully on my pillow to be looked at later. I got out of my organdy prison, scratched the hundred spots that had been itching all day, and stepped barefoot into a pair of cool, crisp shorts and a faded shirt. With my hair braided into two rather stubby plaits, I breathed a sigh of precious freedom.

"It's summer!" I said aloud, as though the change of seasons had just been revealed to me. "Summer!" I repeated, rolling the sound and feel of it on my tongue and in my heart. I ran back down to the kitchen where Granna was measuring rice and water into a saucepan. The chicken was now sizzling in hot fat, smelling a great deal more appetizing than it had just minutes before.

"Granna, just think, it's summer and school's out!"

"So I s'pose you think you can just run free for three whole months, with no responsibilities? At my age, Emily Jean, I need help around this place, and it's high time you learned to take more of a hand with the cooking and ironing."

"I know." I sighed. "I'm nearly twelve."

"Indeed you are. And I expect to hear some good solid improvement in your piano too. At least an hour at the piano every day. I don't sacrifice for you to have lessons from Evelyn Simpson just to let it all go down the drain. And before I forget it, Mittie Nelson asked me if you'd help with the six-year-olds at Vacation Bible School, and I said of course you'd love to."

" 'S'ma'am." Granna had a real gift for taking the joy out of a summer. But she couldn't spoil it all—there were too many hours in a long summer day for even Granna to think of ways to fill them all.

"Slice up a plateful of those good ripe tomatoes, and you'd better do some onion and cucumber too. And set three places in the dining room."

"Three—the dining room?"

"Need I repeat myself?"

"No, ma'am. But, who's coming, Granna?" We usually ate our

supper at the kitchen table, using plain white dishes on the ivy-patterned oilcloth. The dining room was saved for Sundays, very special occasions, or times when we served more than four. "Who's coming?" I repeated.

"Robert phoned. He should be here any minute, so don't dawdle."

"Uncle Bob! You mean, to stay for the summer?"

"Watch that knife, Emily Jean. Don't cut yourself. He'll be here on weekends, he said, and sometimes during the week. He's taken a construction job over at Bradley, and he'll need to sleep there some nights."

"Oh boy, oh boy," I sang under my breath. This was good news indeed. Things took on new life when Uncle Bob was home. He had a way of talking that made everything so interesting and a way of listening that won my heart, and he was fun to be with.

My mother had been Granna's first child. Uncle Bob had been born a year and a half later, and Rogie nine years after that. I couldn't bring myself to call him "Uncle Roger" to save my life; we had grown up in the same house together. He had been only ten when I was born and my mother died. Uncle Bob had been nineteen and already in the Navy before I came along, so my knowledge of him had come in delicious, infrequent nibbles through the years. To have him close by for most of the summer was an exciting prospect. If it had been Rogie . . . well, Rogie and I shared a sort of mutual dislike. To him, I had played the role of a resented, unwanted kid sister; and to me, he was a presence of ill will and meanness. He rarely spoke directly to me; instead, he would assume a pained expression and look past my head.

"Mother!" he would call. "Please remove this infant idiot." Or, "Get this snoopy brat away from me; she gives me the creeps."

Knowing how he felt, I would often stand around and watch him at whatever he was doing, just to see how long he could take it. It generally wasn't long.

Uncle Bob and Rogie seemed like brothers in only one characteristic — their coloring. Both had smooth, medium-olive skin, fine brown hair that tended to fall forward, and brown eyes. Otherwise, they were as different as tomatoes and onions. Where Uncle Bob was calm and cheerful, Rogie was quick-tempered and inclined to complain. Uncle Bob spoke in plain English and warm, matter-of-fact tones, but Rogie used big words and an uppity drawl. Uncle Bob's features were blunt and regular with a wide, friendly mouth. Rogie looked as though someone had placed hands on either side of his face and pressed everything toward the middle. His eyes were close-set, and his mouth drooped sullenly—easy to sneer and hard to smile. He rarely laughed, and when he did, it was either a short, mocking bark or a high-pitched whinny.

However, I could remember a time when he seemed to laugh more easily. When Junior Bailey and I were still good friends, we had followed Rogie downtown on a late winter afternoon. He had said he was going to see a movie. We planned to pop up behind him at the ticket window and beg him to pay our way to the show. Of course, we knew he wouldn't do it, but we hoped he would at least give us enough change for some candy and a new comic book at the Rexall.

Rogie strolled right past the theater, however, without even a glance at the poster ads. Mystified, Junior and I followed, keeping a safe distance. Rogie turned into Park Street, which didn't describe the area at all because there was no park, and the street was hardly more than half a block of a poorly paved alleyway, opening onto a couple of bars, a seedy men's store, and an amusement center. Junior and I paused and looked at each other, our eyes wide. Then, by unspoken agreement, we moved forward cautiously and peered around the corner. At first we thought we had lost Rogie, but then we saw him walking with a girl. Before we could creep close enough to see who she was, they vanished into the amusement center (formerly known as Ed's Billiards), which had tattered green shades blocking the two plate-glass windows in front.

Junior and I strolled determinedly up and down Tatum's half-block of seedy night life a suspicious number of times, but no one paid us any attention. Although the evening wasn't bitterly cold, the December humidity made it seem so, and we began to shiver.

"Come on, Emily Jean," Junior pleaded. "Let's go."

"Don't you dare!" I hissed. "We're staying right here, Junior Bailey, or I'll tell what really happened to Mrs. Silver's birdbath."

"Well, gee whiz! I'm freezin' to death."

"That's okay, so am I. But we've gotta find out what Rogie's up to."

Junior's sigh was a visible cloud on the neon-lit twilight air, and he hunched his jacket collar up around his ears and kept walking. I had found it useful to keep several choice bits of information on hand in those days—not that I ever had to use them—but they made wonderful arm-twisters. I was hoping to collect enough damaging evidence to brandish in Rogie's face the next time he tried to get me in trouble with Granna, which he delighted in doing.

We walked, then pretended to be absorbed in a window display of men's flannel shirts, and walked some more. The neon lights grew more and more gaudy in the deepening evening blue, and we grew colder and colder. We were just pooling our pennies, deciding which of us would keep watch while the other ran to the Rexall for a cup of hot chocolate, when Rogie and the girl came out of Ed's. Junior and I shrank into the entryway of an out-of-business shoe store and quit breathing as they approached.

The girl was Chrissy Cantrell, a large-boned young woman who matched Rogie in height and probably topped him in weight. She had wide-set green eyes above high cheekbones, a smattering of freckles, and square white teeth. The two of them were holding hands and laughing at something funny. Junior and I crept further into the shadowed doorway as they passed us, lighted cigarettes swinging from their free hands. Their laughter subsided, then exploded again in a fresh outburst as they caught one another's eye. They walked on, open and young and unsuspecting, and I stared at Rogie in disbelief. The sulk, the sneer, and the affected drawl he used were not evident. His eyes were bright with tears of mirth, and obviously they shared a special sort of friendship. The wind tousled

Chrissy's short hair as she took a final pull on her cigarette and flipped it expertly into the gutter. She was not really pretty and certainly not very feminine or refined, but there was a feeling about her of pine forests and wood smoke and cold, star-flecked skies.

Granna would just die, I thought, *if she knew Rogie smoked cigarettes and went to pool halls and hung around with Chrissy Cantrell!* But close on the heels of that satisfying thought came the realization that, having seen Rogie with such an unaccustomed expression of happiness, I didn't want to betray him in what might be his only source of delight. What didn't occur to me at the time was the fact that if I *had* told on Rogie, Granna would almost certainly have questioned the propriety of my being in that part of town at that hour of the evening.

Anyway, I didn't think about it because shortly after Christmas that year, Rogie's friendship with Chrissy Cantrell met a quiet but definite end. I suppose that in such a small town someone would inevitably get word to Granna about Rogie and Chrissy. Granna knew the Cantrells slightly—well enough to know that she didn't want her son going around with their daughter, and well enough to invite them over to say so.

I probably wouldn't have known about that meeting if I hadn't been addicted to "The Shadow," which came on the radio at eight o'clock Friday night. I'd already had my bath that night, gotten into my white flannel gown and bunny-ear slippers, and brushed my teeth and hair the required number of minutes—all these so that Granna might be persuaded more easily to allow me my Friday night chills and thrills. "Who *knows* what evil lurks in the hearts of men?" the spooky voice would inquire, and then answer itself—"The Shadow knows . . ."—and go off into a cascade of chilling laughter. I would pull down the shades, turn on both table lamps, tuck my feet under me in the big overstuffed chair, and hug Granna's needlepoint pillow, prepared to be scared silly and loving every minute of it. Once, when Star spent the night, she listened with me, and later she wet the bed and cried until Granna had to call her father to come get her and take her home. I was sorry, but secretly I thought she was a big sissy.

On this particular Friday evening, when I was halfway down the stairs, I heard Granna's voice coming from the living room and realized she was not alone. I hadn't known of any invited company, so I sat on the stairs and eased myself downward, one step at a time, until I could see a portion of the living room through the dining-room archway. Half of the sofa was visible, and on the edge of it perched a woman I had never seen before. She was thin and not very tidy. Her dingy blouse had crept out of her skirtband, and her ragged hair was haphazardly scraped back from her face and held with an assortment of bobby pins placed at odd angles.

Granna's voice was purring. She could spread charm like summer butter when she felt the situation called for it. "And so," she was saying, "I thought it would be best for all concerned — especially for our dear children — if we exercised our adult judgment on their behalf. As much as I hate to interfere in their little friendship, I can't help feeling we must. In view of their differing beliefs and backgrounds, don't you feel that in the long run they'd be happier with companions of their own faith and culture?"

I knew immediately that Granna was talking about Rogie and Chrissy. Then I noticed the gold cross against the woman's rumpled blouse and remembered that the Cantrells were Catholic. I had to admit that Chrissy didn't much resemble her mother.

"I take your point, Mrs. Markham," Jake Cantrell's voice rumbled from the other side of the room, where I couldn't see. "I ain't home all the time, drivin' on the road like I do, so it's hard to keep track of Chrissy. Delores, here, ain't been too well lately, so Chrissy's been on her own a whole lot."

Mrs. Cantrell lovingly fingered one of Granna's second-best tea-cups and took a sip from it, holding it with both hands as a child might. She seemed unaware of the conversation, and her eyes caressed the furnishings in the room, lingering on the brown plush overstuffed sofa set with its crocheted antimacassars.

Mr. Cantrell stood up and came into view — a huge hulk of a

man stuffed into what must have been a secondhand suit, since the trousers were too long and too tight. He bent over his wife, gently loosening her hold on the teacup and setting it back in its saucer. He had wide-set eyes and the air of a lumberjack. Chrissy was his, all right.

"I'll sure talk to Chris, Mrs. Markham. We don't want to cause you or your boy no trouble or nothin'. Kinda hate to do it, in a way, kids bein' what they are these days and all. Seems like your boy was about the onliest one I could trust out with Chrissy and not worry about him gettin' too fresh or nothin'."

"Well, I should think," Granna said proudly. "Roger's been brought up to be a gentleman and a Christian. I don't believe such things enter his mind."

"No'm. Likely not. Come on, honey, time to go."

Mrs. Cantrell allowed herself to be drawn to her feet. "So kind of you to ask us," she murmured. "So lovely. We must do it again sometime."

Granna closed the front door softly after them, then shot the lock in the bolt. She came back through the living room to pick up the teapot and cups and carry them to the kitchen. In the light from the kitchen doorway, her face seemed haggard and old, her mouth drooping in an almost bitter expression. She saw me hunched on the stairs, hugging my knees, and stopped.

"I cannot understand," she said slowly, "why my children see fit to humiliate me by associating with such people."

I was only seven at the time, or eight at the most, but I knew she wasn't speaking only of Rogie. Her daughter Ellen, my mother, had eloped with my father, whom Granna said she had "warned her against from the beginning." A year after the elopement, my mother had returned home alone to give birth to me and my twin sister, Ellen Jane. As often happens with twins, one was larger and stronger than the other. I had survived; Ellen Jane had not. My mother had not survived for long either. My father didn't come for the funeral, and about a month later, he died somewhere in New Orleans.

This had left Granna, already a widow, with a tragedy to mourn and a newborn grandchild to care for. My grandfather had left her well enough provided for financially, but he was not able to leave her protected from unhappiness. So, half-welcome, half-unwelcome burden that I was, I grew up with the knowledge of Granna's grief and rage, her stern sense of duty, and her fierce, protective brand of love that wounded as often as it soothed.

I sat on the stairs and looked at her solemnly, understanding far more than I could say. Because I couldn't bring back my mother, because I couldn't explain that Chrissy was fresh air to Rogie, and because nothing I could say would ease the lines in Granna's face or the bitterness in her heart, I took refuge in the question I had come downstairs to ask: "Granna, can I please listen to 'The Shadow' now?"

She gave a long, ragged sigh. "I suppose so. Although it seems to me that this house has enough shadows as it is."

A few weeks later, the Cantrells moved away from Tatum.

. . . . 4 . . . .

Granna?"

"What? Slice that onion thin, the way Robert likes it."

"Granna, I can't remember — what is it about the Mormons that's so bad?"

Granna waited to answer until she had deftly turned each piece of chicken in the skillet and replaced the lid.

"In the first place, they're not Christian people. They believe in some other book instead of the Bible. And they do perfectly awful things. I read a book about them once, from our church library."

"What kind of awful things? How come they all moved clear out West?"

"Well, I suppose it was because the United States government didn't want a bunch of heathens with harems corrupting our Christian country."

"Harems?"

"Yes, indeed. They all had a whole slew of wives, especially that Brigham Young. This book had a picture of him in a big bed with all his wives ranged out on either side of him."

I put down my knife. "A *photograph?*"

"Well, no. My mercy, Emily Jean, it was a drawing. But it was true, nevertheless. Still is, too. They say they don't do that any more out there, but of course they do. They just try to keep it hidden so they can stay out of jail. Now there's no use your young mind dwelling on such things."

I pondered this for a while. Granna sounded sure of herself, as always, and she usually knew what she was talking about. But something didn't exactly seem right.

"But Granna, if they're not Christians, why do they teach about Jesus? How come they send out missionaries? They—they didn't talk or act wicked."

"My land, child, haven't you ever heard of deception? Of course they send out their handsomest young rascals to preach false doctrines and tempt the sheep away from the flock. When I was a girl, they were said to lure innocent young girls out there to their temples. And the good Lord only knows what goes on *there*."

The word *temple* created in my mind a vision of broken white columns on a bare hilltop with chanting people below. Among the columns, a white-clad girl was bound to a stone altar, gazing up in horror as the sun glinted on the poised dagger. Did they—surely they didn't—that couldn't be what LaRae was being groomed for, so innocent and unsuspecting, riding her Appaloosa over the windy hills of far Wyoming! Or would she be one of twenty wives, sad and neglected among all the others?

"No!" I said suddenly, rejecting the thought as too horrible to contemplate. And those two nice young men—those elders—surely they wouldn't . . . "I'll bet they just don't know!"

Granna looked up absently. "Who?"

"Those two Mormon missionaries. They were so nice—I'll bet they don't even know yet what goes on in those temples."

"Well, maybe not. They did look a mite young, and I have heard they have to be a certain age to go in those places, which in itself ought to tell us something! Now, let's see," she said, surveying her cupboard, "I'll just open a can of peas and save the string beans for Sunday. How were your closing exercises, Emily Jean?"

With an effort, my mind clambered back over the afternoon to the warm, sticky auditorium. "Okay, I reckon. Kinda long and hot. All I got was special mention in language arts. But later, Miss Mary Afton gave me a book of poems by Emily Dickinson. She's so pretty, Granna. I wish I could look like her."

"Who, Emily Dickinson?"

"No, ma'am, Miss Mary Afton."

"She is a pretty girl, though I don't know a thing about her background. Arnelle Chapman seems to like her well enough though. Why did she give you a book?"

"I don't know. I reckon she didn't need it anymore, and it has a poem in it that I like."

"Did Starlett play her piece?"

"Yes, ma'am. It sounded real good. Granna, was my mother pretty? Do I look anything like her?"

She turned away quickly and jerked open a drawer to get the can opener. "You don't look a thing like your mother," she said sharply. "Red hair never ran in our family."

"But . . . was she pretty?"

"Too pretty. Far too pretty. Now get that table set, Emily Jean. Robert'll be hungry when he gets here. I'd better strain the tea."

Defeated again in trying to learn from Granna what my mother had been like, I went into the dining room to set the table with three of the big dinner plates. I admired their ornate, raised border design of plum and gold that matched the satin stripes on the dining-room chairs. Granna was quite proud of her dining room and said it was a comfort to her to have a few really good pieces in the house. She polished them lovingly with a lemony-smelling wax and always kept the room dim except for special occasions. My grandfather had given her the furniture when their first son was born, and Uncle Bob had often remarked that the only real competition for affection he had faced in his early years had been that dining-room set.

I hadn't been allowed to eat at that table until my eighth birthday, and most of the time I still hurried through the room practically on tiptoe. Strangely enough, it was located in the middle of the house, with the stairs leading upward from its inner side, and it opened onto the front hall and the kitchen, so it was by no means isolated. Yet it maintained that atmosphere of quiet elegance—a tribute to Granna's indomitable will.

Granna had timed dinner just right; Uncle Bob's old Nash pulled into the driveway, and I pelted down the porch steps to meet him with a flying hug. He laughed and swung me around, then gave me a kiss on the cheek. He smelled of spearmint gum, and his face felt bristly.

"Hey, pigtails, keep that up and you'll find yourself on the football team!"

"Supper's all ready in the dining room, with fried chicken and cream gravy and stuff, and I didn't even know you were coming home today!"

"Sounds like exactly what I need, and I didn't know for sure until this morning, myself. Hello, Mom, how're you feeling?" Granna had stepped out onto the porch.

"Oh, I'm bearing up," she said, welcoming his hug and kiss with obvious pleasure. We all swept into the house, somehow made more complete by his presence and our proud ownership of him.

Granna hummed against the sound of his splashing from the bathroom. "Amazing Grace," it sounded like, her soprano tremolo coming through even when she hummed. She still sang in the church choir, and though her voice had grown a bit reedy, it was still true to the melodies of the hymns she loved.

"I'm glad you can still eat my plain old cooking," Granna said a little later as Uncle Bob wiped his mouth and leaned back with a satisfied sigh. "There's a bite of dessert, but first, you said on the phone you had a surprise for me."

"And so I do." He leaned forward, a boyishly eager light in his eyes. "I had a phone call from Pastor Welch just this morning, asking if I would take the evening services at the Pine Forest Mission for the summer."

"To *preach*?" I squealed, bouncing on my chair.

He nodded. "It's a good opportunity to get the feel of preaching to a real congregation of everyday folks, week after week. Frankly, I'm a bit weary of all the seminary theory and instruction, and I want to get my feet wet, so to speak. What do you think, Mom?"

Granna dabbed at her eyes with her napkin. "I'm so happy, Robert. Papa'd be so proud."

"Can I go and hear you preach?" I asked. "And can Star come?"

"Oh, by all means. I'll need all the moral support I can get."

"Half the congregation will probably flock out there to hear you," Granna predicted. "The whole church is just real proud of you, and you know Pastor Welch is due to retire before long."

"Oh, well . . . you're going to want a seasoned man to follow Pastor Welch. I couldn't expect to step right in with a big congregation like Eastside."

"I don't know, dear. People think ahead, and I think they may petition for you. After all, they've known you all your life, and they've known me and Papa. They'd be sure of what they were getting."

"Well, don't get your hopes up. Let's just take one step at a time. Now, where's that dessert?"

Granna brought in a fragrant lemon meringue pie, droplets of moisture beading on the stiff, golden peaks. "I had a feeling there'd be something to celebrate," she said.

"You haven't forgotten my favorite!"

"Of course not. Lemon was Papa's favorite too. He could eat a whole pie at one sitting."

"I remember you always made two. Well, I can't eat a whole pie tonight, but then I don't think E. J. would like it much if I did, would you, kiddo?"

"Nope," I admitted. "And I'm celebrating two things—you're here, and school's out for the summer."

"We'll have some fun this summer, okay? What would you like to do most?"

"Picnics and car rides and swimming and the carnival when it comes, and—"

"Emily Jean, your Uncle Bob is going to need some peace and quiet and time to himself to prepare his sermons, so don't you start thinking you can monopolize his time."

"No, ma'am."

Uncle Bob winked at me. "You be thinking, E. J., which of those things you want to do first," he said as he stood and stretched.

When the dishes were done, I wandered up to my room, which was still warm and bright from the late afternoon sun. I could hear the familiar squeak of the front porch glider as Granna rocked back and forth. Uncle Bob was in the bathtub, singing "Peg o' My Heart" in his surprisingly good baritone, and I recognized the voices of Fred Silver and Arnie Blalock and some smaller kids playing any-eye-over next door. I considered joining them, but Fred had been acting downright peculiar to me lately, as if we were strangers and not next-door neighbors all our lives, so I decided against it. Besides, soon enough they'd be asking me to join their afternoon ball games. So I flopped contentedly on my stomach and picked up the worn brown volume of poems.

The next day was Saturday, and while I woke with the peculiar sense of relaxed exhilaration that comes with first days of vacations, I knew that Monday would feel even more delicious. Saturday was Saturday, summer or winter, and precious enough in itself, and Sunday was Sunday all year long. But on Monday there wouldn't be such a bustle of shopping and errands and lawn mowing. Monday would begin quietly. Granna, of course, would do her wash, and the soapy laundry smell and the stillness of the house would make it seem as if I must be missing school — except I wasn't sick, and I knew all the other kids were home too — and the anticipation would begin to build. As soon as it was politic, kids would begin to venture out of their houses and find each other. Last summer's favorite haunts would be hopefully revisited, and plans would be made for more activities and projects than any summer could hold — clubs and con-tests, ball games and money-making schemes, parties and fishing expeditions, picnics and swimming and secret hideouts. By Monday evening, summer would be in full swing.

That Saturday morning, however, felt almost like any other as I ironed the best Sunday tablecloth and napkins, cleaned my white patent-leather Mary Janes, dusted the living room, and practiced an impatient hour at the piano. It was eleven-fifteen when I made my escape and headed for Star's house, and the heat had already taken hold of the day. The uneven sidewalk felt hot through my sandals. Slugs, in their nighttime wanderings, had left silver traceries along the cement. At least we *had* sidewalks — most of the town didn't. Our street, one block east of the business district; Main Street; and Colquitt, one block west of Main; along with four north-south connecting streets, boasted the only sidewalks in town. In fact, the farther you got from the center of town, the worse the streets became, so that the outer streets weren't paved at all—just graded from time to time to erase ruts and erosion.

Our neighborhood was not as elegant as the one around North Main where Dr. Land and Mr. Sumter, retired from the state legislature, lived. But it was still considered a respectable and "nice" part of town. Star's house, three blocks south of ours, was a bungalow with a wide front porch. It had a dim, somewhat oppressive atmosphere to it, although Mrs. Hargrave was considered to have excellent taste in decorating, keeping her house and family polished to perfection. Twin hydrangea bushes flanked the front steps, and a huge bridal wreath bush obscured the dining-room windows.

Mrs. Hargrave answered my knock, a plump, attractive lady with dark hair and eyes that darted here and there. She reminded me pleasantly of a sparrow.

"Hello, Emily. Ready to play so soon? Starlett still has ten more minutes to practice. Do you want to wait for her?"

"Yes'm, thanks. I'll just wait out here."

I sat on the cement steps and listened to Star whipping through a Hanon exercise with careless abandon and accuracy. Then she played "Flower Song" twice through with hardly a bobble, and I heard the lid thump shut over the keys. She came outside wearing a starched white cotton shirt and pink flowered shorts that came halfway to her knees.

"I couldn't come over last night," she said. "We had to go to Aunt Bessie's."

"That's okay. Guess what? Uncle Bob came home."

"Just for the weekend?"

"For the summer. And you know what? He's going to be preaching the Sunday evening services out at the mission church!"

"Well, how nice," said Mrs. Hargrave, who had come out to sweep her porch. Star and I stood up to let her get to the steps.

"Robert's such a fine young man. I know Mrs. Markham's proud to have such a son."

"Yes, ma'am. I reckon she is, all right."

"I'll have to tell Patricia. Just the other day, she was wondering who'd be taking those services."

Star and I glanced at each other. She covered her mouth, and I clenched my teeth to keep from giggling. Pat was Star's older sister and the secretary at our church. She was dark, with quick-moving brown eyes like Mrs. Hargrave's, but she was slender and graceful instead of plump. What Star and I knew, but were not supposed to know, was that Pat Hargrave was very interested in the budding career of one Bob Markham, and the interest was not entirely religious or professional. There had been some evidence, too, that Uncle Bob found Pat attractive, and Star and I approved of their friendship and fostered it as openly as we dared. We'd even gone so far as to try to determine what our precise relationship would be if they were to marry. We decided Star would become my aunt-in-law by marriage.

Mrs. Hargrave left her broom and hurried into the house, presumably to find Pat, and Star and I dissolved into suppressed giggles. Finally, we wiped tears from our eyes, and Star dug into her pocket for her ball and jacks. We played lazily for a while, each going through threesies and foursies before losing interest.

"Let's go for a walk," I suggested, anxious to be out in the sunshine again, restless for activity.

"I'll ask," Star said dubiously, and then brightened. "I know! Mama's been writing letters. I'll see if I can take them to the post office for her."

I saw nothing wrong with a walk for the joy of it, but Mrs. Hargrave seemed to, and for that matter, so did Granna. Star emerged, waving a sheaf of envelopes.

"Okay, I've got till twelve-thirty," she said. "It's eleven-forty now."

I considered the situation. We had a good forty-five minutes, long enough to allow for a couple of detours.

"Let's go this way," I called, leaping ahead of Star and feeling the sun heat my bones and spirits again. At the corner we turned and wandered up Oglethorpe Avenue past the tall wrought-iron spikes that surrounded New Hope Cemetery. I paused by the open gates.

"Let's walk through," I suggested.

"I'd just as soon go around," Star said.

"Why, Star Hargrave, it's broad daylight! What are you scared of? I do it all the time."

"There's nothing to be afraid of," Star said resolutely, eyeing the moss-covered oaks and lichen-decorated tombs in the oldest corner of the block. "It's just . . . kind of sad."

"I know. But I like it anyway, especially in summer."

"Emily Jean, sometimes you're so strange."

I turned in, avoiding the crushed-shell drive with my thin-soled sandals. Star followed reluctantly, kicking at a pine cone or clump of dirt. I wound unerringly between the gravestones to kneel on the coarse grass beside a grave set a little apart from the others in its section. I reached out and touched the dandelions that grew on the little mound like yellow polka dots. I liked them because they looked so bright and cheerful there. Star sat down beside me.

"Reckon this is why you like to come," she said softly.

"Reckon."

"I'm sorry, Emily Jean. If my mama and sister were out here, reckon I'd want to come too."

"It's okay," I told her. "It's not the same, really. My mama and sister aren't anybody I really know, like yours are."

I touched the inscription under the carved stone lamb. "Asleep in Jesus, two lambs in his bosom. Ellen Markham Knowles, 1915–1936. Ellen Jane Knowles, born and died October 31, 1936." I looked up. "Sometimes, I think about my sister a lot. How come I deserved to live, and she didn't? Maybe she'd have been better'n me. Reckon it sounds dumb, but sometimes I kind of miss her. I used to pretend she was with me, and we'd play together. I told Granna that once, and she said it was because I was a half-soul."

"A *what?*"

"A half-soul. You know, because we were twins, and sort of half of each other. Granna says that when one twin dies, the one left goes around looking for the other half of its soul all its life. Reckon maybe that's why I feel lonesome a lot."

Star stared at me for a moment, then gave a nervous giggle. "I'm sorry, Emily Jean, but a half-soul sounds like what Mr. Cutter puts on Daddy's old shoes!"

"I know," I agreed, grinning. Then we both sobered again.

"Do you think that's true about twins?" Star asked.

"I don't know. Maybe, on account of that lonesome feeling I get. But I sort of like to think my soul is just mine, you know? I mean, what if Ellen Jane is up there in heaven feeling lonesome for me and wishing I was with her? Now, that plumb gives me the creeps!" I jumped up and dusted off my knees.

"I don't reckon you need to worry about it though," Star said earnestly. "Because I don't think anybody could feel sad or lonesome in heaven, do you?"

"Reckon not, with the gold streets and harps and Jesus there and all." I flicked a June bug off my shoulder as we started walking. "What d'you reckon they do all the time, up in heaven?"

Star looked surprised. "Do? Well, sing praises to the Lord, I reckon, and look on his face. That's what Pastor Welch says."

"I guess so. Star, I don't mean this to sound bad or anything, but . . . do you think you'd ever get tired of just doing that all the time?"

She considered. "Maybe sometimes you get to do something special," she conceded. "Like — maybe like being a guardian angel to somebody here on earth."

"That'd be fun — saving them from accidents and trying to get them not to do bad things. I'd like that."

"And maybe," she continued, "maybe your sister is your guardian angel right now."

The idea appealed to me, but I had my doubts. "She's just a baby," I said.

Star shrugged. "Is her soul a baby soul in heaven too?"

"I don't know. I never thought about that."

"Well, I know this much — if Ellen Jane would've lived, likely you and me wouldn't be best friends."

"Why not?"

" 'Cause it seems like twins don't very often need friends, 'ceptin' each other. Remember Patty and Polly Pierce, in the fourth grade, how they always stuck together?"

"Maybe it's just easier because they're already so much alike, and like to do the same things."

"Well, we're not much alike, but we're best friends. You're a lot braver than I am, and a lot better at games and stuff."

"That's nothing. You're lots prettier, and more polite, and more talented than me. And likely a better Christian too," I added in a burst of honesty.

"Oh, no, Emily Jean. I am not, either. But listen — are you going to wear your white organdy to church tomorrow?"

"Reckon I'll have to."

"Then I'll wear mine too."

We deposited Mrs. Hargrave's letters in the proper slots at the post office and stood for a minute under the slow-moving ceiling fan, letting the circulating air cool our sun-warmed bodies. I breathed deeply, liking the peculiar smell of paper and glue that somehow made me think of butterscotch pudding.

Mr. Huggins, the postmaster, peered at us from behind his grille. "Mornin', girls," he called. "Emily, here's a letter for your grandma. Might as well take it along to her if you're headed home."

"Yes, sir, I will." I took the envelope and looked it over. It had been postmarked in Turley, a town up in Franklin County, and it was addressed in a thin, spidery scrawl. Likely one of Granna's cousins, I reflected. She had more of those than I knew of, and every so often she would hear from one or get word that one had died. I stuffed the envelope into the pocket of my shorts. Star and I parted at our usual corner, and I ran home, despite the ever-present noon sun.

5

If I sat straight and tall in the eleven o'clock preaching service the next morning and sang with a little more fervor than usual, it was probably due to my inordinate pride at being with Uncle Bob, who nodded and smiled and shook hands as far as he could reach before we settled in our pew. Granna beamed on us from the choir box, which was located just below the glass window of the baptistry. Once a month, white-clad baptismal candidates were led into the water by Pastor Welch, and "buried with Christ in baptism, raised to walk in newness of life." A mural in soft pastels was painted on the back wall of the baptistry, depicting Jesus' own baptism by John in the River Jordan.

I was approaching the age when Granna would expect me to be baptized, but before that time, I'd have to make a profession of faith and be saved. This process consisted of leaving my seat at the close of the service and walking down to the front of the sanctuary during the singing of the invitational hymn. There, I'd confess my belief in Jesus as my personal savior, and then be prayed for and counseled. I had never found the courage to make that long walk, although certain people, including my former Sunday School teacher, Mrs. Emmons, and even Star, would occasionally seek me out and give me an encouraging smile or nod. I suppose my unsaved state was a source of concern to them. Star had gone down twice — once to be saved and once to rededicate her life. I don't know what held me back — fear, timidity, pride? I don't think it was unbelief, because I had never really doubted the Bible stories and lessons I had been taught. But for whatever reason, my feet stayed glued to the floor and my eyes to the hymnal as we sang, "Just as I am, and waiting not . . . ," and I waited.

Dinner that Sunday was a prolonged affair. Granna had invited Pastor Welch, his wife, Pat Hargrave, and, at my pleading, Star. Pastor Welch, a ponderous old gentleman with kind, protuberant blue eyes and an ill-fitting denture plate, could spin a good tale or occasionally wax eloquent from the pulpit. He wasn't much for small talk or dinner conversation but confined himself to good-natured nods at one or another of us while making a hearty meal of Granna's pot roast and hot biscuits. Pat paid close attention to everything that was said, her dark eyes darting shyly in Uncle Bob's direction every time he spoke. Star and I didn't miss much that went on, and when the adults finally withdrew to the living room with their spice cake and coffee, the two of us lolled limply in our chairs for a few minutes before tackling the dishes.

"Did you see Pat blush when Mrs. Welch told her how pretty she looked in yellow?" I whispered. " 'Like a butterfly, dear.' "

"And then your Granna said, 'And just as sweet as she is pretty,' and your Uncle Bob just sat and smiled at her. Pat about went through the floor."

"Star, what if he proposes to her this summer!"

Star gave me a wise look and beckoned me to follow her into the kitchen. "I know something, Emily Jean, but you've got to promise not to let on you know."

"Cross my heart."

"Hope to die?"

"Stick a needle in my eye. What is it?"

"*Well*, I heard Pat telling Mama that she was going to ask Mrs. Simpson to take her place as organist for the evening service so she could be free to go with your Uncle Bob to the mission church. He *asked* her to go along, to play the piano out there."

"Wow! Just like a missionary couple!"

"You know what else? Pat went out and bought herself five pieces of material to make new Sunday dresses." Star's eyes widened significantly. "Mama got after her for being so extravagant, but Pat said, 'I'm not having him see me every Sunday in last year's old dresses!' "

"Oh, boy! Has she got it bad," I gloated, with the superiority of one who has not been touched yet by romance.

The afternoon wore to a close, and our guests left to prepare for the evening service. Later at the meeting, as we sang the hymns with gusto and watched Pat glance furtively in Uncle Bob's direction while she played the piano, Star and I exchanged occasional secret looks and smiles.

I had been right about Monday morning. I woke to the mingled fragrances of laundry detergent and Granna's coffee. I loved the clean, soapy smell of clothes washing and the feel of quiet industry in the house. I rolled out of bed and looked for the shorts and shirt I had worn on Saturday, but Granna had already whisked them away. I pulled on a pair of last year's shorts and a shirt, then took the stairs lightly and headed for the kitchen. I could hear Granna at her washer on the back porch, singing, "There shall be showers of blessing . . . "

"Morning, Granna," I called, pouring myself a bowl of cornflakes.

"Good morning, child. Remember your hour of practice this morning. But before you do that, I want you to weed around the pole beans before it gets any hotter."

"Okay."

"*Okay?*"

"I mean—yes, ma'am."

"Then this afternoon I'll need some help with the ironing. It's time you learned how to press a man's shirt, and you may as well practice on Robert's work shirts."

" 'S'ma'am." I munched happily, absently reading an ad for some blue cereal bowls on the cornflakes box.

"Showers of blessing," Granna sang. "Mercy drops 'round us are falling, but for the showers we plead."

I didn't really notice when she stopped singing, but when she called my name, her tone alerted me to trouble, and I lost no time getting to the back porch. Granna stood by the wringer washer, a pair of shorts in one hand and a crumpled envelope in the other.

"I found this in your pocket," she said in a quiet voice that sounded as if it had to be squeezed past something in her throat.

"I'm sorry, Granna. I plumb forgot to give it to you."

"Did you open it?"

"No, ma'am."

"Are you sure?"

I stared at her in confusion. "Granna, Mr. Huggins at the post office gave it to me on Saturday when I was there with Star. I just stuck it in my pocket and forgot about it. I wouldn't open it. It's not addressed to me."

A little color seemed to flow back into Granna's pale lips. "Indeed it isn't. I'm glad you remembered that portion of my teachings, at least." She drew a ragged sigh. "Go ahead now, child, and do your practicing."

"I thought you wanted me to weed first."

"No . . . yes . . . whichever. I believe I'll just take a little break. The heat's making me tired already."

"Who's that letter from, Granna?"

"Just — a relative. No one you know."

She didn't stop in the kitchen to have a cup of coffee as she usually did while she read the mail, but she went into her bedroom and softly closed the door. My shorts lay on top of a pile of clothes I stepped over as I went outside.

I didn't think any more about the letter until late that evening when I was in bed, pleasantly tired and relaxed after an active day and a long bath. I wriggled my toes contentedly between crisp, clean sheets and paged through the book Miss Mary Afton had given me, only half aware of the murmur drifting up from the front porch glider, where Granna and Uncle Bob were trying to cool off. I must have dozed for a moment, because I started sharply when the glider gave a protesting squeak as though someone had abruptly halted its rhythm.

" — only fair to let her go," Uncle Bob said decisively, and I was instantly alert. Were they speaking of me? And let me go where? Granna didn't answer right away, and the only sounds I heard were some crickets somewhere in the bushes and the old mockingbird in our backyard telling the world good night. Then the glider resumed its rhythm, and Granna said, "But, Robert, we made a bargain years ago, ... honorable-enough woman to keep it."

Honorable woman? No, that wasn't me. Who, then?

I lay very still, attuned intently to the voices from below.

"Well, she's ... nearly twelve years.... dishonorable ... to request a visit. ... near to eighty."

I imagined rather than heard Granna's sigh. Her answer was indistinguishable, and I swiftly turned off my light and crept to kneel at my window.

"You've had twelve years to raise her as you wanted, and she's a good, sensible kid. What harm can a few days with Mrs. Knowles do? I don't think she'll be corrupted."

"Her ways are not our ways. And she's not our kind of people," Granna objected. "Emily Jean's a trusting child. She was even taken in by a pair of Mormon missionaries the other day — plumb scared me to death. She could be filled with all sorts of strange ideas — like your sister was."

"Oh, Mom — haven't you been able to forgive Ellie yet? She was in love, and she was happy that year with Frank."

I held my breath and felt my heart beat fiercely. Ellie and Frank — my parents! And Mrs. Knowles must be — could she be — my other grandmother?

" ... not a matter of forgiving Ellen. She was young and foolish and taken in by that rogue and his promises. He's the one I can't forgive — stealing her away to that wicked city and then packing her back here eight months pregnant with twins and so mortally weary and ill that she died from it."

"But he meant to follow, didn't he, when his job was finished? I thought he sent her home early because she wanted to be here for the birth."

"So she said, the poor girl. I never thought for a minute he intended to come. Glad to be rid of her, no doubt, when she was ill and bloated and about to make him a father. Never even came for the funeral, you'll recall. That should tell you something about Frank Knowles! No, it's a blessing and a just retribution that he died when he did."

"Mom, we really don't know all that happened during that time. Mrs. Knowles said he was terribly ill, and she must have been devastated when she lost him—just as you were when Ellie died. And knowing how you felt about Frank's and Ellie's marriage, Mrs. Knowles did agree to let you bring up the baby without interference. Am I right on that?"

"Yes," Granna admitted.

"Well, look at it from her point of view. Surely all these years she's wanted to see and know her granddaughter too. And like it or not, E. J. *is* her grandchild, as much as yours."

"I'm the one who's cared for her and provided for her all these years. I've borne the burden Ellen left for me. No one can say I've shirked my duty."

"No one's even thinking such a thing. You've done a great job. But it was your decision to take it on, remember?" Uncle Bob's voice was kind, but as always he kept Granna firmly toeing the line of truth, as he did me. It was one of the reasons I trusted him— there was no deviousness in him.

"What else could I have done?" Granna was asking. "I honestly believe Ellie knew she was going when she said, 'Take care of my babies, Mama. You know how, better than anybody.' And who else was there, anyway? It was my duty as a mother and a Christian."

"And you've fulfilled that duty wonderfully, and still are. But speaking of Christian duty—how about a little charity toward another mother and grandmother? She's considerably older than you, isn't she? And from the looks of this letter, she must be frail. Maybe you ought to consider humoring what might well be an old lady's last wish."

"Oh, Robert, I declare—you could talk your way 'round the devil!" I was relieved to hear Granna's chuckle. "But it's the child

I'm most concerned about. How's she going to feel, suddenly packed off to visit a grandmother she knows nothing of? I've felt it best to say as little as possible on the painful subject of her father. Thank the good Lord, she hasn't been too curious."

I hadn't? I'd felt myself to be consumed with curiosity about both my parents, but Granna had been very effective in blocking my questions.

"Seems she has the right to know both sides of her family. As for how she'd feel, why not ask her?" I shrank back from the window. Did he know I was listening? "She's pretty level-headed, Mom. I think if you put it to her right, it'll seem the natural thing it really is."

"Well, maybe it wouldn't do too much harm. But not until after Vacation Bible School! I promised she'd help there, and besides, I need some time to get her clothes in order."

"Mom, you're a true jewel," Uncle Bob said, a laugh still warm in his voice. "I imagine Grandmother Knowles can wait a week for Bible School to be over. But I rather doubt any special clothes are needed for a visit to Franklin County. Just pack her sandals and shorts."

Granna murmured something about "raised to be a lady," and I heard the pinging of the glider springs and the bang of the screened door that told me they were coming inside. I scrambled back into bed and lay in the fragrant darkness, trying to absorb all I had heard, certain that the patterns of my life were about to shift again.

I woke early the next day, with the shadows still long and cool outside my window. The jays in the chinaberry tree were scolding Fred Silver's old cat, who was always stalking some of the smaller animals in the neighborhood. It wasn't really necessary to be up yet, so I plumped my pillow and hunched against it to do some more thinking.

Why had my other grandmother been kept secret from me? Because her son was my father? And was he really so terrible — truly a drunken rascal who had all but kidnapped my mother and then thrown her aside as she grew ill and clumsy with pregnancy? What would his mother be like? Crisp, prickly, and efficient like Granna? Likely not, 'cause they said she was a good deal older. I thought of Star's great-grandmother who had suffered a stroke. Unable to speak, she rocked hour after hour and tapped her cane, her left hand helpless in her aproned lap. When anyone spoke to her, she nodded and smiled and made little humming noises, and the cane-tapping increased. I never knew what to say to her, although Star's mother assured me she understood everything. I wondered how she could tell.

Maybe my other grandmother would be like Emma Tully, who did Granna's hair. She was round and soft and sweet like the wonderful raisin-filled cookies she baked for her grandchildren. That would be a relief, but I didn't place much hope in it. Granna had said something about Grandmother Knowles not being "our kind of people." What kind of people was our kind of people anyway?

Granna had always referred to us as "decent." Did that mean my other grandmother was somehow *not* decent? To Granna, that word meant a whole spectrum of things, it seemed. It meant physically clean and suitably clad, responsible, civic-minded, ethical, morally clean, and religiously inclined. In addition, there was another meaning of which I was very much aware, though I couldn't have put it in words at the time. It had to do with southern class structure, ancestry, and social position. The Cantrells didn't have it. However, the Silver family next door did, even though they were Jewish. They had earned Granna's respect as "decent people" because their family had been in the South since way before the War between the States, and because of Mrs. Silver's quiet kindness and excellent housekeeping skills and Mr. Silver's dependability and business acumen.

But what did decency mean with respect to my Grandmother Knowles? I shuddered. What if she were like Beulah Sneed, who came into town to shop, surrounded by six or seven unkempt children who swarmed all over the grocery store, pinching bread, picking up fruit, pocketing candy and gum, and yelling to each other in their hoarse voices and nearly unintelligible dialect. They all had matted hair and looked as though they never brushed their teeth.

Beulah was just an overgrown version of her children. She had small, mean eyes that peered out over mounds of unhealthy flesh. As she moved through the market, she scolded in a voice as coarse as her children's. Her greasy hair was slicked back into a skimpy pony-tail, and rundown slippers flopped on her dusty feet. I used to stare fascinated at the Sneeds, until Granna whisked me away, whispering that they were "not our kind."

I comforted myself that Grandmother Knowles likely wouldn't be anything like Beulah. The way I saw it, nobody who had been reared by Granna, as my mother had been, could possibly have fallen in love with anyone brought up by the likes of Beulah Sneed.

What, then? Was she poverty-stricken, ignorant, heathenish, worldly, superstitious? There must be something strange about her for Granna to feel as she did. I didn't know how I could get through the next week of not knowing. And worse yet, how would I manage when I was up in Franklin County with her the week after that?

"Emily Jean! You'd best get up if you want to get your practice time in before Vacation Bible School."

Granna's voice sounded so normal that I began to feel better right away. However, I watched her with heightened awareness as I ate breakfast, wondering when she would choose to tell me and what she would say. She chattered about this and that but gave no sign that anything special was on her mind. By the time my hour of practice was up, I did know one thing: I was dying to tell Star.

I spent the morning helping Mittie Nelson's six-year-olds cut out and color their paper-doll apostles, and then I took the children out into the churchyard for games and Kool-Aid. I looked around for Star, who was supposed to help with her mother's class, but they had gone back inside. When we dismissed at noon, I caught up with Mrs. Hargrave and asked where Star was.

"Oh, Emily—well, Starlett wasn't feeling too perky this morning, so I let her stay home to rest up."

"Oh. Reckon she'd like some company later on?"

"She likely would. Why don't you drop over about three or four and check on her?"

I thanked her and skipped home, eager to change from my dress to shorts and get on with my day. But Granna had other plans and took me downtown to shop. We ate chicken salad sandwiches at the Rexall lunch counter, and Granna surprised me by letting me have a strawberry soda. Then we bought my summer wardrobe — shorts, blouses, a new pair of pants, a red and white swimsuit, and, at Lana's Dress Shop, a yellow Sunday dress with petal sleeves and eyelet trim. Miss Mary Afton, who had a summer job there, helped us with the dress. She told Granna how well I read and what a help I'd been that year and how I was a credit to Granna's upbringing — and Granna melted, as everyone did, under Miss Mary Afton's warmth. She had certainly done her best by me, Granna said, but at least part of the credit must be due to the excellent teachers I'd had in both school and church. Miss Mary Afton agreed, but said that surely the major influence must have come from the home. Granna left Lana's, pleased with Miss Mary Afton, with herself, and, miraculously, with me.

Granna said it was too close to suppertime for me to visit Star when we got home, so I called to see how she was. She sounded tired and said she had a stomachache but would likely see me the next day.

"I can't wait to see you. I've got something important to tell you," I whispered into the phone, giving her something to think about.

I went to my room to put away my new things. I was dying to try out my new swim suit, and I hoped Star would swim with me the next afternoon. By some unwritten rule, Mondays and Wednesdays were girls' days at the bend in the river where we swam. On Tuesdays and Thursdays, the boys held sway, and Saturdays and Sundays were family days.

Star came to help out at Bible School on Wednesday, and we walked home together afterward.

"Emily Jean, I'm purely dying to know what you've got to tell me!" she said as soon as we were alone.

"*Well*," I began importantly, "it's still kind of a secret, I reckon.

Granna doesn't even know that I know, but I heard her talking to Uncle Bob, and I'm going on a trip next week."

"Where to?"

"To visit my other grandmother!"

Star's green eyes widened. "I didn't even know you had another grandmother!"

"That's just the thing—I didn't either. I mean, of course I knew. I just didn't think she was alive. Granna's kept her a secret. You know how I told you Granna didn't like my daddy very much? Well, this is his mother. Star, I'm really scared to go. I don't know what she's like at all, except she's old—older than Granna."

Star considered. "Your Granna'd never let you go stay with somebody bad, so she's prob'ly nice. Most grandmas are. Besides, Emily Jean, just think! You've always wanted to know about your daddy, and likely she'll tell you all about him! When are you coming back?"

"I don't even know for sure when I'm going or how long I have to stay. She lives up in Franklin County—Turley, I think. That letter Mr. Huggins gave me the other day—that was from her."

"Wow! Hey, I know! I'll let you take my Brownie camera so you can take pictures of everything. And Emily Jean, you've got to remember and tell me every single thing!"

I promised, gratified at Star's interest in my adventure. We paused in front of her house. The sun was merciless, and it felt good to stand in the shade for a minute.

"Want to go swimming this afternoon? I've got a new suit."

Star shook her head wistfully. "I'd like to, but I can't."

"Why not? What're you doing?"

"Not much. Just practice some, I reckon. Maybe embroider."

"Well, why can't you go? You don't sound like you've got a cold, and your Mama sure can't say it's too chilly today!"

"It's not that. It's just—well, I can't wash my hair either, if you know what I mean."

"Why not?" Her hair, shiny-clean as always, didn't seem to need washing, and I wondered why she'd brought it up.

"Well, you know—the curse."

I stared at her. "*What* curse?" I asked loudly, a little annoyed. Star usually said what she meant.

"*Shhh!*" she hissed fiercely, her cheeks flaming. "*The curse*, Emily Jean," she whispered impatiently. "*You* know—I fell off the roof."

My voice dropped too. "What were you doing on the roof? What curse?" The only curses I knew anything about occurred in ghost stories or in the mouths of blasphemous people.

Star rolled her eyes upward, imploring help from the heavens. "Honestly, Emily Jean!" She leaned closer and whispered emphatically, "*I started my period.*"

I looked at her helplessly. "Starlett Hargrave," I said slowly, "I don't have the slightest idea what you're even talking about."

"Oh." Star looked wise and wistful. "Reckon you'd better ask your Granna. Likely she hasn't had to tell you yet."

"Tell me *what?*" I didn't like to feel stupid, and there was a lump rising in my throat. Star and I had always been able to talk about anything. "Come on, Star," I pleaded. "I told you my secret."

"I know, but—well, this is different. I just don't know how to talk about it. It's kind of—nasty." She looked uncomfortable. "It's kind of about having babies when you grow up."

I frowned. "What do babies have to do with going swimming and washing your hair?"

"Well, not babies, exactly. Oh, Emily Jean, please go and ask your Granna. Ask her what it means to start your period."

"I *will!*" My voice ended on a squeak as the lump in my throat made itself felt, and I whirled away in a temper of frustration.

"I'm sorry," Star called after me, but I didn't look back.

6

Granna was putting cold meat-loaf sandwiches on the table when I burst into the kitchen.

"Granna, I've got to ask you something awfully important," I began.

"And I have something important to tell you," she countered. "But first, go and change your clothes and wash up for lunch. Talk can wait."

I had an idea that if the house caught fire in the dead of night, Granna would insist on my changing clothes and combing my hair before I could be rescued. It was true, however, that I was more comfortable in shorts.

A few minutes later, I hooked my bare feet around the rungs of the chair and bit into my sandwich. "What did you want to tell me, Granna?" I asked, my heart thumping at the thought of what she would say.

"First, your question," she said. I wondered if she was playing for time, and I felt a touch of sympathy for her. But I soon realized that the topic I brought up was as uncomfortable for her to discuss as the one already burdening her mind.

"Star said she couldn't go swimming because she started her period or something, and she talked about falling off a roof and some curse or other, and I don't know what in the world she's talking about. She said to ask you."

Granna eyed me sharply and took a slow, deliberate sip of iced tea. "So, little Starlett Hargrave has become a woman. Who'd have thought—she's such a little thing. Of course, she is almost thirteen. Land sakes, they grow up fast!"

"But what does it *mean?*" I persisted.

"Oh, well, it just means that she's growing up. She's a woman now. All you need to know, Emily Jean, is this: if you ever find spots of blood in your underpants, you drop whatever you're doing and come straight to me, do you hear? Even if you're in school, don't say a word to anyone about it. Just tell Starlett to say you're sick, and come straight home. Is that clear?"

" 'S'ma'am, but—"

"No buts. I'll show you what you need to do when the time comes. And till it does, there's no call to talk about such things. Now, who's that?" she added, in response to the slamming of car doors in our driveway. She peered through the dining-room curtains. "Well, Lord love us, I believe it's my boy!"

I knew she wasn't talking about Uncle Bob—and that left Rogie. Sure enough, he came slamming in through the front door, calling in a voice that immediately set my teeth on edge, "Mother! Mother mine, are you home? This way, Raymond. Don't be the least bit shy. Mother will adore having you."

"I'm here, Roger." Granna smoothed her hair and hurried to receive Rogie's greeting. He kissed her cheek, then turned to the blond young man beside him.

"Mother, may I present Raymond Whitmire? Ray and I are business partners."

"Well—how very wonderful! That sounds just fine. Won't you be seated, Raymond? My granddaughter and I were just enjoying a light lunch, and it'll only take a jiffy to get you some too."

"Don't bother, Mother, we lunched at the Green Lantern on the way. Just a cold drink will do for now. Hello, Emily—still collect crickets? Be a dear child, won't you, and don't let any loose in the house while we're here? You can't imagine, Raymond, what this child put us through. Dreadful! Crickets hopping all over the house—in the sink, in our beds. Ugh!"

"They weren't supposed to get loose," I said stubbornly, as if the incident two years ago had occurred just last night. Raymond gave me what may have been a smile, but it came across as a soft smirk.

"I didn't think young ladies cared for bugs," Raymond remarked, his voice such an uncanny echo of Rogie's that I pigeonholed them immediately as two of a kind—to be ignored when possible and annoyed when not.

"Here you are, gentlemen, just relax and cool off." Granna placed tall glasses of tea before them and uncovered a chocolate cake she'd baked to surprise Uncle Bob.

"Now, I want to hear all about your business ventures. You're here for a week at least, aren't you? I declare, Roger, it's been an age since you were home."

"We'll be here a few days," Rogie said, "depending on how much success we have here in town. Actually, we're on a buying trip for our shop." He helped himself to a large slice of cake and pushed the rest toward Raymond, who also took a piece.

"A shop!" Granna's voice sounded excited, and I could sense her relief at the prospect of Rogie becoming a businessman or respectable shop owner. Any steady, reliable line of work would have pleased her. Rogie had been bouncing from one thing to another for over two years, ever since he had been asked to leave the University of Georgia for reasons never disclosed to me, but which had hurt Granna deeply at the time. She and Uncle Bob had spent long hours closed away in the front bedroom discussing the matter; but Rogie himself, seemingly unconcerned about the whole thing, had taken himself off to Atlanta to make his fortune. Unfortunately, it seemed to take money to make money, and Granna frequently sent off money orders "to help secure an apartment in a better neighborhood," or "to get the dear boy some decent clothes for his job interviews," or "to tide things over until his first paycheck comes."

"Well, mercy sakes, Roger, tell me what you're selling in your shop, before I perish of curiosity!"

"Antiques, Mrs. Markham," volunteered Raymond, his blond eyebrows arching over cool gray eyes.

"Antiques—what a marvelous idea."

"Isn't it? I knew you'd approve, Mother. Ray and I are opening a shop on the outskirts of Atlanta. Actually, we have the most ideal spot you could imagine—a quaint old slave cabin on Raymond's family's property, right at the edge of a busy highway. We're fixing it up to be absolutely charming, and we're out scouring the countryside for merchandise."

"Well, I'm so proud of you both."

"I knew you would be. And I thought how you and your ladyfriends have cherished so many old relics through the years—things that perhaps have ceased to be useful but have the added patina of age. Moneyed people will pay very well for this quaint aura of yesteryear," he added, with a wink for Raymond. "I wondered if you might know of some items that folks around here might be persuaded to sell or donate to us? You see, since Raymond has provided the place and the materials to fix it up—and the prominent old Atlanta name to give us good credentials—I need to have either capital to invest or merchandise to sell if I'm to be a full partner."

"Of course you'll want to contribute your part. Too bad your shop isn't closer to home. As you know, dear, your own family has been rather prominent in this part of the state for many years. The Markhams are a branch of the South Carolina Markhams, and our Henrys are related to Patrick Henry, so I'm sure you and Mr. Whitmire are admirably suited when it comes to background."

"True, but when it comes to the matter of cash in hand, I'm afraid I'm temporarily short. So whatever you can provide, Mother dear, either in cash or in kind, will be greatly appreciated."

I stood up suddenly, feeling a compelling urge to be out in the sunshine again. I clattered my dishes together on the way to the sink.

Granna looked up. "Emily Jean, where are you going?"

"May I go outside, Granna? Or—did you want to tell me something, first?"

Granna looked distracted for a moment. "Oh . . . no, that can wait. Run along, but be sure you're here at four-thirty to help me get supper. Now, boys, let's make a list."

I went to the front porch and plopped onto the glider. "What a stupid day," I grumbled. The only good thing about it was a bank of thunderheads building toward the northwest. If we had a good rain, especially coming from the direction where Bradley was located, it might mean that Uncle Bob's construction crew would quit work early, and he could come home, instead of bunking with the other men in a rooming house close to his job. Tolerating Rogie was always easier when Uncle Bob was on hand. Wordlessly, I prayed for rain.

The heat grew oppressive. I wandered about the yard, unable to settle on a particular pastime or train of thought. I inspected Raymond's white convertible. Rogie aspired to such luxuries, but, as he put it, he had neither credit nor "cash in hand" to achieve his aspirations.

Sitting by the fence, I tried to coax Fred Silver's cat over to be petted, but she was too wary of Granna, who had put the fear of the broom into her for her natural use of our garden plot. She lay in the shade of an oleander bush and washed her face, stopping with paw in midair when I called to her.

After a bit I slipped upstairs to my room, where I set aside a few possessions to take with me on my as-yet-undeclared visit to Grandmother Knowles. I chose my Bible, my jacks, my glass mustard-seed bracelet, my lavender fountain pen, and my book of Emily Dickinson. If I was speaking to Star again by the time I left, I might decide to take her Brownie camera too.

Thinking of Star roused feelings of frustration and resentment. I felt I had been turned aside by both Star and Granna. What were these mysterious allusions and unfamiliar phrases they both understood but couldn't (or wouldn't) explain to me? Why was I too young to know?

Of course, I had taken part in my share of whispered discussions at recess, when several of us had shared tidbits of information and misinformation about where babies came from. Enough of us had witnessed the birth of puppies, kittens, or farm animals to have a pretty good idea of how babies arrived and where they grew. How they got there in the first place, though, was still a matter of speculation among us.

Granna, I recalled, had a medical home reference book—a thick white volume with shiny color illustrations of the human body inside and out, which she kept tucked away carefully in her bedroom downstairs. She was busy in the bathroom, and, with hardly a qualm of conscience, I set out to discover the things I felt I had a right to know.

With its drawn shades and white chenille spread, Granna's room was dim and almost cool. On one side of her mahogany veneer dressing table was a bronzetone photograph of a young man with calm brown eyes beneath an Army cap. Across the bottom in large elegant script were the words "William Markham, May 12, 1917." He was my grandfather, and this picture was taken just before he had marched off to serve in World War I. On the middle section of the dresser, which was lower than the sides, was a small clutter of bobby pins and wave clips and a spatter of pink face powder. As neat as Granna was, there always seemed to be spilled powder on her dresser. It was an endearing thing, somehow—a girlish, careless habit left over from her past.

The medical book wasn't on the dresser or in it, nor was it on top of the closet shelf. I finally found it in the cedar chest atop the woollen blankets. There were little slips of paper marking various pages, but I didn't take time to explore those. I turned to the index and looked up *period,* but there was no listing. I tried *curse* and *roof* and *falls,* but to no avail. None of the listings under *blood* seemed to apply either, so I started leafing through the book at random, hoping to spot something meaningful. I had very little time to search, however, as I was afraid Granna would come into her room and find me there with *The Book*. She had never expressly forbidden me to read it, but there was no doubt in my mind what her reaction would be if I were caught doing so. Stealthily, I slipped it back into place, closed the chest, and crept out into the front hall.

"What were you doing in Mother's room?" demanded Rogie, bumping his suitcase along the hall.

"Putting away a book," I said and walked steadily past him, back up to my room. I groused around for a few minutes, then slipped on my sandals, ran downstairs, and marched out the front door and through the gate. I wasn't sure where I was going, but I felt the need to put some space between me and my family for a while. I walked past Star's house and debated going in, but my pride forbade it.

I puzzled over where to get the information I needed. There was no town library—only the ones at the schools, and they were closed for the summer. I doubted they would have anything on the subject anyway. I walked through the cemetery, pausing at my mother's grave.

"Why did you die and leave me?" I whispered. "Didn't you know I'd need you? I bet you'd have told me the truth about things. How could God need you more in heaven than I do here? I'll never understand it! But I guess it wasn't much up to you, was it? Granna says it was God's will and must be all for the best. But I'm not sure she really feels that way. She misses you a lot." I sighed. "Sorry, Lord," I added, closing my eyes. "It's just that I miss her too, and I know that must sound silly, because I can't even remember her, but I just need somebody who'll tell me how things really are. There's an awful lot of stuff I need to know about. But I'm sorry—and I know you really do know best."

Realizing that what I had just uttered was a sort of prayer, I tacked on, "in Jesus' name, amen." I stood there a moment, trying to feel whether God heard me, or whether my mother knew I was there. My cheeks felt warm and wet, which surprised me. I hadn't known I was crying. It felt deliciously melancholy, and I gave in to the urge to cry a little more. Then I dried my eyes with the backs of my hands. "I'll be back," I promised the dandelions, as I always did.

I scuffed along the edge of the drive with my head down, and that's probably why I didn't see the two men in dark suits until I was almost upon them. They were sitting on a stone bench, their straw hats beside them, eating sandwiches from brown paper sacks.

One of them was new to me, but when the other looked up, I started in recognition. He was one of the Mormon missionaries Granna had sent away so abruptly—the one called Elder Jensen, from Wyoming.

"Hi, there," he said, grinning at me. "How are you today?"

"Fine, thank you," I said, preparing to hurry past them.

"Say, I sure hope you didn't get into trouble the other day on our account."

My feet seemed to stop of their own accord, but my heart beat wildly. I shook my head. "No, it's okay. I'm sorry about Granna. I honestly didn't know she'd feel that way and all."

"Don't worry about it. Lots of folks around here think we're not Christians. Since they already believe in Jesus, they don't see any point in listening to people that don't worship him—or so they think. But we do, you know." He added gently, "We really, truly do."

"Well, I'm real glad of that," I said. "I reckon Granna just didn't understand."

"I think that was it. By the way, this is Elder Comstock. He's new here. And this is—was it Emily?"

"Yes, sir—Emily Jean Knowles. Hello," I said nervously to Elder Comstock, who had a brush of reddish hair above merry brown eyes and a sunburnt pug nose.

"How d'you do, Sister Knowles? Would you like a potato chip? They sure get soggy fast in this climate if we don't eat them up."

"Oh—no, thanks. Uh—do y'all eat here a lot?" I indicated the surrounding graves.

Elder Jensen answered. "When we're on this side of town, we do. There's no park, and we might not be too welcome just sitting on somebody's lawn. On the other side of town, we usually picnic in the schoolyard. Do you come here often yourself?"

I nodded importantly. "I have kin here. My mama and sister and other older folks."

"So that's why you live with your grandmother."

"She's raised me, all my life."

"I see. You know—I wonder, Emily Jean, if you could do me a big favor."

Instinctively I took a half step backward. "What would that be?"

"Well, I had this letter from my kid sister—"

"LaRae?" I interrupted.

"Right—you remembered! Seems she wants me to find her a pen pal here in the South. If I gave you her address, do you think you could find someone who'd like to write to her? She gets kind of lonesome out on the ranch in the summertime."

LaRae—and Stormy—on the far western reaches of the Wyoming hills. "Would it be okay if I wrote to her myself?"

"It'd be super! Would you really? But maybe your grandmother would object."

"I don't think so. She likes me to write letters. She says it improves the mind and the penmanship—and with me, I reckon both could stand some improving."

They laughed, and Elder Jensen tore a page from a small notebook and wrote LaRae's address. I took it and left them, feeling unaccountably good inside, yet wondering how I could feel that way after what Granna had told me. But they were so nice—sort of fresh and clean and open—and they had said they believed in Jesus.

"They'll *tell* you anything," I heard Granna's voice echo in my mind and felt a momentary pang for my gullibility, then another for agreeing to write to LaRae. On that account, however, I felt somewhat justified. In one of my letters, I planned to bring up the subject of those temples and what went on in them. Maybe I could warn her. She might even be able to get word to her nice brother before it was too late, because I was more convinced than ever that he didn't know the truth about the church he belonged to.

The downtown area was sleepy and almost deserted in the afternoon heat. I spent some time in the five-and-dime, looking at stationery, toys, and the small collection of cheap books, then went out again into the heat. I stood irresolutely on the sidewalk for a moment, bored, lonely, and at loose ends. It was an unaccustomed feeling for me.

A blue-green dragonfly buzzed against the sidewalk by my feet and took off again, and from the west came a slow, deep rumble of thunder.

"Comin' on to rain, I'd judge," said old Mr. Moffitt as he shuffled past me.

"Reckon," I agreed, shaken sufficiently out of my doldrums to continue down the street. Mrs. Mavis Buzbee, who owned Lana's Dress Shop (I never did know who Lana was), hurried from the Rexall and back to her shop, her high heels clicking on the pavement. A moment later, Miss Mary Afton came out of Lana's, checking something in her purse. Her heavy amber-colored hair was pinned up off her neck, and her soft print dress clung damply to her legs as she walked. She turned into the drugstore without seeing me, and I surmised that she and Mrs. Buzbee must be taking turns with their lunch breaks. I followed her into the Rexall, not sure why.

I've always loved the Rexall because it was cool when nowhere else was. The store was full of wonderful smells and shiny surfaces and interesting packages, and it always gave me a feeling of confidence, as if it could provide a remedy for every ill.

"Hello, there, Emmy. Come and visit with me while I have lunch," Miss Mary Afton invited, sliding into a booth. Shyly, I sat down across from her, feeling pleased to be asked but a little afraid of presuming on her time.

"Ice cream or lemonade?" she asked, smiling.

"Oh, nothing, thanks. I didn't bring any money, and I already had lunch."

"That's okay. Ice cream or lemonade?"

I grinned foolishly. "Lemonade, I reckon. And thanks."

"It's good for you to have extra liquids in this weather," she assured me with a wink. "Now, what have you and Starlett been up to?"

I bristled at the thought of Star. "Nothing, really. Just helping with Vacation Bible School. But I might go to visit my other grandmother for a while."

"How nice. Where does she live?"

"Up in Franklin County. But—it's kind of scary. I've never seen her before."

"Oh." She leaned back, regarding me seriously. "I can see how that might be scary."

"It's my father's mother, and I never knew my father." I went on to tell her the bits and pieces, somewhat edited, that I knew about my parents.

"Oh, Emmy, this is so exciting! It's such a good chance for you to get to know your father. I mean, who'd know him better than his own mother, and most mothers love to talk about their children." Her hazel eyes began to shine, and gradually her enthusiasm cheered me. "You can ask her so many things—what your father was like as a boy, what he liked to do, what things were like for her as a girl, where her people came from. And, Emmy, why don't you write down in a memory book what you learn, to keep for later? It's so easy to forget things like that unless you do. And you'd do a nice job of it, I know you would."

The idea appealed to me and crowded out some of my fear. I decided to look for an appropriate notebook that very day. I sipped my lemonade and listened to Miss Mary Afton talk about memories of her own father, who had died several years before.

"I've written quite a bit about him in my own little book," she said. "I'll share those things with my children someday, if I have any."

The subject of children reminded me of my most recent source of frustration—Star and her curse. Warmed and cheered and made confident by Miss Mary Afton, and recalling no time when she had ever told me less than the truth, I took a deep breath and made the plunge. However, I left Star's name out of it, from my sense of loyalty to our friendship.

"Have you asked your grandmother about this?" Miss Mary Afton inquired, when I had told her what I needed to know.

"Yes, ma'am," I said with a sigh. "But she wouldn't say much about it. Do you even know what I'm talking about?"

She smiled. "I surely do, and it's very simple. Lots of older folks are a little embarrassed to discuss these things, because it wasn't considered proper to talk about it when they were young. I can see why you're confused." She pushed her plate aside and folded her arms on the tabletop. "You see, Emmy, it isn't really a curse at all. It's a blessing."

I stared at her in surprise. She continued: "Little girls can't have babies, but grown-up girls and women can, right?"

I nodded.

"Well, sometime between being a little girl and being all grown up, things begin to change inside your body so that when you're grown and married, you'll be able to have your own babies. Every month, in a special place inside you, your body gets ready to feed and take care of a baby while it grows and gets big enough to be born. But of course, you aren't ready to grow a baby yet, so when your body realizes that there's no baby there this month—well, it decides to clean house and get ready for next month."

"Clean house?" I asked incredulously.

"Uh-huh. All the food it was saving for the baby, mixed with some blood you don't need any more, is swept right out a certain opening in your body—the same opening a baby would be born from. And that housecleaning is called menstruation, or having a menstrual period."

"Oh . . . well, does it—hurt?"

"Sometimes your body works so hard inside on this cleaning spree that you might feel a little tired or uncomfortable for a few days. But you can feel glad too, because you know that everything's right on schedule, and someday you'll be able to be a mother with babies to love. So you see, Emmy, all this talk about it being a curse or falling off the roof—all that's just old-fashioned nonsense."

I nodded, awed by my new-found knowledge. After we finished lunch, I walked back to Lana's with her, and she gave me a brief hug as we parted.

"Come and tell me about your trip when you get back," she said.

"I will," I promised. "And, thanks a whole lot—for telling me."

"You're welcome, Emmy. I hope it helped."

"Yes, ma'am, it sure did!" I skipped off down the street, a buoyant happiness replacing my earlier gloom. About two blocks from home I started to run in earnest, as half-dollar-sized raindrops began to splat in the red dust of the road and on my bare arms and legs. The drops felt warm at first, but then as the downpour increased, the rain became chilly. I leaped up the front steps and landed dripping on the porch just as a ferocious peal of thunder shook the heavens. Skimming the stairs, I ran for the bathroom and shucked out of my wet shorts and shirt. I wrapped up in a big towel, padded into my room, and carefully placed LaRae's sodden address under my table lamp for safekeeping. I spared a thought for the Mormon elders, wondering if they had found shelter from the rain.

. . . . 7 . . . .

Dressed in dry clothes, I ran back downstairs to unplug the refrigerator and close the kitchen window where Granna's plants were
getting doused. I didn't know where Granna was, but I assumed she
had gone antique-hunting with Rogie and Raymond, as the white
convertible was missing from the driveway. The house was dark and
quiet—all noise seemed concentrated outside in the drumming rain
and incessant thunder. Up in my room, I sat down by the open
window, which was sheltered by the big, leafy chinaberry tree. I
loved the earthy, sweet rain smell, and breathed deeply of it.

Suddenly, a thought occurred to me: my prayer in the cemetery
had been answered—I'd been given someone to tell me what I
needed to know! I believed that prayers in general were probably
heard and sometimes answered—other people's prayers, anyway.
But for the first time, my own had been answered. I felt both awed
and delighted, thinking that God himself was aware of me, Emily
Jean Knowles in Tatum, Georgia! It gave me chillbumps.

"Thank you, Lord," I whispered. "I really do appreciate it."

By the time Rogie and his friend brought Granna home, all of
them stamping on the porch and flipping excess water from their
umbrellas, Uncle Bob's gray Nash swished into the driveway behind
the white convertible. He seemed surprised to see Rogie and greeted
him in a voice that almost succeeded in being hearty.

"Hello, hello, big brother," Rogie replied. "Raymond, my brother
Bob, who's studying to be a man of the cloth. Bob, may I present
Raymond Whitmire, of the Atlanta Whitmires—my business partner."

Handshakes and polite remarks aside, we all gravitated toward the kitchen where Granna was counting pork chops and putting on potatoes to boil. Rogie and Raymond were happily speculating on whether Mrs. Simpson would give up her antique butter churn for the price they had offered her. I sidled up to Uncle Bob, who was trying to read a rather soggy newspaper by the light from the rain-washed dining-room window. Granna insisted that the lights be turned off when there was lightning.

"Hey, Uncle Bob."

"Howdy, Punkin. What's up?"

"Um — do you . . . " I lowered my voice. "Do you think God really answers everybody's prayers?"

He folded his paper together and pulled out a chair for both of us. "Everybody's, huh? Hmm." He frowned slightly, narrowing his eyes in the way he had when making up his mind. "I guess I could give you an easy answer on that and say 'of course,' but — well, you know that sometimes folks just pray words without being very sincere or even believing there's a God to listen to them. I suspect maybe that kind of prayer doesn't get far past the ceiling.

"And other times, people pray sincerely a long time for something they want very badly. When it doesn't seem to happen, they wonder why not. Maybe they just need to learn patience first. Or maybe they get an answer but don't recognize it, or the answer isn't the one they hoped for. God can say no as well as yes — and no is still an answer, isn't it? It's not as though God were in the business of granting wishes, like a fairy godmother. But yes, I think he hears us when we're sincere and answers us according to our faith and his will for what's best for us in the long run. Does that help, kiddo?"

"Yes, but . . . would he — would he have time to listen, even to kids like me, if they needed something? I don't mean like a bike or a present or anything. I mean, just needing to know something."

"I don't see why not. Jesus loved children and wanted them near him. Why wouldn't he listen to their prayers, maybe even sooner than to grown-ups' prayers?" He smiled at me. "Besides, I have a hard enough time saying no to you when you want something, and if God loves you even more than I do—well, I think he'd do his best for you, don't you? Why don't you give it a try?"

"Well, I—I did. And I think God really did listen and answer me. I just wondered if you thought that was likely."

"You'd better believe I do. That's great, E. J., and I'm glad you took your question to him."

It was typical of Uncle Bob that he didn't ask what I had been praying about. He knew I would tell him if I felt inclined.

"Emily Jean, I need you to set the table and take up the turnip greens. You can slice a plate of tomatoes too. There's no call for you to sit talking while I do all the work."

Uncle Bob gave me a little pat and murmured something about Mary and Martha.

The refrigerator was still dark when I opened it. "Shall I plug this back in now?" I asked.

"Not yet. I think the lightning's getting worse. Thank goodness we have a gas cookstove so we can have a hot meal. But you'd best get out the candles for the table so we can see to eat."

As it turned out, the storm was severe and seemingly stalled over our house. By the time supper was ready, we had no electricity, and the yellow utility candles flickering on the table added to the company atmosphere. Even turnip greens tasted better by candlelight.

As the candles burned down and the lightning flashed silver-blue through the rain, our conversation turned to the telling of stories. Uncle Bob told some funny ones from his college and Navy days, Granna recalled a couple of Civil War tales she'd heard from her grandfather, and then Rogie persuaded Raymond to tell some ghost stories from his own family. Rogie revelled in this sort of thing, and I had to admit Raymond was skilled in the telling of them. He folded his arms on the table and leaned slightly forward, his light eyes holding each of ours in turn as he spun a chilling yarn of a murdered ancestress who purportedly still appeared on occasion, smiling on the stair landing or standing wistfully in the doorway of the dining room when guests were present to remark on her beauty. I fought an unreasoning desire to glance at our dining-room doorway.

Ordinarily Granna wouldn't stand for much of this kind of thing, but even she was caught up in the spell and was unwilling to risk offending Rogie's friend and partner. However, when Raymond, who apparently dabbled somewhat in spiritualism, got into an account of a séance he had attended, it was more than either Granna or Uncle Bob could countenance. Granna began to gather up dishes noisily, and Uncle Bob said he was full as a market-bound hog and twice as sleepy, and would we please excuse him?

I wanted to stay and listen, but Granna fixed her eyes on me from the dining-room doorway, and they were even more compelling than those of Raymond's haunt. Obediently, I stacked an armload of dishes and tiptoed into the kitchen with them. We wouldn't wash them now, for fear of drawing the lightning.

"Granna," I ventured, "today you said you had something to tell me. Is now a good time?"

I heard her sharp intake of breath, followed by a sigh. "I suppose it had better be," she said resignedly. "Let's go into my room where we can be private."

I don't know whether the gloom or an unusual display of affection was the reason, but Granna kept her hand on my shoulder as we moved through the candlelit dining room where Rogie and Raymond still talked animatedly. In her room, we sat carefully on the edge of the chenille bedspread.

"You see, Emily Jean," she began, and then gasped, "Oh, my mercy!" as a white bolt of lightning quivered just outside the window. Almost instantly, an explosion of thunder followed it. "Thank the good Lord for these sheltering walls," she added fervently, and I had the feeling she might be reminding the Lord to keep them in sheltering condition for us. From her closet, she took an old-fashioned oil lamp with a red waxed shade and set it on her dresser. "There, that's cozy," she said after lighting it, and I had to agree. The soft light glimmered on the glass of my grandfather's photograph, and Granna's eyes seemed to soften as she glanced that way.

"That letter, Emily Jean, which you so carelessly left in your pocket—that letter was written by your . . . father's mother."

A tight quivering had begun in my chest, but I said nothing.

"She's an old woman now. She wasn't really young when your father was born, and she writes to say she isn't well. Naturally, she'd like to see you, child, before she—uh—gets any older. You're her only grandchild, as you are mine, and I—I feel it my duty as a Christian to grant her that wish."

I found my voice, though it sounded hollow and unfamiliar. "Do you know her?"

Another peal of thunder, not quite so deafening as the last one, shook the house. Granna folded her arms and clenched her elbows with her hands. "I've met her only once, and admittedly I was distraught at the time. She came to the—uh—services—for your mother and the baby, which was decent of her, though she was unable to explain why her son wasn't there. She was sensible enough to agree that Ellen's wishes should be followed, that I should bring you up here. But, to give credit where credit is due, she would gladly have taken you if there'd been a need—even at her age."

Granna's eyes closed briefly, and her mouth drew downward in bitter remembrance. "Lord knows, I'd had to have been on my deathbed to allow her to take you after what her son did to my precious girl. And she acted so proud of him, just as if she had a right to be—standing there talking about her dear boy and what he must be suffering. As though he wasn't a no-good criminal, or near enough to make no difference. Well, I thank the dear Lord for giving me strength to raise you myself in a Christian home. I only hope and pray, Emily Jean, that I've taught you enough—that you're strong enough now to know right from wrong . . ." She paused, and her worried eyes behind her glasses searched mine.

"You've tried awful hard," I said, "and I know I'm not easy to raise. But, Granna, how come she never wanted to see me?"

Her chin lifted, and she gazed at the flame in the lamp. "I reckon it wasn't so much a matter of wanting. We had an agreement—a bargain. I agreed to write to her once a year and report on your progress—which I have done. A couple of times I included one of your school pictures. She agreed not to interfere with my raising

. . . . 65 . . . .

you or to contact you in any way, and she's kept that bargain till now. I could still refuse, but Robert's persuaded me that it's my duty to allow you to visit her this once, to ease her in her age and illness.

"I mailed a letter to her saying to expect you next Monday. She assures me she has a capable housekeeper and nurse who will look after you. She wants you to stay for two weeks, which I think is a mite long, but we'll see. Robert will take you with him Monday morning. You'll have to leave early—her place is up in Franklin County, a good hundred and fifty miles from here. Robert'll have to double back to Bradley, and it'll make him late getting to work. It's very kind of him to take you."

"Granna, is she—a bad person?"

Granna pressed her lips together tightly. "I don't really reckon she is, although I always hold a mother accountable for her children's natures. I think she's an honorable woman in her own way, or I'd never let you go there. But her ways are not our ways. Ellen should have known better than to have gotten herself entangled with that sort of boy. I can only blame myself that she did."

Her face crumpled, and she covered her mouth with her hand. "If she hadn't met Frank Knowles, she'd be alive today."

But I wouldn't be, I thought suddenly. *Or at least, I wouldn't be who I was—would I?* I didn't dare say that to Granna, of course. She might be fond of me, but I always felt that she found me to be a poor substitute for her lost Ellie.

"I'm sorry, Granna," I whispered, wishing I could be Ellie for her. "I'm sorry she died having me."

Granna pulled herself up and swallowed her tears. "She died because Frank Knowles neglected her health and sent her here all alone when she should have been flat on her back in a good hospital. It should never have happened. He as good as killed her himself."

"I'm sorry," I said again. Granna looked at me, stark misery apparent in her eyes. It was an intimate moment, or should have been—a time for grandmother and granddaughter to cling together, mourning the loss of the young woman who linked them. But something snapped shut in Granna's eyes, and she said briskly, "Well, it was no fault of yours, Emily Jean, so don't go having foolish ideas like that. Just be sure you have sense enough not to fall for the foolishness of the Knowles clan." She lifted the oil lamp and carried it with her into the dining room.

"But I *am* a Knowles," I whispered, rising to follow. I tiptoed behind the dining-room table, where Rogie and Raymond were having a second piece of chocolate cake, and started up the stairs, hoping they wouldn't notice me.

"Quit sneaking around, missy, we know you're there," Rogie said. "You can't believe, Raymond, what a brat she is."

I didn't even turn my head. I just wondered if my mother in heaven knew what a rotten little brother she had on earth.

The next day, Star and I walked home from Vacation Bible School, dawdling along the way and enjoying the rain-washed air.

"Emily Jean, you're not still mad, are you? Did you ask your Granna about . . . uh, what I said?"

"Oh, that? Sure, I know all about it."

Star sighed. "Good. I'm awful glad. I wanted to tell you, but I just *couldn't* — you know."

"Honestly, Star, I don't know why you made such a fuss. It's all very simple and natural." I gazed up at the fluffy white clouds that had replaced yesterday's black ones.

"It is?" Star nearly tripped from watching me instead of paying attention to where she was walking.

"Of course," I said confidently. "You see, it isn't really a curse at all. It's a blessing."

"A blessing! Just wait, Emily Jean Knowles, till you're doubled over with cramps and a backache — then tell me it's a blessing!"

I faltered for a moment, but regained my aplomb. "That's only because your body's working so hard, cleaning house inside," I explained. Miss Mary Afton had never failed me yet.

8

Pleased with themselves, Rogie and Raymond left on Saturday morning, the white convertible packed with churns, flat irons, and one treadle sewing machine. They planned a leisurely trip back to Atlanta along the side roads, cultivating the acquaintance of every elderly person or owner of an elderly house that they could find. Granna saw them off, then came beaming back into the kitchen where Uncle Bob and I were enjoying a late breakfast.

"Well, I'm so pleased," she said, joining us at the table. "Roger is including me in his business! I'll be paid a dollar for every good antique I find for him. Isn't that just like him, to want his old mother to be a part of things? And that sweet Raymond—I'm so glad Roger has finally found a friend to steer him in the right direction, aren't you, Robert?"

Uncle Bob stared at the sugar bowl, a sad smile on his lips. He didn't answer.

"Oh, Son, I'm sorry." Granna patted his hand. "Here you are, trying to plan your sermon for tomorrow, and I just rattle on. Go ahead and concentrate, dear—I'll hush. It's just that I'm so proud of both my boys!"

Uncle Bob's smile grew wider, and he winked at Granna. "I hope we both always do you honor, Mom, and I hope things work out well for Roge."

"I'm confident they will, now. Emily Jean," she added in a hushed voice, "come on up with me and we'll strip the beds in Roger's room and change them. The bathroom needs cleaning too. I want everything tidy for Sunday, and we've got to keep out of Robert's way so he can think. What will your text be tomorrow, dear?"

"Hmm? Oh—hope, I think. Our hope in Jesus."

"Sounds just right. I'm sure you'll be inspired." Granna shooed me upstairs, where she sang hymns all morning in her trembling soprano. I don't know where in the house Uncle Bob could have gone to escape the sound of her singing, but perhaps the hymns were meant to provide part of the inspiration she had promised him.

I spent the afternoon perched in the old chinaberry tree below my window, composing my letter to LaRae. I tore up several versions before I hit on one that sounded right, wanting to let her know right off that I was a Christian and not a Mormon. I told her about our Girls' Auxiliary at church and mentioned that Uncle Bob was studying to be a preacher. I figured she'd like to know how nice I thought her brother was, so I put that in, but I didn't mention how Granna had sent him packing. I asked what it was like to live on a ranch and have her own horse, because I genuinely wanted to know. And then, because my impending visit to Grandmother Knowles was on my mind, I told her about that.

I found a stamp in Granna's kitchen drawer and tucked the letter inside my diary, waiting for a chance to mail it. Then, following Miss Mary Afton's suggestion, I found a black-and-white speckled note-book and put it in the bottom of my suitcase in case I wanted to write down anything I found out about my family.

After supper, Uncle Bob drove Star and me around town a while and bought us each an ice cream—the new soft kind that swirled out of a machine into a white, creamy mountain on the cone. When we dropped off Star at her house, he peered past me, as if trying to see into the dim interior of the Hargrave home.

"Pat home tonight?" he asked casually.

"I'll run see," Star offered quickly, but he stopped her.

"No—no need. I'll see her tomorrow. She'll be going with us out to the mission."

"Want me to tell her anything for you?"

"I guess not, thanks. Just — that I'll see her tomorrow. That's all."

"All right. Thanks for the ride and the ice cream. It was real good."

"You're surely welcome. 'Night, Star."

"Bye," I added, winking hugely at her as she got out of the car.

"Nice little girl, that Star," Uncle Bob commented as we pulled away.

"All the Hargrave girls are nice," I replied primly, my voice such an echo of Granna's that he gave me an amused glance. "Well, they are," I said, grinning back at him. Neither of us said another word till we got home.

There was a hushed sense of anticipation in the house the next afternoon as Uncle Bob prepared his sermon for the Pine Forest Mission that evening. When the phone rang at two-thirty, we all jumped and laughed nervously. Uncle Bob answered, murmured some sympathetic words, and came back frowning.

"Marva Topham's got some kind of stomach complaint. She and Pat were going to sing a duet for me — "Whispering Hope" — to preface my message. I was counting on that, but now she can't go, and I can't spring a solo on Pat."

"That wouldn't be fair," Granna agreed. "And the other altos are needed in the choir tonight at Eastside. They're singing at the baptismal service for Joe Simpson. He's finally decided to come into the fold."

Uncle Bob chuckled. "Joe'll be embarrassed to tears to have the choir sing him in." He stared out the living room window. "Guess I'll have to do without the duet."

"I'd help if I could, dear, but my voice just doesn't lend itself to part-singing. I'm strictly a soprano, I'm afraid."

"Um — right."

"I know someone who could do it just beautiful," I said, "if she could just come."

"Who's that, E. J.?"

"Miss Mary Afton. She knows that song, because she taught it to us in school — in parts."

"Miss—who? She's a teacher?"

Granna spoke up. "She's been helping Arnelle Chapman and Mittie Nelson with the fifth and sixth grades as a teacher's helper. She rents that little house behind Arnelle's place. Mary Afton MacDougal, isn't it, Emily Jean?"

" 'S'ma'am. She's super, Uncle Bob, and she just purely loves to sing. Couldn't we go ask her, please, just to see?"

"I don't know, E. J. It hardly seems fair when I don't even know her."

"But I do, and Star does, and Granna's met her! Please?"

"It might not hurt to try," Granna put in. "I don't know where she attends church. Of course, she might already be obligated, but you could ask."

"I don't know where she goes, either," I said. "But I know she's a good Christian. Please, Uncle Bob?"

He reluctantly allowed himself to be pulled outside to his car. Uncle Bob drove down the sleepy Sunday afternoon streets and parked in Mrs. Chapman's drive. Then he and I walked back to the little red-painted house that sat under some ancient oak trees.

As we approached the tiny house, we realized that Miss Mary Afton hadn't seen us yet, for she jumped lightly out of a swing suspended from one of the massive branches and went over to a gray-haired woman in a white lawn chair. "Come on, Mama," she said cheerfully, bracing herself and leaning to lift the woman to her feet.

Uncle Bob put out a hand to keep me from running forward. "Let's wait a minute," he suggested. We stood behind a bridal wreath bush and watched the young woman lead the older one toward the house. The mother moved with shuffling steps, her arms hanging heavily at her sides. When they reached the concrete blocks that served for steps, Miss Mary Afton slipped one arm around her mother's waist and bent to lift her foot onto the step.

"In we go—time for your rest," she said gently, propelling the unresisting woman into the small house.

We stood in silence for a moment, contemplating what we had

seen. My mind was a turmoil of awe and pity. Why was it that Miss Mary Afton had such a mother to care for, and we hadn't known? She had spoken of her dead father and her happy memories of him, but no wonder she had been silent concerning her mother.

"Maybe we'd best not bother her, E. J. It looks as though she has her hands full right now."

I agreed, but just then she came back out to retrieve a book she'd left by the swing and spotted us.

"Emily Jean, is that you?" she called, shielding her eyes against the sun as she came forward. "How nice to see you! Were you looking for me or for Mrs. Chapman?"

"For you," I said, pulling Uncle Bob forward. "This is my Uncle Bob," I began, but they were already reaching to shake each other's hand.

"Bob Markham, Miss MacDougal. How are you?"

"Pleased to meet Emmy's uncle, Mr. Markham. If I'm allowed any favorites among the children, she's one of them. What brings you folks to this part of town—and won't you sit down?"

She indicated the white wooden chairs, and Uncle Bob eased himself down on the edge of one.

"Well, Miss MacDougal, my niece here had an idea that you might be able to help us out of a spot, of sorts. But I'm afraid, E. J., that we'd be imposing too much . . . "

Miss Mary Afton smiled, leaned forward, and clasped her hands around her knees. She looked from one to the other of us, her dark-fringed hazel eyes wide with interest.

"Well, now you've got me curious. What is it?"

Certain that Uncle Bob was about to withdraw his request, I plunged ahead, explaining about the mission church and the sermon on hope and the need for an alto. I barely glanced at Uncle Bob, who sat rubbing his forehead and looking somewhat embarrassed.

"And so," I concluded, "that's why I thought of you, because you taught us that song, and I know you can sing the alto part."

"I do love that song," she admitted. "It really is a temptation. I wonder . . . "

"We realize it's awfully short notice," Uncle Bob said. "If you have other plans or obligations, we'll surely understand."

Miss Mary Afton stood up, and so did Uncle Bob, quickly, but she waved him back down. "I have my mother staying with me now, and she's an invalid," she said. "But sometimes I can get Mrs. Chapman or her sister to sit with her for a while. How long would we be gone?"

"From about five-thirty to eight-thirty, but please don't feel — "

"Excuse me for just a moment," Miss Mary Afton said and ran down the drive to the Chapman home. I threw a triumphant glance at Uncle Bob, but he was turned on his chair, watching Miss Mary Afton with a strange expression on his face. I decided not to say anything.

As she returned to the little house, she reported breathlessly, "Mrs. Chapman and her sister will take turns sitting with Mother." Her cheeks were flushed, and I thought she had never looked prettier. "I'll feed her before I go, so there should be no problem. She'll probably sleep."

Uncle Bob stood up again and smiled at her. "If you're sure this is something you want to do."

She nodded. "It sounds just like what I've needed today. Besides, Mrs. Chapman practically ordered me to go. She seems to think a lot of you." Miss Mary Afton laughed lightly, and Uncle Bob reddened.

"She's my mother's good friend," he explained. "I really am indebted to you, and very grateful. We'll be here shortly after five then."

"I'll be ready," she promised.

"See?" I prodded as we drove home in the shimmering heat. "Isn't she nice? Didn't I tell you?"

Uncle Bob didn't answer at first. When we finally turned down Oglethorpe, he said, "I know one thing — I never had a teacher like that! I wonder though, E. J., if we ought to take her away from her mother for that long."

"Seems to me she wanted to come."

"Did seem so, didn't it? Maybe she doesn't have many chances to get out just now."

"And she does love to sing."

"That must be it," he agreed and began to whistle.

We picked up Star and Pat first. Granna insisted on getting out of the car to straighten her skirt and urged Pat into the front seat to sit next to Uncle Bob. Pat blushed, but didn't object. She sat very still, her hands clasped in her lap. She was wearing a pink and white candy-stripe dress, fresh from the sewing machine and ironing board, and her white earrings and pink lipstick looked pretty against her olive skin.

I explained to them about our substitute alto, and Star gave an excited little bounce.

"Pat, you'll love her," Star declared. "She sings like an angel." Then she laid one thin hand on my arm. "But, Emily Jean, I'm so scared! I'm supposed to play for them, and what if I mess up?"

"You won't," I assured her. "You've practiced it plenty, and you'll do just fine, like always."

"I don't know. Will you sit on the bench by me and turn the page?"

"Sure." I smoothed the skirt of my new yellow dress, glad that there was something I could do, however small, to contribute to the success of Uncle Bob's first service.

Miss Mary Afton came out even before Uncle Bob could knock. She was smiling and wearing a simple tan dress with a creamy rose pinned to it. Her hair was turned under in a kind of long pageboy style. Polite greetings were exchanged as we all settled back into the car, and then an uneasy silence descended as Uncle Bob turned the car onto the highway.

After a few minutes Granna said, "Why don't we all sing? It'll give the girls a chance to warm up their voices."

Uncle Bob took the initiative on that, launching us into one song after another — "Moonlight Bay," "April Showers," "The Old Folks at Home," and a whole collection of hymns. Miss Mary Afton provided a rich enough alto from the back seat to balance the three soprano voices of Pat, Granna, and Star. I tried valiantly to follow her lead, but made a general mess of it. When we began singing, "I was sinking deep in sin, far from the peaceful shore," she just listened, so I knew she likely wasn't a Baptist, but by the second chorus she was able to join in on "love lifted me, even me" and she seemed to know "Sweet Hour of Prayer" and "Master, the Tempest Is Raging," which was one of my favorites.

"What next?" asked Uncle Bob, temporarily out of songs.

"I know," said Star. "Let's do 'Give, Said the Little Stream.'"

"They probably wouldn't know that," Miss Mary Afton said.

"But we do," I said. "Let's teach it to them, the way you taught us at school."

"Sure, let's hear it," encouraged Uncle Bob, so the three of us began,

> Give, said the little stream,
> Give, oh! give, give, oh! give,
> Give, said the little stream,
> As it hurried down the hill;
> I'm small I know, but wherever I go,
> The fields grow greener still.

The simple, catchy tune was easy to remember, and we soon were going through all three verses — "Give, said the little rain," and "Give, then for Jesus give . . . there is something all can give," and Miss Mary Afton was able to blend in her harmony.

The heady sensation of rolling along the open highway, singing, with the fragrant summer breeze blowing in upon us, was so relaxing and exhilarating that I forgot, for a time, my fearful anticipation of the journey I must make the next morning in that very same car. It was enough to be with the people I loved best in the world, all of us together and united, for the moment, in the joyful blend of words and melody.

. . . . 9 . . . .

It seemed no time until we turned off the highway onto the red clay road that led to the Pine Forest Mission. The chapel was a white frame rectangle elevated on concrete blocks. It sat, as its name indicated, in a clearing in a pine forest. We parked and climbed out, stretching and breathing the fragrance of sun-warmed resin and listening to the sighing of a breeze high in the treetops. No birds were singing, but an occasional insect buzzed loudly or hopped on the slippery brown needles underfoot.

We were early, so we took our time wandering through the church. Granna and I went down the pews, seeing to it that the dilapidated black hymnals and the paper fans advertising Kickliter's Hardware were evenly distributed. Uncle Bob opened windows, arranged his Bible and his notes at the pulpit, took off his suit coat, and then put it on again. Pat and Miss Mary Afton practiced their song until people began to arrive, when Star slid off the piano bench and let Pat take over to play the prelude music.

The seats by the open windows filled up first. Uncle Bob tried to shake each person's hand and ask each name, and I wondered how many of them he could hope to remember. A very stout woman, her massive body packed into a purple and black print dress, plodded up the center aisle and plunked a mason jar filled with zinnias on top of the piano. Pat murmured a startled "Thank you," and the woman retraced her journey to the back of the church, where she collapsed, puffing, beside a tiny, white-haired man with a jutting chin and gold-rimmed spectacles. Four children crowded in on her other side.

One of the girls looked about my age. Her dark blonde hair hung straight to her collar, and long, unevenly cut bangs made her blink and toss her head to free her eyes from the untidy fringe of hair. She stood up once and marched impatiently to the doorway to beckon to someone outside. Her faded dress was missing its sash and hung limply to just above her knees. She wore none-too-clean bobby socks with scuffed black patent high heels at least two sizes too large. Even with the socks, they slipped and clattered on the wooden floor as she returned to her place. She kept her head turned toward the entrance until a boy of about ten or so, obviously her brother, eased into the pew behind his family. He carefully squirmed and adjusted his position until he was hidden from view of the pulpit behind the back of the stout woman. She paid the children no mind, but sat vigorously fanning herself and the elderly man beside her.

At two minutes after six, Uncle Bob moved to the pulpit and began the service. "Let us begin this worship service by singing on page thirty-one, 'Bringing in the Sheaves,' after which we'll ask a good brother, Deacon Eli Gurney, to lead us in prayer."

For such a comparatively small congregation, the volume of the singing was surprising. After the hymn, a man stood up in the third row, leaned on the back of the pew before him with cracked, soil-dried hands, and bowed his head, humbly thanking God for the bounties of life—sun, rain, crops, herds, families—and for "this young feller" who had come to try to lead them to Christ. We sang a few more hymns, and then Pat played a soft medley while two men passed the collection plate—a tin pie plate painted white, unlike our felt-lined mahogany ones at Eastside. As the plate went around, we could hear the clink of every coin that was dropped into it.

Afterward, Uncle Bob introduced Star and Pat and Miss Mary Afton and announced their song. Star's hands were trembling, but she launched steadily into the introduction while I sat beside her, ready to turn the pages. The song went well, and even the children were quiet as the sweet harmony washed over them. Then Uncle Bob slipped into his sermon, talking quietly about hope—how it whispers, so that we have to listen for it, rather than demands our attention as the cares of the world seem to do.

"I cain't hear him," complained the white-haired little man in the back. The heavyset woman, still fanning herself, hissed, "Hush, Paw-Paw!" and pressed her finger to her lips. He frowned at her and made a "get-back" motion with his hand.

Uncle Bob accommodatingly made an attempt to speak louder, but a woman on the second row called out, "Never mind, preacher. That's old Paw-Paw Jenkins, and he couldn't hear you 'lessen you yelled in his eardrum. Rest of us hear you just fine."

"What'd she say?" demanded Paw-Paw, as the heavy woman tried to soothe him. The girl with stringy bangs looked behind her, snatched a piece of paper from her brother's hoard, and hastily scribbled a note that she passed to Paw-Paw. He held it a great distance from him, frowned, then gave a submissive grunt and settled into silence. I wondered what in the world she had written.

Uncle Bob took a deep breath and continued: "Paul told us, 'If in this life only we have hope in Christ, we are of all men most miserable.' But friends, we have no need to be miserable, no need to despair. No matter what trials and afflictions we have to bear in this life, not even death is beyond the power of hope in Christ Jesus."

I stole a glance at Pat and Miss Mary Afton, who both looked totally attentive. Star had rolled her handkerchief into a damp ball and was slowly transferring it from one hand to the other.

"We have hope both in this life and in the next, through the redemptive power of the blood of Jesus Christ, who died for the sins of every one of us. What does this mean? It means that Jesus loved us — and God loved us — enough to allow his beloved son to be sacrificed on the cross for you and me. It means that because Jesus paid the price for our sins, we don't have to! Is that good news, friends? He 'took the rap' for us, as prisoners say. He bought us, it says in First Corinthians. We belong to him, and we owe him all that we have and all that we are, for the hope he gives us of a glorious resurrection and life with him and his father in the realms of joy everlasting."

"Amen!" shouted the man who had given the prayer.

Granna, sitting with her hands folded decorously on top of her purse, was trying to subdue her smile, but it kept breaking out in prideful little quivers. Uncle Bob continued, naming the many uses of hope, and we were all beginning to relax and be glad that things were going so well, when a superbly constructed paper airplane sailed from the rear of the church, banked, and took a nose dive in front of the pulpit. Uncle Bob's eyes contemplated it for a moment, but his voice never faltered. The girl who must be Paw-Paw Jenkins's granddaughter turned around and glared with narrowed eyes at her brother, and an outraged murmur arose from several people, but Uncle Bob continued to preach. Presently a large, wet spitwad hit the ceiling, stuck, and then dislodged and fell, splatting on the backrest of a pew about halfway up the aisle.

Still speaking in a normal tone of voice, Uncle Bob stepped down from the pulpit and strolled down the aisle to the back row, where he held out his hand. The boy, his eyes enormous, offered up his ammunition — the sheaf of papers he had brought with him. Uncle Bob gave a little shake of his head, placed the papers on the seat of the pew, and held out his hand again, still quietly talking about hope. The boy shrugged, and Uncle Bob leaned over to take him by the elbow. Maybe it was the look in Uncle Bob's eyes — a certain commanding presence he might have learned in the service — but something compelled that boy to walk back up the aisle and climb the two steps to the simple pulpit with him. Uncle Bob stood behind him, his hands resting lightly on the boy's shoulders, and continued to preach.

On the next to the last bench, the three younger boys sat well forward, their mouths open. The girl kept her head down, scribbling furiously, and the massive woman beside her frowned and fanned harder than ever. Paw-Paw pursed his lips and squinted, as if trying to make some sense of what was going on.

"Now, this boy," Uncle Bob said conversationally, "this isn't a bad boy. I can tell that from looking into his eyes, can't you?" He gazed at the congregation as if appealing for agreement, then continued. "No sir, this isn't a bad boy. What this is, is a *bored* boy. You see, folks, this young man's been growing awfully fast lately, and his young bones and new muscles are just hollering for motion. He wants to be moving every waking minute, don't you, Son? And sitting still in school or church is one of the hardest things he's had to do in a long time. Is that right, fellow?"

The boy tossed his hair and shrugged one bony shoulder. His wrists hung a good three inches below the cuffs of his plaid shirtsleeves, and his ears stuck out like bright red flags on each side of his face.

"Yes sir, he needs to be active. His mind needs activity too, and what it craves above all else at this age is *fun*. Humor, you might say. I'll tell you, folks, a boy like this can find more to laugh at in one day than you and I put together. The strangest things can be funny to him—even a paper airplane sent on a secret mission during a new preacher's sermon.

"But, there's something else he craves, too, at this stage of life— something he needs just as surely as he needs his eggs and grits every morning, though he may not know it. He needs and craves our love and attention. Oh, I know he has a funny way of asking for it, but that's how boys do."

The boy swallowed, almost audibly, and lifted his head a fraction. The quiet in that little building was so intense you could have heard the plink of that proverbial pin, had anyone thought to drop one. I was willing to bet that none of those folks had ever heard a sermon quite like this one—I knew I hadn't! Pat looked a bit uncomfortable, and stared at her white pump bobbing up and down with the nervous motion of her foot. But Miss Mary Afton was looking at Uncle Bob with a strange expression on her face—a mixture of suppressed laughter and sympathetic approval.

Uncle Bob sighed deeply, and when he next spoke, his voice had deepened, grown almost melancholy. "You know, folks, farming's doggoned hard work, isn't it?"

The men in the room cast half-amused glances at each other that plainly said, "If he only knew!" The women nodded solemnly.

"I hope to tell you it's hard work! Backbreaking work. But it's also satisfying and productive—seeing the crops come in and the herds increase, fighting the elements, working with the things God has given us to feed ourselves and our neighbors. What work could be more important? Takes a lot of time, though—daylight to dark and sometimes beyond. But, you know something? All that steady work doesn't look too appealing to a young fellow like this one."

The attention never wavered. You could almost hear folks wondering what he was leading up to.

"Tell you what," he said finally. "I don't know this young man's family, but I'd hate to think he was going to get a licking for what's gone on here today. After all, it hasn't been easy for him to stand up here and listen to himself being talked about. Then, too—right after the service, he's going to help out by picking up any trash and papers he finds around the building and grounds. Isn't that right?"

The boy nodded again, his eyes flicking toward his family in the rear of the room.

"Good. And there's something else I'd like to recommend for this boy. I think he should earn a little money this week, either at home or at a neighbor's—whoever needs a little work done. Doesn't much matter what kind of work it is, as long as he earns his pay. And then, next Saturday I think he ought to ride into town with whoever's going, and he ought to spend the money he's earned, just for fun this once—maybe to see the Red Skelton movie that's playing. Now, Mr. Skelton has a knack for getting as much fun out of life as this boy does, and that's a gift, folks. That movie would satisfy this fun craving I talked about, and I don't think you need be afraid it would give him ideas. He's smart enough to know that pranks like Mr. Skelton's belong up on the movie screen. And if his dad or mom or uncle or somebody could spare the time to go with him, it'd double the pleasure and help out on the love and attention he needs."

The boy twisted his face around to gaze up into Uncle Bob's, obviously unable to believe what he was hearing.

"One thing more—if someone could take time off from working in the fields every so often and play a good game of catch, or wrestle, or run a race — well, this boy'd be getting attention plus the exercise his body needs. Exercise needn't all come from work, folks, for any of us. How about it, you dads — couldn't you spare an evening now and again to take your boys fishing or your little girls for a walk, or drive into town for an ice-cream cone? And do you know why I suggest this? Because these young people are so very, very important."

He patted the boy's shoulder and had him take a seat on the front row. "This young man is important because of what's inside him waiting to show up as he grows. We don't know what's there, and he doesn't either. He's kind of like a seedling that's just poked through the ground and is starting to expand in the sunshine. At first, it's hard to tell if it's going to be a weed or a useful plant. Right now he's growing like a weed, but if we nourish him and take good care of him, he's just liable to bloom and produce some fruits that will astonish us. Jesus said, 'By their fruits ye shall know them.'

"This young man may become a scientist someday and learn how to make better use of our natural resources. He may become a good farmer, or a doctor, or a teacher — or even a preacher. He may even go into aircraft design — he's already shown some talent in that direction! Right now he's a boy, but boys soon grow to be men, and little girls with pigtails become women — wives, mothers of future generations. What could be more important? They are the future, and we can help to guide and shape the future through how we treat them today. That's where hope comes in, folks — hope keeps us moving toward faith, toward a future we can't see . . . "

Thus Uncle Bob eased back into his message, and everyone, even the boy on the front row, was now listening. When the service had ended, and the last person had shaken Uncle Bob's hand, the boy came running up, breathing hard, with a brown paper sack full of trash he had collected.

"Got it all, I reckon, Preacher, 'ceptin' one thing." He dashed inside the church and scraped the dried spitwad off the back of the pew. Solemnly, he handed the sack to Uncle Bob, who accepted it and shook the boy's hand.

"Preacher, I don't rightly know how to say this, but it was plumb ornery what I done, and I reckoned you was carryin' me up front to shame me in front of ever'body." He lifted wide eyes to gaze at Uncle Bob, who stood with one hand on the thin shoulder, his expression intent. I knew that listening look; it was the same one he gave me. The rest of us hung back, as if no one else was allowed in their world just then.

" 'N' then," the boy continued, "you stood there and talked about me like you knowed me inside out. I'd be proud to know how you done that."

"Well," Uncle Bob said slowly, "sometimes when a boy grows up to be a man, he forgets a lot about what it feels like to be a boy. But once in a while, something will happen to make him remember—and when that spitwad hit the bench, I knew that there was somebody back there feeling like I used to feel sometimes. And I knew that your feelings were just as important as mine or anyone else's and that we all needed to know that. You see, Son, some of the things I talked about boys feeling and doing, I know about because I felt them and did them when I was a youngster."

"*You* did, Preacher?"

"He never!" whispered Granna to Pat with an embarrassed little laugh. "He was always perfect."

Pat nodded, but I figured there were probably things about Uncle Bob that Granna didn't know, just like there were about Rogie—and me.

"Did you mean what you said about the picture show too?"

"I sure did."

"I ain't never seen but one picture show. I shore wish my Paw'd been here today to hear you say it. But Maw was here, and my sister Selma wrote down ever'thing you said so Paw-Paw can read it later, 'counta he cain't hear so good."

"Sounds like your Paw will get the gist of it, then. Think he'll let you go?"

"My Paw ain't a mean man. He's just awful wore out all the time, like you said. I reckon he just don't never think about things like picture shows. I hope he'll say yes, and I shore do thank you, Preacher. Us kids'll be good next time. Will you be here next week?"

"I sure will, and I'll want to know what you think of Mr. Skelton."

"Yes, sir. Bye now." The boy ran off to jump into the back of a pickup truck with his sister and brothers, who all waved as the truck bumped off down the clay road.

Uncle Bob sagged against the door frame for a minute, then stretched and shook his head as if to clear it. "Whew!" he whistled. "I've survived, at least. Let's go home."

The drive home was quieter than the earlier one had been. Each of us was absorbed in his own thoughts and reflections, and perhaps we were experiencing the letdown that often follows a much-anticipated event, even if the occasion lives up to expectations.

Back in Tatum, we dropped Miss Mary Afton off first, and Uncle Bob thanked her again. "You ladies sounded wonderful. It really set the mood I wanted—for most of us, at least," he added with a grin.

"I wouldn't have wanted to miss it," she assured him. "That was no easy situation with that little boy, and you handled it superbly. I've no doubt you made a friend for life."

"Well, thank you. I knew I had to take some kind of positive action there, or lose the day. But I hope I didn't ruin the intent of the message! I surely got off the subject, I know that." He chuckled wearily. "The things they don't tell you in seminary."

"You wove it all together again very skillfully. Thank you for asking me."

At home, we ate chilled banana pudding. As soon as I was finished, I whispered to Star, "Come on, I'll walk you home, and then Uncle Bob will get to take Pat by himself."

We strolled slowly down the familiar streets, beautiful in the golden light and long shadows of the summer evening. Star was quieter than usual, and so was I, as the weight of tomorrow's anticipation and dread began to return.

"Well," I said at last when we stopped in front of the Hargrave home, "I reckon this time tomorrow I'll know what my other grandmother is like."

"Are you scared? I would be, to be there all alone."

"I sure wish you were coming with me."

"Mama'd never let me, even if you could invite me," she said glumly, her face shadowed under a cloud of dark hair. "I've prob'ly just got the whim-whams, Emily Jean, but I feel so weird! It's like— like everything's going to change somehow. Like nothing'll ever be the same again. It's kind of sad and kind of spooky and kind of exciting." She stopped and looked at me anxiously.

"Reckon I've had that kind of feeling too. Maybe it has something to do with us—you know—starting to grow up and all."

"Reckon that must be it." She brightened a little. "Oh—I've got a surprise for you. Wait right here."

Presently she returned.

"Here's my Brownie camera. You know how to work it, don't you? And here's your surprise. It's a new Nancy Drew book my cousin in Atlanta sent me. I haven't read it yet, but it looks real scary. You can take it with you. You might want something to read while you're gone."

I was speechless at her generosity. I knew for a fact that I wouldn't be able to let a Nancy Drew mystery out of my sight until I had read it at least once. I stammered my thanks.

"You're welcome. Listen, I've got to go in now. Mama can't wait to hear how everything went. Have fun, and write if you can, and remember *everything* to tell me!"

"I'll try my best," I promised. "See you later."

"Bye."

"Star?" She turned. "I'm glad we're still best friends."

"Me, too," she said and ran inside. As I trudged home with my borrowed book and camera, I wondered if there was a lump in her throat to match the one in mine.

. . . . 10 . . . .

Emily Jean, you have got to eat something, even if it is early,"
Granna scolded the next morning. "I can't send you to Mrs. Knowles
on an empty stomach. It's not polite to arrive hungry."

I mashed a morsel of scrambled egg with my fork and slowly
put it into my mouth. I had no fear of arriving hungry; my stomach
felt as though it still contained everything I'd ever eaten in my life.
When no one was looking, I deposited a forkful of egg in my left
palm, which already held a goodly amount. Then Granna sat down
with her plate, and I couldn't do that anymore. I watched as she
stirred sugar and canned milk into her coffee and mixed a yellow
puddle of melted butter into the little mound of white grits. Ordinarily I loved hot buttered hominy grits, but today even that stuck
in my throat.

"Did you remember to pack your Sunday shoes, just in case?"

"Yes, ma'am."

Granna ate quickly and neatly, not leaving a crumb.

"Drink your milk, child."

"All right. Granna, do I have to wear a dress?"

"Indeed you do. If you want to change into play clothes after
you get there, I expect that's all right. But you will arrive in a dress.
And be sure you comb your hair again, just before you arrive."

" 'S'ma'am. Granna, can I please leave the table? I can't eat any
more, honest."

"Well, at least you ate your eggs. Hurry now so you won't keep
Robert waiting."

I scraped my plate into the garbage pail, letting go of the moist handful of eggs as I did so. "Sorry, Granna," I whispered, then fled upstairs, where I put on a plaid school dress with puffed sleeves. My hair still had a little curl left from Sunday, so instead of braiding it, I tied it back with a green ribbon. I studied my reflection in the mirror. I looked ordinary enough, except for a tight look around my mouth, probably from my clenched teeth. I tried to smile at myself, but I looked as silly as I felt.

"Suitcase ready, E. J.?"

I nodded at Uncle Bob, and when he had taken it, I made my bed and stood looking around my room, which suddenly seemed too clean and bare, as if nobody lived there. I grabbed a white cotton gown from my drawer and looped it around one bedpost, then casually tossed a pair of socks onto my braided rug. That was better. Now the room looked as though it waited for someone who planned to come back.

Downstairs, Granna pressed a dollar into my hand, looked me up and down through her bifocals, and gave me a hug. "Now you remember everything I've taught you. Remember who you are and that you're nearly twelve. And don't don't worry about anything. Robert will come for you a week from Friday, but if you need to come home sooner for any reason, use a nickel of that dollar to make a collect call here. You know how to do that? All right."

She pushed me from her with a little pat just as Uncle Bob came in and said, "Let's go see the world, E. J. It's a beautiful morning to travel."

He whistled as he backed the Nash into the street, and I waved solemnly to Granna, who waved back. It looked, through the screen door, as if she held something white to her face, but I couldn't be sure. It came to me that going away for two weeks was a very different matter than going to spend a night with Star.

After I had swallowed half a dozen times, I asked, "Think the Rexall's open yet?"

"What do you need, honey?"

"Just some film."

"Let's try Burlingame. There ought to be someplace open by the time we get there."

We drove past Mrs. Chapman's. I think we both stretched our necks a bit to catch a glimpse of the little red cabin under the trees.

"Quite a young lady, your Miss Mary Afton," Uncle Bob said.

"She sure is."

"Nice voice. Rich and pleasant — speaking and singing."

"I know. Pat has a nice voice too."

"Sure does."

"Did you like her dress?"

"I thought that light yellow rose set it off nicely."

"No, I meant Pat's dress."

"Refresh my memory, E. J. What did Pat wear?"

I sighed, exasperated. All that sewing, and he hadn't noticed. "Pink and white candy stripe," I told him. "She made it herself, on Saturday."

"That right? I should've complimented her."

"And the one she wore last Sunday — she made that too."

"That is impressive. I think I do remember that one. Do you think Miss MacDougal made hers too?"

"I don't know. Could've done, I reckon. But she also works at Lana's Dress Shop, so maybe she got it there."

"Works at Lana's, teaches school, and cares for an invalid mother. She's a busy lady."

"But the nicest thing about her is, she's never too busy to talk a minute or listen. She's a real good listener."

"A fine thing to be, all right. Where's she from, E. J.? Not around here, I'd think."

"I think one time she said she came from Maryland."

"I see. Seems like I have seen her somewhere before, though, so I guess she's been here for a while."

"I don't know how long —" I raised myself up on the seat and waved vigorously out the open window at two young men in dark suits and straw hats, walking toward town.

Uncle Bob frowned into the rearview mirror. "Who in the world was that?"

"Just some Mormon missionaries. I met them once in town."

He raised his eyebrows but made no comment, and it wasn't a subject I wanted to pursue right then. I was very much aware of my letter to LaRae, currently pinned to my cotton slip, waiting its chance to be mailed.

I slumped into my corner of the seat. We were in the country now, driving a narrow gray road between green cornfields interspersed with occasional farms of tobacco, cotton, or beans. I liked to see the big, dark tobacco barns where the plant was dried—they looked like they'd be fun to play in—and I enjoyed looking at the old farmhouses, many of them weathered to a silvery gray and standing starkly in severely swept yards of hard-packed clay or dirt. Some of the houses were surrounded by ancient trees long since grown tall enough to dwarf the man-made structures they sheltered. I wondered if Grandmother Knowles lived in a house like that. The ceilings would be high, the wallpaper dingy and streaked, and a smell of kerosene and fried pork and musty old quilts would linger in those houses. I wasn't sure how I knew that—had Gramma taken me to visit a cousin in such a place in years past?—but I was certain of it, and I hoped I wouldn't be spending the next two weeks rattling around in one of those houses.

We stopped for film at a drugstore in Burlingame.

"Ice cream, E. J.? No? I guess it is a bit early."

"Reckon so," I mumbled, bending over and unpinning LaRae's letter from my slip as inconspicuously as possible.

"What on earth . . . "

"It's just a letter to a pen pal," I explained. "I don't have a purse or a pocket, and I didn't want to lose it." Quickly I poked it into the slot of a green corner mailbox.

Uncle Bob grinned. "I won't ask how come you didn't just leave it in our box for Mr. Warren to pick up on his rounds."

"Could've done, but he might not stop today," I said, and then went over to buy some film for Star's camera.

"And now what're you going to do with that handful of change? Can't pin that to your underwear," said Uncle Bob, teasing me.

I giggled as I slipped onto the front seat of the car. "Just hold it, I reckon."

"Sit tight, E. J. I'll be right back."

I waited, and before long he had returned and handed me a small flowered coin purse. "For your silver, ma'am."

The little gift cheered me for a while, but as we skimmed over the tops of lush, rolling hills into terrain that was beautiful but unfamiliar to me, I began to feel distinctly uncomfortable. The resident lump in my stomach seemed to have taken on a life of its own, quivering and radiating chills upward into my chest. My head began to ache. My palms were cold and wet, and my fingers felt weak and rubbery. I fought as long as I could, willing it to go away, but finally I reached a frantic hand to tug at Uncle Bob's sleeve. I couldn't say anything; my teeth were clamped against a rising tide of nausea.

"What is it? You look kind of—hold on, kiddo, we're stopping."

The Nash had barely skidded to a stop before I was out and running to lean against a fence post, where I contributed all I had to some good farmer's corn crop. Finally, exhausted and trembling, but relieved, I picked my way back to the car, where Uncle Bob sat on the running board.

"Sorry," I said, wiping my eyes and mouth with the handkerchief he gave me.

"Me, too, honeybunch. It's no fun to be carsick."

I gave him a long, level look. He and I both knew that I had never been carsick nor had any kind of motion sickness in my life. Unlike Star, whose stomach was challenged by the merry-go-round, I could ride any contraption the carnival brought to town and go back for more.

"Want to talk about anything?" he asked. I sat down beside him and glumly reached down to pick sandspurs from my socks. I started to speak but was horrified to hear my voice squeak off into tearful sobs. He pulled me against him, and it felt wonderful and awful to give in to my feelings and cry against his warm, soap-and-starch smelling shoulder.

"I know it sounds dumb," I said at last, "but I reckon I'm just plumb scared to death to meet Grandmother Knowles."

He nodded slowly. "I can understand that. You didn't even know she existed until the other day. I never did agree with that."

"I don't know what she's like. I keep thinking maybe she's like this person, or that one. Did you ever meet her?"

"Never did, E. J. But I did meet your dad once."

"Was he—awful?"

He reached out and flipped the end of my hair, smiling at me. "I didn't think he was awful," he said reflectively. "But you see, I was home on leave from the Navy—all tough and brave and ready to go defend my country, and there Frank was—no job, no steady income, but full of laughs and wild-sounding schemes and dreams. So, we just didn't have much in common except my sister, Ellie. For her sake, I tried to get along with him, which wasn't hard, because he was fun to be around. But I was such a sobersides at the time and so full of my own importance that I couldn't really appreciate somebody who didn't seem to take anything seriously—least of all, my fancy uniform."

"Did Ellie—did my mother—love him?"

"Now that, E. J., is one thing you can depend on. Ellie and Frank were just plain crazy about each other—or maybe just plain crazy. All they had to do was look at each other and they'd start to laugh, like life was some big joke they had between them." He shook his head, smiling at the memory. "Ellie'd always been a pretty girl, but when Frank was around, she glowed." He looked at his hands. "Actually, I only met him on that one leave, but when Mom wrote and said they'd eloped, I wasn't surprised. In a way, I was a little bit jealous. I kept wishing I could find somebody who'd make me feel the way they felt. As for what happened later—nobody really knows, I guess, why Ellie came home without Frank when it was time for you to be born. I don't see any reason not to take what Ellie said at face value—that she simply wanted to be home for the birth where

Mom could help out. Mom always thought the worst, of course, but you have to realize that Frank was nowhere close to what Mom wanted for Ellie, and I'm afraid she didn't forgive either of them."

"Do you think he didn't want me—I mean, us—the babies?"

"Somehow I find that hard to believe, honey. Whatever his faults, Frank seemed the sort to enjoy kids. But if the responsibility was too much for him, I just don't know. He had told Mrs. Knowles he would meet her in Tatum, but he never showed up. After the funeral, your grandmother traveled to New Orleans to see him. I don't know exactly what happened because Mom never told me much about it, and I don't even think she knows for sure. All I know is that he got sick and died there. I knew your father for just a short time, and I liked him a lot. So I feel that if your grandmother is anything like Frank, you don't need to be afraid of meeting her."

I regarded him doubtfully. "You aren't much like Granna," I pointed out.

"No, I guess I'm more like Papa."

"Granna says Grandmother Knowles is not our kind of people."

"Well, you have to understand that your Granna has some pretty stiff notions about kinds of people. I wouldn't take them too seriously if I were you. All she probably means is that your Grandmother Knowles is of a different religion, or is from a different part of the country, or something."

"Is she?"

"I believe so, but I don't know any details."

I took a deep breath. "Okay," I said. "I think I'm ready to go."

He looked at me with worried eyes. "I wish I knew more to tell you, honey."

"So do I, but I feel better anyway."

We got back into the car, and it was true: I felt immensely better, though still nervous. We stopped for gas at a crossroads, and he bought me a slim bottle of lemon soda and a package of peanut-butter crackers. They tasted marvelous to me—my appetite had somehow been restored.

. . . . 11 . . . .

We finally turned north at a crossroads, getting more and more into the forested hill country. At a town called Lynchville, pretty in spite of its sinister-sounding name, I looked at the stately homes that flanked the main street and wondered how it would be if Grandmother Knowles lived in a place like that. I knew it wasn't possible — Uncle Bob had already told me that my father didn't come from a wealthy family.

We missed our turn where the street divided to go around a turreted courthouse that sat square in the middle of town, and we had to double back to find it. About thirty miles east of Lynchville, a small white sign announced "Turley," and Uncle Bob said he was glad, because otherwise he'd never have known. There wasn't a building in sight. Half a mile down the highway we came to a dirt crossroads, a few farmhouses visible along its length. On the northeast corner stood a broad, low building that called itself "Bramley's Feed and General Merchandise." One rusty gas pump sat out front, and the side walls were plastered with peeling signs advertising Bull Durham Plug, Nehi Orange, and Clabber Girl Baking Powder. We pulled up between the gas pump and the sagging screen door, and Uncle Bob got out to ask directions. Just left of the door, two elderly men sat sunning themselves on a bench, watching Uncle Bob with interest.

"Good morning," he said in his friendly, no-nonsense kind of voice and held out his hand to the man on the left, who shook it for a long time.

"Howdy," the man said. "Hep ya?"

"Hope so," said Uncle Bob, withdrawing his hand and offering it to the other man, who shakily extended arthritic fingers for a brief greeting. "We're looking for the home of Mrs. Maureen Knowles. Do you happen to know her?"

The first man scratched above his ear and squinted at his nails. "Y'all be kin?"

The other one stiffly tilted his head and shoulders back so that he could peer up into Uncle Bob's face with his faded eyes. "Who?" he asked.

"Yes, we're family," Uncle Bob answered the first. "I'm bringing my niece down for a visit. She's Mrs. Knowles's granddaughter."

"Who?" asked the other man again.

"Miz Knowles, Hank. Some of her kin," the first man shouted at his friend, who was evidently about as deaf as Paw-Paw Jenkins.

"She ain't dead?" Hank asked anxiously, his chin beginning to tremble. He had a thin face, blotched and mottled by age and sun, but his features could once have been handsome.

"No, Hank, she ain't dead," the first man shouted. "Do hear she's been porely, though," he added in a normal tone. "Hank, here, he used to be kinda sweet on the Widder Knowles. Even proposed to marry her once, as I recall." He winked at me, where I was half hanging out the car window.

"I ast for her hand, once upon a time," Hank said, obviously not having heard his friend's remark. "Turned me down, she did. Don't that beat all? Said she preferred her peace. Law!" He slapped his knee and laughed, a sound as dry and dusty as old leaves. "She be a fine woman though. A mite uppity, but a fine woman."

"Aw, she ain't uppity, neither. Jest sensible."

"Cain't figger how a woman as uppity as her wants to hobnob with that colored bunch down by the creek."

"You mean Miz Vesta Lincoln? Vesta does for her, you know that!" The volume of the conversation made it sound like a public brawl.

"Naw, it's more'n that. They're friends. Sat down together at the same table. I seen 'em."

"Wal, I had me a little colored buddy when I was a boy. A good nigra's a better friend than some whites."

"Uh—could you please tell me where she lives?" Uncle Bob prodded gently.

"Vesta Lincoln? Down by Brown Creek, it's called. You go past—"

"No, no—Mrs. Knowles. Where does she live?"

"Oh! Land sakes—right down that road yonder, purt' nigh a mile or so. Just go beyond the old Jackson place, and you'll see her mailbox. Hope you find her well."

"Thank you. Thanks very much." Uncle Bob got back behind the wheel and gave me a raised-eyebrow grin. I giggled and looked at the two old gentlemen as we backed around. The one called Hank seemed to be gazing into eternity, but the other waggled his fingers at me in a wave. I waved back as we pulled away.

My butterflies were back, but I could live with them. We bumped down a dappled-shaded dirt road that wound between pecan trees and banks of heavenly smelling honeysuckle. I nearly missed the rural mailbox nailed to a post with "Nate Jackson" crudely lettered in paint that looked like tar. The one beyond it had "M. M. Knowles" stenciled neatly on the side.

"There it is! I never even knew her name was Maureen until I heard you say it back there." I sat forward on the seat as we turned into a lane that led to a one-story frame house built in a clearing and surrounded by green grass and bright zinnias. There were trees, but none of them grew close to the house. It rested on concrete blocks and had a sort of latticework constructed around the bottom to hide the dusty darkness beneath. The wooden railing of a fair-sized front porch was crowded with flowering plants potted in coffee and lard cans. A tall Negro woman bent to water one of the plants from a soda pop bottle. As we bumped to a halt, she straightened and moved down the steps to meet us. Her skin was about the color of Granna's coffee after she had stirred in a quick dollop of canned milk, and her graying hair had been brushed back above a high forehead, slanting dark eyes, and high cheekbones.

"Must be the housekeeper," Uncle Bob murmured. Too late, I remembered my promise to comb my wind-tossed hair before we arrived. I smoothed it the best I could with shaking hands and got out of the car.

"Good morning," came Uncle Bob's cheery, confident voice again, and the dark woman nodded, her lips smooth in a serene, pleasant expression.

"Mawnin', sir," she said courteously, then turned toward me. Looking me over thoroughly and shaking her head slowly, she made a helpless little gesture with her long fingers before clasping them in front of her again. It was almost as if she wanted to reach out to me but didn't dare. "And this be the grandbaby—there ain't no doubt about that," she whispered. Her hand rose and fell again. "Would you look at that hair! Miz Knowles gonna just—I don't know how she gonna live through this day. I fear she gonna die for pure joy."

She did reach forward, then, in a gesture to draw both of us toward the house. "Y'all come on in. She be waitin'."

"Is she very ill?" Uncle Bob's voice was quiet.

The woman glanced at me quickly, then replied, "Her heart give her some trouble. She keep mostly to her bed these days."

"And you take care of her, do you?"

"I do for her, yes, sir. And thankful I can."

Uncle Bob rested his hand on my shoulder as we climbed the steps. The small living room was clean and uncluttered. The floor was dark red linoleum with bright rag rugs scattered about, and the tongue-and-groove walls were painted a pale gray. A sturdy, cushioned rocking chair and a stand of plants stood before an open window, and a corner bookcase was filled to overflowing with books and magazines.

"Y'all take a seat. I got some new buttermilk in the icebox— that's good to cool a body down. Then I'll see is Miz Knowles awake."

"What's buttermilk like?" I whispered anxiously to Uncle Bob. I'd heard Granna speak of it, but I'd never tasted any.

"It's good if you just don't expect it to taste like sweet milk. Pretend it's cheese you can drink. You like cheese."

The woman returned with two glasses gripped between the long fingers of one hand and a plate of big, soft sugar cookies in the other. "Me, I forget to say my name. I'm Miz Vesta Lincoln. I'll just go tell Miz Knowles y'all here."

"Thank you, Mrs. Lincoln," said Uncle Bob. He took a long drink from his glass and gave a sigh of satisfaction. I sniffed mine and sipped. It wasn't unpleasant, but I knew it was one of those things I'd have to grow into liking. I carefully poured most of mine into Uncle Bob's glass. The sugar cookies were another matter. They were chewy and delicately browned, the tops crusty with sprinkled sugar. I hoped there was an endless supply.

Mrs. Lincoln came back shortly and nodded to Uncle Bob. "Miz Knowles say she like to see you first, please, sir."

Uncle Bob looked surprised but followed her into a hallway that opened off the living room. I made myself finish my buttermilk and licked the tiny flecks of oily butter off my lips. I looked around the room, liking the airy effect of the light walls and the plants and the cheerful red and green print of slipcovers and cushions. I was squinting, trying to discover the titles of the books in the corner case, when Uncle Bob came back. He was smiling.

"Well, E. J., I'd best be getting back down to Bradley while I still have a job. I'll bring in your suitcase, and then I'll be off."

"I'll help you," I said eagerly, but he stopped me.

"No, thanks, honeybunch. You go on in and get acquainted with your grandmother. She's waited a long time to see you. And thanks, Mrs. Lincoln, for that buttermilk—haven't had any like that for years. And the cookies are delicious."

"Take you some along to have with your dinner," she urged, holding out the plate.

"Don't mind if I do," he said, grinning and taking three. He leaned over and gave me a hug. "Don't worry, you'll like her," he whispered.

"Make sure you come for me a week from Friday!"

"I'll be here. See you then, kiddo. Boy, I envy you a vacation out here in the country!"

At the moment, I'd have traded places with him, but he was out the door and off the porch. Gentle hands turned my shoulders toward the hallway.

"Miz Knowles so proud to see you," Vesta murmured. "Don' you be afeard to meet her. She got a lot of love to give you." And raising her voice, she propelled me into a front bedroom. "Here she be at last, Miz Knowles—the grandbaby."

I stopped just inside the door, which closed softly behind me. At first, I wasn't sure whether the woman on the high bed had heard Mrs. Lincoln's announcement. She continued to lie perfectly still against her pillows with her eyes closed. Her hair was dressed in one long, thick braid that lay over her shoulder. Most of it was gray, with that around her face nearly white, but the tip of the braid was of a color long familiar to me—the same muted red I had seen all my life whenever I looked into a mirror. That touched me, somehow, and I felt a little burst of kinship with this aging woman. I was about to speak when I noticed that her eyes had opened, and she had begun to smile. Her head was turning slowly on the pillow. For a second I was reminded of the familiar portrait of George Washington that hung on the wall of every classroom at J. J. Audubon School— the high-bridged nose, heavy-lidded eyes, and the expression of patient wisdom. She held out one hand, and I moved forward to take it. It felt cool and dry, and her grip was surprisingly firm.

"There are no words," she said, her voice low and husky, "no words for a time like this."

She was right. I had no words either. I stood by her bed, silently regarding her while she held my hand and looked and looked at me. Slowly her eyes filled with tears, which spilled and ran down her smooth, barely lined cheeks. She made no move to wipe them away. A sympathetic lump rose in my throat, but no tears came. I was aware of bees buzzing outside and thin white curtains stirring gently against pale-blue figured wallpaper.

"And were you afraid, little one, when you were coming to meet a strange old granny?"

Her voice was gentle, but her hooded blue eyes were keen and wouldn't let me fib, even to be polite.

"Yes," I said, clearing my throat. "Yes'm, I was scared a little, because I didn't know what you . . . what to expect."

Her smile was unusually sweet, I thought—sunny and young—crinkling the soft, dry skin at the corners of her eyes.

"Good—we will be honest with each other. We have no time to pretend and hide and say what we think we ought, have we? No. So I will be honest with you and tell you I was frightened too."

"You were—of meeting me?"

"Oh, yes. Oh, my, yes." She motioned for me to pull a cane-bottomed chair to the side of the bed and sit down while she made an effort to pull herself higher on her pillows and smooth her quilt. The quilt was the kind I liked best, pieced together in small squares from old, used fabrics and worn soft by washing and loving use. I resolved to ask her about the little squares sometime.

"You see," she explained, "I didn't know what you would be like either. Would you be a prissy miss with no sense of fun? Or grown up beyond your years with none of your childhood left in you? Or angry with me for leaving you alone for so long? Oh, yes, I had much to fear. But I see you're none of those, thank the dear God, and I can breathe again. Now, how did you picture me? Tell the truth," she cautioned, holding up an admonishing finger that shook just a little.

So I told her of Star's stroke-laden great-grandmother, of Beulah and the little "snot-nosed Sneeds," as Junior Bailey called them, and of round Emma Tully and her raisin-filled cookies. She chuckled until tears formed again in her eyes, and this time she dashed them away with the back of her hand.

"Oh, Lord love you, what a wonderful imagination you have!"

She reached for my hand again, which she stroked and patted. "As much as I'd prefer to be like the good Emma Tully, I fear I'm more like the lady in the rocking chair—though I can speak, praise be! And I do hope I don't resemble Mrs. Sneed." She chuckled again. "Oh, my dear, I know I should have written to you before you came and not just to Mrs. Markham, but there wasn't time after I learned you were coming. What did Mrs. Markham tell you of me?"

"Not very much," I admitted. "She didn't know how scared I was, or I reckon she'd've said more."

Her smile grew wistful. "Possibly she didn't know quite what to tell you. She and I are not a great deal alike, I think."

"No'm, I reckon not. She did say something like that."

"But she's a good woman. She's been good to you ... " It was almost a question.

" 'S'ma'am. She's real good to me. And I reckon I'm not always easy to raise."

"Oh? Well, neither was your father, God bless him! But you'll not know much of your father, then?"

I swallowed. "I—I'd really like to know about him."

She nodded slowly. "And well you should know, my lovie. You'll sleep in his old room here and explore among his things to your heart's content. And I shall tell you all I can, but that must wait till later. I'm afraid this old body needs to rest now, so you go and tell Vesta to settle you in and feed you her best. It's such a joy to see you, love! Thank God you were allowed to come."

I stood up and leaned to kiss her cheek, tasting salt tears on her soft skin. She smelled of starch and talcum and age, but not unpleasantly.

"I'm glad too, Grandmother," I said, and she held me against her briefly. I could feel the heavy throb of the heart in her thin chest, and then she waved me away, turning her head to the side so that the tears ran onto her pillow.

I slipped into the hallway and looked for Vesta, who was dusting the living room. She smiled as if she were proud of me for something.

"You gonna be in your daddy's bedroom?"

I nodded.

"Right through there, next the kitchen. I put your satchel in there already. Miz Knowles gonna rest now?"

"Yes, ma'am, she said she was."

"You go get settled in your room, then, while I see does she need anything. Then I feed you your dinner. Law, law — the grandbaby at last!"

I giggled a little, envisioning Vesta tucking me, the grandbaby, up into a high chair and literally feeding me my dinner. But then I sobered, realizing that I was about to occupy the actual room that had once belonged to my mysterious scalawag of a father — and suddenly, I couldn't wait.

At first, I was a little disappointed. It was just an ordinary room — shabby and worn, with walls like the living room and a narrow, brown-painted iron bed. The linoleum here was so thin that the outline of the floorboards underneath showed through. A brown and yellow patch quilt covered the slightly sagging mattress, and there were two pictures on the wall — one a familiar print of a sheepdog howling above a prostrate lamb, and the other a Winslow Homer ship cutting through a painted green ocean. A triangular closet had been built into the corner at the foot of the bed, and my suitcase stood before it. There was a small bookcase beside the bed and a battered chest of drawers opposite. Curiously, I approached the chest and took down a framed photograph. Two laughing young faces looked back at me, and with a shock of recognition, I viewed my parents for the very first time.

The solemn, curly-haired baby pictured in Granna's album bore little resemblance to this slim young woman in a dark dress, leaning adoringly against the jaunty young man who grinned straight into the camera. He had one arm around his bride and the other flipping his jacket back so that his hand could rest on his hip. A corsage on her dress made me sure that this was a wedding picture.

I sank onto the bed, still holding the photograph in both hands, hungrily memorizing each feature. Yes, my mother was pretty — wavy dark hair, heart-shaped face, and round eyes. And Granna was right: I didn't resemble her, at least that I could tell. Did I look like my father then? Lighter hair, a longish face widened by that infectious grin, eyes crinkling at the corners with the joy of the moment—I was, perhaps, a little more like him.

And what if they had lived? And Ellen Jane, too? How different my life might have been with a twin sister and two loving, laughing parents—maybe growing up in New Orleans and just coming to visit both grandmothers in the summer. It boggled my mind to think of it. I leaned against the crisp pillow case, experiencing for a moment the poignancy that only a photograph can bring. There they were, caught forever in that joyous moment of time, unaware of how short-lived their joy would be—unaware, indeed, of how precious little of their own lives remained to them. Young as I was, I sensed a part of this and understood that you can't hold on to special moments very long. They may be savored at length only in memories and pictures. There's no time to pass the kaleidoscope around for others to glimpse a particularly beautiful pattern. Chances are it will have altered before it leaves your hand.

. . . . 12 . . . .

I was aware that some time had passed when I awoke and found myself still clutching the framed photograph and covered with a light sheet. I pushed it away and stood up, quickly becoming aware of two other things — one, that I was hungry, and two, that I needed a bathroom rather urgently. I boosted my suitcase onto the bed and found a pair of shorts and a shirt. I took off my shoes, and the cool linoleum felt good to my bare feet. In the hall, I looked around for a bathroom but couldn't find one. My grandmother's door was closed. Muted kitchen sounds came from behind another door just off the living room, and cautiously I opened it. Vesta Lincoln stood at a yellow enameled stove, cutting slices of green okra into a pot from which a wonderful aroma rose to fill the steamy room.

"Well, well, you done woke up! I saved you your dinner, though it be halfway to suppertime now. I reckon you be near starved."

"I am," I agreed. "But first, I—can you tell me where the bathroom is, please?"

Vesta laughed and pointed with her paring knife out the back door. "You see that little old house out yonder? That be the outhouse. Ain't many folks out this way got bathrooms in their houses. Me, I saw 'em in N'awlins, and I reckon they be fine to have, 'specially in the wintertime. But Miz Knowles, she ain't never bothered to put one in. Said she didn't spend enough time there anyways. 'Course, these days, she cain't get out there, so I just takes care of her. Land, honey, git on out there an' don't stand listening to old Vesta!"

I "got" — sparing a thought to wonder why a puff of cotton was tied to the screen door. The afternoon heat struck me like a blow as I left the shade of the porch and ran to the unpainted privy. Gingerly, I opened the door and saw a plank bench with a conspicuous round hole in it. A shelf nearby held a roll of toilet paper and a sack with the words "Powdered Lime" stamped across it. I closed the door and fastened the hook latch, blinking in the dimness, as the only light now came from chinks in the wooden walls. A faint stench rose from the hole in the bench, and a dirt-dauber buzzed against a corner of the tin roof. I resolutely put aside the thought of spiders and wasps and did what I had come to do.

Grateful to be back in the sunlight, I stood surveying the backyard. Far to one side was a fenced area with a coop for chickens, and opposite the coop was a barn that stood invitingly open and cool-looking. The back part of the yard sloped off and turned into a footpath leading into a pine forest. Beside the back porch stood a rusty old pump, and I wondered if it still worked. I had already seen that water was piped into the kitchen sink. The porch held two wooden chairs and a butter churn, which I vowed right then and there would never fall into Rogie's hands.

As I headed back to the house, a spotted bird dog creakily unfolded himself from a cool place under the porch steps and ambled forward, his head wagging one way and his tail the other. Delighted, I crouched down to greet him. He paused just short of me and gave a great yawn that ended in a squeak and made me laugh.

"Your hinges need oiling," I told him, as he stretched first his front legs and then the back ones. He butted his head against my legs, content to lean there while I fondled his ears and head. "I don't know a whole lot about dogs," I explained to him. "I've never been allowed to have one, but I sure would like to have one like you. Do you belong to Grandmother Knowles or Mrs. Lincoln? Or maybe you're just visiting, like me." I gave him a hug. He felt warm and solid and seemed happy for the attention, and when I went back into the kitchen, he stood and watched me through the screen door.

"You ain't comin' in here, Hunger," Vesta Lincoln told him. But her voice was kind, and he wagged his tail before lying down with a thump and a groan.

"Hunger?" I asked, washing my hands at the sink and drying them on an old piece of clean toweling that Vesta handed me. "Is that his name? Whose dog is he?"

"Well, baby, he be your daddy's old dog! He must be fourteen, fifteen years old by now. They call him Hunger on account of he's always actin' like he be about to starve. He eat anything, that dog."

"Hunger was my father's dog? Really?"

"Shore was."

"Mrs. Lincoln, did you know my father?"

"Oh, law, yes, I knowed Mr. Frankie. Loved that young'un like one of my own. He was a good boy. It hurt me bad when he died, and it like to killed his mama. I ain't never seen anybody take on so, though she tried to do all her grievin' in private. I sho'ly thought we gonna have to bury her too."

Vesta's head was tilted slightly back, her slanted dark eyes staring beyond me into the past. I sat down quietly on a kitchen chair, hoping she'd talk some more about my father, but she brought herself back to the present and set a plate of fried chicken and sliced tomatoes before me. "Here you be, about as hungry as that bird dog claim to be, and I go visitin' in the past. You'd best have a bite of these field peas and butter beans too. They goes good with tomatoes."

The mixed brown peas were delicious, as was the chicken, and I ate hungrily.

"Law, I do love to see a healthy young'un eat! You save you a little room for supper later on though. I made us a pot of N'awlins gumbo."

"New Orleans? That's where my mama and daddy used to live."

"Oh, honey, don't I know it." Vesta sighed. "Me, I've done grieved over that all these years, knowin' the blame lays on my head for them ever goin' down there."

"How come?" I put down my fork, realizing that Vesta might be just as rich a mine of information as my grandmother herself, and a whole lot less fragile. "How come, Vesta?"

She gave me a sad, twisted kind of smile. "Well, honey babe, N'awlins is where I come from. It be where I growed up. My mama, she was a cook for a fine, rich family, name of Beaulieu. They was good to my mama and good to me. When I was about eleven or twelve, my mama took to lettin' me come and help her in their kitchen so's I could learn to do things nice. They even paid me a little bit, and I did feel so proud and growed up! I learned how to make crab bisque and crawfish étouffée, and this little old cream pudding with praline sauce—mm, mmm! And it was pure pleasure to me, workin' alongside my mama.

"We'd get up real early, just at daybreak, and walk all the way up to their place, and then walk home again in the evenin'. Took us a good hour each way, and sometimes we like to froze in the wintertime, I tell you true. But in the springtime, all them azaleas and dogwoods and tulip trees and the like, they smell like heaven must, and it so green and shady out where the Beaulieus live, and so quiet. Downtown where we live, it don't smell the same, and it ain't quiet, neither—but it always so full of life and seem like there be music comin' out of every other doorway. Such tunes! You don't hear the like nowhere else on earth, I do believe." She shook her head, smiling at remembered rhythms and melodies.

"It sounds nice," I said inadequately. "When did you move up here to Georgia?"

"I was about sixteen." Her voice grew wistful. "I always was big for my age—I growed up fast. One summer, one of the Beaulieu boys come home from his boardin' school and took to hangin' around the kitchen, watchin' us work. My mama say to him, 'What you need, young Mister? You hungry again?' and he say, 'No, Lily, I ain't hungry—jus' kinda lonesome.' Then one day he take me aside, and he say, 'Vesta, you right purty for a colored gal. Here's a silk flower for you to wear in your hair.' Me, I jus' giggle and tell him thank you.

"Well, come that evenin', walkin' home, I showed it to my mama, all proud and happy. Whoo! She snatch that red silk flower and stomp it in the gutter till it be all dusty and tattered, and she say to me,

'Vesta, that what *you* be like iffen you let white boys fool around with you!' I say, 'Mama, you know I ain't that kinda gal. You done raised me up to be good.' She say, 'I know that, and you know that, but they ain't no way in the world young Mister gonna believe it when you go and take presents from him. And you ain't doin' young Mister no favors, neither. His daddy'd beat the tar outta him, he find out that boy sweet on you! He be a good man, old Mr. Beaulieu. I like workin' for him. I don' wanna lose my place, me, but I druther lose my place than my girl-child.' I say, 'Mama, they ain't nothin' wrong. Young Mister, he just be friendly.' She say, 'Uh-huh, there be a passel of friendly white men in this town, and they all be color-blind when it pleases 'em. Lordy, lordy, what I gonna do? I wisht you was with my sister up in Georgia, away from this crazy place!' "

Vesta turned to stir her gumbo with a long wooden spoon. "And, honey babe, next thing I know, I'm sittin' in the back of a bus, my clothes rolled up in a brown paper sack, lookin' out a dirty old window at my mama cryin' on my daddy's shoulder. My daddy, he pat her shoulder but he look straight at me, and I look at him till the bus pull away. That the last time I ever see my daddy. Next time I see my mama, I be married with three babies of my own."

"That's when you came to Georgia — on the bus to stay with your mama's sister?"

"Been here ever since, and like it fine too. Married me a good old Georgia farm boy and raised us six young'uns. But I tell you true, honey — I ain't never got N'awlins outta my blood. Come spring, I think on them azaleas — and come fall, I see the fog rollin' in on Lake Ponchartrain. I 'member them big fine stores, and how they all fixed up glittery at Christmas — and the fancy iron trim like lace on them old houses downtown — and the food and music and tom-foolery at Mardi Gras time — oh, honey, you see? I done talk like that to your daddy too. He was always askin' me to tell him about N'awlins. So I told him all that and more, and next thing I know, he done talked his pretty little bride into goin' there with him."

"My mama," I said softly.

"Law, yes — your mama, bless her sweet heart. And when your

daddy got so porely and die there, I say, 'Vesta, you done killed that boy. You done killed him 'thout even knowin' it—you and your fancy talk, dreamin' 'bout that wicked city.' And it be a wicked city, honey, just as wicked as it is purty, like some of them fancy ladies that live there. So here you sits, 'thouten no daddy, and you can blame old Vesta for it."

Twin tears made shiny tracks down her brown face. I searched for a way to comfort her. "Mrs. . . . Vesta, I don't reckon my daddy'd have gone to New Orleans or anywhere if he hadn't wanted to. And it sure wasn't you made him get sick and die. So I don't think you ought to feel like that—honest."

"You be a good child, for true. I knowed you was, soon as I set eyes on you. You like your Granny in there. She say, 'Vesta, it nobody's fault. It just a grief we gotta bear somehow.' But I still rue the day I ever told that boy how I longed for that city." She patted my arm. "There, there, honey, old Vesta talk too much—you done learned that already. Now, your granny say for you to spend the afternoon 'splorin' round and gettin' used to this place, and then you and her can take supper together about six-thirty."

"Vesta, do you stay here at night?"

" 'Deed I do. Right through that curtain's where I sleep."

I looked behind me to see a curtained alcove just big enough to hold a feather bed and a chest of drawers. "That's good," I said. "And I don't mind listening to you talk, not a bit. I really want to know all about my mama and daddy, 'cause I never have known much about them at all."

"Well, honey, 'tween me and your Granny, we'll stuff you so full of memories you gonna swell up and pop!"

"Okay," I agreed cheerfully. "I mean—yes, ma'am. And thanks for the food. I reckon I'll go out and talk to Hunger some more. He's about as close as I'll ever come to having a dog of my own."

She lifted a cloth from a dish and handed me a ham bone with bits of meat and gristle still attached. "You give him this, and he know you speak his same language. Law, law—the grandbaby at last."

. . . . 13 . . . .

Hunger slunk happily off with his ham bone to a certain spot on the grass where he carefully dropped it. He looked from side to side for possible challengers before he flopped down and gave himself up to the enjoyment of his prize. For a moment, I watched how he held the bone upright between his paws and gnawed blissfully on one end, eyes closed. I eyed the barn and the chicken coop but decided to explore them another time.

This first day, the little sloping path leading off into the piney woods called to me. Insects buzzed and plopped, blue jays squawked, and a soft wind made a whispering sound high in the pine boughs overhead. Otherwise, there was silence. Parts of the path were carpeted with slippery, pointed brown needles, and I had to step carefully to avoid sliding or having my bare feet punctured. I thought of going back for my sandals but didn't want to take the time. So I pretended I was a dark-haired Indian maiden and tried to walk as I had read of Indians doing—one foot placed carefully before the other, toeing in slightly. It worked fairly well, and I began to feel a warm contentment stealing over me, mixed with just a tingle of fear at being alone in a strange forest. But it seemed a friendly forest, perfumed with the scent of sun on pine and the subtle fragrance of some other plant that made me think of Granna's blackberry jam bubbling on the stove.

The path wound through the trees and zigzagged down a slope to a weathered wooden footbridge that spanned a brown creek. I crossed the bridge gingerly, pausing to remove a splinter of gray wood from the dirty sole of one foot. Pine gum from the needles had attracted dust until my feet were reddish-brown. At the top of the opposite hill, the path divided. Each half diminished in size, as if two people had customarily walked side by side along the trail, then separated to create one-person pathways.

I hesitated, then chose the left, curious to investigate a flash of sun on something white through the trees. As I drew closer, I discovered a cemetery in the clearing, and the object that had caught the sunlight was a white marble monument. I came up against a flimsy gate of wood and wire and realized that this must be a back entrance. At the far end of the clearing stood an iron archway bearing the name "Zion's," which I read backwards from my position.

Slipping the wire loop over the post and pushing the gate open was easy. The cemetery was small and seemed to have many unmarked graves. I saw a number of old and broken stones, grown over with lichen, and there was a section of newer, more modern markers toward one side. The place was fairly well-kept, though not trimmed and planted like the one where my mother and sister were buried. Curiously, I made my way down the center path, reading unfamiliar names and familiar sentiments, such as "Sweet is the Sleep of the Righteous," and "I Go to My Father and to Your Father." I hadn't been aware of feeling nervous, but at a sound behind me, I whirled in panic. Hunger nosed his way through the gate, tongue lolling. I laughed with relief as my heart pounded away.

"Hunger, you followed me, didn't you, boy? That's good, you'll be company on the way home. Let's go."

But Hunger only gave my hand a perfunctory lick and ambled off to one side of the cemetery. He lay down and began to dig with his short front teeth at something evidently embedded between the pads of one foot. I waited patiently for a few minutes. He didn't seem to be having much success, so I decided to see if I could help.

I was almost beside him when I realized what he was trying to rid himself of—sandspurs! One was imbedded in my own foot, and as I balanced on my right foot to pull out the spiky little ball, I stepped on another as I put my foot down, and then on another with my other foot when I shifted position. Wildly, I teetered forward and grabbed a grave marker to steady myself. I carefully extracted three of the little monsters and sent them spinning over the grass as tiny drops of blood oozed from my punctured feet. I looked for safe footing, but found little.

"Now look what you've got us into," I chided Hunger, who was still struggling with his own problem. Cautiously, I placed my feet on small patches of clear grass and slowly straightened up. As I did so, my own name seemed to leap out at me from the marble grave-stone I had been clutching: "KNOWLES," I read across the top, and underneath, "Frank M., Beloved Son. 15 March 1913 — 9 November 1936." Again my heartbeat gained momentum.

"My father!" I whispered with awe. If I had ever thought at all about his place of burial, I must have assumed it was in New Orleans. But, of course, his mother had had him brought here, close to her. I felt a pang of regret that he didn't lie beside my mother and sister in Tatum. Perhaps there hadn't been room there? But I knew there was.

"Hunger—you knew where to come, didn't you? I bet you've been here lots of times with Grandmother Knowles or Vesta."

I contemplated the simply carved white stone and the rough, sandspur-infested grass of my father's grave. I wondered, as I often had at my mother's grave, if the dead were able to know who visited them. I thought I ought to say something to him just in case, but I never had considered what I would call him. Father—Papa? "Daddy" sounded right.

"Daddy," I began and cleared my throat. "Daddy, I don't have any way of knowing if you can hear me, or if it's even right for me to try to talk to you, but—I just want to say I'm sorry you died, and Mama, too—but I'm doing okay. I just met your mama, and I like her. I reckon maybe you'll be seeing her before too awful long, 'cause she's pretty old and not too well. You remember Mrs. Vesta Lincoln? I like her too. I reckon they both miss you a whole lot— but you probably know that."

My eyes fell on Hunger, who triumphantly pulled the sticker

from his paw and slung it away with an ear-flopping snap of his head. "And I like your old dog Hunger. I almost feel like he's my dog, because I never had one before. Granna—that's Mama's mama— she's been raising me, and she doesn't like pets around because they're too messy. But I like them anyway. I wish you could talk back to me, but likely I'd be scared to bits if you did! I just hope you're happy up in heaven with Mama and Ellen Jane. I—uh—I love all of you." My voice broke at the last, and a strong feeling of loneliness washed over me. I almost felt like I ought to say, "Amen," but I hadn't really been praying to God, so I didn't.

"Come on, now, Hunger," I said, picking my way back to the safety of the path and replacing the wire loop over the post. As he trotted before me down the pine-dotted hillside, nosing out inter- esting smells and moving with a funny sideways lope that made it seem as if his back end wanted to pass up his front, I could picture my father walking through these woods years before with Hunger beside him.

Back at the house, I went up onto the porch, but I didn't dare go inside. "Mrs. Lincoln?" I called softly through the screen.

"Vesta here, honey. Come on in."

"I can't just yet. My feet are too dirty. Does this pump in the yard still work?"

"Reckon it might, but I wouldn't trust it to. Tell you what—I'll give you a rag with some soap on it. That'll clean you up real purty."

The soap took care of the dust and dirt all right, but spots of sticky pine gum still dotted my feet.

"Oh, baby, you been out in them piney woods, all right. Takes more than soap to get that mess off." Vesta came out to the porch and lifted down a jug from a high shelf. "Turpentine," she explained. "Dab a little on the rag and rub real good, then rinse good with water."

That worked, but it also stung all the tiny puncture wounds from the sandspurs and pine needles. By the time I was tidy enough to go inside, my feet were grateful to be put into clean white socks and sandals. I washed my face and hands and combed and braided my hair into pigtails, then settled on the rag rug in my father's old room to look through his books.

I was pleased to see my old friends Tom and Huck, much read and handled, but the other titles were new to me. My father had owned a book called *Freckles* by Gene Stratton Porter, a boy's biography of Thomas Jefferson, a book about King Arthur and the Knights of the Round Table, and one on the Maya, Aztec, and Incan Empires. Sherlock Holmes's *The Hound of the Baskervilles* sounded particularly intriguing to me. One by one, I looked through the contents of each book and examined the frontispiece, where my father had written his name in almost every one. In some of the books, it was "Frankie Knowles," in a childish hand; in others, it became "Francis M. Knowles," in a spiky, self-assured script. I hadn't known his name was really Francis. I wondered if even Granna knew. In the volume on King Arthur, which was very heavy and old and spotted with age, I read, "Edward S. Knowles, Baltimore, 1896. Happy Birthday from Cecily Jane." Edward, I realized, must be my grandfather. Eighteen ninety-six seemed a very long time ago.

I could hear Vesta moving back and forth in the hallway, and soft voices and a chuckle or two came from my grandmother's room, so I knew she was awake. I took the black-and-white notebook from my suitcase and wrote on the first page:

My Father
Francis M. Knowles
born: March 15, 1913
died: November 9, 1936 (when I was 9 days old)

My Grandfather
Edward S. Knowles
born:
died:

My Grandmother
Maureen M.
born:

I nearly wrote "Knowles" for my grandmother's last name too, but I remembered that she had had another name before she was married, and I didn't know what it was. I turned the page and made another heading: My Mother. I found that I didn't know much more about her side of the family than I did about my father's, in spite of having been raised by Granna. I'd heard Granna speak of the Henrys and the Brooks and the Owenshaws, but I didn't know how they fit in. I promised myself I would ask her as soon as I got home. After all, they were kin to me, and I deserved to know about them.

By the time Vesta summoned me to supper, I was ready to eat again, and though I felt a little shy, I was eager to see Grandmother too. This time she was sitting up in her rocking chair, propped with pillows, and a little cloth-covered table before her was set for two. Her smile was sweet and younger than her years.

"Sit down, my lovie," she invited. "This day is so special for me that Vesta let me get up and dress for dinner."

"Wadn't no stoppin' you, is more like it," Vesta said with her warm chuckle.

"You look real nice," I said shyly, and it was true. She had put on a blue-flowered dress that matched her eyes, and her hair had been brushed and wound into a soft twist at the back of her head. I began to realize that she must have been a very pretty woman once.

"All in honor of you, my dear. And you, with your pigtails, remind me of another little girl who once was — only I had to wear hot old dresses and black cotton stockings."

"Even in summer?"

"Oh, yes. Our summer dresses were lighter fabric, of course, and on Sundays, our stockings were white. But the only time we were allowed to go barelegged was on a rare trip to the shore. How we would have envied you young ones your comfortable play clothes! But now I'm old, and even a warm summer evening like this doesn't seem to thaw my bones." She pulled a blue shawl around her shoulders. "Maybe Vesta's gumbo will help."

"What exactly is gumbo?" I asked, as Vesta placed steaming bowls of rice and a thick, greenish-brown soup before us.

Vesta answered. "What gumbo is here and what gumbo is in N'awlins is two different things. Up here, I cain't get the crawfish and fresh shrimp and crabmeat like down there. So I make do with chicken or what fish we get here or now and again a can of crab or shrimp. But the sauce — ever'body has their own recipe. You makes you a roux, add some onion and garlic, tomato if you want, broth, okra, Creole spices and filé powder the very last thing. That be powdered sassafras leaves. Mmm, old Vesta do love her gumbo."

"And she's taught me to love it too," added my grandmother. "Sure you won't sit and eat with us, Vesta?"

"Oh, no, ma'am. You need you some time with this here grand-baby. Me, I'll just sit by the back door and keep old Hunger company."

I watched as Grandmother shakily spooned a bit of gumbo and rice into her mouth, and I followed suit. The gumbo was warm and savory, and just a bit pepper-hot, but not fishy-tasting as I had feared. I already liked okra, but Granna usually sliced and fried them in cornmeal and flour.

"Have you met Hunger, then?" Grandmother asked.

"Yes'm," I replied. "I like him a lot — he came for a walk with me. Was he really, truly my daddy's dog?"

"Indeed he was. Frank loved to fish and hunt, and Hunger was his companion. When Frank married Ellie, he was still quite a young dog and barely trained to hunt, so he was without his master for the most part, after that."

"Where did they meet — my mama and daddy?"

"Oh, down in Tatum where Frank had gone looking for work. The only thing around here was farming, and that wasn't his cup of tea at all. Too solitary. He liked to be around people."

I frowned, wondering how to ask what I needed to know. Was this the best time to bring it up, when I still barely knew her? Yet it was on my mind, and I spoke.

"My Uncle Bob — the one who brought me here today — he says my mama and daddy loved each other a lot."

She nodded. "That they did, to be sure."

"But what I can't figure is why my daddy didn't come to the funeral for Mama and Ellen Jane. Do you — maybe — know?"

Her gaze slid past me and fixed on the still-bright sunlight outside her window.

"You have the right to ask," she said slowly. "I only hope I have the wisdom to answer you truly. I know that Frank's absence added to your Grandmother Markham's grief, though I'm not sure his presence would have given her comfort. It would have comforted me, I know that." She smiled sadly, then continued her story.

Vesta and I went to Tatum for the services for Ellie and the baby. When I spoke with Frankie by long-distance telephone, he had been so heartbroken — so distraught. Our connection wasn't the best, but I was sure we understood each other well enough to get our plans straight. Since there was no bus station in town, we were supposed to meet him about two hours before the funeral at the drugstore on the corner where the bus would stop.

The bus came just a bit late, but Frankie wasn't on it. I described Frankie for the driver, but he shook his head — hadn't seen such a feller, he said — and the next bus coming from that direction would be the next day. We knew that if Frankie had missed his bus, he would have moved heaven and earth to find another way to come. So we waited there as long as we could — two grown women standing on a street corner, hearts heavy with sorrow. Finally, I asked the druggist if Frankie had called and left a message, but no — he hadn't.

The time for the service drew near, and Vesta said, "Miz Knowles, you go on and 'tend that service. You got to. Me, I'll wait right here 'case Mr. Frankie come along."

"But Vesta," I said, "I want you to be there too. You knew Ellie and loved her."

"Now, Miz Knowles, that be the truth, but you know I cain't go in that white folks church no how. I doubt they's a section for coloreds."

I knew she was right, but I dreaded going in all by myself. I'd never met Ellie's people, and I was already so full of emotions. The service was about to begin, and the usher asked if I was kin. When I told him I was Ellie's mother-in-law, he took me right up front and put me in the same pew with Mrs. Markham.

There was little time to speak. I just whispered to her that I was Frankie's mother, and she asked where he was. I told her that he'd planned to be there but must have been delayed. I tried to tell her how awful I felt about Ellie, but she turned away. Her eyes were all red from crying, but she was far more composed than I was during that hour.

Afterward, because I filed out with the family, someone tucked me into a car, and we went to the cemetery. I hung back on the edge of the crowd, watching for Frankie and still thinking that somehow he'd get there. When it was over and everyone began to leave, I spoke to Mrs. Markham again, trying to explain that I was sure Frank was on his way. She just looked at me, tight-lipped, and said that it couldn't possibly matter now. Then she told me that Ellie had asked her to care for the babies if anything should happen to her. I agreed that that was best for the time being, and we parted — not friends, but something less than enemies it seemed.

I went back to find Vesta, who was still standing patiently on the corner. Then we called Frankie's apartment house in New Orleans to see if he really had left. The landlady told me how bad she felt about Ellie. She thought Frankie had left as planned though she didn't actually see him leave. I asked her to see if Frankie was still there. She came back to the phone all out of breath to report that Frankie was in his room, all right — on the floor and delirious with fever. I begged her to get a doctor for him and told her I'd pay for his treatment.

When I told Vesta what I'd learned, she said, "Well, Miz Knowles, looks like you'n me goin' to N'awlins."

I had no idea how difficult it can be for a white woman and a black woman to travel together. The druggist knew a man with a truck who was going to Macon, where there was a train station, and he agreed to take us. I sat up front with him, but poor Vesta had to sit on our suitcases in the back of his truck. Then on the train, we weren't allowed to sit together either. This whole thing was so ridiculous that I marched back to sit with Vesta in the colored car despite the conductor's protests.

"Tell him I be your maid," Vesta whispered, and I did, explaining that I needed to talk with her about our plans. I finally went back to my car just in time to get off in New Orleans. Again, we used the maid ruse to get us both into the same taxi to go to Frankie's place.

He was just barely alive. The landlady had called a doctor, and he had recommended putting Frankie in the hospital. But the landlady had put that off. I think she was afraid that she'd be left with the bill to pay. To give her credit though, she had done her best to nurse Frankie and to follow the doctor's orders.

He must have been ill with what we used to call the "grippe," but it had gone into pneumonia by the time we got there. I've often wondered since if much of it was grief. At the least, I've no doubt that with Ellie's death he didn't have much will to fight his sickness. Vesta and I worked frantically doing whatever we could think of to bring him out of his delirium. We made a steam tent for him and covered his chest with mustard plasters. We tried to feed him sips of broth and fruit juices to nourish his poor dehydrated body. He seemed to rally for a while. He recognized us, but he still wasn't entirely clear in his mind.

"Where's Ellie?" he asked. "Has she gone shopping for dinner?"

We couldn't bear to answer him. Truly, we couldn't say anything for the tears that choked us.

Then he seemed to remember. "It wasn't just a bad dream, was it—about Ellie?" he whispered.

"No, Son," I said. "It wasn't. But you have a dear baby daughter to live for. Ellie called her Emily Jean."

He said, "There were two babies—one to be with me here, and one to keep Ellie company in heaven."

"That be right, Mr. Frankie," Vesta said. "Now all you gotta do is get better so's you can raise your little girl."

"How can I do that—without Ellie?"

"We'll help you, dear heart, and so will Ellie's mother. She loves the baby too," I told him.

"Doesn't love me," Frankie whispered. "Thinks it's my fault. Maybe right—I don't know. But I love Ellie."

" 'Course you love Ellie," Vesta soothed. "We all knows that. Miz Markham know it too, if she admit it. And Ellie loves you, Mr. Frankie. That don't stop when a person—dies."

"I want to tell Ellie—tell her I—love her, more than ever."

"She know, honey. She know."

"We need to get ready—for the funeral. The bus might leave—if we don't hurry."

"That be all over, honey. You too sick to go. But you gonna be all right directly. You jus' sleep now and don' fret yourself. We gonna take care ever'thing."

"Mama?" he said, and I moved to take his hand, which was burning with fever. "I'm real tired right now. Do I have—time for a—nap?"

"Of course you do," I told him. And that was the last sensible thing he said to us.

His fever was on the rise again. For hours, we worked over him to bring it down, but it was no use. The doctor returned to check on him. He said if Frankie made it through the night, he might live. But he didn't. Perhaps it was a blessing for him. He'd have been so lost without his Ellie.

Grandmother Knowles wiped the tears from her cheeks, then sighed.

"I arranged to have Frankie's body brought back here. Then, we packed up just a few of their belongings to bring with us and left the rest for the landlady to dispose of as she chose. They'd been happy there, I think. It was just one room they had, but it was large and sunshiny, and Ellie had made it cozy with bright cushions and potted plants. God bless their memory—how we loved them! It's been lonely for me without them. But now you're here, lovie, and it eases my heart to see you before me. There, I've talked a long time. We'd best get to Vesta's good supper before it grows cold."

We ate silently for a while. *Did my daddy die of a broken heart?* I wondered. Somehow the thought made everything seem a little easier to bear, and I was thrilled to think that he knew my name.

The stories must have also whetted my appetite. I dug eagerly into my gumbo, liking it more with every bite. It took very little food, though, to satisfy my grandmother, who soon ceased eating and relaxed against her pillows, watching me fondly. When I had finished, Vesta brought in two little bowls of custard with a sort of caramel sauce.

"Vesta sure is a good cook," I remarked after she went back to the kitchen.

"She's pleased to have a healthy young appetite to cook for. And yes, she's excellent. She could find a place with a wealthy family any day. Am I not lucky to have such a treasure? But I have no need anymore for much food."

"Reckon you wouldn't get very hungry, staying in bed all the time."

"No," she said, sighing. "But tell me—what have you discovered today?"

"Well, I went for a walk in the woods back yonder. And I—found my daddy's grave."

"Did you, then? Did Hunger take you?"

"Well, kind of. He went over and lay down by the gravestone to dig out a sandspur, or likely I wouldn't have noticed it."

"I was going to have Vesta take you, if you wanted to go. One of the things I detest is that I can't go there anymore. I used to go quite often and talk to Frankie, though there's many would say I was addled and foolish to do it. I don't know why I should feel any closer to him there than here, where I can picture him everywhere I look, but it was still a comfort to me."

"I know what you mean," I said eagerly. "I talked to him too. I always talk to Mama in the cemetery back home. Do you think they can hear us?"

She raised her eyebrows. "Sometimes I feel they do — and other times I hope not. It would be a shame for those in heaven to have to be burdened with our little troubles. If a heaven there is . . . " She broke off and smiled at me again. "Oh, my lovie, I'm afraid I'm not the one to give you answers on questions of theology. Shame that it is, this old granny still has more questions than answers."

I regarded her with interest. Granna never seemed to have any questions, but she had lots of answers. I had assumed that by the time a person became a mature adult, such wonderings as I experienced would be far in the past, replaced by certainty and wisdom. Yet here was this aged lady, openly admitting there were things she didn't know. Was this what Granna had meant when she said that Grandmother Knowles was not our kind?

I put down my spoon and asked, "What kind of questions do you have?" Then I blushed in confusion. "I didn't mean to sound like I could answer them. I just wondered . . . I mean, I'd like to know if any of them are the same as mine."

"I hope not, my lovie. I hope you're snug and secure in a solid, simple faith." She sighed. "My questions seem to go back quite a ways — maybe even before I was born. They were with my parents, I think. But that's such a long story. And I don't think you'd want to sit still long enough for me to tell it."

Right now, there wasn't anything I wanted to hear more about. Just a few weeks ago, I hadn't even thought I had another grandmother. It was like discovering whole new parts of me that I hadn't even dreamed existed. "I want to hear," I blurted. "Honest, I do."

. . . . 14 . . . .

Grandmother Knowles smiled. She folded her arms, hugging her shawl against her as she began to rock. Her eyes gazed out at the long pine-tree shadows on the sunlit grass as she began to speak.

I was born on February 3, 1869, to a Boston Irish family — Francis and Eileen McCullough. I was the youngest of seven children. I had two sisters and four big brothers.

Oh, they were grand. Mum — that was what we called our mother — she was a tiny lady. Such a little waist you never saw — and after seven children at that. She had a pointed chin and the deepest green eyes, and her hair was a soft red, just warmer than brown. I remember she always wore a white apron, cinched tightly — to show off that tiny waist, I do believe, as she was just a little vain about it. Her apron always seemed clean — snowy white — though how she managed that, I may never know! Under the apron was a blue or gray-striped dress. For mass on Sunday, she would put on a dark green silk and fasten a little gold cross brooch at her throat. In summer, she'd pin flowers to her dress. She looked so lovely then, with her white skin and green eyes, that we all felt we should call her "Mother." Later, when we got home from church, she'd put on her striped dress and her apron and make lamb stew with carrots and dumplings — that was Father's favorite. Her face would be flushed with heat from the old wood stove, and she'd be "Mum" again.

We were dyed-in-the-wool, umpteenth-generation Irish Catholics, and proud of it. Father wasn't so faithful as Mum though. He was something of a free thinker and had his doubts. Maybe I took after him with my questioning ways. But he was a good man, my father—proud, stubborn, and unyielding, but a good family man. How he loved us all! We never doubted it. He would lose his temper if we disappointed him, and rail and scold and whip the boys— though he never whipped us girls. But then he'd come with tears in his eyes and hold us close and tell us how wonderful we were and how precious to him.

He was so handsome. His own hair was blacker than black, with just a bit of a wave, and he had bright blue eyes and a marvelous black mustache that he used to tickle us with when we were little.

I hurt him so once, when I was thirteen, and I never forgave myself. Thirteen's such a miserable age! I shouldn't say that, I guess, when you have yet to go through it, but maybe this will help you.

It's a terrible age because you care only for your own feelings, and half the time you don't even know when you're treading on the feelings of others. I was just graduating from the girls' school I had attended. It went only through the eighth grade, and then high school was for those whose parents could afford to send them—and mine could not. In fact, they had scrimped and saved and done without to get me even that far. I don't know how much they sacrificed to send me, decently dressed, to a good school. It was a day school, operated by the sisters—the Catholic nuns—and I had done very well. I was graduating at the top of my class— and one of the youngest too. I was so proud of myself! There was to be a graduation ceremony with all the parents present, and I was to give a little speech on behalf of our class, then lead the traditional grand march around the hall. Each girl's father was to march with her—a custom they'd had at the school for many years. Then we'd finish out in the courtyard and have cake and lemonade with our guests.

But there was a problem—at least in my own mind. My father had only one leg. That is, he wore a wooden leg—a peg leg. He had been a conductor on the train, and one icy morning he had slipped and fallen across a track just as a train was coming through. He scrambled to get out of the way, but his right leg was caught and so mangled that the doctors had to take it off just below the knee.

This all happened long before I was born—before he and Mum were married. They had only just met and begun to get acquainted. Mum was working as a maid for a fine family in Somerville. Her own family lived in South Boston, so that required her to ride the train every morning and evening. She discovered that the conductor on the 6:40 morning train was a fine, handsome young Irishman with black hair and a quick smile for a pretty miss. And he always treated her like a grand lady, though he had never offered to make a date with her. She kept hoping he would, and she kept riding the 6:40. She even gave up the chance to take a room that became available at her employer's house, because if she became a live-in maid, she'd have only one morning a week to see the young conductor—the morning after her day off.

So, the winter wore on, and finally, he asked her name and wondered if she might allow him to escort her on a Sunday afternoon skating party at the pond. She was thrilled, of course. She told him that would be acceptable, providing he came to her home and met her parents first, and she gave him her address. That was on Thursday morning. On Friday morning, a different conductor was on the train, an older man who seemed visibly upset, as he kept dabbing at his eyes and shaking his head.

Mum said she knew something awful had happened as soon as she saw him, but she didn't have the courage to ask. She sat frozen and held her ticket for him to punch, but a passenger behind her said, "Where's young McCullough, then — his day off?"

The conductor murmured something about a terrible accident, and McCullough had slid on the ice and fallen in front of a through train. Mum said she could feel the blood draining from her face, and she half rose and turned to ask, "He's dead, then?"

"No, Miss," said the conductor. "I don't think he was killed. But he was in a terrible bad way, and they carried him off to the hospital. It was an awful thing to see — awful."

Mum sank back in her seat and began to pray, silently fingering the rosary beads she kept inside her muff. All day long, she said all the prayers she knew, over and over, to the Blessed Virgin and every other saint she could think of. She said she never could remember later what duties she had performed that day. That evening, instead of going home, she went from one hospital to another until she found him. Francis Sullivan McCullough, the hospital register said, but no visitors were allowed. She pulled a silk flower off her bonnet and persuaded a nurse to take it to him, with a note that said, "I haven't forgotten our date. I'll come to see you as soon as they'll let me. Eileen O'Shaughnessy."

Then Mum went home to the apartment over the bakery where her family was waiting, frantic with worry.

"And where have ye been, Eileen, and us fearin' ye dead these two hours and more?" asked her father.

Mum took off her wraps and faced them, shivering from the February cold, her eyes big and dark. "There was a terrible accident," she began.

"Ye're not hurt!" her mother cried and ran to grab her arm and look her over.

"No, ma'am, not I. 'Tis a gentleman friend I've known these six months who works for the railroad. He fell in front of an engine this morning and was nearly killed."

"Not the handsome young conductor!" breathed her little sister Annie, who was the only one Mum had told about him.

"The same," agreed Mum, sinking into a chair.

"Ye've not spoken of him to us," her mother said curiously. "He's not been here to call on you."

"No, ma'am. But he was to come this very Sunday to ask permission to take me skating on the common." Tears welled up in her eyes and began to fall. "Now, I don't even know if he'll live to see Sunday!"

"Now then, daughter, don't take on so," soothed her father. "The poor lad was bad hurt, was he?"

"I don't know how bad — they'll not let anyone in to see him yet." Then she raised her pointed chin and got that faraway look in her eyes and said, "But if he does get better, I think — somehow I feel — that we shall be married!"

The family sat stunned, not knowing what to make of this announcement. At last, Mum stirred, got a plate from the cupboard, and served herself some cabbage and potatoes from the stove. "I've not eaten a bite this livelong day, I've been that worried."

"What's his name, Eileen?" asked Annie. "I want to pray for him tonight."

"Bless you, Annie love. It's Francis — Francis McCullough."

"Well, sure and we'll all pray for him," her mother said. "What an awful thing, the poor boyeen. Has he family here?"

"I don't know," Mum said. "We've not had much chance to speak."

"And then, how can ye think of marryin' him so soon?" growled her father.

"I don't know, Father. 'Tis just a feeling I have."

The next day was Saturday, and Mum had most of the afternoon off. Again she went directly from work to the hospital, and again she was told that Mr. McCullough couldn't be seen.

"Please," she begged, "isn't there at least someone who can tell me how he is, what his injuries are?"

The nurse at the desk looked at her kindly. "Are you family?" she asked.

"Well, no—not exactly," Mum said.

"Our records show that he has no family in this country."

"Well, but—I'm his fiancée," she blurted, praying inside to be forgiven for the prevarication.

"One moment, please, Miss," said the nurse and disappeared. She returned shortly with a stern man in a gray woollen suit. "This is Doctor Pierce, Miss. He was one of the surgeons who attended Mr. McCullough yesterday."

Mum gave her best curtsey. "Thank you, doctor, for seeing me. I've been frantic since I heard of the accident. Might you be able to apprise me of Mr. McCullough's condition? Do you expect him—to live?"

Her heart was thumping in fear, but the doctor nodded gravely. "Yes, Miss, we expect him to live. He lost a great deal of blood, of course, so he's quite weak still. He needs a long period of rest and quiet and a lot of nourishing food. But he's a healthy young fellow, and his recovery should be swift if no complications arise. Of course, the leg is gone."

"Leg . . . ?" Mum said faintly.

"Oh, yes, the right leg, just below the knee. Nothing else we could do—it was beyond repair. It would have killed him to try to save it, you understand, and even if we could have, he'd have had no use of it. He's better off without it, Miss, cruel as that seems."

"I—see. And—the other?"

"Sound as a dollar. I don't know how he managed to keep it away from the train, but he was fortunate. In fact, except for abrasions and contusions, the rest of his body is remarkably whole. He's lucky to be alive."

"May the dear Lord be praised! When may I see him?"

"I'd give him until tomorrow at least, Miss. He's in

considerable pain, and he's sleeping a great deal when he can. But by tomorrow, I'd think a brief visit might be allowed." Dr. Pierce nodded at the desk nurse, who made a note in her register.

"I see, yes. Thank you, sir—you've been most kind."

"Not at all, my dear. Good day."

Mum watched the doctor walk away, and then swayed and had to catch hold of the desk to steady herself. "We were going skating tomorrow," she said, "and they've cut off his leg."

The nurse hurried around the desk and eased Mum into a chair. "You've had a shock, dear—sit here for a bit. I'm going to fetch you a cup of tea. Just stay there."

"What must Francis be feeling!" Mum said, as she leaned back, all limp and weak. "And he so proud and fine."

The hot, sweet tea revived her somewhat, and she began to feel a great swelling of joy and relief that he was *alive* and likely to stay that way. At that point, she began to think and plan what to say to him, how to help and cheer him. "What are abrasions and con—con—"

"Contusions," supplied the nurse, looking up from her work. "Scrapes, cuts, bruises. They'll heal."

"Thank you. And I'll be here again tomorrow."

True to her word, she presented herself again at the nurses' desk at 2:30 Sunday afternoon, the hour of their skating appointment. The nurse directed her down a long, dismal hall to a ward where six beds were lined up along opposite walls. Most of the beds were empty, but in one, an elderly man snored peacefully, and in another, a middle-aged fellow stared unseeingly at her with empty eyes. She shivered. Father was in a corner bed with a curtain half-drawn around it, and he lay with his head turned toward the wall, his eyes closed. There was a bandage on his head, and one side of his face was scraped and swollen.

"Francis," Mum whispered, and he opened his eyes. As

Mum came around the foot of his bed, he tried to pull himself higher on his pillows, but it was too difficult. "I've come to keep our date," she said, smiling at him.

"Miss O'Shaughnessy—I don't think—I should skate, this day," he answered, trying to smile, but not meeting her eyes.

"Mr. McCullough—Francis—I think, since we are engaged to be married, that it would be entirely proper for you to call me by my Christian name, which is Eileen."

"Engaged!" He looked at her then, and she gave a mischievous little smile.

"Well, I had to say so to get in here."

"You did that—just to see me?"

"Well, of course. Didn't they give you my note? I said I would come."

"I—yes," he said. "A nurse stopped in, that first awful night, and gave me a note and a wee blossom, and said a lovely young lady with red hair had been to inquire after me. I couldn't seem to focus to read the note, but I knew it must be you. At least I hoped it might be."

"I'm sure it could have been any number of young ladies," Mum said sweetly, "meeting as many as you must in your work."

"Oh, no—I don't. That is, not like you. But I thought—forgive me—that you were a working girl, and here you appear to be a fine lady."

"It's Sunday, and I've been to mass. I prayed for you, Francis, and gave thanks that you're alive."

Father turned his face away. "Aye, I suppose that's worth being grateful for—I've not been certain yet. Did they tell you what they've done to me?"

"Yes, Francis—I spoke with Dr. Pierce. He told me it was impossible to save the leg. But, thank God that it was only one leg—it might have been both!"

"Oh, I know it could have been worse, they've all told me that. But I've always been so free and loved to tramp

through the woods and dance and skate and play football—
and now I'll be a silly damned peg leg, thumping about like
a muggy old sea pirate!"

Mum was quiet for a moment. Then she laid down her
muff and gently took his bruised face between both her
hands and turned it toward her, while she pretended to
examine it critically. Finally she said, "I think that, with a
patch over the left eye and a wee gold earring in one ear—
oh, and a gold tooth, of course—you'll be a proper pirate
and devastating to the ladies!"

He stared at her, hurt and disbelief just waiting in his
eyes, to think she'd make light of his predicament. But she
looked back steadily, challenging him, and finally a corner
of his mouth turned up. "A plumed hat?" he ventured. "Or
a red scarf?"

"Oh, a plumed hat, to be sure—nothing but the best!"
They both began to laugh, hysterically, and when his laughter
turned to crying, she laid her head against his chest and
cried with him, both of them mourning the running and
dancing and skating that would never be. When he drifted
into exhausted sleep, she let go of his bandaged hands, wiped
her eyes, straightened her bonnet, and whispered, "Sleep
then, my love, and tomorrow we'll start to plan."

And so it began that she would spend an hour with him
every evening, and her father would meet her and escort
her home. When it came time for Francis to be released
from the hospital, she insisted that he come to her family
and recuperate in their care.

"Eileen, how can I? I'll not be a burden to your folks;
they don't even know me," he protested.

"How can you not, Francis?" she countered. "You've no
family here, have you? Are they not all in Ireland?"

"Ireland and England. Da's Irish, of course, but Mum was
an English girl, and all her people are there around

Staffordshire. Bein' myself neither fish nor fowl, y'see, I thought I might make a proper American."

"And that you do. But, Francis—who would you go to?"

"It's certain I can't afford a boardin' house, but I could find a cheap hotel until I'm well on my feet again—foot, that is." He grinned wryly. "I can look after myself, Eileen."

" 'Tis likely you'd manage, but you'd wear yourself out trying. And of course, I'd never see you. Father'd never allow me to visit you in a hotel room, cheap or dear! But perhaps you'd welcome a rest from me—is that what you're trying to say?"

"Eileen, it's not! You *know* . . . I—I swear, Eileen O'Shaughnessy, you can be the most exasperatin' girl!"

"On the other hand," she continued calmly, "if you stay at our place, I'll see you morning and evening and Saturday afternoon and all day Sunday."

"Properly chaperoned, of course, by your whole family!"

"Oh, not the *entire* family. My two brothers Eugene and Tim are over in Pennsylvania learning to work iron. It's their bed you'd have. So there'd be only Mum and Father and Annie—she's twelve—and part of the time, me."

"But what does your Da say—and your Mum?"

She smiled in triumph and took a folded piece of paper from her muff. "Mum wrote you a note, or, at least, she told me what to write." She watched with sparkling eyes as he unfolded it carefully and read.

Dear Mr. McCullough,

    Our Eileen has told us of you and your troubles. We'd be pleased to think we could be of some help. We have a spare bed you'd be welcome to for as long as you need, and maybe you've a mind for some plain Irish cooking. Eileen holds you in high regard, so her father and I feel to bid you welcome.
                    Patrick and Sarah O'Shaughnessy

Father looked at the note a long time, and then at Mum. "It would only be until I'm strong enough to get about and find some work," he said, "and then I'd pay back—"

"To be sure. Not one minute longer than necessary. I admire a proud man."

"And I'll not ever, under any circumstances, become a married man until I can take my bride to a place of her own. That is, if ever a girl—"

"Mr. McCullough!" said Mum, laughing. "Are you proposing to me?"

"I was not. But if I had been, what might you have said?"

"I'm not sure, of course, but it's quite likely I'd have said yes, with all my heart."

Father pulled her to him and kissed her for the first time—and that's how it began. He stayed with her family until he was able to get about again, and they treated him like one of their own. The railroad men came and offered him a pension, but he asked for a job instead, and they found him one as a ticket agent. By the time he was learning to hobble around on his wooden leg and able to begin working, he and Mum couldn't bear the thought of a day when they wouldn't be together every possible moment, and so they were married on a Saturday in June.

Mum's employers, who owned a lot of rental houses, gave them a year's free rent in a big old house not far from Father's station. They thought the world and all of her, you see. Mum worked for them until she had her third baby, then settled down to caring for her family full-time—and a fine job she did of it too. She had learned a lot in her years of working—everything from copying a dress style to knowing the value of education and culture.

And so it was on a fine May afternoon that I stood on a little stool in the kitchen, being fitted for my eighth-grade graduation dress. It was made of white organza and was low-waisted with a bouquet of pink roses at the sash. I would wear silk stockings and pink slippers, and my braids would be pinned up on my head with more rosebuds. Father and Mum were so proud of me. I was the youngest in my class, and yet I had the best marks. I'm afraid I was rather proud of myself and anxious for everything to go perfectly on closing day. My talk was all written and had been approved by the head sister, so all I was worried about was that grand march with the fathers. It was a sort of symbol of the nuns handing the "finished product" back to their parents. For the first time in my life, I found myself half wishing I was someone else's daughter.

"Mum," I said, as she turned me on the stool and squinted at the hem of my dress, tugging it to be sure it would hang evenly. "I don't want to lead the grand march with Father."

She took several pins out of her mouth and sat back on her heels to look at me. "Why not? You've earned it."

"Oh, I know — it's not that. It's the way he walks. Step-THUMP! Step-THUMP! And he sort of lurches to the side. I'll be so embarrassed!"

She stood up slowly and stared at me, her eyes flashing green fire. "Maureen McCullough." Her voice was so quiet it chilled me. "Do I understand that you're ashamed of your own father? Fine, brave man that he is! I can tell you *I've* been proud to walk beside him these twenty-four years! I was not quite five years older than you when I looked at him lying in that hospital bed — half dead from shock and the loss of his life's blood — and said to myself, leg or no, this is the man I want for my companion and the father of my children. And why? Because I could tell the fine stuff he was made of! Oh, you'll march with him, my fine lady! Maybe you don't know that he's gone without lunch or any new clothes these three years past so that we could afford to keep you at your grand school. We couldn't afford to do it for the others, but he was determined that for you, the baby — our masterpiece, he called you — nothing but the best was good enough! And you're ashamed of how he *walks?* I'm ashamed of how you *think!* Oh, yes. You'll march, and—"

"Never mind, Eileen. I understand. She'll not have to march with me at all." We both whirled around at the sound of Father's voice from the doorway. For once, I had not heard him coming.

"Francis!" said Mum, her face gone white.

"I understand. She's right," he said, and turned and left the house. The look of shame and sorrow in his eyes was far worse to me than Mum's tongue-lashing—and that had been bad enough. I got out of my beautiful dress, scrambled into my school dress again, and tore out the door.

"Father!" I called frantically, but he was nowhere in sight. "Father!" I ran up and down the street, peering into side streets and alleys, but I couldn't see him. Finally I went back home and hid under our big old cherry tree in the backyard and cried for hours. My cheeks burned to think how thoughtless and selfish I'd been. What had I thought—that he wouldn't mind? that because he was an adult, his feelings couldn't be hurt? He and Mum had been so proud of me— and this was how I repaid them. I wanted to die.

It was a different girl who came to the dinner table that night, red-eyed and very quiet. I couldn't swallow a bite, and Mum didn't say a word, just served the food with her lips tight and her face like stone. My brothers Mick and James stared from one to the other of us but didn't dare ask what was wrong. Finally, I asked to be excused and slipped up to my room. Father didn't come home until later that evening. Never had I been so glad to hear that step-THUMP! I ran downstairs in my nightgown and threw my arms around him, begging him to forgive me.

"I didn't mean it, Father—I'm not ashamed of you! I couldn't be."

"It's all right, chickie," he said, hugging me to him. "I understand, truly I do. We'll not speak of it again."

"And you'll march with me? You'll be there?"

"Now, that's a bit uncertain. I ran into Mr. Arleigh while I was out, you see, and they may need me to come in to work tomorrow after all. It seems that Donald Hayden and Murray Schneider are both off sick, and they may need me. But I'll do my best—I'd truly hate to miss your ceremony."

"Oh, Father, you've got to be there! It won't be the same if you're not!"

"That's kind of you, chickie. I'll do all I can." And that's all he would say.

The next afternoon, I looked out from the platform and saw them, him and Mum, on the next to the last row. I was so relieved, and I sat smiling at them. I got through my speech all right, but toward the end of the program, I noticed Father slipping out the back door. He didn't come back. I looked at Mum, who shook her head at me to let me know not to expect him. The band began to play, and Sister Marie-Mathilde came forward to announce the traditional grand march. "Beginning," she said, "with our top pupil, Maureen McCullough, daughter of Francis and Eileen McCullough."

"Sister," I whispered, tugging at her habit, "my father isn't here—he's left. There's no one to march with me!"

"Your mother?"

"I—I don't know if she'd want to."

"There's no time to find out. I shall march with you—as we did in practice."

So Sister Marie-Mathilde led me off the platform and through the rituals of a Grand March. How I wished for Father! My eyes were brimming with tears, but I smiled as I had been taught to do, and finally it was over. We had lemonade and cake in the courtyard, and afterward, Mum and I walked home together.

"Your speech was beautiful, and so were you," Mum said. "I'm sorry your Father had to leave early, but he was needed at the station."

I looked at her, but she tilted her chin up and stared straight ahead, and I knew the subject was closed. I also knew—and she knew—that his being needed at the station that afternoon was his way of solving my dilemma for me.

Grandmother Knowles sighed and patted her cheeks again with her hanky. "What a man he was! Too proud, perhaps, and too easily hurt by my childish, foolish pride—but such a man as you'd seldom meet. And so, I named my son for him—Francis McCullough Knowles—your father. Now, my lovie, I've gotten far off track and talked myself weary. Will you get Vesta for me? And sleep well, dear heart. Tomorrow, I promise to let you talk!"

I kissed her cheek and left the room in a daze. Vesta was already waiting in the hall. So compelling had been my grandmother's story that I felt suspended between two centuries. At that moment, my great-grandfather, Francis McCullough, was more real to me than Uncle Bob, from whom I had parted so reluctantly that morning. And I knew that I would never look at my grandmother again and see just an elderly woman. For me, part of her would always be the young girl she had once been—ashamed of her thoughtless words, proud of her accomplishments. Something of her girlish remorse lingered in the back of my own consciousness, bringing a small rush of tears to my eyes.

"Write it down," something told me, an echo in my mind of Miss Mary Afton's voice. Sitting cross-legged on my father's bed, I jotted down as much of the story as I could remember: names, feelings, bits of conversation. I wanted to be able to tell my own children someday. With a sense of wonder, I realized that these people were my own people—they were a part of me and I of them. I had a greater sense of family, of belonging to someone, than I'd ever had before.

. . . . 15 . . . .

By the time I finished making my notes, I had just enough light left to pay a visit to the outhouse before true darkness fell. Afterward, I stood on the back porch, rubbing Hunger's ears and watching lightning bugs winking on and off out by the woods. I thought about asking Vesta for a jar to catch some in, but I knew Granna wouldn't want me to. She had read in the paper that they were suspected of carrying polio.

The night air was warm and sweet. A whippoorwill called, and another answered, deeper in the woods. Hunger's solid body leaning against my leg felt good. "I'm glad I'm here," I whispered to him. "I'm so glad I came." A couple of whining mosquitoes convinced me that country life wasn't all perfection, however, and I ducked inside and went to bed.

Before I settled down, I knelt beside my father's old bed to say my prayers as I had been taught. Praying had meant more to me lately, ever since I'd begun to believe that my prayers could really be answered—the way I felt the prayer by my mama's grave had been. For the first time ever, I prayed for my Grandmother Knowles. I felt so warm and expansive that I prayed for practically everybody I knew—Vesta, Star, Miss Mary Afton, Granna, Uncle Bob, LaRae and her missionary brother, and even Rogie, who, I conceded, probably needed praying for almost as much as the Mormons.

Wanting to feel close to my father here in his boyhood room, I decided to read a book he had read and chose *Freckles,* which showed evidence of much handling, and settled against the pillow.

At first it was hard to concentrate, because the events of the day kept intruding. But soon, I was deeply involved in the story of Limberlost Swamp and the one-handed orphan boy, as Irish as my grandmother. I read until I fell asleep, and I didn't even know when Vesta came in to turn out my light.

I woke in the morning with a fresh breeze billowing the curtains and banging the blinds against the window frames. A familiar smell of coffee pervaded the house. I raised the blinds to still them, and sunlight came flooding into the room. A low, intermittent sort of moaning sound brought me to my feet in sharp concern. My grandmother—was she in pain? Or had Vesta hurt herself? The sound came from the kitchen, so it must be Vesta. I edged around the doorway, fearful of what I might find. Sure enough, Vesta was down on the floor, scrubbing the worn linoleum with a soapy brush.

"Oh-h, my Lord," she intoned softly, and I realized she was singing. I stood perfectly still. "My dear Lord," she sang-moaned again, then sat back on her heels and dropped the brush into the bucket as her voice took an upward spiral of mingled joy and pain and then descended, husky and mellow, a wordless flight of pure feeling. I crept back to bed, content to snuggle a while longer and read more of *Freckles*. Vesta's singing, now that I had identified it, made a pleasant background for my reading and thinking.

After a while, when I judged that the kitchen floor must be dry, I dressed, including shoes and socks, and found Vesta working in the vegetable garden.

"I can weed," I offered. "I've done that lots in Granna's garden."

"Well, Lord love it! You finish this here row of beans then, and old Vesta'll go cook you a breakfast that'll set up and say good mornin' to you!"

The breakfast was fried slices of leftover, congealed grits with sorghum molasses and fried ham.

"You're a real good cook, Vesta. Did you work for my grandmother when my daddy was young? Did you cook for him?"

She chuckled. "Bless your heart, honey, I cook for your daddy a passel of times, but not 'cause I was workin' here. Fact is, I don' rightly work here now—not for money. I moved in here so's I could do for your grandmama on account of I love that lady, and 'cause time was when she done the same for me."

I drained a glass of rich milk. "What'd she do?"

"What she do is, she tend me like a baby when I was laid up with two broke legs."

"You broke both legs—at the same time?"

"I surely did. You know them piney woods back there, where the path leads up from the creek? I was comin' down that hill one winter mornin', bringin' some fresh eggs over to Miz Knowles, 'cause she didn't have no chickens right then. I slipped on them old wet pine needles and go feet first right down under that little old bridge, and my toes caught on a tree root, and I reckon somethin' had to give. I best be glad it was my leg bones and not my back or my neck! Law, honey, old Vesta thought she was done for. All I could do was pull me up outa that cold water. I couldn't get up, and I couldn't crawl up the bank. I jus' lay there and wonder whether I was more likely to freeze or starve first, 'cause that path ain't used often, 'ceptin' by me, and I hadn't told nobody where I was goin'. My babies was all growed up and gone, you see, and I was already a widow-woman, so I knew there wadn' likely gonna be anybody out lookin' anytime soon. I figgered it'd be days before anybody come along and find my pore old froze body."

"What'd you *do?*"

"I had on a purty good coat, and it was mostly just wet around the bottom, so I kept that pulled tight around me. I could stretch a little and reach me four or five eggs that was only cracked, so I figgered I could do like an old fox and just suck them raw eggs to keep me alive."

"Yuck."

"Well, I didn't never have to do it, thank the good Lord. You know who found me? That old hound-puppy out there."

"Hunger did? What'd he do?"

"Well, I reckon he was just loafin' through the woods, lookin' for him a rabbit to chase. 'Stead of a rabbit, he comes across this old bundle of bones, and I call him over to me. He knowed me, you see, on account of I'd been through here so much, visitin' with Miz Knowles or takin' a shortcut to the road. So he come runnin' on over, his tail waggin' him to pieces, and act like I'm there just to play with him. I say, 'Dog, you git on home and fetch your missy! Go on, now, Hunger, go home! Fetch your missy.' "

Hunger, hearing his name, thumped his tail on the back porch and whined. I leaned back in my chair and held out my hand, which he sniffed through the screen.

"Did he fetch her?"

"Well, first he thought he had to sniff around and lap up a few broke eggs, but I reckon he finally decided I meant business with all my hollerin' and yellin', so he took out. I just huddled down real still, 'cause my legs felt better that way, and I commenced to pray. Seems like it wadn' no time before I hear footsteps crunchin' down the other side of the hill. I raised up on one arm and says, 'Watch your step, Miz Knowles, or you be down here like me.' "

She chuckled, remembering. "Well, your poor grandmama, she like to jump outa her skin. Then she sees me and comes a'runnin'. 'Vesta,' she say, 'you're hurt. Now I know what that fool dog was tryin' to tell me.' She takes off her coat and spreads it over me 'cause I was all shakin', then wads up her sweater and stuffs it under my head for a pillow. And I tell you true, there ain't never no pillow felt that welcome to this old head! It all warm and perfumey, and I went right off to sleep while she look me over and then go for help. Next thing I know, there be Mr. Nate Jackson and Mr. Henry Brasfield, and they puts me in a car and carry me off to the hospital. Miz Knowles, she stay right with me all the way, and old Doc Booker set both my legs in plaster—said they was fractured. Then he say, 'Vesta, I want you to stay in the hospital for a while.' I says, no-sirree, even the smell of that place enough to do a body in, not to mention all them shiny gadgets and all! He say, 'But, Vesta—all your chirren's gone—you got nobody to do for you at home.'

" 'Yes, she does,' says your grandmama, and sure enough, she come home with me and take the best care of me anybody could.

Ever' day she'd trudge back up here to look after her own place, then she'd come back down to mine and do for me. One day she tote down some books and papers for me to pass the time with, and I tell her, 'Bless your heart, Miz Knowles, I ain't never been to school. I cain't hardly read a word.'

"She say, 'That's all right, Vesta—we'll jest read 'em together. That's more fun anyway.' One day she commenced readin' to me about Huck Finn, and honey, I never did know there's so much pleasure locked up inside a book, or I'da seen to it I learned to read a long time ago! I near split my sides laughin' at that crazy young'un, and when she was done readin', I says, 'Miz Knowles, I wisht I wasn't too old to learn to read.' She jest laugh and say, 'Vesta, ain't none of us never too old to learn anything we want to learn.' Next thing I knowed, she'd fetched paper and pencils, and there I was, propped up in bed with two broke legs and havin' the time of my life!"

"She really taught you to read?" I asked, fascinated.

"She one fine teacher, honey babe. First, she write out little things I can read real easy, then she show me how to make big words into little pieces and figger 'em out, and by the time I was able to sit up in my rocking chair, she was showin' me how to read my Bible. Some of that was easy for me, 'cause I knowed it by heart from hearin' it at church. Then we'd read 'bout old Huck again, 'cause I wanted to start right in and go through that all over again. Sometimes we'd see what was in the newspaper, or she'd write down a recipe and show me how to read that. Them was such happy times, even with my problems. And you know what, honey—I learnt more than how to read words. I learnt to love your grandmama like I ain't never loved nobody else, black or white, since my own mama died. They ain't nothin' I wouldn't do for that lady. That be why I'm here now."

I nodded. "Reckon she's awake yet?"

"Reckon I'd better hustle in there and see."

She was back shortly, smiling to herself. "Sleepin' like a baby. I knowed she'd be tuckered out after yesterday, but I feared she be too wrought up to sleep. Folks get older, they don't always sleep so good. Oftentimes, I go in at night and rub her back, like she done mine when I was down in bed."

"How long did she take care of you, Vesta?"

"Oh, it was some weeks before she come home to stay—and I tell you true, I was the lonesomest thing in the world when she did. Some of my friends from the church, they thought it was a mite strange for a white lady to be doin' for a black woman like that, and they say, 'Vesta, you know we always takes care of our own—there ain't no call for Miz Knowles to be here. We could all take turns.'

"Well, your grandmama, she hear 'em say that, and she says, 'I know you folks'd do for Vesta, same as I'm doin', and we do appreciate all the good food you've brought in to help out, but I jest want you to know I'm here 'cause I want to be, and 'cause Vesta's been a true friend to me ever since I first moved here. 'Sides, you ladies all got families to tend, and my boy's raised and gone, so it feels right to me to be here helpin' out. But I do need to run home for a spell ever' day, so if you ladies'd like to take turns settin' with Vesta whilst I'm gone, I'd be grateful.' "

"What'd they say?"

"Well, they look at each other, and they look around at how my little old house was all spic and span, and they seen how happy I was, so's they allowed as how Miz Knowles was the finest kind of Christian lady. Now, they ain't a week goes by but what one of 'em sends us up a mess of fish or a bait of greens or a pie, and they always askin' me how she doin'. There be a lot of folks love that lady, black and white."

I looked at Vesta with interest. She was the first colored person I had ever known. In Tatum, the schools were separate, so I didn't know any black children, and the only adults I had met were the occasional women that Granna had hired to help with spring cleaning and such.

I couldn't honestly remember Granna ever saying that she felt white folks to be better than colored folks, and I knew she would never have allowed me to chase colored children with dirt clods and pine cones the way Arnie Blalock did. But at the same time, I knew that she would never have been found in Vesta's home, nursing her back to health, though likely she would have donated a little food or money.

A little later, I sat with my grandmother while she ate her few bites of breakfast. She did appear rested. "Did you sleep well, then, my lovie?" she asked, her low voice carrying the slight lilt that fascinated me.

"Yes'm, I did. I've been out pulling weeds this morning, and I started reading *Freckles*."

"You are a busy one! I hope I didn't bore you to grief last night with all my talking and remembering. Old grannies tend to ramble on, you know."

"Oh, no, ma'am. I loved it. I even went and wrote down in my notebook everything I could remember—only I want to check and be sure I've got everybody's name right. I want to be able to tell my own young'uns someday. I mean, if I ever get married and have any."

"Truly—you actually wrote things down—in a notebook?"

"Yes'm. Miss Mary Afton—she was one of my teachers—she said I ought to bring along a notebook in case I wanted to write down things to remember about my daddy and all."

She regarded me with a small, tight smile on her lips, and tears glistened between her eyelids. "Can this old clay vessel contain such a weight of joy?" she wondered, half to herself. "I have wanted, somehow, for them not to be entirely lost, all my dear ones—but that you should find it of enough interest, at your age, to write it down . . . "

"Likely I wouldn't have thought of it myself," I admitted. "But it's awful interesting, the way you tell it—almost like watching a movie. I just feel like they're all folks I know."

She nodded. "Sometimes I think of them so much that it seems they're here with me. Vesta has caught me talking to them, time and again. Tell you what, my lovie—go into my little parlor and bring me the albums on the corner bookshelf—the ones bound in suede leather."

I obeyed, carrying back three floppy photograph albums with black paper pages, and perched on the edge of the bed where we could both see.

"Let's see — here I am, yes, on that dreadful graduation day."

A thinnish young girl looked out at me from a fading brown photo. She was serious to the point of scowling, and the elegant bow and blossoms that topped her looped braids did little to soften the stark misery on her face. Her silk-shod toes were turned out slightly, and her hands were clasped demurely before her. I could barely make out the bouquet of roses at her sash.

"Ah, what a terrible time that was! But the dress was lovely."

"Who's that?" I asked, pointing to a picture of a sweet-faced woman in a flower-decked bonnet, the bow tied under her pointed chin, her gaze straight and calm as she surveyed us down the years. "No, I know — it's got to be your mother!"

"That's Mum. Wasn't she elegant? Those eyes were enough to melt ice. And here's Father."

My great-grandfather's eyes had been light, in contrast to his dark hair and mustache. He held his head proudly, almost defiantly, but there was humor and love in his face too.

We progressed through the pages, with Grandmother identifying the faces and telling me tidbits about each one. To think that all these people were "mine" — linked to me by blood relationship, some with features like my own or similar to those in the pictures of my father! There were a great many photographs of my father, from childhood to marriage, and I viewed them with delight — the big-eyed toddler in sailor suit and bowl-shaped haircut, the lanky teenager who seemed to be all nose and teeth, and the confident young man standing proudly with one foot on the running board of a boxy black car.

"And here's your little mother, lovie," said my grandmother, pointing to a pretty young woman in a silky dark dress with a scalloped neckline. Soft-looking hair framed her heart-shaped face, and she was sitting on some porch steps, hugging her knees and smiling shyly for the camera.

"She really was pretty, wasn't she?" I whispered. "You can tell more from this picture than from the framed one."

"Ah, yes, pretty she was, and sweet. Haven't you seen her before, then?" My grandmother looked at me in consternation.

"No'm, not really. There's one of her in our house when she was about three. But Granna's never showed me any others, and she doesn't talk about her much."

She gave a ragged sigh. "Sometimes, when children disappoint their parents, it's because the children have had so little say in what was expected of them."

I was silent, waiting for her to say more. I knew that my mother had disappointed Granna by running off to marry my father, but I still couldn't see why. I thought he seemed rather wonderful. In fact, without knowing it, I had waited all my life for the story Grandmother Knowles started to tell.

When Frank first brought Ellie home, he said, "Mum, dear, we've got to teach Ellie to laugh. It's inside her, but it's all bottled up."

They weren't married yet, just here for a day's excursion, and I could see that Ellie was nervous and scared. I gave her a big hug, which surprised her, and then I packed them a picnic lunch and told them to go out and enjoy the beautiful fall weather. When they came back a few hours later, her cheeks were rosy from the cool breeze, and they were swinging hands and laughing.

Frank brought her here often. After a while, I realized that she was coming without her mother's knowledge or permission, and I told Frankie that ought not to be.

"I know, Mum," he said, "but her mother won't let her come out with me anymore. She thinks I'm not good enough for Ellie."

"Not good enough! Why ever not?"

He shook his head and looked miserable. "No steady, promising job—no banking or medical career or college diploma or ministerial ordination. I'm just too ordinary a fellow and too frivolous."

"Well, my dear," I told him, "you've got to remember this awful depression we've just got through. Mrs. Markham is wanting Ellie to be safe and secure and well provided for."

"Don't I know it," he said. "But, Mum — I grew up in that same depression. You know we couldn't afford that kind of schooling, and jobs are still tough to get. But don't I bring in regular money from one thing and another? Wouldn't I always be looking for ways to do better? I love Ellie. Wouldn't I do my best for her?"

"Does Ellie love you?" I asked.

He smiled way deep in his eyes. "You know, Mum, I believe she really does."

"Well, then," I said, "you just go and prove that you are good enough and fine enough for anyone! Ellie's a lovely girl and worth working for."

"She is that, and haven't you just seen the difference in her since the first time I brought her home?"

It was true. Ellie had grown open and charming, a little mischievous and ready for adventure. She was always affectionate and full of laughter and high hopes. Frankie had been right — it was all there inside her, waiting to be uncapped. What I didn't tell him was that I'd seen a change in him too. He'd become gentler and more mature and protective. And, I was sure of one thing — they were meant to be together.

As dearly as I loved Frank and Ellie, however, it was still something of a shock the day he brought her here and said they were married. I had hoped they would wait and try to soften her mother's heart so Ellie could have a proper wedding. But the deed was done, so there was nothing to do but rejoice with them.

Vesta was here, and we prepared a nice dinner for them. She made a rich, dark wedding cake with shiny white icing, and we set the table with some flowers from the yard and some plain old emergency candles — it was the best we could do to make it festive. Vesta ran home to get a quilt for them that she had just finished, and I gave them my mother's best dishes and some lace I had made for pillow slips.

We had a fine party, just the four of us, though I thought Ellie seemed close to tears at times, amid the laughter. Finally I took her aside and said, "Ellie, does your mother know what has taken place this day?"

"Yes," she said. "She must know by now. I left a letter on my pillow explaining what we were going to do and asking her forgiveness. But, oh, Mother Knowles, I hate to hurt her — and this will!"

"You both must have wanted to marry very badly, not to tell either of us in advance," I said, for I was a bit stung myself.

Ellie smiled sadly and gave me a little hug. "We know that we belong together forever," she said. "We were afraid that you would insist that we tell Mama, and I knew that she would weep and forbid us. So we decided to slip away and just get married by a justice of the peace, so Mama couldn't say I'd gone over to the Catholics — you know she worries about that. Then we could just begin our life together with no fuss and bother. But I didn't know I'd feel this way — half happy and half sad!"

I put my arms around her and held her while she cried, and finally I said, "That's the way most of life is — half happy and half sad. We make most of our decisions in fear and trembling, hoping for the best — and the moment it's too late to undo them, we begin to mourn the last chance to change our minds."

"I don't want to change my mind, Mother Knowles, truly I don't. I'll always love Frank and want to be with him. It's just that Mama doesn't understand, and she won't give him a chance to prove himself."

"Perhaps she'll come around, now that she knows the decision is made," I said, but wondering if it could ever be.

"I don't know. She wanted me to marry Herbert Maxwell, our pastor's nephew. But he's so dull! I mean, he never *says* anything. We just sit and fidget, and he doesn't quite know what to make of the things I say—and I'm always so relieved when he goes home. But Frankie and I can talk about everything, and we have such fun together, and I'd rather have him than *anybody!*"

Then she ran and sat on his lap, and he kissed her. Vesta got up and whispered to me, and I got a few things together. Then the two of us bade them good night and walked through the woods together to her place. I stayed there until late the next afternoon, and then came home to find the place all cleaned up, slick as a whistle, and a note on the table saying they had left on a wedding trip to New Orleans, where Frankie had heard there were good jobs to be had. They wrote their love and thanks and joy and promised to let me know as soon as they were settled.

I had to be satisfied with that, though already my heart ached at their absence. If I'd known that I had seen them together for the last time on this earth, I'd have followed them on foot, if need be, to bring them back. But I haven't the "sight," as my Granny called it, and I couldn't know.

Well, it wasn't long before Hunger was barking like a mad thing at a strange car that had pulled up out front. A tall, serious-looking young fellow in a black suit came to the door, and I thought, *Oh, dear heaven—is this an undertaker come to inform me that he has the bodies of my dear ones, dead in some awful crash?*

But he said, "Mrs. Knowles? My name is Herbert Maxwell, and I'm here at the behest of Mrs. Ellen Markham, to inquire as to the whereabouts of her daughter, also named Ellen. I believe she is acquainted with your son—er—Frank, is it?"

Well, when I looked at that long, sober face and pursed

lips and heard that formal, preachy tone of his, I nearly laughed out loud just thinking of Ellie squirming and fidgeting and wishing him gone. I was glad to be able to say, "Not only acquainted, young man, but related! They are man and wife, and off on their wedding trip, and while I cannot say where they might be at this moment, please assure Mrs. Markham that Ellie will be in touch before long."

"I see," he said, his face longer than ever. "It's over and done, then."

"Of her own free will and choice," I assured him. "But you say you're Herbert Maxwell? Ellie did mention you—I believe she said you were held in the highest regard by her family."

"But obviously not by her," he said, sounding so glum that I reached out and patted his sleeve.

" 'Twas a surprise to me too," I told him.

He pursed his lips and said, "I'm sure it's all for the best," and ducked his head to leave the porch.

"I'm sure it is too," I called after him—and I meant it!

Grandmother Knowles and I started to giggle. "Boy, I'm glad Mama didn't marry him," I said. "I wouldn't even be me if she had, would I?"

"Indeed not—you'd be a tall, sober-faced young miss with pursed lips and a deep voice."

We giggled like two six-year-olds until my grandmother sent me from her room, declaring that she was ready to take a nap that might last all afternoon.

. . . . 16 . . . .

After a bowl of leftover gumbo, I went for a walk, heading back the way Uncle Bob and I had come the day before, along the sand and clay road that led between banks of bee-laden honeysuckle. The sun was hot, and I thought that if only my grandmother could get outside and bask in it, she would be better. I gave a little skip now and again, when I was sure no one could see me. Granna didn't like me to skip, now that I was nearly twelve. She said it wasn't ladylike. But I was full of such joy and well-being that it was hard not to break into a little dance. I knew how Granna felt about dancing of any kind — it was strictly against her principles — and I wondered if my mother had ever danced. Somehow I felt she had, but only after she had married Daddy.

I walked a surprisingly long time to cover the same distance that we had seemingly flown along in Uncle Bob's car, but finally I crossed the narrow road and approached Bramley's Feed and General Merchandise. The same two elderly men who had directed us the day before still sat on the bench, looking as though they hadn't stirred except to change places. I could imagine them, exactly at midnight, creakily rising and moving like carved wooden puppets, changing positions to greet the new day. *Tuesday — no, it must be Wednesday,* people would say. *You can tell because Mr. Hank's on the left.*

"Howdy, young lady," offered the one who wasn't Hank. "How's Miz Knowles today?"

"She's fine, thank you," I responded.

"Who?" asked Hank, and I hurried into the dim coolness of the store before I could become involved in a repeat of yesterday's conversation. I stood just inside the screen door until my eyes adjusted to the dimness and could take in the wonders before me.

The long, high-ceilinged room was packed full of merchandise of all sorts. Rows of tables filled the center, leaving an aisle on each side that reached clear to the back of the store. A long counter paralleled the right wall, and part of it was yellowed, spotty glass through which I could see a selection of candy, gum, tobacco products, and pocket knives. A little farther along was a display of fishing tackle, then farm implements. A glass-doored cooler held bottles of milk and paper-wrapped butter. Canned and bakery goods lined the shelves, and on the floor stood bushel baskets of fresh string beans, field peas, tomatoes, okra, collards, and yellow onions, while covered buckets marked "Lard" and "Cane Syrup" added to the variety of merchandise offered for sale.

In the front corner to my left was a small, enclosed space with a window grate, over which a sign proclaimed, "U.S. Post Office, Turley, Georgia. Stamps and Money Orders." There was a pervasive smell of grain and feed from the stacked sacks against the back wall, overlaid with a pungent, sweetish odor I later learned was citronella, which effectively kept mosquitoes and stinging flies away. I was the only customer in the store, and I wondered if I had to summon one of the gentlemen from the bench outside in order to buy something. I walked around a black potbellied stove—cold now, of course, but still surrounded by four or five cane-bottomed wooden chairs. I could visualize Hank and his friend and their cronies, huddling around the warmth of the stove against the chill of winter, shouting at one another in an effort to communicate.

Overhead, a wide-bladed fan moved lazily, stirring the hair around my face. The fan made a soft hum, and the dairy cooler sang an octave lower, but those were the only two sounds I could hear in the deep peace of the place—except for—what was it? A tiny sound teased my ears. I quietly tiptoed through a gap in the counter and dropped to my knees before a cardboard box filled with rags and kittens. They were very young kittens, with filmy blue eyes just open and wobbly round heads bobbing and searching for their mother, who was absent.

"Oh-h," I whispered. "Aren't you beautiful!" I reached one finger to stroke a tiny back, and immediately its owner responded, giving little bell-like cries. There were four kittens — two black, one striped, and one mottled black and orange with a dividing line right down the middle of its nose — half one color and half the other. I don't know how many minutes I sat there before I noticed a dusty pair of feet standing perfectly still to one side of me.

Hastily, I stood up and backed around to the customers' side of the counter. The feet belonged to a tall, thin boy with straight black hair, solemn brownish-green eyes, and a sprinkling of freckles across the middle of a longish, tanned face. He looked not much older than I — possibly twelve or thirteen.

"Hey," he said by way of greeting, his voice low and friendly. "Hep ya?"

"Uh — I don't know. I mean — I don't reckon y'all'd have any — white ink?"

The boy looked at me steadily for a long moment — a noncommittal look, neither questioning nor derisive — then turned and went to a wall telephone by the post office corner.

"Three-oh-seven," he spoke into the receiver, and then, "Daddy? We carry any white ink? White ink. Yessir. Yessir. I will. Bye." He replaced the receiver and went to a box on a shelf, brought it to the counter, and rummaged through it.

"Well, I'll be doggoned," he said, as surprised as I was when he drew forth a small white bottle with a gold cap. "Iffen it ain't all dried up . . . " He shook the tiny bottle, and then deftly opened it and set it before me. The ink was fluid. "Need a pen point?"

"I reckon so." I hadn't thought of that. He took down another box from which I chose a small wooden holder for eight cents and a point for two. The ink was nineteen cents. I counted out my coins and put them on the counter.

"There be anything else?" the boy asked, sounding capable and competent.

"Not today, thank you," I replied, primly echoing Granna.

"You from 'round here?" he asked, placing my purchases in a small sack.

"Tatum, not far from Savannah," I told him. "Is this your daddy's store?"

He nodded. "I'm Zack Bramley. I mind the store ever' day while Dad and Granddad take dinner. In the summer, I mean. Generally I know where most things are at. Daddy tries to keep a good stock in—most anything you'd need—even white ink." He smiled, revealing straight white teeth.

I nodded, looking around the store. "I think it's wonderful," I said honestly. "And so are the kittens."

"We generally have kittens. Polly—that's the mama cat—she keeps mice out of the feed bags. Earns her keep."

"What do you do with the kittens?"

"Folks take 'em along home mostly, when they're big enough. Little kids like 'em."

"When are they big enough?"

"Six to eight weeks, after they're weaned good."

"How old are these?"

" 'Bout ten days. You want one? Course, you're likely just passing through. Too bad they're not big enough."

"I'm staying with my grandmother for two weeks, but they'll still be way too little. I know which one I'd take though—the black and orange one."

"I'm kinda partial to her too. She'll make a nice cat." He gave me another of his long looks. "Who's your granny? I cain't rightly place you."

"Mrs. Knowles—just up the road," I said. "Do you know her?"

"Well, don't that beat all! Reckon I just never thought about her havin' any grandkids. How's she feelin'? I ain't been up there for a spell."

"I'm her only grandchild and I reckon she's doing pretty good, but she's in bed about all the time."

He nodded. "She's a real nice lady. I can remember when I was

. . . . 153 . . . .

a little kid, she used to come in here all the time. My granddaddy, he used to like her a whole lot. Story is, he even ast her to marry him one time."

"Is Mr. Hank your granddaddy?"

"Sure is. He's my mama's daddy—Mr. Hank Tidwell. He don't hear so well now, but he's a good old man. Taught me to fish. Hey— reckon if he'd'a married your granny, that'd make us some kind of cousins."

I wasn't opposed to the idea. Zack Bramley outclassed any boy of my acquaintance thus far, and I judged he would have made a satisfactory cousin—a type of relative I didn't have so far.

"Have you got any cousins?" I asked, hoping he didn't.

"Have I! Eighteen or twenty, I reckon. And a brother and two sisters. How 'bout you?"

I shook my head, somehow unwilling to admit my family deficiencies. "One sister that's dead," I said slowly. "But I've got some good friends."

"Not even any cousins?"

"Nope." I brightened. "But I've got two grown-up uncles, so maybe I'll get some cousins someday."

Zack considered. "I don't have all that many girl-cousins," he said. "Reckon I could use another—just between us, you know—on account of we almost was anyway."

I didn't know what to say. A curious feeling was forming inside me, and I didn't recognize it. I stole a glance at the boy with the straight black hair and dark eyelashes. He was digging at a crevice in the battered countertop with a paper clip.

"Reckon that'd be fun," I said as casually as I could, "to—uh— have a secret cousin."

"It'd have to be a secret," Zack warned. "Some girls'd go blab to ever'body, and then it wouldn't be no good."

"Not me," I said staunchly. "I'd never tell. I've got lots and lots of secrets I've never told anybody at all. But I know boys who don't know how to keep quiet either."

I earned another long, inscrutable look from Zack. "I'm part

Cherokee Indian," he said. "Indians know how to keep quiet, even when they're tortured."

I nodded solemnly, impressed.

"How long you gonna be at your granny's?"

"Till a week from Friday."

"Okay—good. See you 'round, then—cuz!"

"All right," I said, dazzled by the suddenly sunny smile on his tanned face. I turned to go. Then, remembering my purchases, I snatched them from the counter and fled.

The heat and sunshine outside were as dazzling as Zack's smile after the dimness inside. I didn't even spare a glance for the two old gentlemen on their bench but crossed the highway and scuffed happily toward home. Home? Had I really thought that? Yes. I recognized home when I found it.

After supper, I brought out my bottle of white ink, and Grandmother delightedly supplied me with names and dates to print under the photographs in her album, stopping only when weariness forced her to.

"But where did you find the white ink?" she asked, as I turned to leave her room.

"I bought it from—from a boy up at Bramley's store."

"That'd be young Zachary, I don't doubt. Tall and thin, kind-natured, with black hair?"

I nodded, noting with annoyance that my cheeks felt hot.

"Yes, that's young Zack. A good boy and smart as a whip. Figures in his head, they say, as fast as an adding machine. Knows the woods too, like his own house. It may be that's the Indian in him."

"He's really part Indian?"

"His father's mother is a little Cherokee lady, dainty and prim. They say she was a great beauty as a young woman."

"Wow! I've been wondering, Grandmother, what was your husband like? Was he Irish too?"

"No, no—neither Irish nor Catholic. See here—here he is." She opened the album to a part we hadn't gotten to yet and pointed out the picture of a stern-looking young man with far-seeing light eyes. My father's father—I was intrigued.

"Tell me about him," I entreated.

"Ned was a thinker and a dreamer," she said slowly. "It all seems so very long ago now. And what good did they do him, all his fine ideals and lofty goals? In truth, they killed him—or at least, he died for them." She sighed. "In the morning, my lovie, I'll try to explain. There's so much to tell."

A short while later, curled up in my father's old bed reading *Freckles*, it didn't even strike me as strange that the image of the hero had suddenly acquired straight black hair that fell across his forehead and deep-set brownish-green eyes.

True to her promise, my grandmother began to tell me about my grandfather the next morning as we lingered over breakfast in her room. She settled more comfortably against her pillows, and her words came slow and trembling at first, then firmer.

Young and proud he was, when we met in Boston. In that, he reminded me of my own dear father. Ned had far the greater education, though. He had been to Harvard, had traveled in Europe, and had read and studied most of the great classics. It was a wonder to me that he found me of any interest at all, when he had known so many wonderful young ladies in his own social set.

He was so far beyond me and such an idealist! It was his dream to improve the lot of the common man. Reform! Strike! Advance the cause of the laborers! As for me and my family—well, we *were* the laborers. And, even though Ned came from an old New England family of silver-spoon patriots—wealthy, cultured, educated—he renounced his inheritance to throw in his lot with the common man.

There wasn't much he could do to become one of them, though—at least in the way of physical labor—because he suffered unmercifully from asthma. So he worked in the office of a great shipping company, and on the side he wrote articles and handbills urging workers to stand up and fight for their rights. He felt that American workers were being exploited by management.

We were married in 1893 and set up housekeeping in South Boston. Of all his family, only his youngest sister, Cecily, came to our wedding. In fact, she was the only one of his people I ever met. She was a lovely girl with shining fair hair and a disposition to match. She treated me warmly, like a true sister, and it was plain she adored Ned and wished him well. She told me that his parents and other sister and brother despaired of him. They couldn't understand why he refused to use his education and social position to fight his battles on a higher level, and not "soil his hands," as they put it. But Cecily knew, as I did, that our Ned was never afraid to soil his hands; indeed, he was eager to plunge in to the elbow!

I often wished he would find a safer, cleaner way to do his work. I was proud of him—he was strong, steady, compassionate, and well-nigh incorruptible. But he was vulnerable too, and it was a risky business he was in. The labor movement was fiery and often became violent in those days. Many times he would smuggle home some labor advocate whose life had been threatened. He never told me, but I strongly suspected his own life was threatened many times.

I'd plead with him to move away and take up the practice of law he had prepared for, but he'd just say, "No, my dear, I can't just now. Perhaps someday when things are different, but right now I want to work at the grass roots and help restore dignity to America's backbone—her workers."

So I waited, and I prayed, and I tried so hard to have children for Ned—and for myself too, as I was lonely and afraid so much of the time. But not until after I had lost three babies and was expecting my fourth did my brother Mick's wife come to stay with me. I spent nearly six months flat on my back; but thanks to Nancy, I gave birth to a fine, healthy boy—my Frankie—your own father. Ned was so happy! Those were good times for us. He stayed closer to home and spent more time with us. We spoke of a house in the country where Frankie could have a dog and a pony and freedom to play. Ned quit the IWW—The Industrial Workers of the World—as he had become disenchanted with them. They felt that socialism was a better system for America than capitalism. Ned was educated and aware enough to see through their logic before long. But while he was there, he had learned some techniques for organizing strikes, and he continued working with various unions, helping them find ways to protest against unfair treatment.

I prayed every day for the time to come when Ned would feel he had done enough. I wanted us to leave the city and find our country home for Frankie, who was toddling around and starting to cry for Ned when he left. But it went on and on—and one night, Ned didn't come home. I spent the hours in frantic worry and prayer, trying to convince myself that he had simply escaped home with someone else. But I think I knew. Deep inside, I felt a cold, black dread that I had lost him. The next morning I checked with all the hospitals, much as Mum had done after Father's dreadful accident, but he wasn't to be found. I contacted others who were active in the labor movement. Yes, there had been a strike scheduled among the garment workers, and Ned was to give the word for the walkout—but no word had come. They were still waiting, and so was I.

He had many friends as well as enemies. It took them two days to find him. He hadn't been harmed outright, but he had been tied with ropes and left inside an unused warehouse where no one could hear his cries. It was March, and the nights were still freezing. A damp wind blew in on him through the broken windowpanes, and by the time he was found, he had developed pneumonia and was delirious with fever. Between that and his asthma, he had no chance at all. He died without ever recognizing me or naming his captors.

Grandmother Knowles's cheeks were wet. "My heart was broken," she added simply. "He was a good man, if not always wise." She was quiet for a moment, lost in thought, and I reached over and touched her thin, white hand. Rousing herself from her reverie, she continued speaking in a voice sparked with renewed life and determination.

"And again, Cecily was the only one from his family who came to his funeral. Cecily was the only one who pled with her father to set up a small trust fund for Frankie, which he did. Cecily was the only one who kept in touch with me through the years — and I have loved her for it. She's written of her own family — her children and her nieces and nephews — so that Frankie and I would have some knowledge of Ned's family. Once, when Frankie was about seventeen, she paid us a visit. I've kept all her letters, saved first for Frankie and then for you, on the slim chance you'd want to read them."

"Oh, yes — I'd love to read them."

"And I know that Cecily would enjoy a letter from you, my lovie, if you'd care to write. She'd be your great-aunt, and she's — oh, in her early seventies, I believe — younger than I."

"Do you think she really would? I mean, I'm just me — and I'm not even twelve yet."

"You're the granddaughter of her beloved big brother, and I'm sure she'd be pleased as punch to hear from you. And so will I, I might add, when you go back to Tatum, though I can't promise frequent replies. I don't write so well anymore."

"Oh, but I'm not going back for more than a week — I don't even want to think about leaving yet."

"You're enjoying your little visit, then?"

"Oh, yes'm, truly I am. I feel so much at home here."

How else could I describe the joyous, secure, yet free feeling that I was experiencing? There were no dodging and apologizing, no secretive thoughts or nagging guilt such as permeated my life at Granna's. There, I never felt quite adequate; here, I felt pampered and adored.

"I reckon you and Vesta are just spoiling me," I admitted.

She chuckled. "I think not. And to be sure, why should you not feel at home here? It was your father's home, and it is mine, and I welcome you here with all my heart."

Grandmother Knowles shifted her position on the bed and gazed out the window. Then she sighed, squeezed my hand gently, and resumed her story.

Frankie was just four when we came here. This place was the best I could do to fulfill the dream Ned and I had cherished of a quiet country place for our little boy to grow up in. After Ned died, I worked for two years clerking in a fine store, yearning for a complete change of scene. Finally, I took what I had been able to earn and save, the little that was left of Ned's savings, a bit that Mick and Nancy were able to give me, and I came South.

I was sick to death of cities and crowds and troubles and icy winters. Though I'd always been a city girl and knew only what I had read of country life, I was of a mind to try it. So Frankie and I took the train as far as Atlanta and began to look at farms for sale. An agent knew of a place near here where a large old family farm was being divided up and sold, and he brought us in his motorcar to see the property.

That particular property was too expensive and too large for us, and I explained to the agent that I just wanted a small house with enough grounds for Frankie to be able to play and roam a bit and for me to raise a small garden.

"Oh," said the old farmer whose place we had just looked at, "if all you want is a bit of livin' space, you might like my sister-in-law's place. Her name's Mrs. Johns, and she's wantin' to move to Montgomery with her daughter. It may be she'd let her place go reasonable."

So he gave us directions to her home, and as soon as we'd turned into the driveway, I knew we'd found our place. The lady was elderly and much taken with little Frankie, and when I had explained to her what we were looking for, the agent interrupted and tried to get her to name a price.

She ignored him, but she looked me up and down and said, "What can you pay, my dear, and not rob yourself?"

"I'm afraid I can pay only nine hundred," I said, thinking that the price would be double that.

"Seven-fifty," she said, and the agent's eyes nearly left his head. I'd wager he'd not had much experience with sellers who asked less than they were offered.

"But, madam, perhaps you didn't understand," he said in a loud voice. "This young lady has offered you nine hundred dollars."

"I'm neither deaf nor daft," she told him. "I know this place and I know my needs, and I know how I choose to live. Seven-fifty, and not a penny more."

"We'll take it," I said, "and God bless you."

"God bless *you* and this wee lad," she said. From her speech, I think she must have been a Scotswoman. "He'll not come to harm in this good place."

And so, we struck a bargain, and Frankie and I moved in, just a month before our country declared war on Germany. I was forty-seven years old, strong and healthy, and alone with my little boy. The war didn't touch us a great deal, though I followed it closely. I had my own battles to fight. Dear old Mrs. Johns had left behind her cow, her chickens, and a pig. And I had no notion of what to do with any of them!

It was spring, and I knew I needed to get a garden in, but I had little knowledge of how to do that either. And Frankie! What I hadn't considered in bargaining for a place for him to run was that he would run so far and find so many places to hide! If I wasn't chasing chickens or the pig, I was chasing Frankie. Some of the neighbor folk stopped by to get acquainted, but when they found out I was both a Yankee and a Catholic — well, they didn't know quite what to make of me, I'm sure. Nor did I, a city girl, know just how to take them, and I'm afraid I seemed cold and unfriendly at first. In my years with Ned and his work, I'd grown wary and suspicious of strangers, and I found it wasn't easy to put aside those feelings.

I remember one warm and windy afternoon a day or so after we'd come, I was sitting on the back steps, crying my eyes out and thinking I'd never be able to manage on my own. The cow was in the barn, bawling pitifully, and I didn't know what to do with her. I'd spent a good hour looking for Frankie, only to find him fast asleep under the porch, all covered with gray dust. On top of that, I'd broken the hoe trying to work some ground for my garden.

Suddenly, I felt someone looking at me. I glanced up to see a colored woman standing back by the edge of the woods, her head cocked to one side. I jumped up, embarrassed to be seen crying, and tried to compose myself enough to ask what she wanted.

She came forward and said, "Afternoon, ma'am. What be ailin' Miz Johns's old cow?"

"I don't *know* what ails her," I wailed. "I think she wants milking, but she scrapes her feet and kicks the bucket over every time I try."

"Ma'am," said Vesta, for that was who it was, as you've likely guessed, "would you mind if I was to try her? She do sound in mortal misery."

"Try her and welcome. I know little of cows, and she knows it."

So I followed Vesta into the barn, and she took the pail and began talking to Penny—that was the cow's name—talking and crooning as you would to a colicky baby, and rubbing her sides and neck. Old Penny rolled her eyes and shook her head and mooed, but she stood still and let Vesta milk her. I watched Vesta's technique, and when Penny had been relieved of most of her milk, Vesta motioned me to take her place. I tried to copy Vesta's way of milking. It wasn't easy—but bit by bit Penny relaxed.

"Now, then, ma'am — you has milk, and old Penny, she has her comfort," Vesta said.

I couldn't thank her enough, and I asked her to tell me about taking care of chickens and the pig and planting a garden. She told me a few basic things, and then said she was on her way to Bramley's store.

"I beg your pardon, ma'am, for comin' through the yard, but I didn't know Miz Johns done carried herself off already. That little path back there — it be a shortcut 'crost the creek to my place. But from now on, I'll take the road."

"Oh, no," I said, "I wish you'd please keep coming this way, especially if you'll teach me something each time you come through!"

Vesta just threw back her head and laughed. "Ma'am, it plain to see you ain't no country lady. But me, I know how you feel. When I come up from N'awlins, I didn't know nothin' much about cows and gardens neither. But you'll learn quick. It'll come. Oh, land sakes! Be that your baby?"

I turned to see Frankie, all covered with dust, rubbing one eye with his fist and peering at Vesta from the other. "My son Frankie," I said. "I'm afraid he's an awfully dirty little boy just now."

Vesta gave a big broad smile. "Good Book says we made from the dust of the earth. I don' reckon a little more dust gonna hinder his growth none — he one beautiful baby! How-do, Master Frankie. I'm Miz Vesta Lincoln."

Early next morning, I heard strange sounds from out back. I pulled a wrap around me and went to the back door. Vesta was there with a mule and a plow, working my garden spot. I ran out barefoot onto the damp grass and said, "Mrs. Lincoln, I can't afford to have you do this — I'm sorry!"

"Oh, no, ma'am. I don't hire out, me. I jus' wake up this mornin' and see it done rained a little, and I think to myself, Vesta, that little old patch of ground be jus' ready to plow this mornin'. So it jus' seem natural to bring old Buster over and do it. Now, ma'am, I got some seeds there on your back porch. You jus' look 'em over and see what you want while me and Buster finishes up. I done my own plantin' already, so they's plenty of everything."

Well, I sat down on the edge of the porch and looked at all the little paper sacks, and a big lump began to rise in my throat. I sat there with tears blurring the whole scene, realizing that there was goodness in people like Vesta and Mrs. Johns—goodness that just spilled over and wouldn't take no for an answer. I wanted to be like those two women—to be able to look, see a need, and then fill it. That seemed to me to be pure human goodness.

Grandmother Knowles closed her eyes, and gradually her mouth relaxed into peace. After a moment, I tiptoed out, not even daring to gather our dishes for fear of disturbing her.

I stood at the back door, gazing past the cotton puff on the screen door—out toward the green yard, the zinnias, the rampant garden, and the darker wood beyond. The colors of my life were green and gold—warm and peaceful and growing. The kaleidoscope was holding steady.

. . . . 18 . . . . .

I stepped onto the porch, where Vesta sat in the weather-beaten old rocker, snapping beans into a dishpan on her lap. Beside her, Hunger thumped his tail and came to flop next to me as I sat down on the top step. The heat, rich and sweet-smelling, washed over me and made me feel sleepy and indolent. I knew if I tried to read I would be asleep in five minutes, and I didn't want to waste my precious time here sleeping.

"Vesta," I said through a yawn, "why is that piece of cotton hanging on the screen door?"

"That keep flies away. Down at my old place, we grow tansy next the doorstoop. It do the same thing; but your granny, she don't want nothin' growin' up next the house. How she doin', honey babe? She need me?"

"She's sleeping right now. She's been telling me about when she first came here and how you helped her with her garden and the cow and all."

Vesta chuckled. "Whoo-ee! That old cow, she was in the most misery I ever did see. She like to bust open, she so full of milk. You know cows — they got to be milked mornin' and evenin'."

I hadn't known, but I nodded sagely.

"That pore child . . . "

It took me a minute to realize that Vesta was speaking of my grandmother, who topped her in age by at least ten years.

"That pore little thing didn't hardly know what seeds was what when we was fixin' to put in her garden. 'I think this some kind of bean—but is this tomato seeds?' she ask. 'Lord love you, no—those be okra seed,' I tell her. 'Vesta,' she say, 'what's okra?' Now, I tell you true, it not easy to explain okra to somebody ain't never seen one. I say, 'Well, they kinda green and pointy and fuzzy on the outside, and kinda slickery on the inside.' She say, 'I don't think we need to plant any of those.' But me, I figger I can teach her how to fix 'em so's she'll like 'em, and I sneak some in the ground. I showed her collards—she hadn't never eat them neither—and we plant pole beans and corn and tomatoes and butter beans and onions. I tell you true, honey, I never see nobody so tickled when them little seeds begin to sprout and grow! She took to gardenin' like it the most fun she ever had. 'Just think, Vesta,' she say to me, 'just think! This real food we growin' here, right in my own piece of earth.'

" 'Been thataway since Father Adam, Miz Knowles,' I tell her.

" 'I know,' she say. 'But *I* never done it before.' She work hard too—hoed and weeded like I showed her. And when the crops come in, I show her how to can and pickle and preserve, and she so proud! She say, 'Vesta, thank you for my garden.'

"I say, 'Honey, the good Lord made the seeds and send the sun and rain—you best thank him.'

" 'I do,' she says, 'but he send me an expert too, 'count of he knowed I'd need one!' "

Vesta shook her head, smiling at the memory. "Her garden done been a pleasure to her too, right on up to a year or so ago when she was took so bad. It kept her and Mr. Frankie through the war and depression and all the hard times, and now it give me a heap of pleasure to work that little old plot of ground. It plumb full of good memories to me. I can see Mr. Frankie out there when he was a little 'un, workin' alongside his mama, and them laughin' together about some nonsense or other. And I see Miz Knowles after Frankie gone, out there hoein' and her tears awaterin' them plants, sayin', 'Vesta, this near about the only place I get any comfort.' I tell you true, honey babe, the good Lord knowed what he's doin' to have Adam till the ground."

I looked at the lush rows of vegetables with new respect. I had always considered gardening just a necessary evil, but perhaps I had something to learn there too.

"Vesta," I said after a minute. "Would it be okay if I picked some flowers to take up to my Daddy's grave?"

"Well, that be fine. Get you a mason jar from under the sink curtain and pick any old flowers you want."

When my jar was filled with red zinnias, I asked if she needed anything from Bramley's store.

"You goin' up thataway too?"

"I thought I might circle back that way. They've got some real cute little baby kittens."

She reached into her deep apron pocket for a knotted hand-kerchief, carefully untied it, and counted out a few coins. "Onliest thing I need is a little piece of salt pork to cook with my collards, but you best get you a drink of sody pop or an ice-cream bar. It be mighty hot out there, walkin' this time of day."

"Oh, thank you, ma'am, but I don't reckon I need—"

"And I reckon you do," she insisted in a tone that brooked no nonsense. I thanked her and crossed the backyard, clutching my jar of zinnias.

It seemed a quicker walk to me now, wearing my sandals against the pine needles and sandspurs. The zinnias made a bright splash of color against the white of my father's marker. "It's me again, Daddy," I whispered. "The flowers are from your mama's yard. I reckon they're not much compared to the flowers in heaven, but I think they're right pretty."

I stood quietly for a few moments, listening to the buzz and snap of the insect population all around me. Katydids sang in concert, their volume increasing and then dying away altogether. From the top of a tall pine, a blue-black crow cried for rain.

"No rain today," I told him. "Not a cloud in the sky." Still, he gave his hoarse, thirsty caw as I picked my way along the path to the rusting front gate, then turned left and followed a road of banked red clay. My road intersected a gravel one that I judged to run parallel to the one on which my grandmother's house stood. Soon, I came to the highway and, looking left again, I could see Bramley's store just down the way. Pleased with my simple success at exploring, I set off along the grassy shoulder.

To my surprise, the bench outside the store was vacant. I entered the dim coolness with a sense of relief and stood uncertainly for a moment, letting my eyes adjust to the dim light. I glanced around to see who was minding the store, but could find no one until a soft squeak drew my attention to Mr. Hank Tidwell, rocking gently in a cane-bottomed chair near the potbellied stove. He must have sensed my gaze, because he opened his eyes and focused them on me. Then he struggled up out of the rocker and stood bent forward for a moment, fingers still touching the chair arms until he felt steady enough to proceed to the counter.

"How do, young lady," he shouted at me. "What can I hep you with today?"

I gave my order in as loud a voice as I thought respectful, but he gave no sign of having heard. Instead, he pushed a piece of paper and the stub of a pencil across the counter to me and said, "Just write your order on there, little lady, and you'd best write it a mite big and dark, on account of my eyes ain't what they used to be, and not a hull lot better'n my ears."

Taking the pencil, I wrote, "A piece of salt pork to cook with collards and an orange soda, and can I please see the kittens?"

Mr. Hank held my note up to catch the light coming in the high window, and then gave a small chuckle as he gestured to the kittens' box and shuffled off to fill the order. I settled beside the kittens as quietly as I could, as the mother cat was there feeding them. She was panting gently and gave a couple of small, anxious cries when she saw me.

"It's all right, Polly," I told her. "I won't hurt your babies — they're sweet."

I ventured a hand to stroke her black head, which rose to meet my caress. She purred for a moment, gave her chest fur a couple of licks, and went back to panting. The kittens pulled and pushed, their purrs sounding like the stop-and-go winding of four small clocks.

Mr. Hank held up my Nehi and gestured to see if I wanted it opened. I nodded, and he pried the cap off and handed it to me, bending carefully from the waist. Gratefully, I sipped the orange fizz and watched the little family before me. At any moment I expected to see a pair of dusty feet and brown legs in rolled-up jeans appear on the edge of my vision, but they failed to show up.

It was silly of me to assume Zack Bramley would be here every day at the same time or whenever I chose to come. Even so, he had said he tended the store while his father went home for his midday dinner, so why was he not here today? Maybe — and my cheeks grew hot — maybe he'd been sorry, when he thought about it, that he had ever mentioned that secret cousin idea. Maybe he had decided it was silly after all. Or what if he was the kind of person who said things like that and never even thought about them again? Likely his daddy had taught him to be nice to the customers and keep them coming back.

Finally, I stood up, placed my empty bottle in the rack provided, and picked up the paper-wrapped piece of salt pork.

"That be all, little lady?" inquired Mr. Hank. I nodded and tried to smile, glad that I didn't have to trust my voice right then. Not for a thousand dollars would I have asked where Zack was — so what in the world was wrong with me?

Mr. Hank held the screen door politely and stepped outside behind me, giving a little grunt of pain as he did so.

"That young Zack's gone fishin'," he said, as if he had read my thoughts. "Reckon as how he'd better hightail it on back 'lessen he wants to git soaked to the skin. It's fixin' to storm." He eased himself down onto the bench and rubbed his knees.

I remembered the calling of the rain crow and the sighing song of the katydids at the cemetery. I glanced up at the sky, which was still as blue as a bowl. The heat bore down with no mercy — not a blade of grass or a weed top moved. How could it possibly be going to rain?

I waved to Mr. Hank and crossed the highway again. Fishing, was he? He had taken himself well out of reach for sure. Well, he wouldn't have to worry about tomorrow. Not for anything would I show up at Bramley's Feed and General Merchandise—certainly not around the noon hour!

I scuffed at the sand and clay of the road until my white socks looked rusty. Little rivers of sweat trickled down the small of my back and the sides of my face. There were no bees on the honeysuckle today—the heat must be too much even for them. I didn't feel like skipping as I had the day before—at least not until I came within sight of my grandmother's house. Vesta was on the front porch talking to—could it be Zack Bramley? I started to hurry, then thought better of it and ambled on at my previous pace.

"Looky here, honey babe," Vesta called, holding up a string of silvery fish. "Zachary here done give us a fine mess of bluegill!"

Zack turned and gave me a sort of nod, but his direct gaze wavered after a moment. "Had purty fair luck," he admitted. "Reckoned maybe y'all could use some."

"We gonna have us a fine fry. You better come on back, Zachary, and take supper with us this evenin'."

"That's right nice of you, Miz Vesta. I'd be proud to, but I reckon by then that storm'll be about here. And Mama, she frets if one of us ain't home when it's stormin' out."

"I know it's comin', me," Vesta agreed. "Air feels mighty close."

I was getting a little impatient with all this talk of storms and rain when the sky above was such a burning blue, and there wasn't even a breeze to bring a cloud.

"Heard on the radio last night that a hurricane's moved in off the ocean," Zack said, "and that ain't usual for this time of year. It's come in down by Savannah and headin' up this way. They always die down a bit once they come ashore, but we'll likely still get a blow, Daddy says."

"Tatum's between here and Savannah," I said. "Wonder if they're getting it."

"Reckon they are, all right. Report said it was a big thing – most of the state'll get rain from it."

"Law, honey, I 'member them hurricanes that come ashore down at N'awlins! Some of them storms are pure killers. I don' know whether the devil brews 'em or the Lord sends 'em to punish folks, but they be mean, mean things. Trees bendin' and swayin' clear over, sometimes the roots pull clean out of the ground . . ." Vesta swayed and bent herself as she spoke, and for a moment I could see how really pretty and graceful she must have been as a girl. "And thunder and lightnin' – whoo-ee! The good Lord, he speak with the voice of thunder, you know, and he done had plenty to say down in N'awlins!"

I was beginning to believe in the coming storm, but I had to ask. "How come the rain crow keeps calling and the katydids sing like they do, and there isn't even a cloud in sight?"

"The critters know first of all," Zack told me. "My daddy, he used to work down in Texas, and he said sometimes they'd have these sudden storms blow down outa the North – drop the temperature twenty or thirty degrees real quick. And they could allus tell when a Norther was comin' on account of the pigs'd start runnin' around and squealin' and carryin' sticks in their mouths, like they wanted to build 'em a shelter or somethin'. Sure 'nough, awhile later the northern sky'd go a dark purple color and the wind'd pick up, and they'd be in for it."

"Well, the Lord gave animals and little things more sense than us in some ways," Vesta said. "Though I coulda told you last night we was in for some weather. My old bones told me – and they're pretty smart too."

Zack grinned. "Grandpa Hank said the same thing. Told me yesterday evenin' not to get too far from home today – and that was before the weather report come on."

I nodded. "He just told me you'd better get home from fishing or you'd be soaked to the skin – but I didn't believe him."

"I reckon he knows – him and the rain crow. Miz Vesta, can I help you fasten down anything around here before I go?"

"Don't reckon so, honey. Thank you, now. I'd best get my collards on and these fish cleaned."

Vesta closed the screen door behind her, and I stood there tongue-tied, wishing Zack would go away, yet wanting him to stay.

"So, you done been up to the store?" he asked.

I nodded. "Vesta needed some salt pork."

"I figgered on gettin' back by noontime, but I got too far downstream. Was Daddy there, or did Grandpa take over?"

"Mr. Hank waited on me."

"And he told you I'd gone fishin'?"

"Yep. I mean I didn't ask or anything. He just mentioned it — about the rain coming and all."

"I'll be doggoned." Zack's grin widened, and his brownish-green gaze examined the far fields. "Well, I'd best be gettin' home to help Mama get ready. I'll come back tomorrow and see how y'all weathered the storm."

"You — will?"

"Sure. You know cousins — they got to look out for one another."

He gave a little salute, picked up his pole and tackle box, and swung off down the drive. I was still watching when he turned by the mailbox to wave.

. . . . 19 . . . .

I stretched out on my stomach across my bed and picked up *Freckles*. The windows of my little room were wide open, but the curtains hung limp and still. From a distance, I heard the rise and fall of the katydids' chirring, but little else. The air was heavy and warm against my eyelids, almost forcing them to droop and close.

When I awoke, a subtle change had taken place. A strange light filled the room; it looked yellowish and felt charged with electricity somehow. I got up and padded into the hall. Through my grandmother's open door I could see that she still napped peacefully, her open mouth emitting soft snores.

"Vesta?" I called softly, but there was no answer. I walked through the kitchen and saw her standing in the middle of the backyard, hugging her elbows and looking at the sky. I went outside and stood beside her. Her light brown skin had turned a honey-caramel color in the strange light.

"I don' like the looks of this, me," she said, with a swift glance at me and then back to the roiling clouds above.

"It looks weird," I said. "It looks like — once I had an Easter basket that came all wrapped in yellow cellophane, and when I looked through the cellophane, everything was yellow, like now. What does it mean?"

"Reckon it mean that old storm's acomin' at us, all right. I done put the chickens to bed and shut up everything loose in the barn, so there won't be none of our stuff flyin' around. Reckon we be in for a blow, right enough."

A swirly little wind whipped around my legs, and I saw that Hunger was trotting around carrying one of his bones in his mouth, poking his nose under the porch steps, then withdrawing it and continuing his search for the perfect hiding place.

"Look what a funny color of green the trees are," I commented. "They're so bright, but it's not sunshiny. It looks sort of like a technicolor movie."

"I ain't never seen a pitcher show, but they must look mighty strange. Tell you what, honey babe — let's draw us up some water and get our fish a-fryin' while there's still light."

"You reckon the lights'll go out?"

"Likely."

I stayed close to Vesta as she filled a couple of buckets with water. Then she cleaned the fish, dredged them in cornmeal, and fried them in a black iron skillet of hot fat. By the time they were ready to eat, Grandmother was awake, and the smell of rain was in the air. More and more frequent gusts of wind rattled the windows.

"Vesta, you must eat in here with us. We'll have a hurricane party," my grandmother said, and so it was that we settled down to an early supper of Zack's fish and Vesta's hush puppies and collards. There was a cozy companionship among us, mixed with a tingle of fear and anticipation.

Vesta turned up the volume on the old console radio in the living room so that we could hear the storm reports. They were not comforting — trees across power lines, beach-front homes flooded or destroyed, three people known drowned as they attempted to ride out the storm in a fishing vessel. The hurricane's fury had lessened a little as it came ashore, but it was still a dangerous storm, and everyone in its path should take precautions. Tornadoes were cropping up as a result of the ferocious winds and climate changes, and a waterspout had been sighted offshore earlier in the day.

Grandmother raised her eyebrows in silent query to Vesta, who slowly shook her head.

"Done about all we can, I reckon," she said. "Put the chickens in, closed up the barn, drawed some water, got the candles and storm lamps ready, brought in the potted plants, unhooked the swing chains—I cain't think of nothin' else. Reckon maybe I shoulda got young Zack to nail a board acrost our windows, but I figgered his mama might've needed help at home to get ready."

"Well done, Vesta. I can't think of anything else we could reasonably do. You had a busy afternoon."

"Didn't take me much time to fix up around here. Then I took a half hour this afternoon and run down to my old place to see did my chirren know what was comin'."

"Had they heard?"

"They runnin' 'round like crazy folk, chasin' down them chickens they let run loose, and the grandbabies was jumpin' up and down like they'd heard Santy Claus was comin' 'stead of a storm. And the Hutchins—you know their little old house is right by the creek—well, they done piled up all their belongin's on a tabletop in the middle of the room. Looks so funny to see a mattress and quilts and chairs and rolled up rugs all stacked up like that. It put me in mind of a lady holding her long skirts up to her knees!"

"They think the creek will flood then?"

"It runnin' high already, though me, I've never knowed it to flood bad."

I swallowed, and both women glanced apprehensively at me, realizing the effect of their remarks.

"Oh, but my lovie—we're on high ground here, and this is a sturdy little house. The worst of the storm will have been spent by the time we get it anyway. I think you need not fear," Grandmother consoled me. Vesta began to bustle around clearing up our dishes.

"Want me to help, Vesta?" I asked.

"No, thank you, sugar. You jus' keep your grandmama company."

"Now, Vesta, if the lightning comes close at all, you take your hands out of the water," cautioned my grandmother, reminding me vividly of Granna.

I wondered if the storm had hit Tatum. How big was a hurricane anyway?

I began to realize that I'd been partly aware of an incessant rumble in the distance. Now I could identify the sound as thunder, one roll after another — the reverberations overlapping, surging, and receding as the rattling wind gusts rose and fell. The rain seemed to come all at once, and it carried a salty tang, as though it had risen undiluted from the sea.

My grandmother turned her face to me, a sweet, puzzled expression crossing it as she said, "Do you know, my lovie, it smells like home! Boston, that is — and the shore."

"It does smell different," I agreed. "How long does a hurricane usually last?"

"If it's as big as they say, I'd guess all night."

"The man on the radio said this one's called Annie."

"Yes, Annie for 'A' — the first of the season. Next one might be Bertha or Betty, then Carol, and so on. A hurricane can change course any minute and head another way. They change their minds like a woman, so they say — which must be why they're given women's names."

I rose and walked to the window. It had suddenly grown very dark outside. The whole outdoors was purplish-gray and moving with wind and rain. Treetops seemed to fling themselves to one side and then the other as they met the onslaught of the storm. Rain dashed against the window in such sheets that there seemed no such thing as individual droplets.

"Does it get worse than this?"

"I think, my lovie, that it probably will. But I also believe we needn't worry too greatly. It makes one uneasy, a great storm like this, but don't you find it a bit exciting too? I used to love a storm when I was a girl! I'd want to run out and lift my arms to the sky, as if to embrace the very elements, or to praise the dear God who created them. 'Come in here, you wild thing,' Mum would say. 'Don't tempt the lightning!' "

"Weren't you even scared?" I asked, as a huge roll of thunder shook the ground.

My grandmother spread her hands on the quilt and looked at

them. "When I was young, I thought I was invincible — indestructible. I thought I would never die."

"But everybody's got to die."

"Oh, I *knew* that — I just didn't believe it. Death was something that happened to other people, and it was so far in the future for me that I couldn't even imagine it. But now, looking back, the distance doesn't seem so great, and I've learned that I *am* one of the other people — the ones who can die. It makes me feel very fragile somehow. I'm not nearly as — solid — as I used to be. I don't suppose that makes tremendous sense, does it? Pay me no mind, my dear. Old ladies ramble on."

I sought vainly for words of comfort. Suddenly a scrabbling sound in the hall caught our attention. It was Hunger, his paws slipping on the linoleum as he turned the corner and scuttled under the bed in my father's old room.

Vesta followed, drying her hands on a towel and shaking her head. "That pore old dog. When it commenced to thunder and carry on, I jus' had to let him come in. 'Sides, the rain was startin' to whip in onto the porch and wet him."

"He's always been afraid of thunder. Frankie used to get up and let him in every time a storm came up in the night, so Hunger thinks the only safe place in the world is under that bed."

"Reckon I'll be glad enough to have him there," I said and ran into my father's room to kneel down and peer at Hunger, who beat his tail against the floor and whined, but refused to come out.

Another hurricane bulletin was coming over the radio, and I went out into the hallway to listen. " . . . winds clocked at one hundred fifteen miles per hour as Hurricane Annie moved onshore last night, leaving destruction and death in its wake in the Savannah area. The winds have subsided considerably, but are still gusting sixty and seventy miles per hour as they move across land. Currently traveling north-northwest at about fifteen miles per hour, Annie is now centered near Athens, Georgia. We advise anyone in the path of the hurricane to take all necessary precautions. Do not leave your home or shelter unless there is an absolute emergency. Those in low-lying areas are being evacuated to schools or other public shelters in their vicinity. We repeat: this storm is dangerous. We expect high winds, extremely heavy rains, and lightning. It's advised that in case of—"

Without warning, our power was gone. The sudden loss of light and sound within emphasized the awful display of nature's power without. I moved quietly into my grandmother's room and sat beside her. She gave my hand a reassuring squeeze. Vesta was lighting an oil lamp on the dresser.

"Maybe it come back in a while," she said, referring to our electricity. "But, anyways—we got light, us."

The light was golden and comforting, and we sat quietly on each side of my grandmother's bed—secure, somehow, in the circle of lamplight, yet each keenly attuned to the rising fury outdoors.

"Miz Knowles," said Vesta softly, "you mind if I make a prayer?"

"Please do, Vesta."

I closed my eyes and held my hands clenched tightly.

"Dear Lord in Heaven," Vesta began. "You know who's here. You know we jus' two old women and one girl-child in the midst of this storm. We got no man here to do for us, and we dependin' on you, dear Lord, to hold this here little old house safe in your hand like you always done. Help us hear your voice in the thunders and lightnin's and know what be your will for us to do. We recommend all our loved ones to your keepin' this night too. And any poor souls who's lost out in this terrible hurricane, we ask you to bless and lead 'em to shelter. Dear Lord, we ain't ever'thing we oughta be, but you knows our hearts, and though we be sinners, we ain't wicked. And we do love you, Lord Jesus. Amen."

I opened my eyes. Grandmother let out a long sigh and put her hand out to Vesta, who took it in both her long brown ones.

"You're my strength, Vesta. You're my greatest source of faith. When I hear you pray like that, I feel you know who you're praying to. I haven't always felt that way about others."

"Well, Miz Knowles, me and the good Lord, we old friends. He done answer my prayer so many times, I *know* he be there. I don' know how he done it, but he ain't never too busy to listen to old Vesta — nor nobody else, neither. He listen to you too, Miz Knowles."

"I don't know, Vesta, I've never been so sure of that. I have prayed many times, it's true, but I can't just talk to God like you do. I feel my words aren't good enough, or I'm not — or I shouldn't be asking for more than I already have. I'm sorry, my lovie," she said, smiling tiredly at me. "At my age, I should have all this worked out and be able to pass on my wisdom and faith to you. But I fear all I can pass on are questions and doubtings."

"Don't worry," I told her. "I think you're wonderful. I think you're going straight to heaven — someday, I mean."

"Anybody deserve to go to heaven, it be this lady," affirmed Vesta. "Now the way I see it, me — if God loves us, and he tell us he do in the holy Bible, then I figger he want to hear from us pretty regular. He want to know how we doin' and how we love him back. Me, I wanna know how my chirren is doin', and I don' need to hear it in no fancy words. I jus' want 'em to tell me the truth, and let me know they still love me, and tell me if there's anything I can do for 'em. I figger it about the same with the Lord, so that's how I do my prayin'."

We were silent for a minute in the lamplight while the winds slammed furiously against the house and the boards in the wall creaked, and then I said, "My Uncle Bob, he's learning to preach, you know? Well, he says good, sincere prayers are always heard and someday answered, but that sometimes the answer is 'no.' "

"That be true," Vesta agreed. "I ask him please not to take my baby girl from me, and he done took her. But he give me such a feelin' of peace and love that I knowed he jus' say, 'No, Vesta, not this time. But I love you, and this be for the best.' "

"I think I got a 'yes' answer one time," I volunteered. "I needed to know something real quick. After I prayed about it, I found somebody who could tell me. Before that, I couldn't seem to find out anything about it."

Vesta nodded approvingly. "It jus' take faith. You gotta believe you gonna be heard, that you talkin' to somebody real and not jus' air."

"I think that was my problem," Grandmother said. "It was probably my own fault, but in my old church, God seemed to be so unapproachable and mysterious and almost spooky. I said my rosary and the other prayers, and the words were lovely, to be sure—but I felt no warmth, no answer. And then when I married my Ned, well—he wasn't of my faith, and I lost touch, you might say. Ned believed in God, but as a great mind or a force directing the universe. He didn't pray. He felt it was useless to pray to someone or something who already knew all things anyway—and who could pray to a force? When Ned was missing, I tried to pray, but I felt so helpless. How could I pray, 'Let him be safe,' when he might already be dead? I just didn't know who God was exactly, or how to approach him. Then, Ned was found, and I prayed, 'Please, God, let him live, let him get well.' But I guess that was one of your 'no' answers." She smiled at Vesta.

"Bless your heart, Miz Knowles. You been through a lot."

"Most of my prayers since then have been silent ones—really just hopes of the heart, you might say. I've been afraid to ask, and sometimes, I confess, too proud to say thank you." She reached her hand, dry and veined, to pat my arm. "But I find I *must* thank him for some blessings, with all my heart," she said. Her old voice was husky with tears, and I knew she meant me.

. . . . 20 . . . .

Our talk turned to other times, other storms, punctuated by respectful pauses during which we gave attention to our present situation. The house never ceased complaining, though its groans and creaks would sometimes drop to a murmur, only to rise again. Often, the entire house would shake suddenly. Night had fallen, and only when lightning flared were we able to glimpse the tall pines bending and bowing before the gale. Awe-inspiring as it was to see the stalwart and usually serene trees so fiercely whipped and battered, it was just as unnerving to sit waiting with each mounting gust for something to blow loose or come crashing down. I was grateful that my grandmother's house sat in a clearing, out of reach of all but the tallest of the pines that might fall. We heard several dull crashes, and once something — possibly a flying board — slammed against the side of the house.

"Sho grateful I gathered in all our tomaters," Vesta muttered. "What's left gonna be smashed to a pulp come mornin'."

"Probably come back," soothed my grandmother, pressing her fingers against her chest.

Vesta didn't miss that gesture. Peering at the clock on the bedside table, she said, "I don' know about y'all, but all this rain makes me plumb weary. Honey babe, you look in the bottom drawer of your chest for an extry quilt, and you know what sets under your bed, 'sides of old Hunger! Ain't nobody paradin' to the outhouse, this kind of night."

I knew about the chamber pot. I nodded and kissed my grandmother. Vesta was giving her a tiny white pill even as I left the room. The illumination of the oil lamp didn't quite reach into my little room, and knowing Hunger lay under the bed was a comfort. I dropped to my knees and talked to him, and he inched forward on his bony elbows and licked my hand. My prayers that night included pleas for the safety of Granna and Uncle Bob and a number of others, as well as those in our little household. Crawling into bed and pulling the covers over my ears was a relief. The sheets felt cold and clammy, and it took a while for my body to warm them so I could relax.

I could hear Vesta moving about, more slowly than usual, and once she came in to check on me. "You be all right, honey?"

"Yes'm," I said drowsily. "Are you going to bed now too?"

"Me, I'm gonna wrap up in a quilt and rest in that rocking chair where I can hear your granny if she need me. So if you need me, you call too, you hear? And Hunger, you mind your manners."

Hunger's tail thumped again, and Vesta moved slowly toward the hall, her feet dragging uncharacteristically.

"You must be awful tired, Vesta," I roused myself to say.

"Bless you, baby, it jus' these old leg bones. Storm like this makes 'em remember where they was broke. I be all right directly."

I dozed restlessly. Once when Hunger whined, I reached a hand down to him. He thrust his muzzle into my palm, and we slept that way for a while. I was vaguely aware of soft voices from the other bedroom a time or two, and sometime during the wee hours I heard Hunger pulling himself from under the bed and being let out the back door.

The next time I awoke, a dim, grayish light filled the room, something was banging crazily somewhere, and a low howl was coming from the back porch. Hunger—he must still be out there!

I slipped out of bed and peeked into my grandmother's room. She slept and so did Vesta, quilt-wrapped in the rocker, her features relaxed in exhaustion. I went to the back door and pulled the bolt, unprepared for the force of the wind. It shifted and flung the door inward along with a barrage of rain. Vesta's cotton puff hung shredded and sopping on the screen, and Hunger sat hunched miserably below it, quivering in terror at flash after flash of lightning.

"Poor old doggy," I sympathized, and then, "Yuck!" as he paused inside the door for a thoroughly showery shake before streaking to his refuge again. Resigned, I found a rag of old toweling and wiped up his path, then shucked out of my damp gown and got into shorts and a shirt that didn't feel entirely dry either. Between sheets of rain I peered out the kitchen window to find the source of the persistent banging. It was the barn door, which had come unbarred and was being slammed back against the building. For once, I was grateful that no animals were housed there; I was in no mood to try to secure it. Although the light was growing stronger, it was impossible to guess the time. I didn't want to tiptoe in to check my grandmother's clock for fear of disturbing her or Vesta. I took two big sugar cookies from Vesta's crock and crept back to my room, which reeked with the unmistakable odor of wet dog. Gingerly, I made use of the chamber pot — my first time — hastily put its lid back on, and shoved it into a corner. I reached for *Freckles* on the small bookcase but picked up Star's Nancy Drew instead.

Star! I had parted from her almost tearfully and had promised to write and let her know the lay of the land, yet hardly once had she entered my mind for nearly a week. Such is the effect of travel and change of scene. Remorsefully, I pictured Star and her feeling that nothing was ever going to be the same again. She had been right — for me, anyway. My world had expanded greatly with this visit.

I found my pen and paper and sat cross-legged on the bed to write her a long letter. Afterward, I picked up the Nancy Drew again, intending to read just a few pages in honor of Star's generosity. But, predictably, the story caught me, and with made-to-order background noises fit for Halloween, I spent an eerily enjoyable early morning helping Nancy solve her current mystery.

When Vesta awoke, stiff and tired, we prepared a simple breakfast of biscuits and leftover fried fish, grateful that the cookstove was gas and not electric, as we still had no power. I was surprised at how tasty I found the fish. My grandmother woke briefly and drank a cup of hot tea, then went back to sleep.

As the morning wore on, the storm abated, and by noon there were just intermittent showers and nervous puffs of wind. After lunch, I helped Vesta replace the potted plants on the front porch and clear the yard of debris — bristly small branches of trees, shingles of various colors, and a ripped square of rusty window screen. The air was unusually fresh and cool; I felt almost as if I should slip on a sweater and start for school — wherever school was. It was easier to breathe now, to move, to plan — even to believe in the future.

As we finished clearing away the mess, Zack Bramley swung into the yard. "Ever'body okay? Have y'all got power yet?"

"Not yet, but we're fine," I told him.

"Reckon it'll be a while. Man came in and told Daddy there'd been a twister touch down over at Lynchville — took the roof plumb off the schoolhouse and caused all kinds of damage. There're lines down all over the place, he said. I seen three utility trucks in a row, heading up the highway — whew!" Zack brushed his palms past each other to show how fast they had been going. "Man alive, that was some storm! Y'all get scared?"

"Kind of," I admitted. "It got awful noisy, didn't it, and it was hard to know what was happening. But it was exciting too."

"Hey, I tell you what. Since we're cousins and all, I'll tell you the truth, but I wouldn't say this to nobody else. My little sister Nelda — she's five — she come crawlin' into bed with me, just acryin', she was so scared, and . . . " He grinned sheepishly. "The truth is, I ain't never been so glad to see somebody in all my life! I grabbed hold of old Nelda and held her tight till she stopped cryin' and went to sleep, and I kept thinkin', 'Well, if the walls fall in, they'll fall on the both of us.' Then I got to thinkin' 'bout how I'd throw my body over Nelda's at the last minute, and later they'd find us, and I'd be dead, but she'd be okay because I saved her, and how good I'd feel — 'ceptin I reckon I wouldn't really feel a thing 'cause I'd be dead and gone. Now, ain't that about the dumbest thing you ever heard? It's funny how a body can think such dumb things in the middle of the night."

"I don't think it's a bit dumb," I said, impressed that he would admit his fears and thoughts to me. "It just shows that you were thinking about taking care of Nelda. I bet you'd feel proud and glad if you saved her life. And even if you died, I still think you'd know."

"You reckon? My mama, she says being dead is just like being asleep till the Judgment Day, but I don't know. Preacher says you go straight to heaven or h—the other place, soon's you die. I cain't seem to get it straight." He grinned. "Reckon I can wait a while to find out though."

"Me, too."

"Wanta walk around some and look at the damage? Parker Savage's barn is leanin' clear to one side, and there's a tree up yonder by the road that got hit by lightnin'. It's all split open and charred black as coal. Only thing is, we cain't go nowhere near the river. I promised Daddy I wouldn't, on account of the high water drove the snakes up higher, and they's likely a whole passel of cottonmouths hangin' up in tree branches. They can climb, you know."

My flesh crawled at the thought of snakes hanging from trees, and I wanted to rush back into the safety of the house. But I also didn't want to miss a chance to be with Zack, especially in this excited and talkative mood of his. So, after promising Vesta that we would stay on the road and not go near any old buildings or damaged trees or power lines, we set out.

Trees were down all along the sides of the road. Tall pines— some already dead and "waiting for an excuse to fall," as Zack's father had told him—and others were cut down in their prime like fallen soldiers. Branches and clumps of needles or leaves lay everywhere, stripped from trees and bushes as if by the whim of a giant, destructive child.

We leaned against a fence post, watching the list and sway of Parker Savage's old barn. "Daddy says that barn's been tryin' to decide whether to stand or fall for years now," Zack said. "He was wonderin' 'bout it last night, whether it was still up."

"It must have been kinda fun with your whole family together last night." Once again, I was feeling my familiar only-child, lonely-child longings. "Did you have oil lamps burning like we did?"

"Yep. We sat around and had popcorn and told spooky stories and such till Mama made us stop. Reckon that was why little Nelda got so scared."

"Who else is in your family?" I asked curiously.

As we continued down the road, he told me of Bobbie Sue, who was fourteen and thought she was all grown up; of his brother, Emmett, age seven; of five-year-old Nelda, his favorite; and of little three-year-old Nancy, who had slept snugly between wakeful parents all night long.

By the time we reached the highway, the sun was shining a few seconds at a time between high clouds that moved swiftly, as if flying to catch up to the storm. When we got to the store, a tall man with straight black hair and high cheekbones looked up to greet us.

"Hey, Daddy," Zack said. "This here's Miz Knowles' granddaughter. We been lookin' over the damage."

"How'd you ladies fare through the night?" asked Mr. Bramley, pushing two Tootsie Rolls toward us across the scarred counter.

"Thank you," I said, pocketing mine. "We did all right except for not sleeping much. We found a few shingles ripped off, but the roof didn't leak and none of the windows got broken. Reckon we were lucky."

"We can take care of them shingles, cain't we, Son? Now, young lady, our phone service was restored a little bit ago, and a call came through from a man said he was your uncle, wonderin' if y'all was all right out here. I told him we were plannin' to check, and we'd let him know was there a problem. A Bob—uh, Martin, was it?"

"Markham," I said. "Uncle Bob. Did he say how they were at Tatum?"

"I ast him about damage down there, and he said there'd been some, right enough, but nothin' too serious. Did say a chinaberry tree put a branch through a winder at your place, but ever'body's fine."

"Wow—that must have scared Granna half to death!" Which window, I wondered. Probably the side window of the front room, as the chinaberry tree stood at the corner of the house on that side.

"I ain't heard no official reports, but I reckon there's been a deal of damage done acrost the state. Utility man said the storm's startin' to die down, but it's still the worst weather these parts ever seen."

After we had visited a while with Zack's dad, and I had petted the kittens, we went out to walk around some more. "Your daddy's nice," I said.

"Yep," Zack said proudly. "Ain't a better man nowhere, I reckon. He can chuck a baseball farther'n you can see and tie flies that'll snag a big bass ever' time. And I ain't never ast my daddy nothin' he didn't know the answer to. Not *never*."

I privately thought there might be a few points of English grammar that could stump the amazing Mr. Bramley, judging from the speech habits he and his son shared, but still I was impressed. He was tall and kind and competent, and he gave promise of the sort of man Zack would someday be. Fine points of grammar just weren't what they cared, or even thought, about.

"Hey," Zack said softly after a minute. "Reckon maybe I shouldn't of bragged on my daddy like that, seein' as you ain't even got yours. I'm kinda dumb sometimes."

"No, you're not. It's okay. I've been finding out lots about my daddy since I've been here, and I think he must have been nice too. I know he liked to laugh a lot and to hunt in the woods with old Hunger. That was his dog—did you know that? And he loved my mama. Besides, I've got Uncle Bob, and he's almost like a daddy. He's studying to be a preacher, but he works construction in the summer, so he's home more . . . "

"Whoo—don't it make you feel kinda creepy, livin' in the same house with a preacher? Would me."

I laughed. "Not Uncle Bob. He's real nice, and he's funny, and he always listens to what I say."

"Well, I've met a passel of preachers—Mama's always invitin' 'em to dinner to talk to Daddy—but I ain't seen one yet I'd want to live under the same roof with. I mean, how could a body stretch out and be hisself?"

"You could with Uncle Bob. He's not a bit stiff or scary." I told him about Uncle Bob's dealings with the Jensen boy at our mission church.

Zack was silent for a few minutes, then he said, "Reckon if a preacher's s'posed to bring folks closer to Jesus, it'd be a help if he was to act more like Jesus did. Sounds like your uncle's kind of that way, but some I've met is enough to scare a person clean away from the Lord, for fear he'd take a notion to drop you right in the fire and brimstone. N'then they turn right around and tell you the Lord loves you! It don't make much sense to me nor my daddy neither. He don't hold much with preachin' and takin' up the collection plate and all. But he sure reads his Bible. Sometimes Mama lets me stay home from church if Daddy promises to read out loud to me. Makes some sense when he reads it—he don't shout and beller and carry on like some. See—that's our house, over yonder on the rise."

He nodded toward a tall, bare, no-nonsense farmhouse, weathered to a silvery-gray. A driveway led past it to a matching silvered barn out back, and I could see a green tractor parked beside it. There were other outbuildings too, but I couldn't tell what they were. Two dark-haired little girls, their faces a blur from our distance, played on the front porch. I gazed, storing the scene away in my mind so that I could call it up and look at it again later.

"Where's your room?"

"Upstairs on the back," he answered, but he didn't invite me to the house, and I was relieved. For all my curiosity about Zack and his family, meeting his father was enough for one day.

We wandered up one roadway and down another, marvelling at the debris scattered by Hurricane Annie.

"Now, don't never go up *that* road," Zack warned, pointing to a narrow, high-centered track that wound under a drooping overhang of branches.

"Why not?"

He lowered his voice confidentially, as though the air around us was listening. "There's a still up there. Old man Potter and his son make moonshine, and they don't take kindly to nobody foolin' around."

"How do you know?"

"I've seen it. 'Sides, you can smell it over half the county when the mash gets to fermentin'. Me and Billy Preston — he's my friend — we just follered our noses one dark night, and sure enough, there it set. It's on Potter's property, of course, so we was trespassin', and we just crept outa there quiet as we come. I told Daddy, and he said yes, he knew, on account of old man Potter'd tried to get him to sell the stuff in our store — just private, under the counter you might say — but Daddy told him no thanks."

"Isn't there a law against making whiskey?"

"I hope to shout there is! But Daddy, he just figgers it ain't his business, and he ain't gonna bring the law down on 'em. But he don't buy it, and he don't drink it — and he told me if I ever went near the place again, he'd whale the tar outa me. He would, too. Daddy don't take no nonsense from us kids."

Zack seemed proud of this fact about his daddy, as well as his other qualities. "I mean," he continued, "it makes sense, on account of me and Billy coulda got shot at. And I hear old Potter's brung him in a couple of German police dogs to guard the place now. So take my word — don't never go up there."

I nodded wisely. I might not be afraid of cemeteries — at least in the daytime — but the thought of following that tangled track in the dead of night to spy on an illicit business complete with guns and watchdogs gave me the shivers. However, I did admit that being just a little bit scared might be delicious fun if you had Zack Bramley along for company, and I envied the unknown Billy Preston.

Vesta was shelling butter beans into a dishpan on her lap as we approached the porch. She held one long finger against her lips. "Your grandmama done had a little spell with her heart," she told me, reaching out to touch my arm. "Let's us be real quiet. I reckon that old storm shook her up a little. She be all right, honey babe, if we just let her rest."

"You want me to fetch Doc Cordner, Miz Lincoln?" Zack asked softly. "The phone's workin' again."

"No, honey—she say not. He jus' humms and frowns and worries at her—cain't do nothin'. She jus' an old lady, is all."

"Reckon I'd best go," Zack whispered, and our eyes caught and held for a moment.

"Just a minute," I told him and got my letter to Star for him to mail at the store.

"See you tomorrow, most likely," he said, and I nodded.

. . . . 21 . . . .

The next day, Grandmother Knowles seemed much improved, though she ate less than ever, and her soft, wrinkle-crossed skin seemed more tightly stretched across the bridge of her nose and her cheekbones. She insisted on seeing me, and I sat by her bed and held her hand while I told her all about Granna, Uncle Bob, Star, Miss Mary Afton, school, and other things. She never seemed to tire of hearing the details of my life, and if I ever flagged, she'd rouse herself to ask a question that would lead me on in another direction. I tried my best to tell my story as clearly and interestingly as she had told hers, and I was too naïve to wonder how a person of her age and experience could sustain such interest in my ordinary and predictable girlhood happenings. Much later, I realized that love was the force that generated her interest — a love long thwarted and denied expression.

This became the pattern of my days for the remainder of my visit — taking meals with Vesta or my grandmother, talking with each of them about my family and a whole lot of other things, helping Vesta in the garden or kitchen, reading my father's books, and going for rambling walks with Hunger — and most often with Zack Bramley. We visited my father's grave, then followed the right fork of the path in the piney woods to see Vesta's grandchildren playing on a huge water oak by her ancient but well-kept little house — decorated, as I might have guessed, with myriads of flowers and potted plants. They were on the porch and in the windows, hanging from low tree branches and even from the clothesline.

I spent a lazy afternoon playing Monopoly with Zack in his daddy's store, listening to the radio about the continuing estimates of hurricane damage. The final figure was in the millions, and the death toll had risen to thirty-four, partly because of a ramshackle old hotel that had collapsed and killed the nineteen people trying to ride out the storm there.

Zack showed me his favorite fishing place, and I kept looking up at the heavy limbs above us to be sure they *were* limbs and not thick-bodied brown water moccasins. But the only reptiles we saw were a pair of turtles who slid off their log into the amber water with twin plops.

Finally admitting to myself that I would be returning to Tatum soon, I began a frantic round of picture-taking with Star's Brownie, recording as best I could the flavor of these days. I snapped the house from all sides, Vesta and Hunger in the yard, the path in the woods, my father's grave, Bramley's store with Zack squinting in the sunlight and holding my favorite kitten.

Not until Uncle Bob arrived on Friday afternoon was I able to photograph Grandmother Knowles. It was his idea for the three of us to lift her in her rocking chair to a spot beside the window where the brilliant afternoon sun spilled in unshaded. He took two pictures—one of her by herself, smiling gently, the other with me kneeling beside her chair. I felt her hand, light and tremulous as a bird, resting on my hair, and I heard her whisper, "My cup is full."

We brought her back into the shade, and Uncle Bob said, "Well, E. J., I'll take your things out while you say good-bye."

"I'll jus' hep you there," Vesta offered, and my grandmother and I were left facing each other. We were no longer strangers, separate and unknown to each other; but somehow we were more than grandmother and granddaughter—equals and, in some ways, sisters. I looked for words to try to say so, but as usual, they didn't come out as I wanted. "This has really been a good time for me," I began and cleared my throat. "I mean, it's been more than fun. I'm real glad I could come."

She reached for my hand and slowly nodded her head. "I know, my lovie. And once again, there are no words for times like these. But I'm just real glad you could come too. Will you thank Mrs. Markham for me?"

"Yes'm, I will. And I'd like to come back real often — whenever I can."

"I'm so glad. And I hope I'll always be here for you."

"Oh, you *will*," I said quickly, willing it to be so.

"And now that you've been here, you'll always be here for me. And for Vesta too."

I realized that she was talking about more than physical presence. She was talking about memories, but I wasn't ready to dwell in the realm of memory. "Oh, I'll be back — maybe later this summer, if I can. Really and truly, I want to!"

"I do hope so, my lovie. Run now, before I begin to think I can't let you go. God bless."

I hugged her as tightly as I dared, feeling her fragility within my arms and wanting somehow to shelter and strengthen her, but I could not. "Bye, Grandmother," I whispered, swallowing the lump in my throat and hurrying from the room.

Through blurry eyes, I checked my father's room for anything I might have left, but there was nothing. All my belongings, plus a few books and the framed photograph of my parents that Grandmother had given me, were already safely in my suitcase. The shabby little room seemed dear to me, and I even gave a farewell pat to the picture of the howling sheepdog as I left.

Vesta waited on the porch, her head tilted slightly back, tears running unheeded from half-closed eyes.

"Oh, baby," she said, taking me in her arms. "You done brought us such sunshine — it be hard to let you go."

"I'll be back," I promised again. "And thanks for all the good meals, and for talking to me and everything."

She nodded, her lips trying a tight little smile. Uncle Bob came and put one hand on my shoulder and extended the other to Vesta. She touched his fingers politely and gave a stiff little movement that was almost a bow.

"It been a pleasure havin' the grandbaby here," she said. "Jus' anytime she be allowed back, she find a welcome here."

"I'm sure of that," Uncle Bob said. "That's plain to see — and we thank you for making it possible. You have our address and phone number?"

"Yes, sir, we do. And iffen there be a need, I'll be in touch."

"That's good. Well, E. J., if we're going to get any supper tonight, we'd better skedaddle."

"I reckon." I hugged Hunger, and then let Uncle Bob hand me into the front seat of the car and close my door as if I were a grown-up lady. I sat quite still while he walked around and got in. Then, impelled by the realization that my visit truly was over, I thrust my head and shoulders out the window, waving and calling, "Good-bye! I'll be back — good-bye!"

Then the little house with its lacy latticework was gone from sight, and soon the banks of honeysuckle and Bramley's store were, too. I waved at Mr. Hank and his crony on their bench. Mr. Hank raised a shaky hand in reply, though I could tell he wasn't certain who we were. A slim, shadowy form appeared behind the screen door. Was it Zack? I couldn't tell.

There were fallen trees all along the roadside, evidence of Annie's stormy passage. They looked as if a giant had played at pick-up-sticks and left his toys where they had fallen.

"So how was your visit, E. J.?" Uncle Bob finally asked, when we had traveled a quiet three or four miles.

"It was super," I told him. "I didn't want to leave."

"You don't want to go home?"

How could I explain that I'd been at home? "Ye-es, I do, but — I just don't want to have to leave here to do it. They were so good to me, and I learned so much! I just feel like there's so much more to me now."

"More to you?" He gave me a sideways look. "Must've been Mrs. Lincoln's good country cooking. No, seriously, kiddo, tell me about it."

"Well, I found out so much about my daddy and his people, and about Mama too."

"Want to tell me any of it?"

I began to tell him, hesitantly at first, the stories that were still fresh and real in my mind. I told them in my own words, of course, but I tried to give them a taste of the rich flavor my grandmother had imparted in her telling. Uncle Bob rarely took his eyes from the road, but I knew I had his complete attention. The ride home went very quickly.

"You know, E. J.," he said as we approached the outskirts of Tatum, "you should write all that down."

"I already did. Miss Mary Afton told me before I went that I ought to take a notebook along to write down things I wanted to remember about my family."

"She said that, did she? Well, I think you've created a treasure for yourself. It'll mean a lot to you in times to come."

"I brought back a picture of my mama and daddy too—the day they got married."

"Is that right? I'd like a look at that, myself. But you'd better not show it to your Granna for a while."

"Reckon not. I know she didn't like my daddy much, but I think she just didn't know him enough."

"That could be. Your Granna has been—well, a little worried is the best way to put it, I guess. I think she's afraid you'll come back changed somehow."

"Oh." I considered this. Yes, I had changed, but I didn't think I had changed in any way that ought to worry Granna. "Maybe . . . maybe I grew up a little, is all—like I told you. Like there's more to me now. But if I changed at all, I reckon it was for the better."

"How's that?"

"For one thing, I don't think I told one whopper the whole time."

Uncle Bob cleared his throat. "I see. Do you usually tell lots of those? I'd have said you were a 'specially honest person, myself."

"I do try to be, but it seems like sometimes I just can't bring myself to tell Granna the whole truth of things. It's like — almost like the truth just isn't good enough — like she expects more of me."

"M-mm. But the truth was good enough over at Turley?"

I nodded. "Reckon that was it. And I feel pretty sure that they told me the truth too — Grandmother and Vesta both."

"I'll bet that made you feel good. Sort of like they were trusting you with their truth, so you could tell them yours?"

"Yes, sir, reckon that's pretty much how I felt, though I didn't exactly think about it at the time. But how come it's not like that with Granna?"

"Well, it could have to do with a lot of things, E. J. For one, your Granna's raised you from a baby, and folks get used to not telling little children the whole truth of everything, only the parts they feel the children can grasp at the time."

"Oh, you mean like Santa Claus and where babies come from?"

"Mm-hmm, and other things. And sometimes, I s'pose, the grown-ups get kind of behind in realizing that as young'uns get older, they begin to know when things are being kept from them."

"I just wish Granna would see that I'm not a baby anymore, and that I can understand a lot of stuff."

"So you can. What do you suppose we can do to help your Granna confide in you more?"

Watching the farmhouses turn to bungalows as we approached Tatum, I considered the question. "Reckon I could hold back on the whoppers and tell the whole truth more."

"Might help," he agreed. "Give it a try, and maybe I'll put in a word too."

"Okay," I promised.

In just a bit, we passed Arnelle Chapman's, and I peered down the long drive to the little cabin in the back. There was no sign of Miss Mary Afton.

"She's busy caring for her mother, who hasn't been doing at all well lately," Uncle Bob commented, as if he'd read my thoughts. "Can't get out much at all."

I stared at him in surprise. "How do you know?"

"Oh, I've talked with her a time or two. She's a fine young lady, your Miss Mary Afton."

"I know she is," I agreed, but an unsettled feeling came over me. While I was gone, had other things—other people—changed, just as I had? Star and Granna—were they the same? Shivering, I recalled again Star's feeling that nothing would ever be the same anymore. What if she was right?

. . . . 22 . . . .

A deep-golden evening light picked out the details of Granna's house, which looked almost the same except for the chinaberry tree by the south corner. My old friend, whose branches had supported my first childhood climbing efforts and whose leaves had often afforded me a bit of precious privacy, had been cut down to a stump with two upraised branches like chopped-off arms. The stump leaned slightly to one side, as though it had nearly been torn from the earth, and the missing limbs were piled in the side yard, waiting removal.

"I meant to ask you about the hurricane first thing," I said to Uncle Bob.

He lifted my suitcase out of the trunk. "It was quite a blow, all right, and you know how your Granna is about storms. We were up all night. We think the tip of a little twister caught the chinaberry tree. Ripped off a good many shingles above it too, but they've been replaced."

"Mr. Bramley told me the tree broke a window."

"Yep. That's all fixed now too. There wasn't too much major damage around town — mostly trees down — but the big striped awning was ripped off the Rexall, and the five-and-dime had a window broken. On the whole, we were pretty fortunate. Hello, Mom — here's your little chickadee, safe and sound."

Granna had come onto the porch, frowning against the setting sun that reflected in her glasses as she dried her hands on her apron. "Well, it's time you were here. I was starting to worry. Come on in, Emily Jean. I've kept your supper warming about as long as it can stand." She gave me a quick, fierce hug and a kiss on the cheek, and, to my amazement, I realized that Granna was trembling. She reached to kiss Uncle Bob, and then shooed us into the kitchen where she fussed about, talking about inconsequential things as she set supper before us — a meal that would have done justice to Sunday dinner with Pastor Welch. Uncle Bob caught my eye and gave me a slow wink, which I took to mean that all was well and this was just Granna's way.

"I don't s'pose this'll taste like much, after the good country cooking you'll have had up at Turley," she said, placing platters of chicken-fried steak and cobs of corn on the table. A three-layer coconut cake stood off to one side. "You know I'm not a fancy cook. I just like to get hot, nourishing food on the table."

"Mmm, this looks good, Granna. Nobody can do chicken-fried steak like you."

"It's nothing special. You know how I do it — just dip it in beaten egg and then in seasoned cracker crumbs, and make sure your fat is hot but not smoking when you put it in. Now, how was Mrs. Knowles when you left her?"

Granna perched on the edge of her chair with a cup of coffee before her and looked searchingly at me through the bottom of her bifocals.

"She stays in bed almost all the time. I think she has a real bad heart. She said to thank you for letting me go see her."

"Well, yes, naturally. But I wonder what in the world you found to occupy your time all day? You must have been lonesome and bored."

"Oh, no, ma'am. It was wonderful, and I want to go back whenever I can."

"Go *back?* Whatever for — what did you do?"

"Well, I spent a lot of time talking to my grandmother and to Vesta, and I — "

"Vesta?"

"Yes, ma'am. She takes care of — of my grandmother."

"Oh, yes, the colored woman. You spent a lot of time talking to *her?*"

" 'S'ma'am. It was real interesting. She told me a lot of things I never knew before." I saw Granna's eyes get rounder behind her glasses. "I mean, she remembered my daddy from when he was just a little boy, and she told me about him. And my grandmother told me all about her life and her family when she was growing up in Boston. I wrote it all down the best I could."

"Wrote it down! What for, Emily Jean?"

It hadn't occurred to me that Granna might not understand or approve. "Um—well—just so I won't forget it all, and so I'll be able to tell my kids—I mean, my children—someday. That is, if I ever get married and have any. But Granna," I added hastily, "what I'd like to do is get another notebook and write things in it about your family."

Granna was clearly taken aback. "Well, I—well, certainly there are things in our family history that shouldn't be lost. But—my mercy, Emily Jean, I had no idea you cared for such things!"

"I really do, but I only found it out myself when Grandmother Knowles started telling me stories and showing me her picture albums. Do you have lots of old pictures too, Granna?"

"Land, yes—I have a passel of them in that blanket box on my closet shelf. I've just never found the time to put them into albums."

"Could I help?"

"Well, I suppose you might. But you'd best eat now and not talk so much." She went on to talk to Uncle Bob about the text for his next sermon, and I dutifully concentrated on my supper, pondering the peculiar experience of coming home again after having been so totally immersed in another environment. Things looked vaguely different, as if there had been subtle changes in size and proportion in my absence. The ceilings seemed higher—was it because I had grown accustomed to the lower ceilings in Grandmother Knowles's little house—and everything stood out in special clarity. Objects I ordinarily didn't even notice, I now saw in detail, as a stranger might.

The feeling persisted after supper when I climbed the stairs to my room. The sun was down by then, and I felt for the cord to the overhead light. Granna had picked up my socks and nightgown after all, so the room looked unnaturally neat. I heaved my suitcase onto the bed, reflecting happily that it was somewhat heavier now, due to the addition of a certain framed picture and a number of old books.

As I released the catches on the case, I stopped to stare in surprise at the maple headboard of my bed. "*That* didn't used to be there," I said softly, tracing a deep, long gouge in the wood with my finger. "What in the world . . . " Then I saw that my old paper lampshade had been replaced with a frilly white eyelet shade to match new eyelet curtains at the window. I looked closely. There were other tiny scratches on the bedposts, and patches of the rosebud wallpaper behind them looked as though a very big cat had sharpened its claws there.

"Granna?" I called, leaping down the stairs two at a time. "Granna, Uncle Bob—what happened in my room?"

Granna threw a quick look at Uncle Bob. "Oh, I had a little accident, is all, while I was trying to reach the cobwebs with a broom—"

Uncle Bob stopped her. "I think she's old enough to know the truth, Mom," he said quietly. "E. J., that was where the chinaberry limb came in—at your window. The force of it carried the branch clear over to your bed. When we saw that, we were both mighty thankful to know that you were visiting Grandmother Knowles." He put his arm around Granna's shoulders and gave her a hug. "Mom was afraid you'd be frightened to know about it."

"I—I reckon I am, just a little. But I'd rather know the truth. Besides," and I grinned, "you'd really have to have a doozy of an accident to do all that damage with a broom!"

"Now, don't make light of it, Emily Jean! I was purely petrified—and then it came to me how the good Lord had blessed me for doing my Christian duty in letting Mrs. Knowles have you for a visit. If I'd've kept you here at home as I wanted to do, you might well have been lying injured or even killed in that very bed. It was a big, stout branch that came flying in, and there was glass everywhere—and dear goodness, what a racket and commotion! I thought the roof had gone for sure."

I swallowed. "I knew a limb broke a window, but somehow I thought it was most likely in the living room. It got awful scary where we were too, but none of us got hurt."

"Thank the dear Lord," murmured Granna. "We'll have to see about some maple stain to help cover that scratch."

"Thank you for the new curtains and lampshade. They're real pretty. Well, reckon I'll go finish unpacking."

It felt good to be back in my own room, I admitted to myself, and the fact that the room had changed somewhat seemed appropriate, since I had changed a bit too. Carefully I lifted the framed picture of my parents from my suitcase and set it on my dresser. I put away the speckled notebook that held my treasured kin—or, at least, my best efforts to capture my Grandmother's memories of them. I made room for my father's books on the closet shelf, and I replaced my little white Bible on the bedside table, on top of Star's Nancy Drew. Granna had taught me that no other book should ever be placed on top of a Bible.

I slipped into a cool gown and turned back my sheet. It was late, and I thought of telephoning Star, but part of me didn't want to yet.

"She's my best friend," I said aloud, as if to convince that reluctant part—but I still felt I needed a little more time to myself, to get back to being the Emily Jean Knowles who slept in this room, whose best friend was Starlett Hargrave, and whose world was in Tatum, Georgia, not too far from Savannah.

When I heard Granna's step on the stairs, I hastily scooped up the photograph of my parents and slipped it into my underwear drawer. "Sorry," I whispered to them as I smoothed my winter undershirts over the frame.

"If you're through with that suitcase, Emily Jean, I'll just store it in the stairs cupboard again. All settled in, are you?"

She glanced quickly around the room and seemed relieved that no obvious souvenirs were in sight. What would she have said, I wondered, if I had brought back the carved wooden crucifix that hung over Grandmother Knowles's bed, or the old sheepdog and lamb picture from my father's room. Or even if she saw what lay under my winter "vests," as she called them. I didn't want to hide my precious picture; I wanted to show the world that I had not been born an orphan of unknown parentage, that I too had a mother and father who gave me life and would have given me love. And yet again, I was content to hug the picture to myself for a while longer. Basically, I was feeling mellow toward Granna, and I wished I could find an acceptable way to show my affection.

"Now, child, I don't want you to feel afraid in here," she was saying. "The storm is over and gone, and such a thing is not likely ever to happen again, so you can lie down and sleep in peace."

"I know. I'm not afraid, Granna. Truly."

"Well, but you cannot imagine what a terrifying time that was, with the power off and the wind roaring and the lightning flashing blue and so sharp and near—I just knew we were done for. And then that terrible noise, like a freight train coming through the house, and we rushed up here with the oil lamps to see that great limb right in this room, the window shattered and the rain pouring in, and that awful gash in your headboard. Well, I surely thought I would faint dead away. I don't know how my poor heart stood the shock. But, thank the dear Lord, you weren't in that bed, and all's well. But don't you be afraid, now, because it won't happen again."

"All right," I said faintly and resisted describing our hurricane experience to Granna. I knew that in her mind nothing could compare with what she had come through—which was considerable, I admitted. "Maybe I'll just read a little and then try to go to sleep."

"Yes, that might help you relax. Now, I want you up and at the piano first thing in the morning, you hear? You've got quite a lot of catching up to do, and I don't doubt you've gotten all rusty, being away from your music for two whole weeks."

"Yes'm, reckon I prob'ly have," I agreed happily. Maybe things hadn't changed so much after all.

Granna paused at my door, looking uncertain whether to say

anything else. "Did you — um — learn anything much about your father? Did Mrs. Knowles talk much about him?"

"Yes, ma'am, she did, and Vesta did too — about how he grew up there. And did you know his old dog is still alive?"

"My mercy!"

"And she told me lots about Mama too — about how sweet and pretty and nice she was, and . . . ," I paused, gathering my courage, "and about how much she and my daddy loved each other and how happy they were. Grandmother Knowles felt bad too, you know, when Mama and Daddy ran off and got married. Not because she didn't like Mama — she loved her a lot. She was just disappointed they didn't have a proper wedding with everybody there and all."

"You mean she wasn't with them for the ceremony?"

"Oh, no, ma'am. She didn't know anything about it till after, just like you. Except they went there after the wedding instead of leaving a note."

Granna stared at me. "I never knew that. I thought Mrs. Knowles was in on the plan all the time," she said slowly, easing into my rocking chair.

I grew bolder, feeling important at having information to impart. "No'm, they didn't tell anybody ahead of time. They just slipped off to a justice of the peace on account of they didn't want you to think Ellie had gone over to the Catholic church 'cause she knew that would upset you. And they didn't tell Grandmother Knowles 'cause they knew she'd insist on them telling you."

"She said *that?*"

" 'S'ma'am. And she said Ellie — my mama — cried because she felt so bad about leaving you with just a note like she did, and she was half happy and half sad on her wedding day because of it. But she was still glad to be married to Frank — I mean, my daddy."

Granna's eyes glistened with tears. "Ellie — cried?"

I nodded. "Didn't she ever tell you about all that when she came home to — to have us?"

Granna's chin quivered. "Well, I s'pose I didn't give her much encouragement to speak of those things. I was not favorably disposed toward the marriage, as you must know, and I was hurt by the way she flat-out ignored my wishes and advice."

I understood my mama's silence. I knew very well how stubborn and unyielding Granna could be when she didn't want to discuss something. "I know," I said. "You were hoping she'd marry somebody like a doctor or a minister — like Herbert Maxwell."

"You know about Herbert Maxwell? He was a fine, upstanding young man!"

" 'S'ma'am, but he was so serious, and he and Mama didn't have anything to talk about, and she'd just sit and fidget when he came to see her. It wasn't any fun with him like it was with my daddy. They could talk about anything."

"Fun! Is that what life's about? No disrespect to the dead, Emily Jean, but Frank Knowles was a nothing — a ne'er-do-well who stole Ellie away from the life she should have had and then abandoned her in the end! Didn't even have the decency to come and bury her when she died from giving birth to his children!"

"He knew you felt that way about him, and he was determined to make something of himself and prove to you he was worthy of Mama. Grandmother Knowles said that Daddy was s'posed to meet her at the funeral, but he couldn't come, on account of — "

"Oh, yes, I know. The story was that he was ill with pneumonia or something, but I've always suspected he was dead drunk trying to escape his guilt — if he had the grace to feel any guilt!"

"But, Granna, how come you think he was drunk? I haven't heard anything about him drinking."

"All the Irish are terrible for whiskey; it's a well-known fact. Not that his mother would admit such a thing."

"Well, I don't know anything about that. Did Mama say he drank?"

"Certainly not! She knew how I felt on the subject. But he had such a hold on her, she'd have defended him to the death — and did." Granna drew a ragged breath, remembering.

I was silent for a moment, trying to gather my courage to say what I wanted to say. At the same time I tried to find a way to say it that wouldn't anger or hurt Granna. Finally I just plunged ahead.

"Maybe—maybe she defended him because it was just the truth. Grandmother Knowles said he was delirious when they got there, and thought Ellie—Mama, I mean—was out shopping. When they got his fever down a little, he remembered she had died, and he talked about hurrying so he wouldn't miss the bus to come to the funeral. Then he got worse again and died that night. I think—I think she told me the truth, Granna. I think that's how it really happened."

Granna shook her head and gave a soft little "hmph" sound, but she had lowered her eyes and was gazing at her hands, folded tightly in her lap. "I s'pose we'll never know the whole truth of it till Judgment Day. And if I've judged wrongly all these years, I pray I'll be forgiven. But I just know how it's looked to me, and what pain I've suffered . . . "

"I know, Granna. And it was awful hard on Grandmother Knowles too. She loved my daddy. He couldn't have been *all* bad."

"I know it was hard for her, of course—I never said otherwise. And I suppose even Frank Knowles had some good points."

Coming from Granna, this amounted to praise, and I drew courage from it.

"And he said he was going to come a little later—um—to get me. He—he wanted to raise me himself."

"Oh, a fine thing that would have been!" Granna stood up.

I smiled a little. "Grandmother Knowles said there'd have been a battle over it."

"Indeed there would. Imagine him caring for a young baby . . . "

"But he could have been part of my life," I said. "He could have come to visit me so's I'd know him. But it doesn't matter anyway, since he died. Granna, how come he's not buried here next to Mama and Ellen Jane?"

Granna's eyes faltered. "Well, I didn't feel—I thought he didn't deserve a place here. I just—Emily Jean, you're far too young to understand all this."

"I don't think so, Granna," I said quietly, and she looked at me in astonishment. "Anyway, I reckon it's better he's buried up in Turley where Grandmother Knowles and Vesta can visit his grave, 'cause they truly loved him. Even his old dog knows the way to his grave."

She gazed at me for a long moment. "My mercy," she said again, softly, and turned and made her way down the stairs.

I heard her say to Uncle Bob, "Only time will tell the full effects of this."

"She'll be fine," Uncle Bob said. "She's made of good stuff."

As I finished my prayers and climbed into bed, I heard Uncle Bob slam the front door and start up his old Nash. He was whistling, "I'm looking over a four-leaf clover that I've overlooked before," and I wondered if he might be going to see Pat and maybe take her for a drive. I'd ask Star tomorrow.

· · · · 23 · · · ·

As soon as Granna allowed me to leave the piano bench the next morning, I was on the phone to Star, who was so excited that her voice squeaked, and whose delight erased the last of my peculiar shyness. I raced through the sunny morning to meet her halfway, and we hugged happily.

"Oh, Emily Jean, I can't believe you're back! I got your letter, and I couldn't believe you wrote to me in the middle of that terrible storm! I want to know *everything,* right now."

"Wait'll you see what that storm did to my bedroom," I said.

She laid one hand on my arm. "Emily Jean, I *know,*" she said in a hushed tone. "Everybody knows. They were talking about it at church."

Granna told everybody?

"Well, I know she told Mama and Mrs. Baxter and Mrs. Chapman."

"She told everybody," I agreed. "Come on, I'll show you."

She was properly impressed with the scar on the headboard and with the new decor. "I do like it so much better," she declared. "The curtains really dress up your room, just like a movie star's bow-door."

"And look, Star, here's my mama and daddy," I said proudly, handing her the framed picture. She sat on the edge of my bed and held it reverently in both hands.

"Oh, aren't they young!"

"They were awful young when they died," I reminded her. "This was taken the day they got married."

"They're a handsome couple, don't you think? Aren't you proud of them? But it just plain breaks my heart to see them looking so happy and to know what happened to them later."

"I know. I like to think they're together now, though, and happy."

"Do you really think so?" she asked, handing the picture back to me. "I mean, your Granna hasn't acted like she thought your daddy would . . . " Star paused, her face flushed in confusion.

"Go to heaven?" I completed. "I know, but I've found out a lot about him, and I think Granna just didn't know him very well. So I think they are together."

"What'd you find out?"

I curled up on one end of my bed and told her the story of my parents' courtship. She hung on every word, frowning or giggling or looking amazed, and I found it very gratifying. "And there's lots more," I ended with a sigh, flopping back against my pillow. "I've hardly got started telling you everything."

"Oh, I can't wait! It's as good as a movie."

We took the exposed film out of Star's camera and sauntered lazily toward town, telling each other about the storm and the events of the days that had separated us. I wondered why I had ever felt shy about seeing Star again. She was soft-cotton comfortable to be with.

"Star," I said suddenly, "I meant to ask you — did Uncle Bob take Pat out last night?"

"No — why?"

"I just wondered. I heard him go out somewhere."

"No, Pat stayed home and sewed on another new dress for tomorrow. Here's Lana's — let's go see Miss Mary Afton."

The small, stuffy shop was crammed full of new clothes and smelled of sizing and dyes that made my nose prickle and my eyes water.

"Hello, girls. What can I do for you today?" asked Mrs. Buzbee, using considerable muscle to shove aside some dresses on a rack and to force others into the resulting space.

"We just wanted to speak to Miss Mary Afton," I said. "Has she gone to lunch?"

"She had to leave me, dear. Her mother was took real bad, and she has to look after her. Lord only knows what they're living on — I hope there's some income from somewhere. I keep meaning to get over and see her, but I've been so busy I haven't done it yet. I've just got my back-to-school inventory in. Got some real sweet matching sweater sets, girls."

Lana's wasn't air-conditioned, and the thought of sweater sets in the heat of summer nearly stifled me.

"Okay. Thanks, Mrs. Buzbee," I managed and dragged Star out by her elbow. The heat outside was at least fresh and free of the overpowering smell of new clothes.

"Miss Mary Afton's mother is sick," Star said. "Reckon we can do anything to help?"

"Likely something. The thing is, I *knew* about her mother, but I didn't think she'd had to quit her job. Uncle Bob told me yesterday when he brought me home."

"He did? How'd he know?"

I shrugged. "Things get around. Maybe Mrs. Buzbee or Mrs. Chapman told Granna."

"Let's go ask your Granna what we could do. Maybe run errands or take some flowers?"

"Okay," I agreed.

We found Granna in the kitchen, putting away the contents of a sack of groceries. She patted her upper lip delicately with a lace-edged hanky, which she then tucked under her belt.

"I declare, it's all I can do in this weather to tote home a few tidbits of food. Robert offered to take me in the car, and if I'd known how hot it was going to get, I'd have let him. But I knew he needed time to work on his sermon, so I told him no. I see he's taken himself off somewhere, though, so I might as well have had a ride."

"It surely is hot," Star agreed politely, giving me a nudge while Granna's back was turned and handing her a can of milk from the table when she turned back.

"Granna," I began, "did you hear about Miss Mary Afton's mother getting real sick?"

"Yes, I did. A stroke, most likely, Arnelle said. Be a blessing if the woman could go, I suppose. I hear she's been sick for a long time. Nobody knows just what's wrong, but I understand she's not right." Granna tapped her silver curls significantly.

"Well, we thought maybe—that is, Star suggested maybe we ought to take something to them, or help out somehow—Miss Mary Afton being our teacher and all."

"What a thoughtful child you are, Starlett. Emily Jean could do well to take a leaf from your book, I always tell her."

Star stared at her toes and looked uncomfortable. The fact that our friendship survived Granna's approval attested to its strength.

"So what should we do, Granna?"

"Well, food's always welcome. There's little time to shop and cook when you're caring for an invalid. I have a nice little chicken I could roast, and maybe a cool garden salad would go well."

"Mama's making rolls today for Sunday dinner, and maybe she'd let me have some to take."

"That sounds lovely. You bring them over here when they're ready, and we'll pack a hamper for you girls to carry over."

"I'll do that," Star promised. "See you later, Emily Jean."

I watched her hurry as far as the front gate, where she met our postman, Mr. Miller.

"Here's your mail," she called, taking it from him and hurrying back to the kitchen to hand it to me. "Top one's for you," she added curiously. "Who's it from?"

I stared at the round, back-slanted handwriting in bright blue ink. The postmark was Thayne, Wyoming. "Oh," I said offhandedly, and then paused to clear my throat, "it's just from a girl I wrote to who wanted a pen pal. She lives out in the country and gets kind of lonesome in the summer."

I paused, waiting for Granna's question to fall, reminding myself that I had vowed to tell no more whoppers.

"I had a pen pal once—in England," Star said.

"How very improving," Granna said, beaming at Star. "Letter-writing is becoming a lost art."

"It didn't work out too good for me," Star confessed. "I wrote her all about school and Girls' Auxiliary and asked her a lot of questions about England that she never answered. She wrote me a whole bunch of letters, but they were all about field hockey matches and her brother's cricket team, and I didn't even know what she was talking about. I'm not very sporty," she apologized. "You know how I am, Emily Jean. If I ever catch the ball, I forget where I'm supposed to throw it. Anyway, I just couldn't think of anything else to say to her, so I finally quit writing, and she did too. But I still have her letters. It seemed kind of rude to throw them away. Well— bye-bye, Emily Jean. Thanks, Mrs. Markham."

Granna's gaze followed Star affectionately. "Such a dear child. Far too delicate to worry about sports," she murmured. I blessed Star for distracting Granna and slipped the envelope under my shirt. There was a curious object lying on the table, and to change the subject, I picked it up. It was a bolster-shaped cello bag filled with a substance that looked a little like lard. There was an orange-colored capsule in the middle of one side.

"What's this stuff, Granna?" I asked, turning it over.

"It's called oleomargarine," Granna said. "It's a butter substitute. Years ago, we used to get yellow oleo in the stores, but the dairy people objected, and it disappeared. Now they get around that by putting that little bead of food coloring in, and folks can color it yellow themselves if they want. Butter's getting so dear, I thought we'd try it."

I wrinkled my nose. "What does it taste like?"

"Oh, it's a bit like butter, though it's made from vegetable oil. You go ahead and mix the color in—that can be your job."

Shortening was made from vegetable oil too, and the thought of spreading shortening on my toast or melting a puddle of it on my grits turned my stomach, but it was fun to pop the little capsule and then work the plastic pillow with my fingers to mix in the color.

"When you're through with that, I want you to bring Robert's three shirts in from the line and dampen them. I'll want to iron them later so they'll be perfectly fresh for tomorrow."

"Golly," I said, "does he use three white shirts on one Sunday?"

"I don't like slang in the mouths of young ladies, Emily Jean. Of course he doesn't, but it never hurts to have an extra. What if he should spill cherry pie on one—there'd only be the one left, if you see what I mean."

"Are we having cherry pie tomorrow?"

"Land, no, we're having pineapple tapioca! That was just an example. I don't know, though, how he managed to use all three white shirts during the week. I know there was a clean one still hanging in his closet just last Monday evening. But, today, all three were in the hamper—and him doing construction work all week! I can't imagine."

"Why don't you ask him?"

"Well, he's a grown man, and I don't want to pry into his business or make it sound like a burden to do his shirts. Heaven knows I'm glad enough to do them! But it does make a body wonder—you don't suppose he's taking Pat out? Has Starlett said . . . ?"

"He didn't last night," I stated, and Granna looked at me with interest.

"He didn't? Then where did he go? He was out rather late."

I shrugged and thought about it. "Maybe, since he's been training to be a preacher, he's been making visitation rounds with Pastor Welch. That would need a white shirt, wouldn't it?"

"Why, Emily Jean, I do believe you've hit on the answer! Though why he wouldn't mention that to me, I don't know." She smiled to herself. "And here I've been thinking he might be out courting a girl. Of course he won't want to do that till he's ordained and established. He's not foolish and romantic like some."

I collected the shirts from the clothesline, first making sure that my letter from LaRae was secured inside the waistband of my shorts. I didn't want Granna to be reminded of that and wonder where I had obtained my pen pal's name and address. I filled a tall Pepsi bottle with water and plugged the little sprinkler cap in the top.

Carefully I sprinkled the dazzlingly clean white shirts and rolled each into a damp little bundle in the laundry basket. Then for good measure, I set up Granna's ironing board and took her electric iron from the cupboard before escaping upstairs to the bathroom and shutting the door.

Granna's blue-tiled bathroom was her pride and joy, and it was the one spot I most appreciated after my experience with chamber pots and outhouses. In addition, it was the one place in the house where I could count on a few minutes of relative freedom and privacy. I sat on the chenille-covered toilet seat and pulled out my letter. It was a nice fat one with several pages.

Dear Emily,

I was so glad to get your letter, because I wanted to write to somebody my age down south there where my brother Doug is on his mission. I really miss him alot. But I am glad he is serving the Lord and teaching people about Jesus and the True Church. He said you gave him some cold lemonade on a hot day and I am glad. I hope everybody is nice to him, because he is a good person and a good brother.

Maybe you'd like to hear about what I do. I live on a ranch not far from Thayne, Wyoming. My dad and my Uncle Brad have got about 1,280 acres. Dad raises beef cattle and Uncle Brad has a dairy herd. This part of Wyoming is famous for cheese, kind of like Switzerland, and we have mountains too, like the Alps. Do you ever get any Wyoming cheese down there? It's real good. I like it melted on the bread my mom bakes.

Well, anyway. I have two little brothers. Jimmy is eight and just got baptized and Bradley is six. He will start school this year and is real excited. Then I have a little sister named Eva Carol because she was born on Christmas eve. She's three.

I like to go to school, do you? Mama drives us in the

pickup to the highway, and the school bus comes there. I will be in the sixth grade this year. Sometimes in winter the snow is so deep the bus can't come, and we get to stay home. I like to read or play paper dolls in front of the fireplace. I make paper dolls from the Sears and Roebuck catalog. But my favorite thing to do in good weather is to ride my horse, Stormy. She is an Appaloosa that has been mine from the time she was born, but Daddy wouldn't let me ride her until this year. But she knows she's my horse, and we have alot of fun. She's my best friend, next to Patty Brimhall, and I only get to see Patty at church on Sundays and Wednesday afternoon at Primary. My mom is the Primary president. Next week, Patty is coming home with me to sleep over till Sunday! I can't wait!! Well, I better go. Write me again real soon, and say hi to Doug.

Love from LaRae Jensen

I started right in and read the letter again straight through. I thought it was very satisfying. I could tell I would like LaRae, and I could imagine us snowed in, playing with Sears paper dolls in front of a fire , and eating melted cheese on homemade bread. I'd hardly ever seen snow, and I'd never seen a real fireplace fire. But I had made paper dolls from the Sears catalog, though I hadn't played with them for a long time. It might be fun, I thought, to pick out one or two and send them to LaRae in my next letter. I couldn't wait to write; I had a lot to tell her.

. . . . 24 . . . .

By the time I had finished my reply to LaRae's letter and selected a pair of paper dolls and their wardrobe to send her, there was a savory smell of roasting chicken drifting up the stairs. I reread my letter quickly to see if I had included everything I meant to say. I had told her a little about my visit to Turley and about the hurricane, as I didn't think it likely she'd ever been through one. Then, remembering my good intentions, I had written,

> I've heard your church has temples. What are they for?
> We don't have temples in our church — just church
> buildings and hospitals and missions and things. What is
> Primary?
>
> It sounds like fun to ride Stormy. What color is she? I
> haven't ever had a chance to ride a horse, but I sure
> would like to. I take piano lessons and I have to practice
> every morning, but I'm not very good. My friend Starlett
> is a lot better. I like to read too. I just finished *Freckles* by
> Gene Stratton Porter. (She's a lady.) What do you like to
> read? Hope you like the paper dolls. I made them a
> couple of years ago.
>
>   love,
>   Emily J. Knowles
> P.S. I haven't seen your brother Doug for a while.
> Write soon.
>
>   EJK

When Star came, we helped Granna pack a basket with the chicken, salad, warm rolls, and several pieces of lemon sponge cake that Mrs. Hargrave had included. Then we started walking to Miss Mary Afton's house.

"Bet if Uncle Bob was home, he'd drive us over," I said as we trudged along.

"Where do you think he is?" Star wondered.

I shrugged. "Been gone all day," I said. "We thought maybe he was out doing visitation again with Pastor Welch."

"Mmm. Could be."

"Wait a second." We paused while I extracted my letter to LaRae and poked it into a green corner mailbox. "Letter to my pen pal," I explained.

"You sure answered back fast," she said admiringly. "Did you get a good letter from her?"

"Yep." I appraised Star speculatively. "Star—can you keep a secret?"

"I always do, Emily Jean," she said, switching hands on the hamper.

"Well, this isn't just any old pen pal I'm writing to. I mean, I'm writing to her for a special reason."

Star frowned as we came out into the sun from under a protective canopy of magnolia trees. "What special reason?"

"She's not a Christian," I said triumphantly. "Anyway, she's a Mormon, and I think that means she isn't a Christian. So I'm trying to help her."

"Oh, Emily Jean—that's—that's just plain noble!" Star said, stopping stock-still in the middle of the street. "I can't believe how brave you are!"

"Not really," I disclaimed, tugging at the hamper to get us out of harm's way. I wasn't *that* brave! "You see, it's just that they seem so nice, LaRae and her brother, that I thought they deserved to know the truth about Jesus and all."

"How'd you get her name anyway?"

"Have you seen the two Mormon missionaries walking around town?"

"In the dark suits and straw hats? They always look so hot. I don't know why they stay around here. Nobody ever talks to them, that I can see."

"Well—I talked to them."

"You did! Emily Jean Knowles, what would your Granna say?"

"She was mad when she found out," I admitted. "But I didn't know who they were."

"What'd they *say?*"

"They were real nice, you'd be surprised. But the thing is, one of them is my pen pal's big brother. He asked me to write to her because she wanted a pen pal from around here."

"And your Granna *let* you?"

"Well, see—that's the secret part. Granna doesn't know."

"Oh, but don't you reckon she'd approve if she knew why you were writing and all?"

I shook my head. "I don't think so, and if she didn't, I'd either have to quit writing or sneak around to do it. And if she did approve, she'd want to tell me what to write."

"I see what you mean."

"It's just sort of my own project, but I wanted to tell you."

"Well, I think it's plumb thrilling! Just like the heathens in Africa or China. But I'd be scared to death to talk to a Mormon! You're so brave to witness to them, Emily Jean. Just think—maybe they'll be saved because of it."

"I don't know. You know me, I'm not even sure for positive that I've been saved yet. But I did want to warn them about their church and all. Granna says they do awful things."

"Reckon that's so. Isn't that . . . " Star was squinting at something farther down the street. "Look—isn't that your Uncle Bob's car coming out of Mrs. Chapman's driveway?"

"Looks like it, all right." We watched as the gray Nash sped away from us, out toward the highway. "Reckon he's been to visit Mrs. Chapman or Miss Mary Afton?"

"Likely Mrs. Chapman—she's in our church," said Star.

With the loaded hamper jerking wildly between us, we covered the remaining distance in good time and slowed to a panting walk as we approached the tiny house under the massive oak trees. Miss Mary Afton answered our knock. She looked tired but pretty as ever, and she smiled at us. Her long, syrupy hair was pulled back and tied with a scarf into one long ringlet down her back, and she wore slacks and a print blouse.

"Well, hello, Emmy, Star. How nice to see you!"

"We were awful sorry to hear your Mama's sick," Star said as we offered her the hamper. "My mama and Mrs. Markham fixed some food for you so you won't have to cook."

"That's very, very kind of them, and thoughtful of you girls to bring it. Come on in and have a cool drink—you look warm."

Shyly, we entered and sat side by side on the edge of a worn sofa while Miss Mary Afton poured us glasses of red punch. It was hot inside, but a small table fan was tilted upward toward the ceiling so that the air circulated a bit. In one corner, on the only bed in the little house, lay the ill woman, breathing raspingly and open-mouthed, her only movement the rise and fall of her chest. Her face was flushed, her half-open eyes glazed looking. She wore a pretty flowered gown, and her hair had been smoothed back.

"Will we disturb your mama?" I whispered, as we accepted the drinks.

"Not at all, Emmy. She isn't aware of much that goes on anymore. The doctor isn't sure she can even hear."

"Reckon she's awful sick," Star said, gazing at Miss Mary Afton's mother.

"Yes, she is. She's had a really hard time these past few years. I've tried to make it easier for her, but it's hard to know how a person feels or what she needs when she can't communicate. At least I've been able to have her with me this summer, instead of in a hospital. She's always hated hospitals."

"You must be a good nurse," I said.

"Well, you learn how to do things when you need to. And I

couldn't do enough for her, because I remember what she's really like — how she used to be and what she did for me. She gave me so much love when I was growing up. The only really hard thing is turning her. It helps to have another person on hand for that. Mrs. Chapman helps when she can, and . . . " — her face brightened — "your Uncle Bob stopped by," she said to me. "He just left, in fact. He helped me turn her and change the sheets while he was here. He's a nice person, Emmy."

I nodded happily. "I know." I looked around. "This is just like a cute little doll house," I said.

"I've enjoyed this little house."

"But where do you sleep?" Star asked.

"The sofa does me just fine — it's easy to jump up from when I'm needed. Here, girls, let me just write a couple of thank-you notes for you to take back with you. Everything looks so delicious."

She sat at a small table and penned a note for each of us. Then we rose to go.

"Thanks so much, both of you, and please come again when you can. Emmy, I understand your trip was a great success, and I'd love to hear about it sometime."

"I did what you said," I told her. "I took a notebook and filled it full of things my grandmother told me. I'm real glad you said to do that, 'cause likely I wouldn't have thought of it."

"Well, then — so am I." She hugged each of us, and we went away, smiling to ourselves.

The next day being Sunday, we went again to hear Uncle Bob preach. By now he had the congregation in the palm of his hand, which seemed to be a pretty comfortable spot for them. All the children dragged their grown-ups to the front pews instead of sliding reluctantly into the back ones. There were no spitwads, and during the invitational hymn, two ladies, along with old Paw-Paw Jenkins and his granddaughter Selma, came forward to give their lives to Jesus. Granna leaned over and whispered to me that while I was away, D. W. Jenkins (that was the boy's whole name — D. W. didn't stand for anything) had come forward to be saved. I hoped I'd be forgiven for wondering whether D. W. had really given his heart to Jesus or to Uncle Bob.

On the ride home, Granna insisted on sitting in the back with Star and me, and Pat sat up front with Uncle Bob. We gaily sang all our good old songs — "Kum-ba-yah" and "Jacob's Ladder" and "In the Garden." I kept thinking of Miss Mary Afton and wishing she could be with us instead of cooped up in that hot little house with her sick mother. Uncle Bob may have thought of her too, because he asked Star and me to refresh our memories on the words to "Give, Said the Little Stream," which we did. We sang all three verses through twice, but Pat seemed a little subdued after that.

Granna had made pineapple tapioca, and after we had eaten it, Uncle Bob offered to drive Pat home. Star and I exchanged bright glances, sure that he would spend some time with her. But when we arrived on foot some fifteen minutes later, Pat was idly swinging all alone in their big front porch swing. In answer to my question, she said that Uncle Bob had intended to visit the sick.

Summer began to wear on in the wonderful way it has of making you believe, against all knowledge to the contrary, that it will go on forever. Star and I did what was required of us in the cool of the mornings — practicing, dusting, weeding, and sweeping — and the balance of the hot, lazy days were spent wandering between our houses, desultorily playing jacks or Monopoly or Old Maid, picnicking in the deserted schoolyard, saving our nickels for ice cream, and talking — always talking — defining and redefining our experiences, hopes, and attitudes. Occasionally we went swimming, cooling our sun-soaked bodies in the tepid but clear water of the river-bend swimming hole. And in the evenings, when Star wasn't with me, I'd get in a game of baseball with Junior Bailey and Fred Silver and whoever else was available.

Gradually, my time with Grandmother Knowles receded in my thoughts, becoming more like a dream or a much-loved storybook than the reality it was. The only thing that kept it close to the forefront of my mind was the never-ending variety of material it furnished me for entertaining Star, ever a willing listener.

We spent the Fourth of July as we always did—first attending a flag-raising ceremony by the VFW on the schoolhouse grounds, then rushing home to finish preparing our picnic for the annual church outing. Star and I played childish games with the younger children; crammed ourselves full of fried chicken, deviled eggs, cake, and watermelon; and anticipated the sparklers, snakes, and bottle rockets that we would set off at first dark.

Granna sat on a striped canvas chair and fanned herself with a limp handkerchief. Even for a picnic, she wore a print dress, stockings, and white shoes. Mrs. Chapman sat next to her. Mrs. Hargrave had gone to supervise the sack races for the younger children, and Pat and Uncle Bob sat on a quilt nearby. Star and I, stuffed and tired, sprawled on the grass and watched ants while we half listened to the adults' conversation. Bob was telling Pat some of his Navy experiences, and Granna and Mrs. Chapman spoke of recipes for fig preserves and scuppernong jelly. I chose to tune in to Uncle Bob, but a sudden little movement from Mrs. Chapman caught my attention.

"Ellen, I can't think why I forgot to tell you—we had to take the MacDougal woman to the hospital last night. She'd got to where she couldn't swallow, and she was having trouble breathing. The doctors didn't give much hope that she'd last very long."

"Well—be a blessing if she went."

"It would be, both for her and Mary Afton. That poor child's absolutely worn out from the strain. But I'll tell you what—I'd like to hope my children would be as good to me, under the circumstances. She's been just wonderful."

"Too bad the mother couldn't have known and appreciated all that good care."

I didn't know Uncle Bob was listening until he spoke. "Yes," he said, "but that makes it all the more admirable, doesn't it, that she couldn't know and realize. But Mary's never neglected a detail or complained a word that I know of."

"I've never heard a word of complaint," Mrs. Chapman agreed.

Pat spoke up. "I think it's what any loving daughter would do. I know I'd do the same for my mama, though heaven forbid she'd ever get that way. We went through a stroke with Grandma, and it's not easy."

Granna leaned back in her chair and gazed bleakly up at the canopy of green leaves above us. "It's a fine thing when children are grateful and return kindness for all you do for them," she said, "but so very hard to bear when they don't."

I knew she was thinking of my mama, and I wanted to cry out, "But that's a whole different thing!" However, knowing that I'd best pretend ignorance, I grabbed Star's arm and said, "Let's go see if there's any watermelon left!"

"You can. I'm plumb full-up," she said, but allowed herself to be dragged away under the massive branches of a neighboring oak tree.

"I don't really want any either," I explained. "I just didn't want to hear any more. I don't like it when Granna talks like that."

Star threw me a puzzled look, but I didn't feel like elaborating. After a few seconds, she said, "Poor Miss Mary Afton. Wonder what she'll do if her mama dies."

"Just go back to working at Lana's, I reckon, and teaching when school starts up again."

Star shook her head sadly. "Not around here. I heard Mrs. Chapman telling Mama that the school board can't afford to keep on any teachers' helpers this year."

"You mean she might—move away?"

"I don't know. She'll have to earn enough money to live on. Mrs. Chapman's real upset about it. Said her and the other teachers have come to depend on Miss Mary Afton."

"Golly, Star—I'd feel real bad if she was to move away."

"Me, too."

The thought of Miss Mary Afton's troubles lingered with me through the evening, and Uncle Bob seemed a little preoccupied too. Although he clapped and cheered at our small fireworks ceremony, he kept falling into long, sober silences that were unlike him. He was on the phone for quite a while that night, and early the next morning I heard him making another call before he left for his construction job. I tiptoed out of my room just as he came slowly up the stairs, rubbing one palm over his face and head as though to dispel a lingering shred of sleep.

"Uncle Bob?"

He looked up, surprised, and gave me what almost amounted to a smile. "Sorry, E. J., did I wake you?"

"What's going on? Who were you calling?"

"Well—I just thought I'd check with the hospital about Mrs. MacDougal."

"How is she?"

"She passed away during the night," he said gently.

I leaned against the doorframe. "Poor Miss Mary Afton. I'll bet she's awful sad."

"I'm sure she is. I wish—oh, well. Nothing we can do for her right now, E. J., except say a prayer that she'll be comforted."

"Reckon so."

"Why don't you just go on back to bed now, kiddo? It's still pretty early."

Padding back into my room, I knelt on my rug and asked God to help Miss Mary Afton not feel too bad. Then I crawled into bed and picked up the thin volume of poems by Emily Dickinson.

It seemed such a long time since Miss Mary Afton had given it to me, and I still hadn't read very much of it. So many of the poems seemed to be about dying, and they were sad and even frightening. As Miss Mary Afton had predicted, I didn't really understand most of them, or even want to—but two or three appealed to me. One began, "Hope is the thing with feathers—That perches in the soul—." I thought it was nice to compare hope to a bird, because birds were always active and singing and cheerful—and yet, even the birds die. Did that mean hope could die too? The poem didn't say so. I decided my very favorite was the most positive of all.

I never saw a Moor—
I never saw the Sea—
Yet know I how the Heather looks
And what a Billow be.

I never spoke with God
Nor visited in Heaven—
Yet certain am I of the spot
As if the Checks were given—

Lying there in the early morning, I decided to memorize the poem. I liked it because I had used my imagination so often to see places where I'd never been—Freckles's Limberlost Swamp, Grandmother Knowles's Boston, LaRae's Wyoming ranch, and the heaven where I pictured my mama and daddy together and forever young.

. . . . 25 . . . . .

Later that day, we learned that Mrs. MacDougal's funeral was to be held on Saturday at the Hooper Funeral Parlor on Davis Street. Star and I felt we ought to go, but we were petrified at the idea. Neither of us had ever attended a funeral, nor had we been in the presence of a dead person. Granna had scrupulously kept me from funerals, saying that such occasions were no place for a child. I had wondered what took place but didn't dare ask—it'd seem morbid of me. But this was different—we loved Miss Mary Afton. Were we willing to put aside our fears to show our love and support?

Star took a deep breath, held it, and closed her eyes. "I will if you will," she said in a rush.

"Okay, I will too. But I don't think I'd better ask Granna. She'd say no for sure."

"Same with Mama. She'd say I should just write a little note."

We debated various methods of achieving our purpose and decided that it would be simplest if I spent Friday night with Star. This was arranged easily enough, and I was relieved at not having to tell a whopper, although my pesky conscience suggested to me that withholding information might be closely related to lying.

I packed my Sunday dress and shoes along with my nightgown and toothbrush, and that night we folded Star's dress into the small case too. We curled up on Star's big old double bed and whispered until after eleven o'clock, at which time her father, who rarely seemed to say anything at all, paused outside her door to remind us, "Morning comes early, girls," and we subsided.

It took me a while to get to sleep. Long after Star's breathing had grown steady and the peculiar little twitches that always accompanied her going-to-sleep process had stopped, I was still alert, watching the changing shadows made by moonlight on the floor and feeling rather guilty that someone's death was providing us our small adventure.

At nine-thirty the next morning, wearing our usual shorts and shirts, we strolled casually down the Hargraves' front steps and turned toward town. Star had risen early and practiced while I made her bed, straightened her room, and helped her mother put the breakfast things on the table so that there would be no reason to refuse Star permission to "walk me home" and stay for a while.

Once around the corner from her house, we paused and eyed each other warily. "Emily Jean, I'm scared," Star said. "First I was scared we wouldn't get to go — and now I'm scared *to* go."

"Come on," I urged, though my heart was pounding too. "The scariest part's over. All we have to do now is change clothes, walk in, and sit down."

"But Mama always says funerals are sad and depressing. I'm scared I'll start to cry. You know how I am."

I knew. "But, Star, we're doing this for Miss Mary Afton — so she'll know we care about her and all."

"I know. Reckon I'll just have to be brave."

We changed clothes in the rest room of Parker's Cafe. Star brushed out her hair and applied something to her lips with the tip of her little finger.

"Starlett Hargrave! Is that *lipstick?*"

"It's just Tangee," she explained, holding out the tube of translucent orange that turned a delicate pink on her lips. "I thought it might make me feel a little braver and more grown up. Want to try some?"

I shook my head, appalled and fascinated that Star owned a tube of lipstick, and I hadn't even known.

"Come on, Emily Jean, you'd look real pretty. Pat gave it to me, and Mama 'bout had a conniption. But she let Pat start wearing real lipstick when she was thirteen, and I almost am. Here — just a dab, and rub it on with your fingertip."

It felt waxy and smelled pleasantly sweet, and it made very little difference in how I looked. But, as Star said, I felt wonderfully grown up as we paraded past the coffee-and-donut crowd at the counter. The fact that no one in particular seemed to notice us soothed my fears, and we gave our attention to our next problem: where to stash the overnight case while we were at the funeral.

We surveyed our choices. We considered going into Lana's and slipping it under the edge of a table of clothing. Lana's was so crowded that it would likely remain unseen. However, I was afraid that we'd run right into Mrs. Buzbee, who was a great one for asking questions. Maybe she was even going to the funeral herself, since Miss Mary Afton had worked for her. We didn't feel right about leaving the suitcase in anyone's yard either. Suddenly, the obvious dawned on me, and I pulled Star into a fast trot. "I know the perfect place — between my Mama's gravestone and the bush behind it!"

"Oh — do you reckon that's all right? I don't know, Emily Jean, it doesn't seem . . . "

"It'll be fine — honest, Star. Who has a better right? And it won't be for long."

We hurried down the familiar path, and I thrust the case into the shady little cave between bush and stone. It was hardly visible.

The Hooper Funeral Parlor was a gracious home that had once belonged to Mr. Hooper's wife and family. Since its conversion into a mortuary, it had taken on a sleepy atmosphere. Blinds and curtains on the ground floor were always drawn, and stone urns of white petunias graced the front porch. What went on in the nether regions of that house had long been a matter of speculation to the children of Tatum, and a favorite Halloween dare was to walk slowly all around the house without running or screaming. No one dared ring the bell for trick-or-treat. This sort of thing went on for several years until the Hoopers' fifteen-year-old daughter, Linda, decided to give a Halloween party for her classmates, one of whom had been Rogie. It was one of the few times I had seen Rogie really enthusiastic about something. He told of tours between dimly lit rows of caskets on display and glimpses of the instruments and tables of the embalming room. Of course, it was just the sort of thing that would excite Rogie's imagination, but I had listened with morbid glee, myself—and slept with my light on for a week. Some indignant townspeople had taken Mr. Hooper to task for allowing such a breach of dignity, but he explained that he had allowed nothing improper to take place and that by satisfying the curiosity of his daughter's classmates, he had relieved her of being such a curiosity herself. "The girl who lives with the dead," she had been labeled. But after the party, the lively redhead had been accepted by her classmates as a good sport. Besides, as Mr. Hooper assured everyone, he had no departed clients on the premises that night.

I don't know what Star expected as we mounted the steps and entered the screen door, but I was pleasantly surprised at the cool, well-lit interior. The floor was polished, and a vase of fresh roses stood on a side table, doubled in volume by a framed mirror behind it. Soft organ music drew us forward into the chapel, where we saw about twenty-five or thirty people already seated on folding chairs. We signed the guest register in our best script, then slipped into seats on the back row.

"There she is," whispered Star, nudging me. I followed her gaze toward the front, where Miss Mary Afton was bending forward to catch the words of an elderly man who held her hand. She drew back with a smile and a nod, then brushed away tears with a hanky as she turned to greet someone else.

Then, I became aware of the metallic-looking casket resting on its trestle just behind Miss Mary Afton. Part of the lid stood open, revealing a pale, composed profile that I would never have connected with the flushed, perspiring woman I had seen at the small cottage. I stared, stiffening myself against the fear and revulsion I had always expected to feel at the sight of a dead person, but those feelings didn't come. All I felt was a sense of wonder at the immense mystery of life and death. I sat still, slowly relaxing as the soothing melodies and hushed bits of conversation eddied around me. Finally, when it seemed that no one else was coming, Mr. Hooper drew a curtain across the area where the casket stood and ushered Miss Mary Afton and three other people behind the curtain as well. For a few minutes, nothing was audible except a quiet murmur from that region and one or two restrained sniffs. Then the curtain was partially opened to reveal the flower-decked casket, now closed. Evidently Miss Mary Afton and her companions had been given seats behind the edge of the curtain so that they could view the service in relative privacy.

Star suddenly gripped my hand. I turned quickly, fearful that she would be overcome by the emotions of the moment, but she was making small pointing motions ahead and to our right. All I saw was a collection of heads. "What?" I whispered.

"On the third row," she mouthed. "Isn't that your Uncle Bob?"

I looked again, peering around the lady in front of me. It was Uncle Bob. He turned to look toward the curtain, and I realized that from his angle, he probably could see Miss Mary Afton. He looked a long time, his expression calm and serious, and I felt that he was somehow trying to send her comforting thoughts — and maybe wishing he could go and sit beside her. It was nice of him to be here, I decided, when he really didn't know her all that well. I nodded at Star, who raised her eyebrows, and I shrugged in reply.

The music stopped, and a man rose and went to the podium. "Brothers and sisters, friends and family, we have met here today to pay a farewell tribute to Sister Mary Leah Turner MacDougal. This service is under the direction of the Wimshaw Branch of The Church of Jesus Christ of Latter-day Saints, of which Sister MacDougal was a member. The family prayer was offered privately by Armitage J. Turner, a brother of the deceased. The opening prayer for this service will now be given by Elder Thomas Stonewell, a full-time missionary serving in this area."

Elder? Latter-day Saints? It was my turn to grip Star's hand. "Mormons!" I hissed in her ear just before we bowed our heads for the prayer. My mind was churning. Was Miss Mary Afton's mother a Mormon? Did that mean that she, too — surely not! Did Uncle Bob know? Should I say anything — should we *be* here?

Finally, a few words of the young elder's prayer filtered through to me. He was giving thanks for the gospel of Jesus Christ, for the Atonement, for the assurance of the resurrection, for the life of this good sister — and much as it surprised me, I could find nothing objectionable in his prayer. In fact, it was a nice prayer — one that any good Christian would have been proud of giving.

Star leaned close. "Are you sure?" she whispered. "They didn't *say* Mormons. It was something else — about Jesus and Saints."

I nodded slowly. "I'm sure." I had just spotted Elder Doug Jensen, LaRae's brother, on the very front row. Star was limp with astonishment, and I wasn't far from that condition myself.

Another man stood and gave a brief sketch of Mrs. MacDougal's life, telling of her birth and childhood in Virginia; her education and move to Maryland, where she married John MacDougal, a schoolteacher; the birth of their only child, Mary Afton, in 1927; and the death of John in 1940. He spoke of her conversion to the "restored" church in 1942, and her never-realized desire to be sealed to John in the holy temple.

He told of how Mary MacDougal had become ill in 1944 and had been hospitalized. One night, through a simple human error, she had been given a large dose of medication intended for the patient in the next bed. The mistake was quickly realized, and appropriate treatment was given that had saved Mary's life, but not before she had gone into deep shock. Her body had partially recovered, but her mind had not. She had required almost constant care since that day and had never spoken a word since. The family, being compassionate people, had elected not to sue the hospital or the nurse, but the hospital had discharged the nurse and awarded the family a generous sum of money, which had quickly been eaten up by the care Mary required.

The nurse responsible for the accident had begged to come and live with Mary and her daughter, insisting that devoting her life to caring for the invalid was the only way she could ever begin to forgive herself for the tragic error. She would accept no pay, but asked only to be allowed to live with the little family. Her presence made it possible for Mary Afton to go to college for two years, pursuing her dream of becoming a teacher like her father. In their shared grief, Mary Afton and the nurse became good friends, overcoming the guilt and sorrow and anger that might have made them enemies.

Impressed with Mary Afton's faith and courage, the young nurse began to study the tenets of her faith and was baptized into the church, where she met and married a young widower — and they were here today. The speaker paused and nodded with a smile at those in the curtained alcove. Then he spoke of Mary Afton's continuing devotion to her mother when money had begun to dwindle. She had left school and gone to work, first placing her mother in the best nursing facility she could find, then coming to Tatum to accept a post as teacher's aide and living as frugally as possible to supplement their funds. Finally, when the nursing care became too costly, the loving daughter had brought Mary to her own small home where she could care for her personally with the occasional aid of neighbors and friends.

"I, for one, have never heard Sister Mary Afton complain these past few weeks, or ever," he continued. "To all appearances, her mother wasn't able to comprehend all that was done for her after her tragic accident. But now she knows — her eternal spirit has been freed from the physical body that was no longer a fit tabernacle for that spirit. Now she knows — she remembers and recognizes and loves and feels gratitude and compassion. How proud and grateful she and John must be to have a daughter such as Mary Afton, such faithful friends, and such a loving Heavenly Father who provides for his children the opportunities of growth and progression and association with one another in this life and the next."

I peeked around the woman in front of me to look at Uncle Bob, who was smiling a small, steady smile toward the curtained area. He seemed to blink away a certain moisture from his eyes, and I found my own eyes were wet too. I could hear Star sniffling beside me.

There were other speakers. One talked of eternal marriage,

referring to the opportunity John and Mary MacDougal would ultimately have to be together forever as husband and wife — their love and relationship not broken by death but strengthened and made lasting through ordinances that would be performed for them in the temple of the Lord. I didn't understand about the temple, but I liked the idea of their being together forever. That was the dream I cherished for my own mama and daddy.

Then Elder Doug Jensen rose to speak. His talk was brief but powerful. He spoke of the reality of the resurrection of Jesus and how we can all look forward to the same blessing of having our spirits reunited with perfect, immortal bodies and living forever. He told of the spirit world where Mary and others who had left their bodies through the separation called death now lived — a beautiful place where they could learn and progress while they looked forward to the resurrection. He made it all seem very plain and very close — like a natural part of our existence. I wished Zack could hear him, because he had told me of his confusion on the subject. Maybe I could remember some of this and tell him about it when I visited Grandmother Knowles again. And Grandmother! She should have a chance to hear it all explained like this too.

I glanced again at Uncle Bob. He was listening intently, a small, puzzled frown evident as he turned his head. I wondered if he believed what we were hearing. I would ask him later. I thought LaRae would be proud of her brother. It was hard to believe that this was Mormon religion I was hearing — it all sounded so right and true! And if Miss Mary Afton believed it, it couldn't be all bad. But then — maybe they just weren't preaching the bad, wrong parts today.

There was a song at the end of the service for Mrs. MacDougal that brought me nearly to tears again. After a closing prayer, Mr. Hooper asked all those present to please rise and follow the family out row by row, beginning with the front.

The casket was rolled down the aisle and carried from the building. Miss Mary Afton followed close behind it with her three companions, whom I now knew to be the repentant nurse and her husband and the uncle who had offered the private family prayer.

Miss Mary Afton's tears still flowed, but she lifted her head to glance over the congregation and nod greetings here and there. When she saw us, she looked surprised and touched and gave a tiny wave of her fingers. I heard Star's subdued gulp and willed her not to burst into tears. As Uncle Bob came down the aisle, I shrank against Star and tried to become invisible, but it was not to be. His eyebrows flared, and I knew he'd be waiting for us outside. When we came through the doors, he pulled us to one side and stood with an arm loosely around each of us, though his eyes kept straying to Miss Mary Afton where she stood beside the black hearse, hugging people and thanking them for coming.

"I had no idea you girls were planning to attend—we could have come together," Uncle Bob said thoughtfully. "It's funny Mom never mentioned it."

I remembered my vow to tell no more whoppers and took a deep breath. "Granna didn't know," I confessed.

"Oh? *Oh.*"

"Mama didn't know either," Star added in a small voice.

"I see. You both felt it was so important for you to be here that you didn't risk asking—is that it?"

Star and I exchanged glances. There was Uncle Bob, getting to the heart of the matter again. He gave our shoulders a little squeeze. "Fact of the matter is," he admitted, "I'm not sure I mentioned to Mom that I was coming either."

I glanced up to exchange a grin with him, but he was still looking at Miss Mary Afton, his expression intent. The crowd around her was thinning out, and he propelled us forward. She saw us and held out a hand to him.

"Bob," she said, "thank you so much for coming—it means a lot to me. And Emmy and Star—bless you both." She stooped to hug us.

"It was a beautiful service, Mary," Uncle Bob told her. "It gave me plenty of food for thought and lots of good ideas to remember when I'm called on to preach my first funeral."

"I was pleased. I hope Mother was, too."

"Surely she would be. Is there anything at all that I can do for you now? When will you be back?"

"Thanks, but everything's arranged. I should be back in about a week or ten days."

"Let me know, and I'll meet your bus."

"There's no need—please don't bother. You're very busy."

"I'm the one with the need. Please, Mary, let me know when you're coming. I want to be there."

She looked at the ground, blinking rapidly as if trying to keep back a fresh flood of tears. "All right," she whispered. "I'll—try."

. . . . 26 . . . .

Some other people came forward to claim Miss Mary Afton's attention, and Uncle Bob steered us toward his car. We waved at Mrs. Chapman, who was walking toward town with Mrs. Buzbee.

"Offer you ladies a ride?" Uncle Bob asked.

"No, thanks—not for me, Bob. I'm just going to my sister's in the next block," Mrs. Chapman said. "Beautiful service for a funeral, wasn't it?" Her nose and eyes were still suspiciously pink.

"Haven't the faintest idea who that young minister was—the last one who preached—but that was as good an Easter sermon as I've ever heard," Mrs. Buzbee declared. "Plumb gave me chills, didn't it you, Arnelle? Never heard the resurrection made to seem more real. I declare, I felt like it was Easter Sunday all over again. And here these two pretty young things are, wearing their Easter dresses, and both from my shop, if I recall! Don't they look sweet, Arnelle?"

"They do, and I'm sure it made Mary feel good to see them here, bless her heart. I'm surely going to miss that girl—I've grown to love her like my own."

"Why—why are you going to miss her?" I asked fearfully. "Is she going away, for sure?"

"Well, honey, if she can put together enough money or get her a scholarship, she wants to finish her college and become a certified teacher."

"She'd be a fine one too." put in Mrs. Buzbee. "And she's as pretty a girl as I've seen in an age. Don't you think so, Mr. Markham?"

"Uh—yes. Yes, indeed—fine young lady in every way."

I was surprised to see the color rising in Uncle Bob's face and wondered why he seemed flustered all of a sudden.

"Who was that young minister, anyway, Mr. Markham—reckon you'd know him?"

Uncle Bob shook his head and cleared his throat. "I don't. Someone from their church, I believe. Very thoughtful talk from such a young fellow, wasn't it?"

"I know him," I whispered to Star. "That's *him*—my pen pal's brother."

Star's eyes widened, and she stared at me as the two ladies took their leave.

"Uncle Bob," I said suddenly. "Is Miss Mary Afton—a Mormon?"

"Well, yes, E. J., that's one name for her faith. The real name is—let's see—The Church of Jesus Christ of Latter-day Saints."

"But, Granna says Mormons aren't even Christians, and I just know—or at least I *think*—that Miss Mary Afton is."

Uncle Bob sighed. "I don't pretend to understand all their doctrines, E. J., but I do believe they worship the Lord in their own way. Thinking back on the few members of their church that I've known, they've all been fine people. Outstanding, as a matter of fact. So even though we may not accept their teachings, we can respect them for the good lives they lead and let God judge their hearts."

"And we can witness to them," Star suggested, nudging my arm meaningfully.

"Why, yes, Star, we can do that." A perplexed look crossed his face. "But, don't be too surprised if they witness right back!"

The Nash was hot and smelled of dusty wool upholstery. We sat in it and waited until the hearse had pulled away, followed by Miss Mary Afton and her friends in another car. She lifted one hand in a little wave as they passed us, but for once she didn't smile.

Uncle Bob cleared his throat again. "Now, ladies, where may I take you?"

"We need to go to the cemetery first," I said.

"Oh—didn't you realize, E. J., that they're not going to bury Mrs.

MacDougal here? They're sending her body back to Maryland to be beside her husband."

"I know. But—well, we left something there that we have to get, so could we just circle through?"

He raised his eyebrows but obligingly turned in through the gates and slowed down. "Where?"

"Behind Mama's stone. I'll get it."

I retrieved the suitcase, relieved beyond words that it was still there. "Thank you, Mama," I whispered, as if she had guarded it for us, then ran back to the car.

"What an elaborate plan you two cooked up! Where to now?"

I giggled, happy that he wasn't angry. "Now we need a place to change back into our shorts."

"Oh—well, two quick-change artists like yourselves can do that right in the back seat. I'll just walk over here a ways. Signal when you're ready."

He strolled to a stone bench and sat down, stretching his arms and rolling his head around as if to rid himself of tension. We squirmed out of our dresses and pulled on our shorts and blouses. I straightened up just in time to see two young men in dark suits coming along the path toward Uncle Bob. To my surprise, Uncle Bob stood up and went forward, extending his hand.

"It's *them*," I whispered, poking Star's arm. "It's the Mormon missionaries!"

"Where?" she gasped, feverishly buttoning her shirt.

"Over there, talking to Uncle Bob."

"Oh," she said, relieved. "Likely he's going to witness to them."

I bundled my dress and slip into my suitcase. "I'm going over there," I announced, opening the door.

"Emily Jean! Why?"

"Too hot to sit here."

Star followed me at a safe distance, kicking at tufts of grass and pretending to read tombstones. However, I wasn't as brave as I let her think. I angled up to Uncle Bob and stood just behind his left elbow, stealing a glance at Elder Jensen, who hadn't noticed me, and then at Elder Comstock, who gave me a surprised sort of wink.

"One of the most touching discussions of the Atonement I think I've ever heard," Uncle Bob was saying. "In fact, the whole tone of the service was quite—um, remarkable. Positive, you know—not so solemn and depressing as most of the funerals I've been to. I found it to be most inspiring. I wonder, would you fellows possibly have a little time this afternoon when we could talk over a few concepts? Have you had lunch?"

"Er—no, uh—we haven't. But we can eat later. We'll be happy to talk with you, you bet!" Elder Jensen saw me then and grinned. "Well, howdy, Miss Emily Jean. I didn't see you there at first. How are you?"

"Fine," I said shyly. "This is my uncle."

"You've met, have you?" asked Uncle Bob, drawing me forward.

"Emily Jean's been kind enough to write to my little sister back in Wyoming, who asked me to find her a pen pal down South here. Heard from her lately, Emily Jean?"

"I've just had one letter," I mumbled, trying not to meet Uncle Bob's speculative glance.

"Tell you what," he said, apparently deciding not to comment on this new revelation, "why don't we drive down to the Rexall for a sandwich and a malt—my treat? It's fairly cool there and quiet enough in a back booth so we'll be able to talk undisturbed. Can you spare the time?"

"You bet," they agreed in concert, and then laughed. "That's very kind, Mr. Markham," Elder Comstock continued. "But please don't feel you have to treat us. We can . . . "

"Only too happy to," Uncle Bob insisted. "Emily, Star, we'll drop you both at home first, okay? My old car, gentlemen."

I made a beeline for the car. But Star, wide-eyed in realization that the Mormon elders were going to get into Uncle Bob's car, backed off and declined a ride. "I'll just walk, Mr. Markham," she said hastily. "It's not but a block and a half. I'll get my stuff later, Emily Jean." Then she was gone, walking very quickly toward the north gate of the cemetery—a high-shouldered walk, stiff with the effort of not breaking into a run.

I got into the car with Uncle Bob and the two missionaries and said not a word in the five blocks it took to circle the cemetery and arrive home. I grabbed the suitcase and bolted from the car with a quick, "Thanks, Uncle Bob," so that Granna wouldn't have much time to look out the window and recognize the other occupants of the car. Luckily, she wasn't in sight. I ran upstairs and put the suitcase in my closet, then headed for the kitchen, where I could hear the tinkle of ice being stirred into a pitcher.

"Well, at least you're home in time for a bite of lunch. I thought Robert surely would be, too, but we won't wait. Did you have a nice time at Starlett's?"

"Yes'm, real nice."

I slid into my place before a plate of fried ham and hominy, grateful that apparently neither Granna nor Mrs. Hargrave had discovered our little escapade.

"There's a letter for you under your plate, Emily Jean." Granna eyed me warily. "Seems you're getting to be a real correspondent, and that's fine. But see that you don't neglect other things, such as your piano practice. I want a good solid hour, right after lunch."

" 'S'ma'am, I will." Was the letter from LaRae? That would be good timing. I hurried through my meal, eager to find out. I glanced at the letter as I picked up my plate to carry it to the sink. It wasn't from LaRae. It was from Grandmother Knowles, addressed in her careful, spidery handwriting. Nonchalantly, I took it and headed for the upright piano in the parlor, where I perched on the stool and ripped open the envelope.

My dear lovie.

I go over and over our visit in my mind, and it gives me such great pleasure to think of each moment. I am so grateful to Mrs. Markham for permitting you to come and humor this old lady. I had a letter from Cecily, my Ned's sister, you recall? I think you will be hearing from her— she was enchanted to know of you.

Vesta and I go on. Our days are much the same, but now we have something special to remember and talk about. We wish you could come again, but we mustn't be selfish. Young Zack brought us a mess of bluegill—pan fry, Vesta called them—and a chunk of his mama's home-churned butter. He asked after you, and I let him read your letter. He says to tell you the kitty runs all over the store now and purrs like a tractor. Also said to tell you he is kind of lonesome since his cousin went back home. Said you'd know which cousin he meant.

Write to us when you can, my lovie—and know that you have made this old heart sing.

With love from your Grandmother

I sat in reverie, lost in what I privately thought of as my "other world." I didn't notice the other slip of paper in the envelope until I started to fold Grandmother's letter back inside. It was a letter from Vesta, set out in her careful printing.

Dear Mis Emily I think you shuld know Mrs Knowles she porely. We had the doctur and the preest to her. I dont know me how long she got left. She dont want you to worrie none and she so hapy since you come but I thot you shuld know. My heart breaks to think we lose her but I trust the Good Lord Above to take care all of us. Your frend Vesta M. Lincoln.

P.S. It tuk her 2 hole days to rite your letter, she that weak.

I sat with both letters held limply on my lap and stared unseeingly at the empty music rack on the piano. *Oh why, why did people have to get old and sick and die? Why?* My eyes brimmed over. Granna paused in the hallway, looking at me curiously.

"Well, Emily Jean, what is it, child? Bad news?"

Silently, I held out both letters. She wiped her hands quickly on her apron and took them, frowning through her bifocals as she read. Her lips moved slightly as she formed the words in her mind. Then she sat down next to me on the piano bench.

"Well, now," she said hoarsely and cleared her throat. "I suppose it's good you went when you did. She'd have been too sick to have you now. We knew she was ill, of course, that's why I—"

Suddenly, I started to cry, sobbing into my arms folded on the piano. All of the confusing, suppressed emotions—attending the funeral, discovering that Miss Mary Afton was a Mormon, and realizing that Grandmother Knowles truly wouldn't always be alive in my idyllic other world—combined to shake me as I had never before been shaken. I cried so hard that part of me was astonished at myself. Granna patted me awkwardly and fretted uncertainly. Finally, she turned me toward her and put her arms around me, rocking and patting me in a way I could never remember her doing before.

"Now, now, Emily Jean, you mustn't take on so! Everything's going to be all right," she soothed. "There's nothing for you to cry about—everything's fine."

I knew everything wasn't fine, but her concern comforted me even if her reassurance did not. "Granna," I said, as soon as I could control my voice, "I want to go back just one more time for a teeny visit, just to see them one more time—please."

"Well, I—I don't know if that's wise . . . "

"Please, Granna. Oh, please, just once before . . . " My voice, harsh and husky from crying, squeaked off as my throat tightened again and my eyes filled.

"We'll talk about it a little later. You're overwrought, Emily Jean, and I want you to come right upstairs and get into bed. A good nap will do more for you now than anything else."

She accompanied me to my room, tucked me between the sheets, pulled the blinds to keep out the afternoon sun, and bathed my face with a cool washcloth.

"I'm not sick," I protested feebly, too exhausted to object more vigorously.

"Heartsick," I heard her murmur as she set a small electric fan on my dresser. "I know the symptoms."

. . . . 27 . . . .

When I awoke, the light had the quality of late afternoon, and I was aware of feeling hungry again but still very tired. Slowly the events of the morning came back to me, and I lay thinking of them. Granna had been right—somehow the hours of sleep had smoothed away the rough edges of my distress. I still wanted to visit Grandmother Knowles again—urgently—but I felt calmer about it, able to reason with Granna and Uncle Bob and try to persuade them without me dissolving in tears. My own storm had subsided, as had the hurricane that scarred my bed. As for Miss Mary Afton's religious beliefs—I decided that I simply didn't know enough to judge one way or another, and I was beginning to suspect that maybe Granna didn't either. Uncle Bob didn't seem unduly upset to know she was a Mormon—but then, he didn't feel as strongly about Miss Mary Afton as Star and I did.

I dressed and went downstairs. Uncle Bob was in the dining room with a Bible and several other books spread out before him on the table, but he was gazing out the window. Soft music came from the radio in the parlor. I knew he must be working on the next day's sermon, so I tiptoed through the room without disturbing him. Granna was in the kitchen, taking a pan of bubbly, yellow macaroni and cheese from the oven and replacing it with a pie. I picked up a curl of green apple peel from the oilcloth cover and began to munch it. Granna glanced at me warily.

"Well, there you are, and no wonder you're hungry—you slept the day away. Do you feel better?"

I nodded, basking in the peace and normalcy of Granna's kitchen. "I'll set the table," I volunteered and began to clear away the pie makings.

"Let's eat in the dining room. Just work around Robert—don't make him move. It's too beastly hot in here with the oven lit. I don't know what possessed me to use it on a day like this, but I just purely craved a good pie and casserole. There's coleslaw in the icebox, and I've got some cold stewed tomatoes. After supper, I'll let you help me fry up a chicken. Robert suggested having a picnic lunch tomorrow. It's not much notice, but I'll do my best. I could stir up some biscuits, but maybe light bread will go better—and we'll take some green onions from the garden, and radishes, if they haven't gone all pithy and strong."

I shook my head to clear it. "Isn't tomorrow Sunday?" I asked. Picnicking, along with movies and swimming, were activities our good Christian household didn't engage in on the sabbath.

"Well, yes, of course it is, but this'll save us trying to buy decent food on the road on Sunday. You never know what you're getting, or how clean—"

"On the road? Do you mean—"

"Well, I showed your letters to Robert, and he decided that if we leave right after church tomorrow, we can get to Mrs. Knowles's house in time for you to have a little visit with her, and we'll try to get back here in the evening, before it's too dark."

"He did! We *will?*" A warm bubble of joy rose and burst within my chest, and I ran to the dining room to hug Uncle Bob.

"Thanks, Uncle Bob! You knew how much I wanted to go, didn't you?"

He set aside his Bible and smiled at me—a sad sort of smile, I thought, as he gently tugged my braid. "Yes, I did, and apparently you made that desire pretty plain to your Granna too."

"I never meant to get so upset, honest I didn't. But you saw Vesta's letter."

"Yes, and I went one step farther. I put through a call to Mr. Bramley at his store."

"Zack's daddy? Why?"

"They've been keeping a pretty close eye on Mrs. Knowles and Vesta, so I thought he might know how things are."

"How are they?"

"Not very good, E. J. Vesta's right to be concerned, and so are you. The doctor said she could go any minute. Somebody sits with her all the time. His wife and some of Vesta's friends have been spelling Vesta off so she can get some sleep, but she's with your grandmother every waking minute. You need to be prepared to see a change in her, E. J. Apparently it's about time for her to go home."

"Oh, why?" I dropped to the floor and leaned my head against his knee. "I only just found her, and now—"

"It's always hard to let go of people we've learned to love," he said softly. "We just have to trust in the good Lord to be kind and do what's best for her. We wouldn't want her to lie there and suffer a long time, would we?"

I shook my head. "I'd hate that. I don't want her to hurt any at all. I guess I'd rather let her—go—than that."

"There—you see? You are growing up, kiddo, by leaps and bounds."

"Why'd you say that?"

"Because you're learning how to love. First, you see, all we can feel is a selfish kind of love that wants to bind the loved one close to us, no matter what—even if it isn't best for that person. We just want to be close and never let go. It's natural. But then, if we're lucky, we move beyond that and learn to want what's best for the loved one, even if it isn't what we personally would prefer. Lots of folks never seem to get past that first stage, even grown-ups. That's why I'm proud of you, E. J."

I frowned. "Well, I don't know if I'm really past it, because it still makes me really hurt inside to think about letting her go—so I reckon maybe I'm not."

"Well, the hurt—that's always there when you part from a loved one, for a little while or forever. That hurt is from the love stretching and pulling between you. It doesn't break, but after a while, it's not so sore anymore. Who's that poet you like—Emily Dickinson? Know what she wrote about parting from loved ones?"

I shook my head, surprised that he knew about Emily Dickinson, although of course he'd been all the way through college.

"In one of her poems, she said, 'Parting is all we know of heaven, And all we need of hell.' "

Startled, I gave him a quick look. "What'd she mean by that?"

"Why don't you think about it for a while, honey, and then tell me what you think it means."

"Well, but . . . "

"Emily Jean? Dinner's all ready to put on the table, and you haven't even set out the plates! I declare, I don't know what you two find to talk about so much. Robert dear, would you mind turning off that radio? No point in having it playing with nobody in that room. Get the coleslaw, Emily Jean."

Uncle Bob winked at me in the wake of Granna's bustle and went to do her bidding.

Later that night, not at all sleepy after my long nap, I tucked up in my bed with several books for company. I read my assigned Bible verses for Sunday School, a couple of chapters in *Dark Frigate*, one of my father's books, and then opened the volume of Dickinson again to look for the lines Uncle Bob had quoted. I didn't find them. There were all those poems about death, but most of them gave me the willies, so I finally put the book down and slid to the floor to say my prayers.

I wasn't quite sure how to go about praying for the two people I was most concerned about—Grandmother Knowles and Miss Mary Afton. I loved them as much as anyone in my life, and yet—what could I say? Should I pray for Grandmother to get better? Was it lack of faith not to? And if I prayed for her to escape suffering, was I really asking that she die? Had either she or Miss Mary Afton really been saved and accepted Jesus? I didn't know. In the end, I just said, "Dear Lord, you know what they need better than I do. Please bless them and me too, so that I can understand what's right. Help me to be brave if Grandmother Knowles has to die. Bless Granna and Uncle

Bob and Vesta and Star, and all the sick and poor and needy. And Rogie. Amen."

I turned my pillow over to its cool side and switched off my lamp so that the bugs would quit spanging against my windowscreen, trying to get in. I pulled my sheet over me, more as a protection against the dark than for warmth. I settled down to what I thought, after my long nap, would be a wakeful night of contemplating life's mysteries. But a mockingbird was singing, and I heard the monotonous staccato of a radio announcer giving the news downstairs, and I was young and healthy — so I slept.

I was awakened the next morning by the ringing of the phone. Still dizzy from sleep, I flung myself into the hall to lean over the bannister and listen, fearful that it was Mr. Bramley calling with news of the worst. Granna's delighted tones allayed that fear, however, and I went back to my room. I didn't much care who it was, as long as it wasn't someone from Turley.

On the way home from the eleven o'clock church service, Granna cleared her throat and remarked offhandedly, "Well, it looks like I won't be going along on this outing today, but you two might as well go ahead and make it a pleasant trip."

"What's this? Not come? Why not?" asked Uncle Bob.

"Well, that was Roger on the telephone this morning. He and that nice friend of his are coming in this afternoon, just for a brief visit, and I really feel I should be here."

Was there a note of relief in Granna's voice? I wasn't sure, but I felt a tiny spark of it within me. Somehow I wasn't quite ready to share my other world with Granna, or even Star, except with what I chose to tell them.

We loaded the picnic into the car. Granna insisted we take all of it, as she would prepare a hot dinner for Rogie and Raymond. At the last minute, she brought out a quart jar of her home-bottled peach nectar and gave it to me.

"This is for Mrs. Knowles, if she can use it. It's easy to digest and full of nourishment for a sick person. And give her—my best wishes, Emily Jean."

"Thanks, Granna. I will."

"Say hello to Roge if we miss him," said Uncle Bob. "And, Mom—be prudent. Don't let him bleed you dry. He's a big boy."

"Oh, Robert, I don't think he—at least, he didn't mention . . . "

"Well—be careful, anyway."

I contemplated this exchange as we rumbled down the highway, viewing scenery that seemed blurry and unreal through heat waves that rose from the pavement. There was always a mirage of a stream crossing the road at a certain point in the distance.

"Uncle Bob, I don't see how you and Rogie can be so different and be brothers."

He chuckled. "Brothers are often very different, E. J. Look at Cain and Abel or Jacob and Esau. In our case, the only way I can explain it is that I grew up with the benefit of Papa's presence, and Roge didn't. He was only three when Papa died, whereas I was twelve."

"What was your papa like?"

"He was gentle, kind—very efficient in a quiet way. Didn't say much, but when he did, he meant it."

"Did Granna—did she boss him around?"

"No, indeed, and neither did anyone else. That's how he built up his own hardware business from scratch. Everybody respected him. I know I did. It hardly ever occurred to me not to mind him—I knew he'd just quietly and firmly see to it that I did. He *expected* us to behave, so we generally did."

"I reckon Rogie can't even remember him."

"No, and that's a shame. A lot of things would be different, I suspect, if Papa had lived."

"Like what?"

"Oh, like—I think maybe things would've gone differently for Frank and Ellie. Papa would probably have given Frank a decent job in the store and talked your Granna around to accepting him."

"And then they might not have gone off to New Orleans—and maybe be alive right now." *And Grandmother Knowles would have been a part of my whole life and not just this brief summer, and I would have been different—maybe not even an only child—and Granna would have been happier, and Rogie not so mean.* Suddenly, "Papa" seemed real to me, he who had been little more than a face in the bronzetoned photograph on Granna's dresser. "Uncle Bob, I just don't understand why God lets people die when other people *need* them."

"That's a tough one," he agreed. "And I honestly don't know the answer. Maybe it's a different reason in different cases. All I can say is that God sees the whole picture of our lives, while we, as it says in the Bible, see 'through a glass, darkly.' Maybe one day we'll learn to see as God sees, and then it'll all fall into place."

"I hope so, 'cause there's sure a lot I can't figure out now."

Uncle Bob sighed. "Me, too, kiddo. But I keep trying, and looking for answers, and hoping. That's about all we can do."

A sudden thought struck me, showing me how self-absorbed I had been. "What about your mission church? Don't you have to preach tonight? We won't get back in time!"

"It's okay, E. J. They'll be enjoying a guest pastor from Moultrie tonight, so I had the evening free."

"Oh—good." I leaned back and watched the farmlands streak by. Most of the fields were high and green; a few were freshly plowed for a second crop. This trip was so different from the first, I reflected. I greeted each new landmark with joy, as an old friend, and I felt I knew a little better what "coming home" was all about.

We tried to picnic at a small park in Lynchville, but the horseflies and ants were so pesky that we compromised by spreading the folded cloth between us on the front seat and eating as we continued to drive. At length, Bramley's Feed and General Merchandise came into view, sleepy and deserted in the Sunday sunlight, and we negotiated the right turn across from it. There was no sign left of the old barn that had been demolished by the storm. Even the spot where it had stood for nearly a century was already being erased by the growth of grass and weeds.

Nothing else seemed changed, however. Tendrils of fragrant

honeysuckle still waved from the bee-laden clumps along the fence, and the same plants still flourished in their coffee cans along the railing of Grandmother's porch. Zack Bramley sat on the steps with his arm around Hunger. My heart beat faster. Zack rose as we bumped to a stop, and Hunger came with his silly sideways lope to whimper and twine around my legs and then stand leaning against me while I rubbed his ears the way he liked. I didn't trust my voice to speak, but Uncle Bob introduced himself to Zack and thanked him for his family's help with Mrs. Knowles.

Zack shook his hand solemnly and then addressed me. "Miz Knowles is real poorly. It's good you come."

I felt his straight green gaze was trying to tell me something he didn't want to put into words. I nodded to let him know I understood.

"Miz Vesta's with her. I'll fetch her," he said and slipped inside.

Uncle Bob stretched and plucked at his wet shirt where it was plastered against his back. In the woods behind the house, a crow was calling, and the buzz of cicadas rose and fell in scratchy symphony.

Vesta came quickly to the porch, moving rather stiffly, as if her legs hurt her, and looking a little thinner through the face. "Oh, Lord be praised, I done prayed y'all here," she cried, grabbing me in a fierce hug and then touching her long, elegant fingers to Uncle Bob's in what was, to her, a handshake.

"We thought we'd best come when we got your letters," Uncle Bob said. "How is she, Mrs. Lincoln?"

Vesta shook her head slowly, her lips compressed into a straight line. "She come and she go," she whispered, her voice cracking. "One minute, she say, 'Vesta, you get some rest; this too hard on you.' Next thing, she say, 'Frankie, you got that dog in your bedroom again?' Then she drift off into a deep sleep for hours, and I cain't wake her for nothin'. It be two days now she ain't took no nourishment but a little water. You know a body that don't take nothin' cain't last long." She glanced at me. "I thought maybe . . . maybe the grandbaby do her some good — at least ease her last days."

"Is she in pain? Did the doctor give her anything?"

"Yes, sir. He left some pills, but she won't take none."

"Can I see her?" I blurted.

" 'Course you can, honey lamb. I hope she wake up and know you, but don' you feel bad if she don't, all right?"

I nodded, and we went inside as Zack stepped out onto the porch again. He gave me just the ghost of a smile in passing. I realized this was hard on him too.

"That Zack, he sure one good young'un," Vesta whispered. "He stayed here all this last week and done whatever I ast him."

I went straight to my grandmother's bedside. My first impression was that she had shrunk. Her head seemed smaller against the pillows, too small for the heavy braid. Her cheeks were sunken under the delicate cheekbones, upon which appeared round spots of red like a clown's rouge. Her lips, partly open, were tinged with blue, and her heavy-lidded eyes seemed to have retreated deeper on each side of her prominent nose. Her eyes were closed.

At first, I panicked, thinking she wasn't breathing at all, but then I saw the slight rise and fall of the thin chest under the white cotton gown. I counted five full seconds before it rose and fell again. A tiny, whistling sound accompanied each breath. I turned to Vesta.

"I hate to wake her," I whispered.

"Honey, I don' even know if you can. But I do know it be her greatest wish to see you one more time. Miz Knowles," she called out, as if to someone in another room. "Miz Knowles, see who's here."

I picked up her hand, light and dry and cold even in the midsummer heat, and tried my voice, which quavered. "Grandmother? Grandmother, it's me—I got your letter."

She moaned and turned her head slightly on the pillow.

"Try again—she wakin' up," Vesta encouraged.

"Grandmother? I've come to see you again. It's me, Emily Jean."

Her eyes opened just a fraction, revealing a dull glitter, and her breathing quickened slightly. I squeezed her hand and leaned over to kiss her forehead. As always, she smelled of soap and talcum, and I blessed Vesta for keeping her fresh.

"It's me, Grandmother—I came to see you," I repeated.

Slowly the blue lips worked to form a word. "Lovie?"

"Yes," I said excitedly. "I'm here."

Her eyes opened wider and fought to focus. "Lovie? Are you real?"

"Yes, ma'am, I'm real. I'm right here with you."

A slight pressure from her fingertips told me she understood. "I'm going away on a far journey—did you know?" she whispered hoarsely.

"Are—are you?" I asked, not knowing how to reply.

"Yes, and I'm not afraid at all. Not any more."

"Well, that's—good. I'm real glad you're not afraid."

"Not afraid, because my Ned—is he here yet?"

"Who?"

"My Ned—said he'd come back for me. Is he here?"

"I don't know, Grandmother. I don't see him."

"He'll be back. It was such a joy—to see him. He looked so well."

I squeezed her hand again, not knowing what to say. Had she really seen my grandfather? Was such a thing possible? Her eyes opened again and sought mine.

"Will you mind too much, my lovie, if I leave—while you're here? I may need to go soon."

I looked helplessly at Vesta and Uncle Bob. Vesta spoke. "You do what you need to, Miz Knowles. We'll all be fine here, don' you worry."

Grandmother relaxed then, and I laid her hand back on the sheet. "We'll all take—our good bright memories—with us," she whispered, and I knew then that she understood exactly what was happening to her. Tears spilled from my eyes, and I bent to kiss her again on her soft, papery cheek, but she was asleep.

"That the way she do," Vesta whispered. "Wake a few minutes, then sleep. You all go on out to the kitchen. I got some cold buttermilk, or a pot of coffee brewin' if you'd ruther, Mr. Markham. I call you if she wake again."

Uncle Bob nodded, and we left the room quietly. By mutual consent, we bypassed refreshments in the kitchen and walked out into the backyard, where we stood and looked at Vesta's garden, overgrown with weeds and vegetables. Huge, overripe tomatoes lay on the ground where they had fallen and burst, mute testimony to the hours and days Vesta had spent nursing her friend.

I pointed out the path into the piney woods, and told Uncle Bob of Vesta's ordeal at the little brown stream and the resulting friendship that grew with the young Yankee widow who knew how to love people, even if she didn't know one seed from another or how to milk a cow. I told him my daddy's grave was up that path — and neither of us voiced the thought that perhaps soon there would be another grave close by. Then we stood silently for a while, until Zack suddenly bolted through the back door. "Miz Vesta says fetch y'all fast," he said. "She thinks it's time."

We ran then, Uncle Bob pulling me through the door and into the sudden dimness of the little house. Vesta was standing by Grandmother's bed, holding both her hands and crooning, "It be all right, honey lamb. Your Mr. Ned, he be here soon. Don' fret yourself, Miz Knowles. The good Lord love you, and your friends gonna sing you home to rest."

The spots of color had drained from Grandmother's cheeks, and her breath, still sporadic and jerky, now had a sort of bubble to it, as though she needed to cough. Vesta threw us a despairing glance and continued to rub the thin hands. We stood on the other side of the bed, Uncle Bob with one arm firmly around my shoulders. Zack hung back behind us until Uncle Bob drew him forward with his free hand, which he kept on Zack's shoulder. Zack didn't seem to mind.

Grandmother's eyes opened slowly. She looked at Vesta. "Thank you, my dear friend." Her whisper was barely audible. Then her eyes moved — searching, it seemed.

Vesta motioned me closer. "I think she want you, honey babe."

It seemed Vesta was right, for when the dim old eyes rested on me, Grandmother gave a tiny smile and formed the words, "I love you."

"I love you too, Grandmother," I said, wondering where the strength had come from to speak the words aloud at that moment. She smiled again, apparently satisfied, and closed her eyes. For several minutes she seemed to breathe a little easier, though less often. We were silent, watching and waiting. Suddenly, her eyes flew open and she cried out strongly, joyfully, "Yes, love, I'm ready!" Her breath caught then, and she exhaled what seemed a long, weary sigh. Nobody moved. For a moment, I didn't realize she was gone until Vesta leaned forward and gently closed her eyelids.

"You be happy now, Miz Knowles," she said softly, and holding her apron hem to her own eyes, began slowly to rock back and forth.

"I'll go tell Daddy," Zack said in a strained voice and hurried out, his head turned away to hide his emotion.

Uncle Bob held me against him, patting my shoulder, but strangely, I had little desire to cry. The stretching of the cords of love between me and my grandmother at her passing was painful, it was true, but what I felt, overwhelmingly, was a growing sense of awe and wonder, and a very real sense of the continuation of life. Heaven seemed quite near in that moment.

Mr. Bramley came quickly, and while he and Uncle Bob conferred in the living room, I sat in the sun on the front porch as Zack had done, with my arm around Hunger. There was a deep Sunday peace on the land, deepened even more by the solemnity of the moment I had just been privileged to share with my grandmother. I knew even then that it was a privilege, although I had never seen anyone die before nor lost anyone I really knew. I was comforted by the feeling that the time had been right and by the knowledge that we had for some reason been blessed to be there a bit before it happened rather than a few minutes too late. If Pastor Welch had been long-winded that morning, or if Granna hadn't had our picnic ready to go, or even if there hadn't been so many ants and flies at the park in Lynchville, we might have arrived too late. God had been good, both to us and to grandmother. Good, too, to let Grandfather Ned come to meet her. I was sure that really had happened, and I wondered if every soul on the brink of death was met by a familiar face and given a welcome into heaven. I would ask Uncle Bob.

I had every opportunity to ask him on the long ride home, but the occasion had subdued me, and I found I had no inclination to talk. Uncle Bob respected that and seemed lost in thought himself. He drove more slowly than usual, and I felt at times as if we were floating through the shimmering heat waves and vibrant greens of the Georgia midsummer evening.

Uncle Bob glanced over at me once when we were stopped for a slow-moving freight train that groaned and creaked its way through a crossing. "You okay, E. J.?"

"Fine," I said, nodding solemnly.

"It's okay to cry, you know, if you want to. Or talk about it."

"I don't need to."

"All right."

Raymond's white convertible was in the driveway when we got home, so we parked out front. I helped to carry in the remains of our picnic, trying to tiptoe inconspicuously past the archway to the parlor, where Rogie and Raymond sat sprawled, listening to the radio. But Rogie saw us and came to lounge under the arch.

"Hello there, brother and pest," he greeted. He looked better than I could ever remember him looking. He wore a casual blue-striped seersucker coat and white trousers that looked nice against his tanned skin.

"Hey," I said, hoping to escape in time to preserve the special feeling I had of being protected by a silk cocoon. I didn't want anyone or anything to intrude on my private world at that moment.

"Hello, Roge. Raymond, how are you?" Uncle Bob was saying, shaking hands with each.

Granna, hearing us, came quickly from her bedroom. "Well, you two are back in good time. How did you find Mrs. Knowles?"

I set the sack I was carrying on the dining room table and drew out the mason jar filled with pinkish-gold liquid. "There wasn't time for her to try your peach nectar," I said. "She—she—" But a lump so large and painful grew in my throat that I couldn't give my news.

"She passed away while we were there," Uncle Bob explained. "Very peacefully."

"Oh, no! Not—did the child see?"

I raised my face, wet with tears at last. "It was beautiful," I said between sobs. "Just beautiful."

Granna frowned wonderingly at Uncle Bob and came to comfort me, patting my shoulder briskly, as if she were trying to burp a baby.

"I'll explain later," Uncle Bob told her. "They'll be letting us know tomorrow about the funeral."

"I see. Well, I certainly don't think there's any call for Emily Jean to be subjected to that. She's had enough—"

"Oh, yes," I said, as firmly as I could. "Yes, Granna, I am too going to the funeral. I have to!"

"It probably will be a very simple, brief service," Uncle Bob said.

"Well, I'm sure where there's no family to—"

"*I'm* her family! *I* am!"

"Emily Jean, you're getting overwrought again. That's not healthy for a young girl. All this is most disturbing."

Rogie chose that inopportune moment to speak to Raymond. He probably didn't intend for any of us to hear, but just for a second the radio fell quiet and no one else was speaking, and I caught the last of his statement. "—be a good idea for us to show up there just after the funeral. Old lady might've left a real treasure trove of stuff we could pick up cheap."

If Granna thought I was overwrought before, she'd seen nothing yet. Something snapped in me and unleashed a fury I hadn't known I possessed. "You will not!" I shrieked. "Not one thing! Don't you dare touch one thing! Granna, don't let him! Uncle Bob—"

"Here, E. J., it's all right. He won't—"

"Not very respectful of you, Roger, at this moment. Perhaps later there'll be something—"

"No! Not later, either! Not ever! *Ever!* Oh, you're so hateful! I've always despised you!"

My fury and outrage contrasted so ill with my previous tender feelings that I felt about to split into pieces and fly in all directions at once. The rich and peaceful gold-and-green pattern of the afternoon had shattered and been replaced by one of violent reds and purples.

I felt Uncle Bob's hands on my shoulders, firmly steering me up the stairs, where I flung myself across my bed and sobbed out my rage and grief. Much later I awoke and heard the rhythmic creak of a rocking chair on my hardwood floor. I roused myself enough to see that Granna rocked there, eyes closed and gray head resting against the back of the chair in the moonlight. As I watched, Uncle Bob came in, stocking-footed, and touched her shoulder. She slowly stood up, kissed his cheek, and went downstairs while he settled into the rocker with a sigh. I closed my eyes and slept.

As it turned out, we went to the funeral — Granna, Uncle Bob and I — two days later. We arrived first at the small country mortuary at Lynchville, where we could see Grandmother's body — or "view the remains," as the undertaker put it. I felt rather nervous about this, even though I had been present when she died. I feared that she might have changed since then and become a stranger somehow. For a moment, my fears seemed realized as I approached the white casket. Then I saw that she looked different only because I had never seen her dressed up. Now she wore a dusty pink dress with lace down the front. Her hair was carefully braided and arranged in a loose crown at the top of her head. Her hands were folded at her waist, and a dainty white handkerchief had been tucked in one, as though she might have cause to shed a tear or two at her own funeral. There was a small gold cross at her throat, and her face was serene, composed and queenly. I gazed at her in awe, experiencing two levels of feeling at once. One told me that my grandmother was as regal and beautiful in death as she had ever been in life — someone I could be very proud to belong to — and the other told me, simply, that she was gone. Familiar and lovely and dear as her features were, her spirit had obviously fled; she simply didn't live there anymore. But I knew where she was — or, to be more exact, whom she was with. She was with her Ned — and probably with Frank and Ellie and Ellen Jane too. I felt sure of it.

"Come away, Emily Jean. It's not good to dwell too long on these sad things," Granna murmured, fidgeting nervously behind me.

"But isn't she beautiful?" I whispered, drawing her reluctantly forward to stand beside me. Her gaze flickered toward the casket and away again.

"She's — not as I pictured her," Granna admitted, a note of surprise in her voice.

Uncle Bob turned toward the undertaker, a small anxious-faced man who had been hovering in the doorway. "Has there been a visit from a Mrs. Vesta Lincoln? Has she had a chance to see Mrs. Knowles?"

"Er—that'd be the Negro woman? Yes, sir. In fact, she came in to—er—dress the body and arrange the hair."

"Good. Thank you."

"Yes, sir. Er—Father Murray is here, when you and the family are ready."

"All right."

Uncle Bob stood with his arm around my shoulders as he had in Grandmother's bedroom just three days before. I looked and looked, trying to imprint the dear features on my memory forever, fearful that I would forget them. I was glad to think that Vesta had been the one to "do" for her friend that one last time, and I wished she was with us now.

"Please come, Robert," I heard Granna whisper. "I can't bear to be in the presence of death. It reminds me . . ."

He squeezed my shoulders and gave me a questioning look. I nodded and sent a thought message of "I love you" toward the casket, and we turned away to greet Father Murray, the Catholic priest who was in charge of the funeral.

A youngish man with very pink skin, receding brown hair, and glasses greeted us kindly, and having been told that we were not Catholic, carefully explained what the procedure would be. We followed the hearse bearing the casket to a small white Catholic church, where Father Murray met us and preceded the casket into the church, sprinkling holy water and murmuring some phrases. This, he had explained, was symbolic of the soul entering into heaven. Granna and I, having put on the hats which we knew women and girls were expected to wear in a Catholic sanctuary, followed with Uncle Bob.

The church was dim and fairly cool inside. I knew that Granna was doing the same thing I was as we sat through the brief service, much of which I couldn't follow—we were letting our eyes wander, taking in the altar rail ("Just like the Methodists'," I heard Granna declare later), the altar with its embroidered cloth cover, and the large crucifix hanging behind the altar. At this hour, the morning sunlight shone through the one stained-glass window in such a way that it colored the wooden image of the drooping, dead Christ on the cross with vivid ambers and blues. It was beautiful but infinitely sad. I gazed at it while Father Murray celebrated the mass, then said a few kind things about Grandmother Knowles, whom he admitted he hadn't known very long or very well. But he had heard her confession and had administered the extreme unction of the Church to her not long before she died. He then offered a few words of comfort about the resurrection, which he had taken from the Bible and a prayer book.

Suddenly we were standing, and the service was over. There were only a handful of people at the church, because Grandmother hadn't actually attended mass there and become acquainted in the town. Somehow I had thought it would be the same at the cemetery, but as we pulled up to park at the gate, we saw a crowd of people, all dressed in their Sunday best, waiting for us.

My throat constricted as I recognized Zack and his daddy, the two elderly men from the store (Zack's grandpa, I remembered, who had once offered to marry the widow Knowles), a dark-haired lady who must be Mrs. Bramley, and a number of other folks I didn't recognize. Where was Vesta? I searched for her dark face among the lighter ones as we were ushered forward to take our places beside the grave. I was vaguely aware of Granna trying to hang back a bit, and I glanced at her. Her face was a study in conflict and confusion, and she was staring, not at the grave or the white brocade casket before us, but at the neighboring marker, which bore the name of Francis Knowles — my father and her son-in-law. Then she raised her eyes and peered through her bifocals at the people clustered quietly around us, as if wondering who in the world they could all be. Somehow, I felt I should be the one to comfort and welcome her here, and I slipped my hand into hers and squeezed. She looked at me distractedly, then reached to tuck a flyaway bit of hair back under my straw hat. She kept possession of my hand.

Finally, I spotted Vesta. Dressed in gleaming white, she carefully picked her way forward to speak to Uncle Bob. He listened attentively and nodded, and she turned away, but not before I caught her eye and motioned her to join us. She gave me a look of mingled longing and regret but shook her head slightly and retreated to a position several yards behind the edge of the crowd.

The day was getting hot and sticky, and many of the flowers that had been brought from yards and gardens to heap around the gravesite were already beginning to droop and wilt. A warm, sweet, aromatic fragrance drifted from the pine forest as did the cries of the rain crows and the rising chorus of cicadas — smells and sounds that would remind me always of this spot.

The prayers at the gravesite were brief, and when someone handed me a paper cup filled with soil, I knew it was nearly over. Two men stepped forward and turned the crank that allowed the casket to be lowered on straps into the ground.

"Ashes to ashes, dust to dust . . . " The words droned, but had little meaning to me. Father Murray tossed a handful of red clay into the grave, and I added my cupful as I had been instructed. But it seemed wrong somehow, as if we were dishonoring Grandmother's dear body just because it had worn out. Several ladies stepped forward to choose a flower to toss in too, and this pleased me better. I chose a bright red zinnia because I knew she and Vesta liked them. Self-consciously, I hesitated a moment, then kissed the petals and dropped the flower in after the others.

The priest's murmured benediction was nearly drowned out by old Mr. Hank Bramley, who said clearly, "Well, she was a good woman, even if she was a Yankee." It was a toss-up whether the subdued chorus of amens that followed put the stamp of approval on Mr. Hank's statement or Father Murray's prayer.

Uncle Bob, hiding what I suspected might be a smile behind a big white handkerchief, stepped aside for a moment to confer with the two men who had lowered the casket, and they nodded and retreated to lean against the fence in a shady spot. In the meantime, I found myself and Granna in a sort of receiving line, accepting the greetings and condolences of the people who had come to pay their respects. They all seemed to know who I was. Even Zack came through, solemnly shaking my hand and politely saying, "How do, Ma'am?" when I introduced him to Granna. She seemed about ready to sink into the earth herself, but she stood her ground and listened to everyone relating their memories of Grandmother Knowles and the kindnesses she or "young Frankie" had done them. When Uncle Bob appeared at her side, she gripped his arm and pleaded that the heat was making her feel faint, so we moved to the shade of a large tree, where she took off her hat and fanned her face with it.

Uncle Bob accompanied Father Murray to the gates, shook his hand, and started to walk back toward us when his attention was caught by the arrival of a gleaming black car, large enough to rival the hearse itself. The driver emerged and came around to assist a silver-haired lady from the back seat. And lady she was—no doubt of that. People stopped and frankly stared as she stepped forward, leaning on her chauffeur's arm, and looked about her in dismay.

"Oh, Arthur—I'm afraid we're moments too late," she cried. "Is Miss Emily Knowles still here? Or Mrs. Vesta Lincoln?"

Uncle Bob approached her. "Emily Knowles is right over here," he said politely, indicating our direction. "I am her uncle, Bob Markham. May I introduce you to her?"

"Yes, if you would, please. I'm her grandfather's sister, Cecily Whitestone."

I gasped.

"Who's that?" hissed Granna, pinning her hat back into place as they advanced toward us.

"It—it must be my Aunt Cecily—that is, my daddy's aunt."

"My mercy! Well, don't slouch, Emily Jean—stand up and speak up. I've trained you how to behave."

"Emily Jean," said Uncle Bob, "May I present your grandfather's sister—your great-aunt, Mrs. Cecily Whitestone."

Aunt Cecily looked so grand I felt I should drop a curtsey. Her silver hair was arranged in careful, shining waves under her navy blue pillbox hat, and she wore a navy blue suit with a faultless white silk blouse. Her pearls, I knew instinctively, were real. But it was her face that arrested my attention. Her brimming blue eyes were kind, and her lips were trembling as she tried to smile at me. She put out both gloved hands to touch my shoulders.

"Oh, my dear," she said. "You have such a look of her when she was young! And your hair—the exact color. Oh, I loved her so and admired her! She had such spirit and pride and generosity, and she made my brother so happy in his short life."

"Hello, Aunt Cecily," I ventured. "Grandmother told me about you. She loved you too."

She hugged me then. After all her travel, she still smelled cool and wonderful, even in the heat and dust. She released me and extended her hand to Granna with an expectant smile.

Granna responded. "I'm Ellen Markham, Emily Jean's maternal grandmother."

"Yes, I knew you must be. What a wonderful influence you've been in her life! Thank you for bringing her up so beautifully. Maureen wrote me how delighted she was, and how grateful."

"Oh, well—I did my duty. And it's been a pleasure, of course," Granna murmured, abashed.

"Now, where have they laid Maureen? Over there, I see. I'm so upset that we were late! I'd only been here once, and I'm afraid my memory played me a trick. I got my driver completely turned around, and we've been one step behind everyone all morning."

"Where have you traveled from, Mrs. Whitestone?" asked Uncle Bob.

"My home is in Maryland—Silver Spring. I don't know whether you'd be familiar with it. I wonder—do you think it would be appropriate for me to slip over and pay my respects to Maureen?"

"Allow me," responded Uncle Bob and offered his arm to assist her. Granna's expression was one of stunned amazement. They came back after a few minutes, Aunt Cecily patting tears away with a lace-edged handkerchief.

"I guess we're never quite ready to let our dear ones go, are we?" she murmured to Granna, as if they were old friends. "I'd so hoped to visit Maureen again, and then when Mrs. Lincoln called and I realized I wouldn't have that privilege in this life, I wished I had put off other obligations and made the effort. Now I only hope

I can be where she is in the next life. I've never known a finer woman."

A low keening sound reached our ears. It rose, fell, and rose again—a throaty cry that was half song, half moan of pure anguish and love. I recognized it—I had heard it once before when Vesta was scrubbing the kitchen floor. Turning toward the sound, I saw Vesta standing at the foot of the open grave, a little apart from another group of black women who were dressed in white too. Her song rose in a spiral of wordless pleading toward heaven. Her head was back, her eyes closed, her body straight and slender as that of a much younger woman. My eyes filled with tears, as they had not done during the formal service. Granna's voice came as a harsh whisper, breaking the silence that had fallen on all who were still in the cemetery.

"What in the world! Robert, you can't allow—what do they think they're doing?"

I answered softly, not wanting the spell to be broken. "It's all right, Granna. I know what they're doing—they're singing her home to glory. Vesta told me about it once. It's something they do in their church."

"Well, for one of their own, perhaps, but—"

Uncle Bob put an arm around her shoulder. "Just an expression of love and respect," he explained. "She was kind to them, and they to her."

"Respect!"

"Shh-h."

The other women had joined Vesta now, arms linked as they swayed back and forth and joined their voices in a song that was familiar to me. They started softly, and then the song increased in rhythm and joy: "I got a home in Glory-land that outshines the sun, way beyond the blue. Do Lord, oh, do Lord, oh, do remember me . . ." In my heart I sang with them as we made our way to our cars.

Aunt Cecily turned back for a last look. "We'll see Vesta at the house, won't we?" she asked.

Surprisingly, it was Zack Bramley's daddy who answered. "Yes, ma'am, she's been asked to be there, along with Emily Jean here and Mr. Markham. Reckon they're gonna read the will after we all take dinner."

"Will!" Granna turned to Uncle Bob, who smiled and gave a small shrug. Granna looked a little disgruntled. This had been a day of surprises for her, and she had never been overly comfortable with surprises.

I didn't know much about wills myself, but I associated them with wealth and family feuds. That didn't seem to relate to this situation, so I was curious and a little afraid—glad, however, to be going back to Grandmother Knowles's house for midday dinner. At least that sounded normal and appealing. Not to Granna, though, because she said, "Robert, I'd feel more comfortable getting a bite at a cafe, if there's one within driving distance. I don't think a house of mourning is the appropriate place—"

"I don't know of a cafe within twenty miles, Mom. And just think of the hundreds of cakes and hams and pies you've supplied over the years for funeral-day meals. Besides, when in Rome . . ."

I didn't know what Rome had to do with it, but Granna must have, because she subsided into her corner of the car with a sigh. The house seemed different crowded with strangers, their cars standing around the front yard. Most of them stood stiffly in the living room or on the porch, talking in subdued tones as we approached. I hardly knew any of them, except Zack and his family, and even his mother and sisters were strangers to me. Everyone seemed to know who I was, though, and they stepped forward, one by one, to tell me again how sorry they had been to hear of Grandmother's passing and what a fine woman she had been. Mrs. Bramley came out of the kitchen, wiping her hands on a dish cloth, and hugged me.

"I'm so glad you came in time—it eased her last days so much," she whispered.

"I'm glad I could, too." We followed her into the kitchen, where the table was filled with dishes of meats and salads, chicken and rice, fried corn and sliced ripe tomatoes. There was blackberry cobbler and banana pudding and layer cake.

"Reckon there's enough food, Zack?" Mrs. Bramley peered out doors and windows to assess the gathering crowd. "I could stir up a batch of biscuits real quick."

"I reckon there's aplenty," Zack told her. "Miz Burch is comin' with a big bowl of potater salad and some butter beans — I just saw her. And Miz Luster's got a covered basket that looks to be full of bread rolls or biscuits."

"My," breathed Granna, allowing her gaze to travel from the table around the spotless, if somewhat shabby, kitchen. "People certainly have been generous."

"Yes, ma'am. Miz Knowles had a passel of friends," Mrs. Bramley agreed. "More than she knew, I reckon."

I took Granna's hand and led her through the hallway and into the back bedroom. "This was my daddy's room, where he grew up."

She gave a quick, frowning glance at the narrow bed, the book-shelves, the picture of the howling sheepdog.

"And this," I continued, pulling her across the hall and opening the other door, "is Grandmother Knowles's room. Only it doesn't look right. She wouldn't like it all dim and closed up like this."

"Emily Jean!" Granna gasped as I went to fling open a window and raise the shade so that sunlight and pine-scented summer air filled the room. I pulled the rocking chair close to the window and sat down, rocking defiantly.

"This is the way she liked it," I said with satisfaction. Granna clung to the doorframe, looking fearfully around the room as though she expected to see the ghost of the woman who had died there.

"Emily Jean," she whispered. "Come *on* — it isn't right!"

"I like it in here," I insisted. "This is the only place I ever saw her. I can remember her better in here."

"I — know. But, please — "

"You'd have liked her, Granna. Honestly, you would."

"Please — please come away, Emily Jean."

I rose, stilled the rocker, and obeyed. Granna closed the door quietly behind us.

After all the white guests had partaken of the wonderful food —
Granna had to remind me that the bereaved shouldn't show excessive
appetite — Vesta allowed her black friends to slip into the kitchen
and fix plates for themselves. Then they grouped together on the
back porch to eat. Aunt Cecily watched this proceeding with a funny
quirk to her mouth, but Granna seemed to see nothing amiss.

As I finished my banana pudding, I felt the magnetic pull of
someone's gaze upon me and looked around. Sure enough, Zack
was trying to attract my attention without seeming to do so. He gave
a little sideways jerk of his head that I knew meant, "Come outside.
I want to talk to you."

I set my dish in the sink and slipped out the back door. The
sunlight was dazzling on the white dresses of Vesta and her friends,
and I thought how much nicer that was than the somber dark colors
worn inside the house. "Y'all sung real pretty," I said shyly. "I just
know my grandmother appreciated that." The ladies murmured politely and shifted aside to make a path down the steps for me. I
circled around the house and met Zack in the sketchy shade of a
tall pine, out of sight of the living room and kitchen.

"I gotta go tend the store," he said. "Daddy closed up for the
funeral, but he wants me to open up now, 'case anybody wants
anything on the way home."

"Oh."

"Think you'll be comin' back anymore, now your Granny's
gone?"

"I don't know. I want to real bad, but I doubt Granna'll let me without a good reason."

"Well—be nice iffen you could. I mean—it'd make Miz Vesta Lincoln real happy."

"Make me happy too. It'll be a little lonesome without Grandmother—but she did say she'd always be here for me. Not—you know—not like a ghost or anything. Just like a memory."

Zack kicked a tree root with the toe of his shoe. "Reckon her memory'll be here for me too. She was always real nice to me."

"You were good to her—checking on her and bringing her fish and stuff."

I looked at him as he shrugged this off. I'd never seen him before in anything but overalls or cut-off jeans and a faded shirt. Now he wore dark blue pants and a short-sleeved white shirt. His skin looked darker than ever in contrast with the shirt, and the sprinkle of freckles had all but disappeared into his tan. Suddenly, I realized that I might never see Zack again. Something inside me rebelled mightily at that notion, and I couldn't shake the sense of loss it brought. I wanted to reach out and grasp his hard brown boy's hand, but I felt my ears and cheeks burn at the very idea. He moved restlessly, and I knew he was getting ready to go.

"How are the kittens doing?" I asked, to stay the moment a little longer. His smile was swift and white.

"Funny little buzzards—they're up and ready to be took home. Fact, one already went home with Miz Leachy to be a barn cat. Not yours, though. Nobody seems to fancy her much but you and me."

"Wish I could see her. Reckon I could slip away and walk up to the store with you, just for a minute?"

"You might could, 'cept—look yonder."

A shiny dark green car was pulling into the yard.

"Who's that?"

"Reckon it's the lawyer with the will and all. Daddy says you gotta be here for that."

"Why would I need to be here? I don't know anything about

wills. I could be back by the time they got through, and I bet they'd never know I was gone."

"My daddy says it's likely your granny done left you somethin' nice in her will. Reckon you'd better be around for that."

I stared at him. It hadn't occurred to me that there might be anything for me in the will. I'd just assumed wills were for grown-ups.

"So—reckon you'd best stay. But maybe when y'all get ready to go, you could stop by the store for a minute and see the kitten then."

"Maybe. I can try."

"Okay. Well—reckon I'd best skedaddle. Daddy's expectin' me to open." He rattled the keys importantly in his pocket.

I nodded. "Bye."

"See ya later."

"Okay."

I watched him go, straight and slim in his unaccustomed Sunday clothes. He paused out by the bank of honeysuckle and turned, calling out something I couldn't quite catch except for the last two words—"... still cousins?"

I nodded vigorously, and he waved and disappeared.

The arrival of the lawyer, Mr. Radcliffe, was a signal for the neighbors and guests to take their leave. Those of us who constituted "family and legatees" were asked to seat ourselves in the living room. Granna made a move to go sit in the car, but Mr. Radcliffe stopped her, saying that as my legal guardian, it was appropriate for her to be there. He summoned Vesta from the kitchen, and, taking off the long apron that covered her white dress, she sat down on a straight chair beside the kitchen door.

Zack's daddy was there too, and Aunt Cecily and Uncle Bob. Mr. Radcliffe called us each by our full names, examined us lengthily, then finally sighed deeply and picked up the will. I felt he had somehow found us all sadly lacking. Granna fidgeted, and I tried not to. Uncle Bob cleared his throat and leaned back, one arm along the back of the sofa. Aunt Cecily gazed lovingly around the room, and Mr. Bramley leaned forward, his elbows resting on his knees, a slight frown between his eyes. Vesta sat perfectly still, her face serene and composed, but every little while her eyes would wander toward the window. I wondered if she longed to be out in the sunshine as I did, where the cicadas and rain crows were beginning their afternoon plea for moisture.

I jumped as Mr. Radcliffe began to speak. "As you know, we are met here today to carry out the wishes of the deceased, Mrs. Maureen McCullough Knowles, with regard to the disposition of her earthly goods. To wit, and I quote from the document: 'I, Maureen Mc-Cullough Knowles, being of sound mind and memory, but weak in body and well-stricken in years, do make and ordain this to be my last will and testament . . . ' "

It wasn't really long, but even so, my mind wandered from the formal legal language, and I nearly missed the part that pertained to me. Mr. Radcliffe paused, took off his glasses, and kindly explained to me that Grandmother Knowles had given me her house and property, with the stipulation that Mrs. Vesta Lincoln be allowed to live there for the rest of her natural life, or for as long as she desired to do so.

How wonderful! I looked at Vesta. She continued to sit perfectly still, but now tears ran unheeded down her cheeks and dripped onto the bodice of her dress.

Mr. Bramley was named executor of the will and guardian of the little money that was in the estate, which he was charged to use judiciously and carefully for the upkeep of the house and land, so long as it would suffice. There was also a sum of five hundred dollars to go to him for his services as executor and for his many kindnesses to her during her life.

"I—uh, I don't have to accept that, do I, Mr. Radcliffe? She was a friend, you understand. I don't need no pay for nothin' I done for a friend."

Mr. Radcliffe smiled. "She apparently anticipated that you might feel that way, Mr. Bramley, and she instructed me to tell you that if you won't accept it for yourself, she requested that you do so on behalf of your son—Zachary, is it?—toward his future education."

Mr. Bramley put his head down and shook it slowly, but he made no further protest.

Aunt Cecily was to be given several small personal items. Vesta was to receive five hundred dollars, several books, including *The Adventures of Huckleberry Finn,* and all of Grandmother's clothes, to be worn or distributed to the needy as she saw fit. There was a donation to the Zion Cemetery maintenance committee for upkeep of the graves, and everything else, including everything in the house and barn, was mine. There was one other stipulation: I wasn't to sell the property until I was at least twenty-one years of age, unless the proceeds were judged by Granna, Uncle Bob, and Mr. Bramley to be urgently needed for my personal health or education.

I sat stunned. It never occurred to me that as the only living heir, the place would one day be mine—*mine*—my own house! Surely Granna wouldn't say I couldn't come to visit my own house—and Vesta would be here to take care of me. As for selling, I didn't plan ever to do that.

Finally, the necessary papers were signed and witnessed, and Mr. Radcliffe rose to leave. He shook hands with each of us, and I ran to Vesta and hugged her. She guardedly returned my embrace in front of these white strangers.

"Oh, Vesta, it's so perfect that you'll still be living here! You will, won't you?"

"I be here, me. That what your sweet granny wanted, and that's what I do." Her lips stretched in a smile. "And I tell you true, honey, it do relieve my mind to know I don't have to go back down the hill and live with that passel of noisy grandbabies of mine! Much as I love 'em, I believe we all be better off with short visits."

I laughed and hugged her again, then caught Granna's eye. Her lips were pressed together in a way that promised, "You'll hear from me later, young lady."

I moved away from Vesta and went to speak to Aunt Cecily, who was gathering up her purse and gloves. She drew me to her and approached Granna with me. "What a kind and wonderful young lady you've reared, Mrs. Markham. I'm hoping you might agree to send her to me sometime soon for a visit to my home in Maryland. I'd so love to show her around our area and introduce her to our side of her family. I have several granddaughters close to her age — her second cousins — who would be so pleased to meet her, and who would profit greatly from observing her beautiful manners."

Aunt Cecily was a born diplomat. Granna couldn't find a polite way to refuse. "How very kind of you," she said slowly. "It would be a fine opportunity for her — perhaps when she's just a little older."

Aunt Cecily turned to me. "In the meantime, we'll keep in touch, shall we? Will you write to me, Emily?"

"Oh, yes, ma'am — I'd be happy to."

"Thank you, my dear. I'll look forward to that."

The moment finally came when we left Vesta waving tearfully on the front porch and bumped down the sand-and-clay road to the highway.

"Um — Uncle Bob — do you think we could stop for just a minute at Bramley's store? I mean — don't you need some gas or something?"

Uncle Bob peered at his fuel gauge. He didn't really need gas — I could see that from where I hung over the back of the front seat — but he said, "Well, it wouldn't hurt to top off the tank. Then I won't have to remember to buy some tomorrow."

He pulled up to the rusty pump, and I was out of the car before Granna could say more than "Emily Jean, I hope you're not — "

I could see Zack through the screen door as he slipped down from his perch on the high stool behind the counter. "Hey — you did get to stop by!" he called, sounding pleased.

I grinned at him. "Uncle Bob wants some gas," I reported, "and I want to see my kitten."

He stepped out onto the porch. "She's right there," he said as the screen door swung shut behind him. I looked where he indicated, and there was the kitten, snuggled side by side with her mother like a major and minor sphinx atop a feed bag.

"Hi, baby cat," I crooned, touching her funny orange and black fur, and she began to purr. I stroked Polly, the mother cat, so she'd know I was a friend, and she put up her head for my caress. "Oh,

I wish I could take you home and keep you for my very own," I whispered. "I know Granna'd never allow it—she doesn't much like cats—but I do. Let's go show you to her anyway." I lifted the kitten, who purred louder and snuggled under my chin as if she understood my affection. Zack had told me that cats knew who liked them and who didn't. He said dogs expected everybody to like them.

The kitten's gray-green eyes narrowed against the sunlight as we approached the car. Her tiny claws clung to my dress, but her purr never wavered.

"Look, Granna, isn't she cute?"

"Oh, my mercy, Emily Jean, why are you handling that filthy thing? Who knows what disease you could pick up, and think of the fleas!"

"She's not dirty, Granna. She's lived in the store all her life, and her mama's a real clean cat. Look at her fur—isn't she different? I think she's real pretty."

"Ugly as sin, I'd say. I've seen a few cats I thought were handsome, but that's not one of them."

"I don't know," Uncle Bob said, scratching the kitten under its chin. "Looks like there's a long-haired ancestor somewhere in its pedigree, and it's kind of cute how the colors divide right down the middle of its nose."

"Well, that's unusual, all right. Go put it back, Emily Jean—we don't want to hold Robert up unnecessarily."

"Oh, we've got a minute," Uncle Bob said, winking at me. "I think I'd better check my tires while I'm here. Can I get you a cold drink, Mom?"

"How long are you going to be?"

"Oh—long enough for a lemon soda."

"Well—all right. It is a warm afternoon."

Zack finished with the gas and accompanied Uncle Bob into the store. I stood in the shade and cuddled the kitten, talking to it until it pulled its little head back and gazed seriously up into my face.

"Well, my word, Emily Jean, you've got the creature mesmerized."

"She's so sweet, Granna. I think she remembers me. I've known her ever since she was newborn. She was my favorite out of the whole litter."

"Oh, cats just respond to anybody who'll stroke them. A cat is all for itself, I've always said."

"I've never really been around them much. In fact," I added wistfully, "I've never had a pet of my own."

"Well, they're a lot of work and trouble, and I know exactly who that work and trouble would fall on."

"Oh, Granna, it wouldn't, honest—you'd never have to feed her or clean up after her or anything. I'd do it all, I really would. I'm responsible, you know I am—I'd take care of her!"

"And I've heard that before too," Granna said, with a significant glance at Uncle Bob, who chuckled as he handed her a slim bottle of lemon soda.

"Well, now—I know you're remembering that little puppy that followed me home when I was about nine or ten. But don't hold E. J. responsible for what I did—or didn't do."

"That dog chewed a hole in the corner of my best damask Sunday tablecloth, then proceeded to relieve itself in a corner of the dining room. And we were expecting guests to Sunday dinner right after church!"

"I know," Uncle Bob said sheepishly. "It was all because I forgot to put it out before we left for church that morning."

"It was all because I was foolish enough to allow you to keep the creature in the first place!"

I exchanged bleak looks with Zack. This wasn't going well.

"How old did you say you were, Mr. Markham, when that happened?" Zack asked respectfully.

"Let's see—it was when I had my paper route, and I gave that up when I broke my leg, which was the day after my tenth birthday— so I was nine."

"So—" I took up the train of thought quickly. "I'm nearly twelve—three whole years older, almost."

"And a girl," Zack added. "My mama says girls grow up and take better care of things a long sight sooner than boys. 'Course, boys catch up," he added, in response to my surprised glance.

"Cats catch songbirds," Granna said, dabbing at her mouth with her hanky. "I've never been able to forgive them that."

"And mice," Zack added, nodding solemnly. "Polly does a good job keeping our store free from mice. My daddy says he wouldn't be without a cat for nothin'."

"Well, I don't *think* we have mice at our place. But we do have a passel of songbirds all year long, and I'd just hate to have a vicious cat run them away."

Uncle Bob stood up from checking the air in the tire. "It is distressing to see a cat harm a bird," he agreed. "But then I always remember who gave them that instinct, and I try not to criticize."

Granna looked taken aback.

Uncle Bob continued. "A lot of very knowledgeable people seem to feel it's healthy for a child to have a pet to care for. It gives them some idea of the effort and responsibility involved in parenting— to a lesser degree, of course. It's even better than dolls, so I've heard. A child can put a doll down for days at a time and not feed or care for it, but an animal depends on people for its very life—like a baby."

"My mama says a well-fed cat is too lazy to chase birds," Zack put in. "So maybe iffen it was fed real good, it wouldn't bother 'em none."

Granna looked sharply from Uncle Bob to Zack and back again. "Do I understand, Robert, that you think I should allow Emily Jean to take this little thing back to Tatum with us?"

Uncle Bob shrugged, and Zack began vigorously cleaning the windshield. "It's totally up to you, Mom. All I'm thinking is that E. J. hasn't had it too easy lately. Maybe a little cat to love and make over would do her good. But it's up to you—don't let me influence you one way or the other."

Granna's lips pressed together, and she frowned out across the green field where Mr. Parker Savage's barn used to be. I held my breath.

"I wouldn't allow it in the house," she warned.

"Oh, Granna, thank you! You won't be sorry! I'll take perfect care of her." I dived toward the window to kiss her cheek, but she pulled back.

"Keep that thing out of my face, child! I don't want to get clawed! Now get a box for it to travel in, or I won't allow it in Robert's car."

Zack dropped his cloth, and we made a beeline for the store. He punched a few small air holes in a cardboard box and fitted it with a clean, folded burlap sack.

"I can't believe she's letting me have it!" I rejoiced. "Thanks, Zack, you helped convince her."

He shrugged but looked pleased. "Reckon you couldn'ta got nowhere iffen your uncle wasn't for it though. He's okay—for a preacher."

"I told you he was nice. Now help me think of a good name for the kitten."

Zack regarded the little cat as she sniffed the corners of the box. "Well, to me she looks just like the burned-out cinders from that old potbelly stove yonder. Her colorin', I mean—all orangey and rusty black. So maybe Cinder, or—"

"Cinderella!" I shouted. "Because even though she looks like she's been mopping up the fireplace, she'll grow up to be beautiful and good."

"Okay, cat," Zack admonished the kitten. "You got a lot to live up to."

. . . . 30 . . . .

Unaccustomed to the darkness of the box and the motion of the car, Cinderella cried plaintively until I worked my hand through the folded-down lid and comforted her. She slept then, and before many miles, so did I. I roused as we pulled into the driveway, memories of the emotion-charged day returning as I carefully carried the kitten's box around to the back porch and lifted her out to explore her new home.

"Emily Jean, come and change out of your good dress before you start playing with that cat."

"Oh — sorry, kitty, back you go in the box — but just for a minute. I'll be right back."

I made good on my promise, changing into shorts as quickly as I could, but taking time to fold my dress carefully into the laundry hamper. After what Granna had done for me that day, I didn't want to do anything to displease her. Besides, I had learned that grand-mothers were not permanent fixtures in this world, no matter how firmly entrenched they seemed. Parents weren't either, of course — but I had always known that.

Cinderella cautiously walked the perimeter of the porch, pausing midstride to gaze in fascination at a scolding jay that teetered on a crepe myrtle branch.

"No, no," I told her gently. "Don't pay any mind to those old birds — they're trouble for you."

She continued her inspection, sniffing and touching things she didn't understand. She stared for a long moment at Granna's clothespin basket, as if expecting it to stand up and walk away. Then she slowly raised one paw, hit it a challenging slap, leaped backward, and hissed. I laughed out loud. There was a sound suspiciously like a chuckle from the back door, and when I turned, Granna was disappearing into the kitchen.

After dinner—a simple meal of pancakes and sausage—I helped Granna clear up and played again with Cinderella. Uncle Bob joined me on the back porch, teasing the kitten with a twist of newspaper on the end of a string. She finally tired of chasing it, climbed onto my lap, and went to sleep.

"I expect you're probably about that tired too, aren't you, E. J.?" Uncle Bob asked, locking his hands behind his head and leaning back against the leg of Granna's washer. "I know I am."

"It's kind of funny," I admitted, "but I'm not tired. I feel—I don't know—good somehow. Like I want to run or do something real active. I don't know why."

"Well, you've had a lot on your mind lately. Some strong feelings have been chasing each other around your head too. I expect you're still keyed-up."

"But it doesn't seem right to feel happy and like running when—when my Grandmother Knowles is—dead and can't do anything."

"Oh, I don't know about that. Maybe she can do more—enjoy more right now than she's been able to for years—maybe forever, for all we know. I expect you're just rejoicing with her."

"I reckon. Uncle Bob?"

"M-mm?"

"This funeral today sure was a lot different than the one for Miss Mary Afton's mama, wasn't it?"

"Yep, it sure was. Very different."

"Which one did you like the best?"

He narrowed his eyes, considering. "Well, in each case, I think the important thing was that a lot of love was shown for the lady who died. I liked the natural warmth of the people today at the cemetery, and the send-off that Vesta and her friends gave Mrs. Knowles was quite touching. But I surely was impressed with a lot of the doctrine preached at Mrs. MacDougal's. There was such a good, positive feeling there — sort of a deep happiness that overrode the understandable sadness of the occasion. I can't quite figure — unless . . . "

He paused, deep in thought. I knew he had started out answering my question, but along the way he had forgotten me and started talking to himself. It didn't bother me — I was used to it. I sat gazing at Cinderella, still filled with wonder that she was actually here with me in Tatum, and I was allowed to keep her.

"Hey, Knowles! Wanta play softball? We need an outfielder."

I looked up. It was Junior Bailey, calling across the hedge from Fred Silver's yard. I glanced at Uncle Bob.

"Uh — I don't know," I responded. "I kind of do, but . . . "

"Might be just what you need," Uncle Bob said, "a chance to run and be active, like you wanted."

Granna spoke from the door. "I hardly think it's appropriate to consider playing sports on the very day you've buried a — a loved one, do you, Robert?"

"Oh, I don't know, Mom. Maybe in this case it's just the thing to ease her back into the normal life of a little girl again. And I could stroll along and keep an eye on her."

I started to protest that I wasn't exactly a little girl anymore, but I decided that that might squelch my chances of playing, which I suddenly wanted to do very much, so I kept quiet.

"Well, if you think so, Robert. Perhaps some exercise would do her good. But you be home, Emily Jean, well before dark!"

"Yes'm, I will. Thanks." I deposited the sleeping kitten carefully in her box and took off with the two boys for the schoolyard. I couldn't throw as far as most of them, but I could hit and catch with the best, and they knew it. I would have preferred to pitch or play shortstop, but I didn't quibble. It was enough to be there, perspiring in the early evening sun, breathing the red dust that rose from the bases as I skidded to a halt, and feeling the satisfyingly solid *thwack* of my bat against the ball. Sweet though I had learned they could be, I'd had my fill of age and dying.

Sunday evening, we sat in the mission church, listening to Uncle Bob preach. I sat between Star and Granna, idly fanning myself with the Kickliter Hardware fan and trying to ignore the trickles of perspiration that kept dampening the edges of my hair and tracing the outline of my spine.

Uncle Bob spoke of the Bible—of how it came to be, how valuable it had been to people through the ages, and how it continued to be so to us. He explained how it told of God's dealings with his chosen people in the Old Testament and quoted many of the prophecies that were fulfilled with the coming of Jesus. He showed how the story of Jesus' earthly life and ministry and the ministries of his chosen apostles were detailed in the New Testament, together with the promise that someday the living Lord would return to earth to meet his faithful followers.

"And I know that will take place one day, my friends, just as he promises. The Bible is a true book—the word of God. Now I don't know whether the Lord has ever given other inspired words to other peoples or whether he ever will. Some Bible scholars say the canon of scripture is closed, that the Bible is all we'll ever have or ever need. But others say that God is just as capable of giving further scripture to us, should it be needed, as he ever was. In fact, some folks expect that to happen.

"I do know that the Lord will answer our prayers if we ask him humbly for help and inspiration. He says in James, 'If any of you lack wisdom, let him ask of God, who giveth to all men liberally, and upbraideth not; and it shall be given him. But let him ask in faith, nothing wavering.' Maybe the answers that we get to such prayers, when we ask in faith, become like personal scriptures to us for our own inspiration and edification. Maybe in that sense, the canon of scripture is not closed. And if the Lord ever sees fit to give us further volumes of his holy word, I, for one, will welcome them. But in the meantime, we know the Holy Bible is his word..."

Beside me, Granna's fan had stilled. I stole a glance at her. A small pucker had appeared between her eyebrows, and she gazed at her son speculatively. I knew she had something on her mind that Uncle Bob would hear about, and I was right.

"Robert, dear," she began, when we were on the highway again, heading home in the relative cool of the evening. "I wanted to ask you to clarify something for me. You were speaking tonight as if you thought perhaps God might one day add to the holy scriptures. Pastor Welch has always preached the sufficiency of the Bible, and quoted Revelation where it says something about if any man shall add to the things in this book, he'll have plagues added unto him, or something of that nature. Has the thinking changed at seminary on that matter?"

Uncle Bob didn't answer for a minute. Then he threw Granna a smile. "That's my good Mom, keeping me honest," he said. "No, to my knowledge, the attitude at seminary hasn't changed on the sufficiency of the Bible. But I think we need to remember that the Bible is not really a book in and of itself, so much as it is a collection of books — a library. In fact, that's what the word Bible means — a library. It's God's library of holy books, written by his chosen servants. And you see, research has shown that John wrote the book of Revelation before some of the other books of the New Testament were written. So I think we can safely assume that the warning not to add to or take from the prophecies in that book refers only to Revelation itself. In fact, there's a similar warning in Deuteronomy, and we're not going to throw out everything that came after it, are we? That would include the whole New Testament and a great deal of the Old."

Granna looked at Uncle Bob for a long moment, then smiled in satisfaction. "I knew you'd have a good explanation," she said. "Perhaps you might have included that in your sermon, dear — although I really rather doubt that any of those folks would have thought to question it as I did. And you know, Robert, I can't help thinking that they might respond to a little more — oh, you know — um, fire in your preaching. Not that I don't appreciate your quiet, thoughtful way of speaking, but you know that most country folk expect a — well, a more forceful type of delivery."

"Do you think so? Has anyone complained?"

"Oh, no, dear—they love you. It's just my own suggestion."

Uncle Bob frowned at the road ahead. After a minute, he said, "Well, I'm afraid I may not be much of a fire-and-brimstone type of preacher. In fact, when it comes right down to it, I might be more of a teacher than a preacher."

Pat spoke up. "But somebody does come forward nearly every time, either to be saved or to rededicate his life. And that's what counts, isn't it?"

"Of course it is," Granna said. "You're absolutely right, dear." Pat blushed under Granna's approving eyes.

Two days later Cinderella and I were entertaining each other on the front porch when Mr. Miller brought the mail. I was delighted to see LaRae's round blue writing on one of the envelopes, and tore the letter open eagerly.

Dear Emily,

Thanks for your last letter and for the cute paper dolls. I like them, and now they live with mine and they're friends, like us. (At least that's how I like to think of it.)

Doug wrote and said that you went to a funeral where he gave a talk. I'm glad. He said he was scared because he never talked at a funeral before. I'll bet it helped to see a friend there. That's what I do when I have to give a talk and I'm scared. I just look for my friend Patty and talk to her.

That hurricane you had sounds real scary. Doug said all the missionaries prayed real hard that nobody would get hurt, and nobody did that they knew. I'm sure glad you weren't home when that branch came through your window, aren't you?

You asked what Primary is. Its where we go after school one day and have classes at church for the kids up to age twelve. We learn about Jesus and the gospel and stuff, and sing songs and sometimes we have parties and activities and like that. Its fun, I like it alot. I wish you could go with me.

You wanted to know what a temple is for. Well, its like where people get married for time and eternity, not just while their on earth. And where kids can get sealed to their parents, too. Like, I had this other little sister who died, she was just a year younger than me so I can't remember her because I was only two when she died, but after that my Mom and Dad, they had never been married in the temple but just for this life, by a judge, and they wanted all of us to be a family forever, so they got worthy and when I was four we went to the Idaho Falls temple and got sealed together, and my little sister too. My aunt Rachel (my sister was named for her) took my sister's place and we all kneeled down around this sort of cushiony altar and held hands and a man sort of said a prayer that made it so we won't be separated up in heaven when we die, but we'll still be a family there too. I can just barely remember being there. We were all dressed in nice white clothes and it was real pretty in there, I remember that. And afterwards we all went out and got ice cream sundaes. I hope that makes some sense. They do baptisms in the temple, too, and I don't know what else.

Appaloosa horses are gray with sort of white spots on them, like a cloudy sky, thats why my horse is named Stormy. She is sure fun to ride, I wish you could ride her too. I would let you have turns.

I guess thats all for now. Thanks again for the paper dolls. Write back soon.

love,

LaRae

I leaned back against a porch pillar and watched Cinderella bat at the torn envelope flap, but my mind wasn't on her playing. I was trying to make sense of LaRae's explanation of what went on in Mormon temples. I liked the idea of families staying families in heaven—that part sounded right—but I didn't understand the part about being sealed together. The only kind of sealing I knew anything about included the use of glue or wax. Then, too, LaRae admitted she didn't know about everything that went on in the temples, which was what I had suspected all along. I wondered how I could tell her what I had learned. Primary sounded all right—not too different from my Girls' Auxiliary meetings—and she said they learned about Jesus, so it couldn't be all bad. But I would have to do some discreet study and question-asking to be able to help her with the temple business. I wondered if there was some way I could get Miss Mary Afton to talk to me about it—if I ever saw her again. How in the world, I wondered, could someone as wonderful as Miss Mary Afton be deceived into being a Mormon? And Doug was nice too, and Elder Comstock—and Uncle Bob had said that most of the Mormons he had known had been outstanding people. It didn't figure.

I scooped up Cinderella and my letter and headed for the back-yard, where Granna was picking a basin of pole beans for dinner. I slipped my letter under a pot of caladiums on the porch and set the kitten down on the grass. She thought grass was strange stuff, having been brought up on wood floors, and picked her way among the blades with high-stepping caution. I started helping to pick beans.

"Granna, do you believe we'll be together as families in heaven?"

Granna gave me a quick, assessing glance through the bottom of her bifocals. "Those that make it to that blessed state, maybe," she replied. "At least, I hope to be with my loved ones. That is, if we even recognize one another as individuals in the hereafter, which I've never been perfectly clear on. It may be that we'll all be so caught up in praising and worshiping the Lord that we won't even pay attention to one another. But in my present mortal way of thinking, I surely do hope to see your grandfather again, and Mother and Father—and others. Land, Emily Jean, you do ask the most impossible questions sometimes! What gets your young head thinking on these things?"

"I don't know. Questions just pop into my head. Um — Granna? When could we start to look through your box of pictures and label them? I'd really like to learn about your side of the family."

"Oh — well, once I get these beans on to cook for tonight, maybe I could spare a few minutes for that. Be sure you get the most mature beans, Emily Jean. I don't want a lot of tough old pods hanging on the vine and sapping strength from the young growth."

Later, we spent a pleasant hour with old snapshots as well as studio portraits spread over the kitchen table, separating and labeling them according to generation and place on the family tree. Granna seemed to open up and relax as she told me of the lives and personalities pictured before us, chuckling at some and growing a bit misty-eyed over others. I could now attach faces to names that I only vaguely remembered hearing over the years, and Granna promised to buy an album for the photographs and a notebook in which I could record her memories of her family history.

. . . . 31 . . . .

The next Sunday after morning worship service, I caught up to Mrs. Chapman in the hallway of the education building and asked her if Miss Mary Afton had returned from Maryland.

"She's expected in tomorrow evening on the nine-twenty bus," Mrs. Chapman said. "And I do hope she's had a good rest. That poor child was absolutely exhausted after these last weeks."

"Is she — is she going to move away?"

"Well, I suppose she'll tell us that when she gets back. I rather expect she will — unless, of course, a really good reason to stay happens along — if you know what I mean."

I didn't, but obviously Mrs. Chapman thought I should, so I returned her smile and tried to look knowledgeable.

"Um — Mrs. Chapman, I wonder do you know — "

"*If* you know. I wonder *if* you know. Know what, Emily Jean?"

" 'S'ma'am. I wonder if you know why Miss Mary Afton is a — a Mormon. I mean, she seems so nice and all, like she was a real Christian, and she's smart too, and I just — "

Mrs. Chapman smoothed her black hair and tucked a strand of it under her hat, glancing backwards over her shoulder as she did so and speaking in a lowered voice. "It's been my experience, Emily Jean, that Mormons are just as good Christians as Baptists or Methodists or anybody — and Mary Afton MacDougal is one of the finest of them. She knows her Bible and she loves the Lord, and I've never met a higher-principled young woman in my life. That's not to say I agree with all her beliefs, but then I don't agree with the Presbyterians or the Catholics or even the Free Will Baptists on everything either. Now don't tell anyone I said that, because I'd be in Dutch for sure. But you can rest your mind about Miss Mary Afton. The girl's a Christian, all right."

"Thanks," I said, feeling a degree of relief at Mrs. Chapman's assessment. She should know, I reasoned; she was Miss Mary Afton's landlady and coteacher at school.

At the mission church that evening, the heat was so oppressive that everyone seemed wilted and unable to sing or even listen with much enthusiasm. Uncle Bob tried to liven things up a little by telling more stories than usual and by putting Granna's fire-and-brimstone suggestion into practice, but I didn't think his heart was in it. Finally, he closed his sermon early, and after a brief invitational hymn, during which no one went forward, the service ended, and people filed gratefully out into the breathless air, flapping handkerchiefs at their perspiring faces.

"Warm evenin', Preacher," one man commented, as he shook Uncle Bob's hand.

"You're faithful to come to meeting on a night like this, Mr. Brazeal."

Mr. Brazeal chuckled. "It's hot, sure enough, but I reckon the fires of hell'd be a mite hotter."

"Likely so," Uncle Bob agreed, smiling.

"Unquenchable," Granna put in, standing proudly by Uncle Bob.

"Yes, ma'am. Preacher, you reckon them fires are real? I mean, is there an actual place with a lake of fire and brimstone?"

"Well, such a thing is surely mentioned in the Bible several times, but whether there's a physical place where sinners suffer physical torture, or a spiritual condition where they suffer spiritual torments as painful as fire, I don't really know. I guess the thing for you and me, Mr. Brazeal, is to make sure we never have occasion to find out firsthand."

"That's right, that's right," Mr. Brazeal agreed, chuckling.

"Robert, sometimes you astonish me," Granna said, when he was out of earshot. "Can it be good for a preacher to admit he doesn't know the meaning of a passage of holy scripture? These are simple people — they need firm, strong leadership."

Uncle Bob sighed and gazed out over the pine-dotted landscape. "I wish I could give it to them," he said. "I wish I had all the answers I need. But to tell you the truth, Mom, my questions sometimes outweigh my answers."

It was so close to what Grandmother Knowles had once said that I glanced at him in surprise. Like Granna, I had thought he was the definitive authority on anything to do with the Bible.

"Well, surely at seminary they supply you with answers, don't they?" Granna asked.

"You might be surprised at how much diversity there is, even at seminary. Practically every person who opens the Bible interprets it a little differently, even among the faculty."

"Well, that doesn't seem right. The Apostle Paul said there should be one Lord, one faith, and one baptism."

"But unfortunately, in this imperfect world, the gap between what is and what should be is a pretty big one."

"Maybe so," Granna retorted, "but Paul also said 'If the trumpet give an uncertain sound, who shall prepare himself to the battle?' Seems to me you preachers are the trumpeters, and you ought to all give out the same clear sound so folks can know what to believe and how to prepare."

Uncle Bob nodded. "That's true enough," he said. "Now if we could just all learn to read the music accurately, maybe nobody's trumpet would be out of tune."

We walked toward the car, but were reluctant to get in. We stood with the doors open for a bit, trying to coax a little air through the interior.

"What sorts of things do they disagree about at seminary?" Pat asked. "Just little picky details or important things?"

"Pretty big things, sometimes. Even the divinity of Christ comes into question. We have one student — a brilliant fellow — who can't quite bring himself to believe that Jesus was literally the son of God. He feels that the Lord was just an inspired, specially prepared person chosen by God to be our supreme example of how to live a perfect life."

"Well, what's he doing in seminary, then?" Granna asked. "I shouldn't think he'd be allowed to stay."

"There was a movement to expel him, but some of the faculty stood up for him because he's an excellent speaker and very good with people. I think everyone's hoping he'll come around in his thinking before he graduates—but I don't know if he'll ever be ordained. The surprising thing is, he told me personally that two faculty members confided in him privately that they felt the same way. Others disagree on such things as whether a saved individual can ever completely fall from grace and whether baptisms of other denominations are valid. Some differ on whether all dancing is sinful, and even whether women should wear lipstick or curl their hair. A couple of our fellows even side with the Church of Christ and feel we should ban musical instruments from our meetings."

Pat and Star looked at each other in wonder.

"Well, my mercy!" Granna said. "You'd think they'd have better things to worry about than that."

"That's the tip of the iceberg," Uncle Bob said.

The next morning, Granna asked me to collect Uncle Bob's white shirts for washing.

"And be sure to check the pockets, Emily Jean. There's nothing worse than a wad of soggy paper or a leaky fountain pen in the wash. You might as well get in the habit of noticing such things now that you're nearly twelve."

Dutifully I did as I was told. There was a mint Lifesaver in one shirt, which I appropriated for my own, knowing that Uncle Bob wouldn't mind. Several folded sheets of thin blue notepaper were in the other shirt. I laid these on his dresser, and then, as if compelled by a curiosity even greater than my normal allotment, I slowly reached for them again and unfolded the pages.

I recognized the handwriting immediately; I had seen it on lots

of school papers, on the blackboard, and in the front of a volume
of poems by Emily Dickinson.

Dear Bob,

(And you are dear to me—just how dear you have
become during these last few weeks I've only begun to
realize)—this is such a difficult letter to write. You've
been wonderful, and so kind. So have a great many other
people, but not with the steadfast support and
understanding that you have shown me at a time when I
could so easily have despaired. It was hard watching
Mother die, even though I'm confident it was the right
time for her and the will of the Lord. I was sad, and
lonely, and so very tired—and your visits became the
bright spots in my life—the thing I looked forward to the
most.

For a long time, I tried to convince myself that what I
felt for you was simple gratitude—and that what you felt
for me was Christian charity and sympathy—and certainly
those elements are present. But that last visit we had, just
before Mother had to go to the hospital, when you
mentioned how your affection for me was deepening, I
realized that gratitude was by no means all I felt for you
either. I'm sorry if I seemed short with you and unable to
respond to your questions that day. I was astonished and
confused and—yes—thrilled by what you were saying, but
I was also so wrapped up in my concern for Mother that I
felt I couldn't even consider your proposal with any
degree of rational thought at all.

Since I've been here, I've had a chance to rest and
think it all over, and I must tell you how honored I am
that you would consider me as your life's companion. My
love and respect for you is such that, given slightly
different circumstances, I wouldn't hesitate one minute to
give you a resounding YES! But circumstances are what

they are, and I feel I must force myself to be as practical and wise as possible, though it isn't easy.

Dear, dear Bob—what would a Baptist minister do with a Mormon wife? I'd be a handicap to you in your chosen profession, and I'd never convert—I suspect you know that as well as I do. I love my faith so much and feel it so deeply that I just don't think an interfaith marriage could work for me. We'd be forever hoping to change each other, and that in itself would put a strain on our relationship that I'd never want to be there. I want to be free and open with my husband in all things. Also, going through Mom's passing and realizing that now she and my dad can be together forever, sealed by priesthood authority in a holy temple so that their marriage becomes an eternal one—all this has made me realize that I want nothing less for myself.

So, Bob, I think we must go our separate ways, much as I hate to put the words down on paper, as that makes them so real and final. Don't meet my bus on Monday. Let's not, as they say, prolong the agony. Just please ask Mrs. Chapman to meet me, if she can. If not, I'll walk. It wouldn't hurt me! It does hurt me to say good-bye to you, though, and to think I'll never be your wife or Emmy's aunt (that would have been such fun—I adore her), but you will find a good Baptist girl who will just fill the bill for you, I'm sure, and forget all about the funny Mormon girl you knew one summer.

Thanks, Bob, for everything. You're a wonderful, wonderful person, and I'm sure you'll be richly blessed for all the good you'll do with your life.

Love, Mary Afton

I sat down on the edge of Uncle Bob's neatly made bed, a lump so big in my throat that it was painful. My world had just tilted again, and sorrow and joy warred with each other in what seemed an unwinnable battle. To think that Uncle Bob and Miss Mary Afton had fallen in love right under our noses, and we hadn't even suspected! At least, I hadn't, and I didn't think Granna knew. I was sure Star didn't—she was still whispering and giggling about Pat's efforts to look lovelier each Sunday. And poor Pat! Did she have any idea that Uncle Bob was looking right past her with hardly even a glance for her shiny dark hair and dainty hand-sewn dresses? That he, about to become a minister, was in love with a Mormon?

Not that I blamed him for loving Miss Mary Afton—Star and I and most of the kids in our class had loved her ever since September. Yet, here she was—turning him down, even though she admitted she loved him back—just because she liked the way her church let people get married forever! Well, I had to admit that was a pretty powerful idea. I knew how it had appealed to me to think that people who loved each other and were families here on earth could still be families in heaven someday. It only seemed fair when you looked at it that way—especially for people like me who got cheated out of their families and couldn't even remember them. But what did I know? Maybe like Granna said, once you got to playing your harp and singing praises, you didn't care who was with you.

I looked back at the letter and reread the part about how Miss Mary Afton would have liked to be my aunt, and my vision blurred. It would have been fun to have Pat as my aunt too—it would sort of make Star and me related—but the truth was, I much preferred Miss Mary Afton for that position.

"Emily Jean! Where are those two shirts? They can't be that hard to find. Are you dawdling?"

I jumped as if I'd been caught with my hand in her purse.

"Coming, Granna," I called, trying to sound normal.

What to do? I couldn't risk putting the letter on Uncle Bob's dresser and have him knowing it had been seen and possibly read. I refolded the thin sheets and stuffed them back into the shirt pocket; then I hung the shirt carefully on the chair back the way I had found it. Grabbing his clean white shirt from the closet, I ran into the bathroom and flushed the toilet to account for my slowness, wadded the clean shirt together with the used one, and smeared a light tracing of toothpaste down the front. It was bad enough that I knew Uncle Bob's secret; I didn't want Granna to know too—not until he saw fit to tell her.

For myself, I hadn't realized what a burden it was to carry someone else's secret—one that you're not supposed to know. It weighs heavily on your soul and colors all your thinking about the people involved. It's rather like knowing the future and seeing other people rush blindly about in ignorance of their fates. Of course, I didn't know the future, and by nine o'clock that evening I was wishing I didn't know quite so much about the present.

"Granna, are you expecting Uncle Bob home for dinner tonight?" I asked about three-thirty in the afternoon.

"No, not that I know of—he didn't say he'd be here, and it's only Monday, after all. Surprises me, though, how much he's managed to be here this summer, what with that construction job he has and all. He's spent a lot of time driving back and forth, but I guess he's felt an obligation to help Pastor Welch with visitation, like you said."

"M-mm." *Visitation.* I had said that, hadn't I? Well, surely he had been visiting the sick and the bereaved, so I wasn't too far off. I tried another angle.

"Has Mrs. Chapman said whether Miss Mary Afton's back in town yet?"

"She hasn't mentioned it. Just said how sorry she'd be not to have the girl's help this year at school."

"I'll miss her."

"It's too bad, but it won't affect you, Emily Jean. You'll be in junior high."

"Yes'm. I know."

"Well, you don't sound very happy about it. Land, the summer's two-thirds gone already. We need to be thinking about school clothes before long. Let's plan a trip to Lana's to see what Mavis has got in, all right? Emily Jean, do you hear me?"

"'S'ma'am. I do. That'll be fine."

She peered at me through her bifocals. "You look a little bit peaked. I believe the heat's got you all washed out. Why don't you go on upstairs and take a little rest before dinner?"

"All right, Granna." Willingly I trudged upstairs and turned back my sheets for whatever vestige of morning coolness might be left in them and stretched out. I needed the time to plan how to get to the bus station by nine-twenty that evening. I had to see for myself who met Miss Mary Afton's bus.

. . . . 32 . . . .

I hung around the downstairs part of the house all evening, listening to "Your Hit Parade" on the radio and trying to write a letter to LaRae and one to Aunt Cecily in Maryland, who had sent me pictures of her granddaughters. My cousins were pretty girls with brown eyes and long dark hair tied back with ribbons. Granna had said that they looked remarkably well-bred. I had a hard time concentrating, but finally I sealed the envelopes with a sense of relief.

Just before nine o'clock, I heard the sound I had been waiting for. Uncle Bob's Nash veered into the driveway with more speed than caution, and the driver himself flung into the house and took the stairs two at a time, calling out to us in passing, "Hi, Mom, Emmy— sorry to be in such a rush, but I have an appointment."

Granna looked at me. "Good thing we got his shirts ready. That boy's pushing himself too hard. He's going to plumb wear out."

I stood up, stretching with elaborate slowness. "I need some exercise," I said. "Granna, would you mind if I walked down to the mailbox and put these in? I'd be back before it gets dark."

"Well, I suppose that'd be all right, as long as you're sure you can get back in time. Tatum's no big city, thank goodness, but I still don't want you on the streets after dark."

"Yes'm. I understand."

I strolled down the steps and out of the yard, and then hit the street at a dead run. It was already five after nine, and I needed some time to select my vantage point before anyone else arrived. I thrust my letters into the corner mailbox by the Rexall, and then looked around for a hiding place. The Rexall, where the bus station was located, closed at seven, so anyone waiting to meet the bus just stood on the corner or under the awning if the weather was bad. The opposite corners were taken by the Commerce Bank, Woolworth's, and Parker's Cafe. Behind the Rexall was the old Sanborn house, said to be at least a hundred years old. Young John Sanborn had restored it and turned the front parlor into a real estate and insurance office. He didn't live there, however, and the office was closed, so no one would be around to notice me hiding in the corner of the picket fence. It was perfect.

I strolled around the yard a bit, admiring the flowers, which were old-fashioned varieties that might have grown there back before the War between the States, Granna said — verbena and phlox and climbing roses. Casually, I wandered toward my chosen observation post and sat down in a spot that afforded me the best view of the bus stop through the pickets.

It wasn't long before Uncle Bob's Nash pulled into the shade of a huge oak tree across the street. He turned the engine off and sat very still for several minutes. Then he folded his arms on the steering wheel and rested his head on them. He didn't look up until we both heard the sighing exhaust of the bus as it lumbered around the corner and stopped. Then he got out of the car and stood leaning against it, his hands in his pockets. Even from where I huddled, I could see the anxiety in his expression, and it surprised me. It wasn't a familiar look for Uncle Bob, who always seemed calm and in charge of any situation that confronted him.

Miss Mary Afton was the only passenger to get off in Tatum. She carried her purse and a small bag, and the bus driver helped her with a larger suitcase. She didn't see Uncle Bob's car until the bus slowly pulled away, and he started to cross the street. She had picked up the larger case, preparing to lug it home herself, and now she slowly set it down again and tilted her head to one side as if to admonish him for being there. But a smile came and went on her lips, and I knew she was glad to see him.

"Bob, you needn't have come," her clear voice called. "I told you not to bother. But I — I'll bet you didn't get my letter yet, did you?" Her voice dropped as he drew closer. "I wrote you from Maryland, telling you not to meet my bus. I'm sorry you went to all this trouble. I can easily . . . "

"Mary." Uncle Bob's voice was quiet, but it cut through her nervous chatter like a warm knife through butter. "Your letter came."

"It — did? But then . . . "

"It was a lovely letter, Mary, but — " His voice softened yet more as they came face to face, and I could catch only occasional words: "overlooked . . . possibility . . . you? . . . not positive, but . . . maybe I might . . . trying to discover . . . give up . . . patient . . . ?"

I strained to hear her reply. Her higher voice carried more clearly. "I — please don't feel you need to do this for my sake."

"No . . . both our sakes . . . vitally . . . me, and . . . know . . . true, then . . . more time? . . . must . . . Mary, one way or . . . help me? . . . your prayers."

She just stood and looked up into his face, as if trying to read something written in his eyes. Then she simply nodded and closed her eyes as if against the tears that were forming. I felt a sympathetic lump in my own throat as she bowed her head and allowed Uncle Bob to hold her against his chest as he might a child. He raised one hand and caressed her hair, then kissed the top of her head and gently pulled away to pick up her suitcase. They walked together to his car, neither one speaking as he deposited her case in back and opened the front door for her.

Just as his engine caught and came alive, I felt something sting me. For several seconds, I had been dimly conscious of slightly itchy, crawly sensations on my bare legs, but I had ignored them in my effort to remain undetected and to hear the conversation. Now, I rolled over onto my bottom, slapping at the red ants that evidently had formed a battle attack against this huge threat to their home. I had disturbed a large anthill, just where the grass ended under the edge of the picket fence. There were so many that I didn't know where to hit first. I ran my hand down one leg, wiping off several little soldiers, only to find that one of them stung me between my fingers—a tender spot that I knew would bother me for days.

"Oh, help!" I muttered, hoping no one could see my contortions. "I'm gonna pay for this one." As soon as I thought I was relatively free of ants, I hightailed it home, running harder than I had on the way to town. Banging into the house, I took the stairs in threes, ran into the bathroom, and turned on the bathtub faucets full blast.

"Emily Jean? What in the world?"

"Red ants all over me," I yelled. "Gotta take a bath, quick."

Granna, bless her, came up to the bathroom with a yellow box of bicarbonate of soda, which she sprinkled liberally into the tub. "Land, child, I can't imagine how you managed to get covered with red ants on a simple walk to the mailbox. What did you do, park on top of a bed of them and have tea?"

I giggled. "All I know is, they were all over me before I realized it. It must have been—um—when I was waiting for the bus to pass."

"Well, it must have been a slow bus. You come on down when you're done, and we'll put calamine lotion on the worst ones. I'm going to be scraping together a bite for Robert to eat. He can't have had time for any supper. Wonder what his appointment was?"

I just shrugged at this, not trusting myself to utter a word. Granna leaned over the tub, peering at my bites, which were starting to swell and redden. I always had quite a reaction to ant and mosquito bites, and I knew I was in for some misery.

"Well, my mercy, they even—oh." She drew back as I protectively folded my arms across my chest, where lately, much to my alarm, my breasts had begun to soften and swell.

"My mercy!" she repeated softly, as she closed the bathroom door behind her and started down the stairs.

Later that evening, I slipped back upstairs to bed as soon as the calamine lotion had dried, not wanting to face any discussion of Uncle Bob's whereabouts, my tangle with the red ants, or the evidence of my budding womanhood. I also wanted a little time to myself to think over the conversation I had heard between Uncle Bob and Miss Mary Afton.

. . . . 299 . . . .

As I lay in bed listening to the comforting evening sounds of cricket and mockingbird, I realized there were things about that conversation that puzzled me. What exactly was it that Miss Mary Afton didn't expect Uncle Bob to do for her sake? And what was it that was vitally important to him that would take a little more time? I knew of only one problem between them. She had spelled it out quite plainly in her letter to him, and all I could imagine was that he needed a little more time to convince her that she could be just as good a Christian in his church as in her own. And if she wanted to get married for eternity, well — couldn't they just ask Pastor Welch to put that in their marriage ceremony instead of the words about "until death do you part"? I felt sure he would do that as a favor to Uncle Bob. And I knew for a fact that Miss Mary Afton had enjoyed hearing Uncle Bob preach that time she came to sing at the mission church. I was pretty confident it would all work out.

Sometime later, I awoke and started rubbing one foot against the other leg to appease the miserable itch that had set in, as I'd known it would. I squirmed my shoulders against the hot sheet to scratch a bite between my shoulder blades, then turned over with an irritated flop that set my bedsprings squeaking. The squeaking seemed to go on for a very long time, until I finally realized that it came from the glider swing down on the front porch. It felt late — there was no moon, and I couldn't see the face of my clock. Everything was quiet: no crickets sang, no one's radio played, there was no sound of traffic on the streets. Then who was swinging on the front porch in the middle of the night — Granna or Uncle Bob? I decided to go see and also to find some relief for my itching. I walked softly so as not to disturb anyone and looked out the open front door.

"Oh, dear Lord," Uncle Bob's voice sighed, "what should I do?"

I hesitated, not wanting to disturb him if he was praying. I'd been taught that you could pray anytime, anyplace, but it still seemed funny that he would choose the glider swing in the middle of the night. However, Uncle Bob wasn't one to take the Lord's name in vain, so I thought it must have been a prayer of sorts. I strained to catch his next words, which were in a different tone.

"All you ask for is food and affection, isn't it? A simple enough life. Maybe I should be more like that—satisfied with simple, basic things that are readily available."

Who was he talking to now? Not the Lord, that was certain. I craned my head and could see a dark, elongated shape resting on his chest as he reclined on the glider cushions—Cinderella. He kept one foot on the floor, idly continuing the gentle motion of the swing. I opened the door and stepped out onto the porch.

"Hi," I whispered, touching Cinderella's head as she lifted it. Her purr intensified, but she made no move to leave her place.

"E. J., did I wake you with this old swing squeaking?"

"No, I woke up itching from a batch of ant bites I got today."

"Oh, is that right? Friend of mine in the service showed me how to stop insect bites from itching and stinging. You use ice and ammonia. What say we go try it out?"

"That's okay. They're not too bad now that I'm up." I was fibbing; they were worse now, but I made a face at myself in the dark for bringing up the subject. What I really wanted to know was what was on *his* mind and troubling him so.

"How come you're out here? Isn't it awful late?" I asked.

"I guess it is. I couldn't sleep, to tell you the truth. It's so hot and still, and I've had a lot on my mind lately. So I decided to get up, cool off a bit, and try to deal with my problems head on."

"What—kind of problems?"

He chuckled softly. "How does it go? *Something or other and sealing wax, and cabbages and kings?*"

"But I'm not Alice, Uncle Bob! I'm nearly twelve, and I can understand some things."

"I'm sorry, E. J. You're right. But I'm afraid my problems would sound about as outlandish to you as some of the things in Wonderland. It's just that I have some big decisions to make about my life, and they'll affect you too—and Mom, and everyone I know. I feel a lot of responsibility to make the right choice—but it's hard. Being grown-up, you know, doesn't make everything clear and easy."

"No. I reckon not."

He was silent for a few minutes, stroking Cinderella's back with long, slow motions. "You know, E. J., I care a lot about you. In fact, I really love you, kiddo."

I didn't know what to say. I had always known he loved me—known it and depended on it—but he had never come right out and said so before. We didn't say such things easily in our family. I felt warm and embarrassed and wonderful.

"Uh—thanks—and me, too."

"I know. I wouldn't ever want to disappoint you or be less than you think I am. I just feel I should stand in for your daddy, I guess."

"I kind of feel that way too. That you do that, I mean."

"So that's why my decisions weigh heavily on me right now. I want to do what's right and best for all of us. It's not just myself I have to think of."

"Um—what kind of decisions? Like—um—who you might marry or something?"

He chuckled again. "Well, that's a big part of it, all right. And I think you'd approve my choice. But it's more complicated than that. Much more." He sighed. "Oh, well, I'll work it out. Listen, kiddo, do you feel hungry at all? Mom left me a nice supper in the kitchen, but I haven't felt like touching it till now. Want to share it with me?"

"Sure, I reckon I could eat a little."

He placed Cinderella gently on the porch and stood up, quieting the squeak of the glider with one hand. "I keep trying to oil that thing, but I never get the right spot," he muttered.

It was fun, tiptoeing through the darkened hallway after him and listening outside Granna's open door to her soft snores, then quietly getting the macaroni salad, fresh pickled okra, and lemon pie out of the icebox for an after-midnight feast. In fact, as I glanced at the kitchen clock, I was surprised to see that it was three hours and forty-two minutes after midnight. I couldn't remember ever being up at that hour, much less eating then! I grinned to think what Granna would say if she caught us.

. . . . 33 . . . .

After our wee-hours feast, Uncle Bob showed me how to apply household ammonia and an ice cube alternately to my ant bites, then he helped me with the ones on my back that I couldn't reach. By the time we were done, Cinderella was at the back screen, leaping to catch the moths that kept banging against it. We hastily turned out the light, and I slipped a bite of food out to her to settle her down before we climbed the stairs to our rooms like a couple of conspirators.

It should have been no surprise to me that I slept late the next morning. The clock read ten-fifteen by the time I groggily rolled out and pulled on my shorts. Granna felt my head as I forced my way through a small bowl of cornflakes.

"How do those bites feel, Emily Jean? When you slept so long, I worried that you might have got a feverish reaction."

"I think they're some better," I told her. "When I got up with them itching again last night, Uncle Bob had me treat them with ammonia and ice, and that helped."

"You saw Robert last night? Land sakes, he was out late—and then gone again by the time I got up at seven."

"Was he really?" I wondered if he got any sleep at all, poor man.

"I declare, I don't know what's going on with him. He doesn't quite seem himself somehow. I reckon I'm going to have to speak to Pastor Welch and see if he doesn't think Robert's taking on too much."

"Oh, I expect he'll work it all out."

"Well, it's true the summer'll be over before we know it," she replied. "He'll soon be back at seminary and not have to chase back and forth to that construction job. That'll be a blessing."

"I'll miss him, though. It's been nice having him around."

"Yes," she sighed, "and when he gets his first church, who knows where it'll be? Oh well—the Lord will provide."

"Yes, ma'am. I reckon so."

"A mother can't expect to keep her children always under her wing, I know that," she said, as though talking to herself. "But it's hard when some leave so young—and some never return. I don't worry about Robert though," she added resolutely. "That one's always had good sense."

I wondered what she would think if she knew he hoped to marry Miss Mary Afton! Granna seemed to like her—but liking her as a person and accepting her as a Mormon daughter-in-law might be two different things. As for me, I hugged the knowledge of their love close to me and cherished it. I thought it was the most wonderful thing in the world, and I had faith that they could work out their differences. There was only a tinge of regret that it wouldn't be Pat— Star and I had hoped for that for so long, and I felt sad for both of them. But this was beyond my wildest dreams. The only trouble was, I couldn't run to Star and share my joy and hopes and regret. I had chosen to burden myself with this secret that belonged to other people, and now I was bound to carry it alone.

"Emily Jean, stop your dawdling and get in there to the piano. You have a lesson this afternoon, and there's not to be any running off with Starlett or playing with that cat or any such nonsense until I can hear some real improvement in your pieces."

"Yes'm."

Obediently, I practiced until a spot between my shoulder blades burned with fatigue and my hands felt heavy on the keys. Surprisingly, the time went fast, and my pieces did sound considerably better by the time I got through, even though my thoughts hadn't been solely on notes and technique. I stretched, and Granna handed me a broom.

"Now get yourself a little exercise by sweeping the front porch and walk. Then bring in the clothes from the line and fold and dampen them, and then sweep the back porch. I don't want dust swept onto the clean clothes, so mind you do it in that order."

"Okay."

"Okay is slang. 'Yes, ma'am' sounds much more appropriate in the mouth of a young lady."

"Yes, ma'am." Granna was in fine form today, I thought, and smiled a secret little smile. Her admonishments didn't bother me as much as usual, and I wondered how much of that had to do with the fact that I knew something she didn't know! Or maybe it had more to do with the fact that I knew Uncle Bob loved me. For that matter, Granna did too, in her own way, though I wasn't sure what ratio of love, anxiety, and resentment there was in the emotional mix she presented to me.

There were a small black book and some pamphlets by the edge of the glider swing. I set them in the swing while I swept, then took them upstairs to Uncle Bob's room, realizing he must have left them there last night when he came inside with me. Curiously, I glanced at the spine of the black book where gilt lettering, nearly worn off, proclaimed that it was the Book of Mormon.

"Hmph," I said to myself, randomly opening the book to a page that seemed to read remarkably like the Bible. "Weird." I looked at the pamphlets. One was labeled "Ten Points of the True Church" and the other was titled "Joseph Smith Tells His Own Story." I left them on the dresser, pondering Uncle Bob's reasons for reading them. Obviously he wanted to know what Miss Mary Afton believed — probably so that he could show her where her church went wrong. I nodded to myself. That would be it.

Later that afternoon when I had completed all the chores Granna had asked me to do, I went upstairs to get a book to take out where there were two white wooden lawn chairs in the shade of a pecan tree. I wanted to avoid Granna and Star, who I expected would call, until this business about Uncle Bob and Miss Mary Afton was settled. Outside Uncle Bob's room, I paused. Did I dare? He wouldn't be back until evening at least, and maybe not then. But should I be looking at things from the Mormon church? I knew what Granna would say. But then, she didn't know about LaRae and my project to help her. Maybe these materials might give me some idea what to say in my next letter. Besides, I knew what I believed, didn't I? I had always gone to church and Sunday School, and now I was in the Girls' Auxiliary, and my own uncle would be ordained a minister soon. Surely I was fortified against false teachings!

I collected the book and pamphlets and headed out back, pulling one of the chairs behind an althea bush, where I couldn't be seen from the house. Granna was resting in her room, having felt obliged to work twice as hard as she asked me to do, so I felt relatively safe. Cinderella came and sprawled in the grass at my feet, playfully grabbing my toes when I wiggled them. I rubbed her tummy with my foot, and she promptly went into mock-battle position, locking her front legs around my foot and kicking with her hind feet.

"Ow, that tickles — cut it out," I told her, but she wouldn't let go until I picked her up and put her in my lap, where she pretended to bite my hand. Her eyes, which had turned from the kittenish blueberry color to the green of ripe gooseberries, watched my face for reaction. I didn't show any, and presently she relaxed into a purring slumber. I picked up the pamphlet about Joseph Smith, whoever he was. I had heard of Brigham Young from Granna, but I didn't recognize this name. I read his story through, at first in total disbelief at the fantastic ideas of angels appearing to a young boy and of ancient records being buried in the earth. But then, compelled by a desire to understand if any part of it could possibly be true, I read it again more carefully, trying to sense the character of the young man who said he had actually experienced these things. Was it possible? There was something about it that made me feel that Joseph Smith had been an honest person in spite of the incredible story he told. I decided that either he was telling the truth or he was somehow tricked into believing that he told the truth.

I tried to picture any of the boys I knew being serious enough about religion to warrant angelic visitations, but that was beyond even my imagination — until I thought of Zack. Somehow, I could envision him a year or two older than he was now, straight and slim and honest enough to admit that although he wasn't comfortable with any of the preachers of his acquaintance, he really did want to know what was true and right and what God expected of him. Knowing Zack made it easier to believe that there had been such a boy as Joseph Smith.

I opened the black book, The Book of Mormon — which was supposed to contain the words that had been written on those ancient buried records and translated into English through the gift and power of God by this Joseph Smith — and began to read.

To begin with, it seemed to be about another boy called Nephi. He said that he was exceeding young — whatever age that was — and had quite a frightening and adventurous time trying to obey his father and get along with his brothers. They were traveling in the wilderness to escape the destruction about to come upon Jerusalem, where they used to live. It seemed an angel had told his father in a dream that their city was going to be destroyed. The father, who was a good and righteous man, was warned to take his family and escape — to leave behind what sounded like a nice home and a lot of expensive things. Two of Nephi's older brothers, Laman and Lemuel, didn't want to do that, and they fought against the whole idea all the way. They weren't a bit nice to Nephi, and I felt sorry for him. For some reason, I pictured Lemuel as looking like Rogie, and Laman as being bigger and a really mean bully.

There were angels appearing to people in this story too, and since it all took place back in Old Testament times, and since I was used to things like that happening in the Bible, it all seemed quite believable. I didn't find the book hard to understand either, because I had done enough reading in the Bible to more or less get the gist of what was meant.

I read happily until Granna got up from her nap and called me to help with dinner. I hid the book and the pamphlets under my pillow so that I could read some more when I went to bed, or whisk them back into Uncle Bob's room if he came home — whichever happened first.

He didn't come home that night or the next, so I just kept reading during every private moment I could steal. Parts of the book I found more interesting than others, and though I didn't quite understand a lot of it, I felt compelled to keep reading. By the third day, I had figured out one thing: that book hadn't been made up by Joseph Smith if he was the uneducated country boy he claimed to be. It came from somewhere though, and it sounded true—like the Bible.

It talked a lot about Bible people too, such as Joseph, the son of Jacob, who had had the coat of many colors and had been sold into Egypt by his brothers. I knew all about him; he was like an old friend. This Nephi and his family were supposed to be descendants of that Joseph. It mentioned Moses, and it talked a lot about the Messiah who would come, and of course I knew who that would be—Jesus.

Suddenly, I remembered the conversation between Granna and Uncle Bob about whether the Bible was all the scripture we would ever have or need. What had he said? Something about how if God ever saw fit to give us more, he would welcome it? Was this—I closed the book and looked at it with awe—was this that scripture? Had God seen fit to give us more? I would ask Uncle Bob the very next chance I got, even if it meant admitting I had been reading his things without his permission.

On Thursday, Star came over looking for me, and I quickly hid what I was doing and greeted her.

"Have you been shopping for school clothes yet, Emily Jean?"

"No, but Granna said we'd go soon. Have you?"

"Mama got me a plaid dress, a striped one, and a green skirt and sweater. But talking about clothes, you ought to see the dress Pat made to wear next Sunday. She's just sure your Uncle Bob will like her in it! It's light blue with little flowers embroidered all around the neck and on the sleeves. It plumb took her forever to get the flowers done—but it's so pretty."

I felt a pang of pity and guilt, knowing what I knew, but I couldn't say a word to dispel Star's hope. Besides, if things *didn't* work out for Uncle Bob and Miss Mary Afton, maybe he would notice Pat in her dainty dresses. Star and I talked for a while and played with Cinderella, who made it impossible for us to play jacks on the porch. She pounced on the ball and scattered the sharp little metal jacks in all directions, as if we had invented the game just for her amusement.

"She's so funny, Emily Jean. You're lucky to have her. I never ever thought your Granna'd let you have a pet."

"Me, neither. I really love her too—she's good company, and she reminds me of—of people up in Turley."

"I reckon she reminds you of your cousin there."

"Cousin?"

"That boy cousin—Zack."

"Oh. Well—he did give her to me."

"You ought to write and tell him how much you like her."

Write to Zack? I stared at Star. The idea had never occurred to me. But why not? This surely had become a letter-writing summer! I had corresponded with a Mormon girl in Wyoming, a dying grandmother, a great aunt I'd only just met, and the only black person I had ever truly known. Why not Zack, who meant almost as much to me as any of them?

"Reckon maybe I'll do just that," I said, grinning in anticipated delight.

Star's eyes lit up. "You're brave, Emily Jean. I think it's super, but I wouldn't dare write to a boy. I'd say something stupid, I know."

"Well, Zack's—different from the boys we know around here. He—" I paused, unsure of how to describe him exactly and unsure of how much I wanted to share, even with Star. "He's nice," I said. "He doesn't make fun of people. He wouldn't tease and try to make you feel stupid—like Junior and Fred and Arnie do."

"He sure must be different, then," she said with a sigh.

. . . . 34 . . . .

That night, Uncle Bob came home from his construction job again. He appeared in my doorway while I was sitting cross-legged on my bed, trying to compose the perfect letter to Zack. He looked tan and fit, but a worried little frown had settled between his eyes.

"E. J., I left a book and some pamphlets around somewhere. Mom says she hasn't seen them, and I wondered if you had?"

"Oh—I think so," I said, knowing full well that they were just behind me, under my pillow. I hadn't expected Uncle Bob home until Friday evening, and I'd planned to have them safely back in his room before then. I tried frantically to think of a way out of this, then remembered my resolve to avoid whoppers. I also wanted to know what he thought of the ideas in those publications.

"Um—are these what you're looking for?" I asked, pulling them from behind me and holding them up.

His eyebrows lifted. "They sure are. What were you doing with them, kiddo?"

"Well, I found them by the glider, and I figured you'd left them there, so I—kept them for you. And—I read some of it too."

"Oh, did you? What did you think?"

"I reckon I just thought you were reading them so you could learn more about the Mormons and what they believed and all. Maybe so you could witness to them better."

"No, I mean—what did you think about what you read?"

I straightened my shoulders, flattered that he would ask my opinion. "Well, I don't know exactly. I got the feeling that Joseph Smith believed what he was saying about the angel and the gold plates and all. But I can't figure how he could write a book like that—or how anybody could. It's so much like the Bible, but it's different too—I just don't know exactly. What do you think, Uncle Bob? Did it really come from old buried records, or did Joseph Smith just make it up?"

He stood there at the end of my bed and gazed at me, his expression one of pained uncertainty. "If I knew the answer to that, E. J., all my problems would be solved."

"Is this—is it something to do with the decisions you were worrying about the other night?" I asked, my voice subdued.

"It has everything to do with it," he said. "You see, honey, if this all turns out to be true, if this book really is scripture and Joseph Smith was telling what really happened to him, then I'm duty-bound to do something about it. If the Lord has given us further scripture, then I have to accept it and live by its teachings."

"But why would the Lord give the Mormons this book to live by and give everybody else the Bible? Why wouldn't they use the Bible too?"

"Oh, they do. They use the Bible and the Book of Mormon both—and some other scriptures too."

I nodded. "I thought they fit together." Another thought struck me. "But why would God give the Book of Mormon to a country kid like Joseph Smith? Why didn't he give it to—I don't know—a Christian minister, or the Catholic Pope, or somebody—somebody who knew a lot about religion already and who could tell a lot of people about it?"

"I'm not entirely sure, but I suspect it might have been because they were already too steeped in their particular denomination's beliefs to accept it. Maybe the Lord needed a young, fresh mind searching for truth, not someone who was a member of another church."

"He did say he was confused, and that's why he prayed to the Lord to find out the truth. But wow! He got a vision of God and

Jesus when he prayed. That'd be so scary. Do you think he really saw them, Uncle Bob, or was he telling a whopper?"

Uncle Bob frowned. "I've read a bit about his life, and I can't think of anybody who would go through what he went through for a lie — being tarred and feathered, run from place to place, put in prison, and eventually murdered for what he believed."

"He was *murdered?*"

"Shot by a mob of men while he was in jail. He could have gone back on his story anytime, and people probably would have left him alone."

"That shouldn't happen to a nice person just because he said he had a vision of angels and Jesus and all. But if he really did, why didn't God save him from being killed?"

"E. J., do you know what a martyr is?"

"No."

"Well — it's someone who gives his life for what he believes."

"Oh, like Stephen in the Bible."

"Exactly, and many others of the early Christians. It's not an uncommon thing for prophets to be persecuted. In fact — think of the Lord Jesus himself."

I was quiet, thinking of the spitting and scourging and the crucifixion. Jesus hadn't deserved that either, but God had let it happen — for our sakes. "I reckon I see. Uncle Bob, you sound like maybe you think Joseph Smith was telling the truth."

He shook his head slowly. "I'm just not sure yet, E. J. But if his story is true, I can't ignore it."

"Well, how can you find out? Wouldn't God tell you too if you prayed about it? I mean — you're almost a minister. Wouldn't he listen to you if he listened to a farm boy? Why don't you do that?"

His smile was wistful. "I have been, believe me. And I plan to keep on trying. I have absolutely got to know, one way or another." Uncle Bob bowed his head and shook it, covering his eyes briefly with one hand. "But what you have to realize, honey, is that if I really do get an answer from God that this book is true scripture — then I can't become a Baptist minister at all."

I sat up real straight when I heard that. The thought that Uncle Bob couldn't be a preacher was too awful. And Granna—she was so proud of him. "But—but why not?"

"Because—while there's room in the Baptist faith for quite a number of different attitudes and interpretations, there's no room at all for a preacher who believes in the Book of Mormon. Mormons aren't even regarded as real Christians by our people."

I remembered Granna's horrified attitude toward the two Mormon missionaries, Elder Jensen and Elder Taylor. "That's just what Granna said. But—I mean, it doesn't figure. I can't imagine Miss Mary Afton not being a Christian. And the Book of Mormon—at least the part I've read—talks so much about Jesus."

"I know. In fact—how much did you read, E. J.?"

"Um—to the place where the pamphlets are tucked in. About the man called Alma and his sons."

"I see. There's a place further along where it tells of Jesus' appearance to the Nephite people, just after he was resurrected. That, more than anything else, makes me *want* to believe the book. It sounds so right—so like him. In the New Testament he said he had other sheep he had to bring into the fold. Well, he told these Nephites, over here in this part of the world, that they were those other sheep. It made sense to me that he would visit them if they belonged to the house of Israel."

I didn't know much about sheep or about the house of Israel, but it gave the Book of Mormon new stature in my eyes to know that Uncle Bob took it seriously. But that he wouldn't be able to be a Baptist preacher—that was unthinkable. "Uncle Bob, what will Granna say if she finds out about all this?"

He shrugged and grinned. "I take it she hasn't discovered these things?"

I shook my head. "They've been right here."

"That's probably just as well. I don't know whether to feel glad or sorry that you've read them though."

"I kind of wanted to know what Miss Mary Afton believed—and LaRae."

"Who's LaRae?"

"Remember? Elder Jensen's little sister. I write to her back in Wyoming."

"Oh, yes, I'd forgotten that. Well, here's a surprise for you — I've invited Elder Jensen over for supper tomorrow evening. Elder Comstock, too, of course."

"You *did?* Uh, but Granna . . . "

Uncle Bob laughed. "You just leave your Granna to me. I'll get around her."

"And Uncle Bob — reckon if you were to join the Mormon church, you could marry Miss Mary Afton."

His eyebrows quirked, and he looked at me for a long, silent moment while his cheeks slowly reddened. Finally he said, "Is my feeling for Mary Afton something the whole town is gossiping about behind my back, or are you just making one of your famous educated guesses?"

"Oh, no — I'm just guessing. I mean, Granna doesn't even suspect, and neither does Star or anybody, I think, except maybe Mrs. Chapman. I didn't even figure it out myself for a long time. But I think it's super! There's nobody nicer. Are you — mad 'cause I know?"

He let out his breath on a relieved sort of laugh. "No, E. J., I'm not mad. In fact, I'd love to tell the world, but there are too many complications just now — too many uncertainties." He tapped the book in his hand. "I have to find out about this first, and then I'll know how to proceed." He turned to go. "Thanks, honey, for keeping these safe. Feel free to borrow them anytime I'm not using them."

I nodded, then sat staring after him for a long time after he had gone into his room and closed the door. Life had just taken another turn, and the colors had shifted again. Was the pattern ugly or glorious? I wasn't sure.

All the next day, I was apprehensive and watched Granna closely. She seemed a little distracted, and she had me help her clean and polish the living and dining rooms until they shone more than ever.

Finally I could stand it no longer. "Are we having company or something, Granna?"

"My land, Emily Jean, do you think we only clean and care for our things when company is coming? Is that how I've brought you up?"

"Oh, no. ma'am. It just seemed like you were making things look especially nice."

"Well, as a matter of fact, Robert is bringing some people over tonight, and he asked me to prepare a little dinner for them, which I'm always happy to do. You and I, however, will eat in the kitchen as usual."

"Who's he bringing?"

Granna fidgeted. "Well, if I tell you, I'm afraid you're going to want to linger around and try to listen in. In fact, I wondered if you might not enjoy spending the night with Starlett one more time before school starts. Why don't you call her and see if that might be allowed?"

"Granna, I promise I won't hang around and bother. Please just tell me who's coming!"

"It's that young woman who was your teacher's helper—Miss MacDougal, and two—um—young men from her church. They're just going to be discussing matters of religion—far beyond your interest or need to hear. I believe Robert will be trying to help them see the error of their ways. I'll serve their dinner and then retire to my room, and I think it best if you are out of the house. I know you care for Miss MacDougal, and I don't want you to disturb them."

"Oh," I said, being unable to think of any other response. So Miss Mary Afton was going to be here with the elders too. I would have been willing to hide under the dining table to be present at that meeting, but I could see that Granna was determined. Dutifully I called Star, who was puzzled but said she would ask about my spending the night as soon as her mother came back from shopping.

We cleaned and cooked and set the table way ahead of time with four place settings of Granna's best china. She went about her work grimly, but the results were impressive—a baked ham with raisin sauce, au gratin potatoes, fresh garden beans, fluffy bread rolls that filled the house with a heavenly fragrance, and a devil's food cake with glossy white frosting. I yearned after the rolls and the cake, and Granna finally relented and allowed me one roll. She took one too, and we ate them on the back porch.

"Granna, you sure have gone to a lot of trouble for this dinner," I said.

Granna frowned. "It's a matter of setting a good example, Emily Jean. I might not approve of these people or what they believe, but I feel it my duty to help Robert in the only way I can — by showing them what a well-ordered Christian home is like."

"Well, the rolls sure are good," I told her.

"Do you think they're light enough? It's been a long while since I've made yeast rolls."

"Honest, they're wonderful. They'll think you're the best cook in the world — which you are!"

"I'm not doing this for flattery and praise, Emily Jean. Now go and get your night things together so that you can be gone before Robert and the others arrive."

And I had thought a well-deserved compliment to her cooking might please her! I never could outguess Granna. I put together a small bag with my nightgown, toothbrush, comb, and a book to read, said goodnight to Granna, and circled around the block. I had told Granna I'd be leaving at five-thirty and told Star I'd be arriving at six-thirty. That gave me nearly an hour to try to catch a glimpse, at least, and a few words, at most, of Uncle Bob and his guests. Granna had said they were expected about a quarter to six.

I crept through Fred Silver's backyard next to ours, to their scuppernong arbor. Stalactites of sour-sweet grapes drooped on vines from the ceiling in a near cavelike effect. Stashing my bag there, I cautiously moved to the back part of our yard behind Granna's garden, and then slipped over to the althea bush. In a few minutes, I recognized the sound of the Nash's engine, and when I knew that the passengers would be getting out and distracting Granna's attention, I made a dash across the open grassy area of the yard and edged around the house to where I could see but not be seen.

They all appeared solemn as they came up the front walk, and I thought Miss Mary Afton looked as though she had been crying. Uncle Bob slipped a hand under her elbow as they climbed the steps to the porch, and she glanced up at him with a small smile. No one spoke until Granna met them at the door, and I could hear the stiff formality in her voice as she welcomed them and showed them to the dining room. Elder Comstock and Elder Jensen tried to sound hearty in their appreciation of Granna's efforts, and Miss Mary Afton's expression was warm and sincere. But somehow, their voices took me back to the day of Grandmother Knowles's funeral and the stiff pleasantries of the folks who had provided and helped to eat the dinner after the services. They too had chatted and praised the food, but their hearts weren't in it.

I scrunched down against the wall so that my head didn't quite come to the sill of the double dining-room windows and prepared to listen. I knew when Granna finished serving the dinner and went to her room, and I knew she must be just as curious as I. Would she be listening at her door? No—Granna might be curious, but her iron self-control would prevent any such behavior. And as for me— I knew it was wrong to eavesdrop, of course. Hadn't I proved it to myself time and again by hearing things I wished later I hadn't heard? By even now carrying secrets that burdened my thoughts? But I was too deeply involved. I loved these people, and the decisions they made affected me too—and I simply had to know what was going on.

"Now what exactly happened?" I heard Uncle Bob ask. "You say it was a moonshiner who shot him?"

"Apparently so," Elder Jensen said. "It seems Elder Taylor and his companion were tracting out the country roads around the Turley area—"

"Tracting out?"

"That means going from house to house, inviting folks to listen to our message, and leaving tracts — pamphlets — with anyone willing to take them."

"I see. And they came to this man's house?"

"I don't think anyone knows for sure yet. The elders were walking down a dirt road in a wooded area where the local people say there's an illegal still. But no one seems to know whether they were headed toward or away from the woods. Elder Taylor was killed outright, and his companion hasn't been able to say much. His lung was punctured, and he's in pretty serious condition."

I sagged against the wall. Turley — a dirt road leading into the woods — and Zack's voice cautioning, "Don't never go down there . . ." But there hadn't been anyone to warn Elder Taylor and his companion . . .

"What a shame!" Uncle Bob was saying. "Here a young fellow comes out to preach the gospel of peace and gets gunned down by those law-breaking, money-hungry ambassadors of Satan! I hope they clean out that nest of vipers for good."

"We were told that the sheriff's office is investigating. Elder Taylor was a good man — a good companion and a fine missionary — one of the best." His voice cracked, and I felt a lump rise in my throat. It registered now — the other missionary had been Elder Taylor, drinking lemonade on our front porch on a warm June afternoon. I remembered the nice smile, dark hair, and kind, intelligent eyes behind his glasses. I pictured him walking away with Elder Jensen, clapping him on the shoulder as they tried to encourage one another after Granna's curt rejection. Tears welled up in my eyes and spilled down my face, and I slid down the wall into a sitting position, my head bowed on my knees.

"Elder Taylor was Elder Jensen's companion earlier this spring, before Elder Comstock," Miss Mary Afton explained to Uncle Bob. "They get transferred from place to place in the mission every so often."

"Listen, folks, if you'd rather not go ahead with our discussion this evening, I'll surely understand. You have a lot on your minds."

"No, indeed, Brother Markham." Elder Jensen's voice was

stronger now. "I think I can speak for all of us when I say there's nothing that would comfort us more right now than to spend some time talking about the gospel of Jesus Christ. That's what Elder Taylor died for, and we know he's in good hands. We just have to deal with our own feelings, and the best way to do that is to dwell on the good news of the gospel."

"I agree," put in Elder Comstock. "We have a saying in our church that sacrifice brings forth the blessings of heaven. I can't help thinking that the sacrifice of this elder's life, as sorrowful as it is for his family and all who knew him, will call forth great blessings in the Lord's work in this area. For one thing, everyone will hear about it—and good people who might otherwise have turned us away unheard will open their doors to us and open their ears to our message."

"That's a good attitude to take, " Uncle Bob said thoughtfully. "And you may be right. I have a question for you, gentlemen—and Mary too, of course, if you care to respond. Why do you think that your church is regarded as non-Christian by so many, when your scriptures preach of the divinity and redeeming sacrifice of the Lord Jesus, and his very name is part of the real title of your church? Now, don't stop eating to answer that—just think about it while you have another roll and some more ham. Help yourselves."

After a moment, Elder Jensen replied. "From my experience, I think it has to do partly with a thing called sectarianism. Each religious organization tends to think of itself as having the most true, the most correct interpretation of the Bible. And each regards all other churches as less correct but more or less Christian, depending upon how alike or how different they are from its own views.

"We have many similarities to all churches who accept the Bible and the Savior, but we have many more differences from all of them than they have among themselves—so we're the most suspect. Plus, we openly claim to be the one true church of Jesus Christ on the earth. We can't claim otherwise, knowing what we know and having what we have—but many folks don't understand and regard that as an arrogant and impossible stand to take."

. . . . 319 . . . .

"It does sound bold—but perhaps, as you say, they all secretly feel that way about their own churches. Tell me more about why you feel justified in making that claim."

"First of all, we were told about this by the Lord himself. When he appeared to Joseph Smith in the Sacred Grove, . . ."

My mind wandered. I remembered what Joseph Smith said he was told by the Lord—to join none of the churches because none of them really had the truth. And there was something about denying his power. But who did that? And power to do what? I had always been taught that God had all power to do anything he pleased, so surely we weren't guilty of that! But if God had all power, I mused, then why hadn't he used it to warn or save Elder Taylor? Did that mean he *wanted* Elder Taylor to die? Why? To be a martyr, like Stephen and Joseph Smith?

I couldn't listen any longer. My mind had plenty to grapple with already. I stood up and walked slowly through our backyard and Silvers', collecting my night things from the arbor on the way, not even bothering to wonder if anyone saw me.

. . . . 35 . . . .

I wasn't very good company for Star that evening. I had thought I might tell her about the missionaries coming over for dinner, leaving out the part about Miss Mary Afton, of course, so I could tell her about Elder Taylor, but I decided I'd better not. She chatted about school clothes and beat me at Monopoly and jacks, but my heart wasn't in any of those things. It didn't help either that Pat sat at the piano for over an hour, playing and singing love songs in her pretty soprano voice. I knew she must be hoping that Uncle Bob would make an appearance, but it wasn't until bedtime that she asked me, very casually, whether he was home for the weekend. I said I thought he was, but I hadn't talked to him yet.

Star's room was hot, and not a single breeze blew that whole night long. I don't think I slept at all, and at one point I started to cry, thinking about that nice Elder Taylor and wondering about his family and how they would feel when they learned of his death. What if it had been Elder Jensen? What could I possibly have written to LaRae to make her feel any less pain at the loss of the big brother of whom she was so proud? I began to understand a little of what my grandmothers must have felt at losing my parents. They had died young too — and it must have seemed senseless. Why did God allow such things to happen? It seemed that anything could happen to anybody, anytime! What if I had been at home in my bed when the chinaberry branch came hurtling in? Then Granna and Uncle Bob — and yes, Miss Mary Afton too — would be mourning my loss.

I sniffled some more, and Star, ever a light sleeper, turned over.

"Emily Jean, what's the matter?" she asked sleepily. "You've been strange all evening."

I swallowed and cleared my throat. "I think I'm getting a little cold," I whispered. "Do you have a hanky?"

"Summer colds are plumb miserable. Do you want a drink of water?" she asked, handing me a tissue.

"No, thanks, I'll just try to get back to sleep."

I lay and stared at the dark. I would die someday too, just like Grandmother Knowles and my parents and my sister and Elder Taylor. I had always known that, of course. Everybody knew it—but it had never sunk into my heart before. Why did some people get to live long, full lives, while others died as tiny babies, like Ellen Jane?

It didn't seem right that some people had a good chance to learn about God and get ready for heaven, and others didn't. Would they go to hell, even if it wasn't their fault? That's what a missionary couple had told us when they came to our church to give a talk and show pictures of the people they worked with in Africa. They said they were serving there so that as many of those people as possible would have a chance to learn about Jesus and avoid the fires of hell if they died unsaved. It had sounded right and noble at the time, but now I wondered. Wouldn't a loving God be more fair and just than that? It wasn't those people's fault if they died before someone like that good couple arrived to teach them about Jesus, was it? And yet— my mind boggled at all the questions that crowded in—unanswerable questions, it seemed. I finally dropped off in an exhausted sleep just as the objects in Star's room became distinguishable in the pink light of dawn.

I awoke several hours later and lay listening to Star faithfully practicing the piano. Then I dragged myself out of bed and dressed, feeling as if I were just recovering from some wasting illness that had sapped all my strength. I ate a bowl of cereal and bananas with Star, who had waited to have breakfast with me, and she gratifyingly fussed over me the whole time. Then I thanked Mrs. Hargrave and set out for home. I found my feet heading for the cemetery, however, and I sat in the sun beside my mother's grave for a while and thought about things. I even bowed my head and prayed for everybody I could think of, including Elder Taylor's family and Uncle Bob, so that he could find out the truth about the Book of Mormon.

As I walked home, I felt tired but peaceful and laughed when Cinderella sprang out of the bushes to scare me as I came into our yard. I cuddled her for a moment, which was all she would allow me to do when she was in her wriggly, wild-eyed, playful mood.

"Well, about time, I'd say," Granna remarked, when I went to find her to say I was home. "My mercy, child, you look ready to drop. How late did you girls stay up? I certainly hope you didn't keep the Hargraves from getting their night's rest!"

"No, ma'am, we didn't stay up late. I just couldn't sleep very well. It was real hot."

"Well—go up and get a bath and lie down for a bit. You can skip your practicing for one day, I guess. If you feel up to it this afternoon, we'll go see what Lana's has in for fall."

I could feel her gaze still on me as I climbed the stairs. The bath was relaxing and cooling, and I was asleep almost before I turned back my spread.

When I got up a few hours later, Uncle Bob was just coming out of his room. He didn't look as though he'd had much sleep the last while either. There were shadows under his eyes, and he looked drained. He gave my shoulders a friendly hug, and we went downstairs together.

"Well, the dead have risen!" Granna exclaimed when we went into the kitchen where she was grinding leftover ham to make a sandwich spread. "Come and have a big glass of tea and a piece of that chocolate cake. I don't know what you've eaten all day, Robert, but I know you must be hungry. Emily Jean, you can have a piece of the cake too, but you'd best have milk with yours."

I lost no time in cutting myself a piece, but Uncle Bob said, "No, thanks, Mom. I'll wait until tomorrow. And don't plan on me for supper tonight either."

"Oh? Are you invited out?"

"No, no. I'll be here, but I'll be—um—fasting."

"Fasting! Whatever for? I've never heard of such a thing!"

Uncle Bob smiled. "I'm sure you have. Jesus did it for forty days in the wilderness in order to prepare himself for his ministry and to draw closer to his Father."

Granna looked a bit abashed. "Well, of course I know about *that*. But I've never known anyone who—but then I've never had a minister living in the house before!" She glanced at him. "Er—how long . . . ?"

"Don't worry. I won't carry it to extremes. I don't think I could manage forty hours, let alone forty days."

"I should hope not!"

I swallowed a mouthful of Granna's delicious cake and washed it down with cold milk. I wondered how going without food could bring a person closer to God.

"Have you done that before, Uncle Bob?"

"No, Emmy. I never have."

"Do you think it'll—you know—work?"

He smiled. "I have it on the best authority. But it has to be coupled with prayer and meditation, for which a person needs solitude. So if I disappear for a few hours, don't either of you be alarmed. I'll be back. Also—tomorrow morning I'm going to be visiting a church over at Wimshaw—just to observe. So I won't be here for the service at Eastside. But I'll be back in time to preach out at the mission—and probably for dinner."

"All right, Son. Thanks for telling me," Granna said, and when he left the room, we exchanged looks that said something like, "Well, what do you know!" I felt I knew more about what was going on than Granna did. Uncle Bob had plenty to fast and pray about, but as for me, I didn't know how good I would be at fasting, though I wanted some answers too. However, I could add my prayers to his, for whatever they were worth.

At that moment, I remembered the scripture that had led Joseph Smith out into the woods behind his dad's farm to pray for wisdom, and I thought about the answer he got. Wanting to go find a place to be alone, to pray, seemed to be a natural thing. I had done it myself at the graves of my parents—just that very morning, for that matter. It felt right.

"Emily Jean, are you still tired? You look about a million miles away!"

"No, ma'am. I feel lots better. I'm ready to go look at school clothes when you want." I wasn't terribly interested in spending time in Lana's stuffy shop when it was so hot, but I knew that was what Granna wanted to do—so we went. I dutifully tried on wool skirts and sweater sets and plaid dresses, and then some stiff new saddle shoes. I wanted penny loafers instead, but Granna said they didn't give enough support to my feet. I sighed. For my part, I'd much rather have gone to school in my soft old pants and sandals, but girls weren't allowed to wear pants to school—which made it rather risky to slide into third on the baseball diamond!

That evening, I took up my letter to Zack again. I now had even more of a reason to write. In addition to thanking him for Cinderella, I could ask if he knew anything about the shooting of the two young missionaries. I was sure it would be the talk of the whole community. I was gladder than ever to recall that Zack's daddy had refused to sell bottles of the killers' moonshine whiskey under the counter of his store. I just wished that he—or someone—had alerted the lawmen to that illegal whiskey earlier, so that Elder Taylor and his companion would have been safe walking down any country road they chose.

True to his word, Uncle Bob drove away in his Nash and didn't return until late at night after we had gone to bed. He was gone again early the next morning and came home just in time for Sunday dinner. He still looked tired, but he didn't seem as tense as he had lately—and he joked with Granna and kidded her about the dinner being the best he'd ever had.

"They do say that hunger is the best sauce," she replied. "How many meals did you miss anyway, Son?"

"Enough to make me appreciate plain bread and water, if that were all I had," he replied.

"Did—did it work?" I whispered across the table to him, when Granna went to slice some more pot roast.

He looked at me and nodded. "It did, E. J., beyond my wildest hopes. I'll tell you soon."

I could hardly restrain my curiosity, but Granna came back in with the meat, and I had to be content with my own speculations. Had he, like Joseph Smith, seen a vision? Had God answered his questions about his ministry and about the Book of Mormon?

After dinner, he disappeared again—this time into his room to put the finishing touches on his sermon for the evening. Not surprisingly, Uncle Bob's sermon that night was on the theme of fasting and praying for answers to personal questions. I had heard lots of sermons on prayer before, but I couldn't recall Pastor Welch ever mentioning the idea of ordinary people trying to fast. Uncle Bob gave several examples from the New Testament, and I noticed people beginning to perk up and listen.

"I testify to you, folks, that a short season of fasting from food and drink will humble you before your Lord. It will make you realize how dependent you are on daily nourishment for physical strength, and if you add to it sincere prayer about your sins or your problems or your needs, you will realize your dependence upon the Lord for spiritual nourishment and strength as well. You'll come to see that a person can be spiritually starved, just as he can be physically hungered. And friends, when the Lord sees that you're as eager for spiritual food as you ever were for a plate of good home-cooked chicken and dumplings, he'll feed you a banquet you will long remember! He will open the windows of heaven to you and pour out a feast of wisdom and guidance and truth and comfort and love the likes of which you've never before tasted. It is a true principle and it's right here in the Bible. But how many of us have taken notice, except to say, 'Oh, well—fasting is something they did back in those days'?"

I gazed at him, fascinated, wondering what his experience had been—what answers he had received.

His voice dropped to a lower key, and he leaned on the podium in a friendly, confidential way. "Folks, have any of you ever noticed that life doesn't always go the way you planned or thought it would? That it springs little surprises now and then? Some of them are pleasant and easy to accept, and some—like the death of a loved one, or the loss of a crop or even a farm, or a disappointment in a career or a romance, or the loss of health—are not so pleasant. But they do come, don't they, these little surprises? They come to all of us. They're part of what we're put here on earth to learn and experience, and often we don't know why.

"With the best of intentions, we may plan a course of action that seems to us exactly right, and then the Lord says, 'No, Son—or no, Daughter—I have something else in mind for you,' and we have to adjust our thinking. Sometimes we may not understand—and sometimes those around us may have a hard time understanding too. But I testify to you, my friends, the Lord has each of us in his hands. He knows us each, thoroughly and personally, and he loves us. He waits to bless us. He wants us to turn to him, through fasting and sincere prayer, for answers, for guidance, for understanding of things beyond our ken. He will answer—not always when and how we want or expect him to, but according to his own will and our best interests. He sees the whole picture of our lives, while our view is limited. We still see through a glass, darkly, as the Bible reminds us—but if we will turn to the Lord, he will illuminate our way, one step at a time, even through the deepest, darkest passageways of life."

He took a deep breath, looked down at his folded hands for a moment, and then continued. "This summer I have walked some pretty dark passageways at times. I've so much enjoyed my association with you good folks and appreciated your kind encouragement and your faith. Now it's time to turn my steps down a slightly different path—one that I never expected to be asked to follow. But the Lord does ask it of me, and I follow, one step at a time, praying only that he continue to lead me.

"My friends, I love the Lord Jesus Christ—more than life itself— but that's a poor comparison, because he *is* life itself. And I publicly rededicate my life at this time to follow him wherever he leads me, even if I don't immediately understand how or why—and even if those I love don't understand either." He glanced at Granna, who sat straight and still, frowning a little. "I know that he *does* see the way, and I trust him with all my heart and soul. Let us all draw closer to him through sincere fasting and prayer, that we may be led back to his presence and have joy with him in the kingdom of our Father. May we sing now, 'Savior, Like a Shepherd Lead Us.' "

Pat led the song, Star played the piano, and Granna's soprano rang out—all apparently absorbed in the music. Did any of them know what they had heard? I knew, and tears found their way down my cheeks, as person after person quietly made their way to the front of the small church to offer their lives to Jesus and to be counseled and encouraged by a young preacher who was about to leave the church—who was about to become a Mormon.

. . . . 36 . . . .

Uncle Bob was gentle and polite with Pat and Granna on the way home. They didn't seem to understand what had just taken place, but they were impressed with the number of people who had come forward during the invitational. Star kept looking at me anxiously, and finally she whispered, "Emily Jean, are you all right? You look like you don't feel too good. Have you still got a cold?"

I shook my head. "I'm fine," I told her, but I kept wanting to cry, and I think she knew it. I was remembering something she had said earlier in the summer — something about everything being about to change and never being the same again. Somehow she had known — and now I knew. This summer had changed me, there was no doubt about that — and I suspected I wasn't done with changing yet. I was filled with such a mixture of feelings — happy and sad, excited and terrified — and I couldn't pin anything down.

It all came out when we got home and I had a minute alone with Uncle Bob in the front room. We looked at each other, and I burst into long-suppressed sobs and threw my arms around him. "I know," I told him, when I could get my breath, "I know what answer you got. It's true, isn't it, and you're going to join that church, aren't you?"

"I have to, E. J. And I want to. Yes, honey, the Lord has made it plain to me in a way I can't deny that Joseph Smith really was a prophet, and that the book he translated from those ancient records really is scripture, just like the Bible." He held me a little away from him and wiped my face with his soft handkerchief.

"What — happened?" I asked, almost fearing to know.

"I didn't see a vision, but I did hear a voice, quite plainly, in my mind — one that I know wasn't my own. It told me that these things are true, and that the Lord has a work for me to do in his church, and that I mustn't fear to go forward and follow him. I was also told that a way would be prepared for my loved ones to see and follow the truth as well."

I stared at him. "Wow," I said softly. "Wow. And Miss Mary Afton — are you going to marry her?"

"I hope to." He smiled. "Of course, I've known that I wanted her to be my wife ever since that first afternoon when you took me to meet her."

"*Really?* I can't think of anything nicer. Except — poor Pat. She'll be so sad."

"Pat? I never gave Pat any reason to think I . . . did I?"

"I don't know — but she does. At least, I know she hopes — you know."

He frowned. "I guess I'd better have a talk with her. Anyway, she'll soon lose interest in me when it becomes public knowledge what I'm going to do. E. J., dear heart, you've more or less been with me through all this. Nobody else knows what I've decided yet, and I have to trust you to let me tell people, all right? Please don't tell Mom or Star or anyone?"

I swallowed. "All right. I won't. Um — what you said in your message today, about making changes? I think it kind of — you know — went over their heads."

He nodded. "I think so too. Well, I'll pray for the right moment and the right way to explain to everyone. And Emmy, you pray about these things too — okay? And do some more reading and studying."

"All right."

"Now, I'm going over to visit Mary. I'll trust you to keep our secret for a while longer, all right?"

I sighed, agreeing. "I'm getting real good at that," I told him. I was thrilled that Miss Mary Afton was going to be my very own aunt, a part of my family forever — and frustrated that I couldn't even tell

Star, and sorry that Pat would feel sad about it. I was awed by Uncle Bob's testimony of the truthfulness of the Book of Mormon and his plans to change churches and careers—and frightened because I didn't know what all the changes would mean. I didn't know what Granna would do, or what I would be expected to do, or what people would say and think. And what did *I* think? My head was full of my own questions. What about those Mormon temples? Were they just about families being together forever, or was there more to it, as Granna suspected? And what were their church services like, and where did they meet around here? Nobody I knew was a Mormon, except for Miss Mary Afton and the elders. And what would Uncle Bob do? Could he just sort of transfer over and become a preacher in their church?

"I declare, Emily Jean, you've been so moody and preoccupied the last while. What's on your mind?" Granna demanded on Thursday as I sat staring at my tuna sandwich.

"Oh—nothing, Granna. Just thinking."

"I wonder. It could be that you're becoming a woman. I've noticed you're beginning to develop. Have you seen any spotting in your underwear, or . . . ?"

I blushed furiously. "No, Granna, honest. It's not that. I know all about that stuff."

"Oh, you do!"

"Well, a lot about it, anyway. And I haven't started yet."

"Maybe you're just concerned about going to junior high school then. But you're a good student, Emily Jean, and if you just apply yourself, you shouldn't have any trouble."

"Yes'm. I reckon that's true. I hope so anyway." I let her think that that was what was troubling me. Funny thing—early in the summer it had been bothering me; but lately, it seemed to be the least of my worries. What I was facing now were not gentle taps to the kaleidoscope of my days. Instead, it seemed like an accelerating whirl, and the pattern never had a chance to form and settle before it changed again.

On Friday I had a letter from Zack, which pleased me greatly, because it meant he had answered back almost immediately. I took it out back and read it behind the althea bush.

Dear Couzin,

   Yes I know about the two guys who was shot in fact it was Daddy what found them. He said the one who was living had crawled over to the other and had a little bottle of oil out putting some on the dead man's head and trying to pray over him, but he couldn't get any words out on account of he was hurt so bad. Daddy said it made him plumb sick he felt so sorry for them. They was some kind of preachers or missionarys like you said, and I was real supprised to hear you knew the one that was killed, and your right—it was that road to the still where it happened, the one I showed you. Potters must of thot they was tax men. Daddy said to his mind the strangest thing was them dogs the Potters had to guard the still was just sitting by the side of the road, just as perlite as you please, and not barking nor nothing. They just wagged their tales at Daddy when he come up to help out. Them Potters aint been arrested yet because nobody knows where they got to I hope the law gets them they sure do desserve whatever punishment they get. The sheriff went in and smashed the still though. Im glad the little cat is working out for you, she was a good one I thought, and my favoright too. I caught a mess of bluegill and took some to Mrs Vesta Lincon Shes fine but kinda lonesome with Mrs Knoles gone and she said she be writing to you soon. I hate to think of going back to school soon dont you. I like summer best. Right again.
                                   Your freind (couzin)
                                   Zack Bramley

I read Zack's letter over and over and tucked it into my shirt before I went back to the house. I was dying to show it to Star. But I didn't dare, because I was too heavy with secrets I couldn't share — and explaining about the death of Elder Taylor might just lead into everything I didn't want to talk about. I knew Star wondered why I wasn't spending much time with her and probably felt hurt. But someday I'd tell her everything — that is, if she was still allowed to be friends with me when everything came out. I wondered what kind of kids there were in the Mormon church, and if I'd find any friends my age if I went there. If they were like LaRae, I didn't think I'd mind.

I prayed and prayed about the Book of Mormon and the Church, half hoping I'd get an answer and half afraid I might. I didn't seem to really get one though, just a good, interested feeling that kept me reading the book Uncle Bob had tucked under my pillow before he left Monday morning.

Friday night, Uncle Bob came home, but Rogie beat him to the driveway. We never knew when Rogie was coming. He just appeared when the notion took him, it seemed. This time he was alone and had borrowed his friend Raymond's white convertible. I heard him in the kitchen buttering Granna up for some more "capital to invest in the business." I knew Uncle Bob didn't think Granna ought to give Rogie any more money, but Granna had a hard time saying no to Rogie — she really hoped something would work out for him.

"You have to understand, Mother dear — and I'm sure you do — that in order for me to be a partner in the business, I've either got to invest capital or goods. I've tried and tried to find some really valuable antiques around here — and you've helped — but I just don't know where to turn next. People are beginning to realize the value of the old things they have, so it's getting hard to pick up any real bargains anymore. Oh, I've found a few churns and flat irons and such, but we need some bigger items, such as furniture. There's an absolute rage in the city for those big old oak pedestal tables. The trouble is, they're expensive to acquire, plus we really couldn't tuck one of those into Ray's car, could we?" He laughed. "We were hoping to make a run up into the Carolinas and Virginia — a finding trip, you know — but it would be so much more sensible if we had a truck or a van to transport our valuables in. I said to Raymond, 'My mother is the grandest jewel. She simply never fails her children when they need help, and I'm just positive she'll be able to find a way to assist us in building up our business!' "

"Well, I — certainly I want to help, Roger, but I don't think you realize how little I actually . . . "

"Brother Bob's pretty much on his own, isn't he, and earning his own way through seminary? And the brat's still pretty young — she doesn't need a lot of money for frilly stuff yet . . . "

"Roger, I don't like to hear you speak of your sister's daughter that way. It's disrespectful and unbecoming to a young man of your station and character! And Emily Jean's becoming a fine young lady. She's growing up fast and starting junior high school this month. She deserves better from you than that."

I couldn't believe my ears! After all these years, Granna was actually taking up for me! Of course, Rogie usually didn't let Granna hear his comments to me, so he must have known how she'd react even better than I. It pleased me that for once, he'd been caught and reprimanded — and right in the act of asking for money too! I listened to hear how he'd try to wriggle back into her good graces, but just then Uncle Bob arrived, whistling and carrying a huge watermelon, which he deposited on the kitchen table with a grunt of relief. I followed him into the kitchen, and he winked at me.

"Hi, Mom, Roger. How's everything? How do you like this baby?"

Granna looked dubious. "It's a bit late in the season for good melon, but that is a beauty — and so big!"

"It's probably been growing since March," Uncle Bob said.

"Well, put it in the tin washtub on the back porch and cover it with cold water," Granna told him. "We'll try it after supper."

Supper was a tense affair for me that evening, wondering when and if Uncle Bob planned to say anything about the changes coming in his life. He seemed cheerful, and both he and Rogie complimented Granna's cooking and exchanged small talk. It wasn't until the meal was over that I knew the time had come.

"Mom, E. J., leave the dishes for a while and let's go out on the front porch where it's a little cooler. I have to talk to you. Roger, you might as well hear this too."

Granna frowned, wiped her hands, and undid her apron. "Well, I don't like to let the dishes set too long, but I suppose for a few minutes . . . "

We settled onto the porch, with Granna and Rogie in the glider and Uncle Bob and I on either side of the steps. Uncle Bob leaned back against a pillar of the porch rail and clasped his hands around one knee.

"Mom, what I have to say is going to come as something of a blow to you, and I deeply regret that." He paused, frowning, seeming to search for a way to soften the impact. Cinderella wandered onto the porch and went to investigate Rogie, whom she hadn't met.

"Where did that hideous thing come from?" he demanded. "Get out of here!" He lifted her with the toe of his shoe and sent her flying.

"She's mine!" I said defensively. "And she's not hideous; she's beautiful. And don't you touch her!"

"Take it easy, honey," Uncle Bob said, scooping up Cinderella and handing her to me. "Um—Mom—I know how much you've counted on my entering the ministry and how pleased you were when I felt I had a call to do so. And I've enjoyed studying toward that end, except for a number of questions that have arisen in my mind from time to time regarding certain practices and points of doctrine that I wasn't entirely comfortable with. I wasn't sure they were compatible with the Bible teachings as I read them . . . "

Rogie broke in. "So what are you saying—that you're not going to be a preacher after all?"

Uncle Bob took a deep breath and directed his answer to Granna, who sat like a stone.

"That's right, I'm not," he said gently. "That's part of what I have to say. I have struggled with the decision all summer, Mom, and I've counseled with Pastor Welch and others, and I've prayed constantly to be led to do the Lord's will."

. . . . 335 . . . .

Granna's mouth opened, and after a second, she gave a little laugh, unbelieving of what she heard. "But, dear — you had a call, and — why would the Lord want you to do anything other than serve him? You've done so well . . . "

"What I thought was a call to the ministry was really a desire to serve the Lord in whatever way he wanted me to — wherever he wanted me to be."

"And where's that?" asked Rogie, regarding Uncle Bob with narrowed eyes. He looked resentful, and I wondered if he was angry with Uncle Bob for upsetting Granna just when he needed her attention.

Uncle Bob still looked steadily at Granna. "The Lord has made it plain to me that my place is in another church — "

"Oh, this is grand!" Rogie cut in. "A minister switching churches!"

"Another . . . church," Granna said faintly. "And Pastor Welch hasn't breathed a word . . . "

"No. He wouldn't. I asked him not to, and he's a man of his word — a good man — and understandably concerned about my decision."

"I — I don't see why our church isn't good enough. It always has been for me."

"I know, and I've loved it too. It's given me a good start in life — it, and you, and Papa. If I hadn't had such a good foundation, I might never have recognized the truth when I found it."

"The — truth. The — what is the name of this church?"

"The Church of Jesus Christ of Latter-day Saints."

"Mormons!" Granna gasped. "Robert, you'd never . . . "

I thought Granna was going to faint right there in the glider. Her head had started to wobble slightly, like a person with the palsy, and she pressed her hand to her chest. I held Cinderella to me, feeling her rapid heartbeat above my pounding one, taking comfort from her purring warmth.

"I think the problem is that we've all had some misconceptions about the so-called Mormon church," Uncle Bob continued, and I wondered how his voice stayed so calm. "All of the Latter-day Saints

I've known, in the service and elsewhere, have been outstanding Christian people, and I've wondered how a church as far off base as I'd been told it was could produce such fine members. Now that I've studied its history and doctrine and prayed about it and received my answer concerning it, I understand. As Luke points out, a good tree brings forth good fruit—right? I've learned that this is a very good tree—the best, in fact—and planted by the Lord himself. It's his *true* church, restored to earth in the same form and power it had when he first organized it in New Testament days."

"So—will you enter the ministry in that church?" Rogie asked, idly swinging the glider with his foot. Granna sat like stone.

"They don't have a paid ministry. No, I'll continue in construction work until I decide what I should do. I'm thinking of teaching, but I'm not sure at what level or what subject."

I felt sorry for Granna, seeing all her dreams crumble before her eyes. But I was also excited listening to Uncle Bob's confidence about the truth of his new church. I liked the Book of Mormon, and I had grown fond of Joseph Smith, and I wanted to know more about all of it.

Rogie laughed suddenly, and I jumped. "Well, I think it's a hoot—our strait-laced old Bobby turning into a Mormon! What a flap! The tongues will have something to wag over for many a day."

Granna gave him a look of pure reproach, but Uncle Bob didn't seem to be offended. He grinned sheepishly and said, "I'm afraid you're right, and I'm sorry to be the cause of it and of any embarrassment that comes to the family. But it's not as though I'm turning to riotous living. In fact, if you thought I was strait-laced before, just wait! I won't even be drinking coffee and tea anymore."

Granna stared at him in even deeper shock. "What in the world is wrong with coffee and tea? I mean, I know too much of either will make a body nervous, but I don't think I could get through a morning without my cup of coffee!"

"Exactly," said Uncle Bob, smiling at her. I think he was glad that she was showing some of her normal spunk and that her head had stopped shaking. "The Latter-day Saints are taught that it's best not to take anything that's harmful or addictive into their bodies. I never have had a problem with alcohol or tobacco—thanks to you, Mom—and I'm not overly fond of coffee. So all I really have to get used to is doing without my iced tea in the summer."

"I noticed you had milk with your supper," she said. "Oh, this is all so disturbing! I don't know how to take it—it doesn't make any sense to me."

"The elders are coming," I said quietly, watching the two young men in white shirts and straw hats turn the corner a block away, putting on the suit coats they carried over their arms.

"Yes, I asked them to stop by and help me answer your questions," Uncle Bob said.

"Seems like I heard about one of their sort getting shot to death up Turley way," Rogie commented. "Appears he disturbed somebody's whiskey-making operation."

"Elder Taylor," I put in. "Remember, Granna, on the day school let out, the two missionaries were here on the porch? The one with the dark hair was Elder Taylor. He got killed up in Turley, not too far from Bramley's store."

"My mercy! What do you know about all this, Emily Jean?"

"Um—not a whole lot," I answered, sorry I had spoken. I believe Granna had temporarily forgotten my presence.

Rogie couldn't miss a chance. "Oh, you can be sure Miss Nosey there knows about all there is to know. She doesn't miss much, whether it concerns her or not."

"I know a few things about you too!" I flung at him.

He ignored my remark. "Well, since it seems to be time for true confessions, I might as well say that I'm no longer officially a Baptist either. I'm a communicant of St. John's Episcopal Church in Atlanta."

"You are!" Granna's astonishment suddenly turned to sorrow. She tried valiantly to hold her head up and to keep her chin from trembling, but tears formed and fell. "I have tried. The good Lord knows I have tried to bring up my children in the church of their fathers and in a good Christian home. But what becomes of them? One goes to the Catholics—married without benefit of clergy and without the permission or blessing or even the knowledge of her family—and comes to ruin and untimely death because of it. One leaves the service of God in the ministry to become a—a Mormon! And now the youngest tells me this. How much am I expected to bear? What will *you* do to me, Emily Jean?"

I fervently hoped I didn't have to answer that right now.

"Mother, dear, you'd be pleased if you could see the quality of people at St. John's," Rogie said. "You'd want me to be there, I know it, mingling and fellowshipping with the finest families in Atlanta, hobnobbing with all the outstanding citizens and successful merchants and professional people . . . "

"Business contacts?" Uncle Bob suggested in a low voice.

"Some of them—but what of that? Do poor people have money to invest in antiques? And it's still a Christian church—a very elegant one, I might add, with the most magnificent stained glass window above the altar, and a marvelous choir! Most inspiring."

"But Roger, the doctrine—it's so close to Catholicism!"

"So? It doesn't bother me. The prayer book is nice—even eloquent in places. I enjoy it."

Granna made a little whimpering sound and shook her head, as if to clear from her ears the painful things she was hearing. "I— I thought, when I weeded that awful Chrissy Cantrell out of your life, that you'd be safe from false—"

"You what?" Rogie's expression was grave and attentive. "What about Chrissy?"

A certain fear flashed in Granna's eyes, as if she realized she had said more than she had ever intended. But then she straightened and pressed her lips together and faced him. "Yes, Roger. I was responsible for the Cantrells moving away and taking Chrissy with them. I made it plain to her father—and he agreed, of course—that your friendship with her was detrimental to the best interests of both of you. He assured me he'd see to it that you never saw her again. It was for the best."

"Chrissy," Rogie said, his voice small. "Things might have been different if . . . I thought she . . . but it was your doing, wasn't it?"

"Well, yes, it was. But I can't believe it still matters! What was she to you? She was just a wild little hoyden with no decent upbringing! She wasn't even our kind."

"And you thought it was for the best, did you?"

"Absolutely."

"Well, mother mine, you thought wrong. She was the only—" He flung himself out of the glider with a force that sent it twisting, pinging wildly and banging against its frame. Granna hung on for dear life. Cinderella sprang from my lap, dived off the porch, and crouched under Raymond's convertible, leaving twin scratches on my arm.

"I'm leaving." Rogie's voice trembled. "There's no way I can stand any more of this conversation, and I'm certainly not hanging around to listen to any whey-faced missionaries!"

"Roge, I think you owe Mom an apology," Uncle Bob began, but Roger stopped him.

"Apologize yourself, you hypocritical, self-satisfied bigot! Do you think she's exactly thrilled with your good news? I hope you roast in hell with all your Mormon friends!"

He lunged past us, down the steps, and swung himself over the door of the convertible and into the driver's seat. All I could see was Cinderella, crouched behind his right front tire. I thought she would run when the car's engine roared to life, but I didn't want to take any chances. I ran toward the car, calling the kitten and yelling to Rogie to wait a minute—but he either didn't hear or didn't care. I heard Uncle Bob calling, "Hold it, E. J.!" and Granna screaming a warning to me. But just then I saw Cinderella appear in front of the white car. I grabbed for her, but when I looked up, the enormous chrome grill of the white convertible was hurtling toward me.

. . . . 37 . . . .

At first, everything was dark. I could hear people talking to me and talking about me, but I couldn't see them, and I couldn't seem to tell them that I was conscious. I couldn't feel any pain, and I wanted to tell them so, but I couldn't feel my mouth either. In fact, I didn't feel anything at all.

"Oh, dear Lord, not this," Granna was moaning. "Not this on top of all else! What have I done? What sin has been so great for me to be punished in this way?"

"Easy, Mom," Uncle Bob soothed. "Dr. Barker's on his way."

"But she's not breathing! Do something—pray, help her, do something!"

Not breathing? Of course I was breathing. If I weren't breathing, I would be dead, wouldn't I? And if I were dead, I'd be in heaven and not just floating in this peaceful, pain-free darkness.

"Oh, dear God, please restore her to us," Granna prayed. "I beg you to forgive me if I've been too strict! I never meant it but for her own good, her own safety. Oh, Lord, I love this child! Please don't take her from me—she's everything to me."

Granna was just being silly, I thought. She ought to be able to see that I was fine. Now, even the darkness was going away, and I could see that there were more people there than I had thought. In fact, there was a whole crowd of people standing together just a little distance from me, but they didn't look as worried as Granna sounded. They were smiling, though they didn't say anything. It was strange—I could see one group of people and hear another group!

I felt drawn to the people I could see, and I tried to figure out who they were. There was a young girl with long, reddish hair tied back with a white ribbon. She nodded and smiled encouragingly at me, and the name "Ellen Jane" formed in my mind. My sister! But my sister was a baby. She shook her head slightly, still smiling. "My spirit is full-grown," she said, but not with her lips. She just sent me her thought. I gazed at her, entranced. She was lovely—fresh-cheeked and vibrantly alive and healthy-looking.

Ellen Jane stepped back a little, and another young woman in a light blue dress moved forward. She too smiled at me, almost wistfully, and I felt a great yearning toward her. The word *Mother* came to me, and I recognized her as the bride in the hidden photograph in my upstairs drawer. She was radiant and sweet, with a heart-shaped face and dark hair, and a white rosette fastened to the neck of her dress. I was so grateful that she was my mother! And if my mother was there, then—and yes, as if in answer to my unspoken question, my mother turned and motioned a man forward to stand beside her. His eyes clung to hers for a second, then he too turned to nod at me. Yes, he was my father, Francis. I knew the jaunty smile and the hint of laughter in his eyes. And behind them I saw someone I recognized immediately as the man in the bronzetone photograph on Granna's dressing table.

"Robert, do something!" Granna's voice pleaded. "Surely—there's something more—"

Uncle Bob's voice sounded exhausted and strained to the point of tears as well. "I'm doing my best, Mom, but she's still not breathing on her own. Dear Father in Heaven, help us, please! If it be thy will, wilt thou restore this child to our home? We love and need her presence. We beseech thee . . . "

I heard a murmur of voices that I thought belonged to Elder Jensen and Elder Comstock, conversing with Granna and Uncle Bob, but my attention was caught by the next person who stepped forward to smile at me—a woman, neither young nor old, with a coronet of soft reddish braids. She inclined her head, and I felt a great rush of love flow between us. "My lovie," was all she said, and I knew her.

I tried to fling myself into her arms, but she shook her head and moved back slightly.

"But I want to be with you — with all of you!" I cried out silently.

"I know, my lovie, and we want you too. But you can do more for us — and for yourself — by staying there for now. You have a life to live and a special mission to perform for us."

"I don't understand. What mission? What can I do for you?"

"Everything that we can't do for ourselves. You'll learn what to do. Elder Jensen will teach you."

"But I don't want to leave you. Wait! Where's Grandpa Knowles — are you together?"

She indicated a tall, serious young man with intelligent eyes. "We want to be," she explained. "But we can't right now."

Reluctantly but helplessly, they all began to recede slowly in different directions, as if drifting apart. "You can help," Grandmother Knowles emphasized as she faded backward. "Listen to Elder Jensen."

Then they were gone, and the beautiful, bright light that seemed to contain all the colors I had ever seen faded. I didn't even wonder how Grandmother Knowles knew Elder Jensen — it just seemed natural that she did. The darkness was back, and my attention was drawn again to the voices beside me.

"Elder, will you anoint?" asked Elder Jensen, and I felt I had to pay close attention to the words they were saying.

Elder Comstock's voice shook as he spoke and addressed me. "Sister Emily Jean Knowles, in the name of Jesus Christ and by the power of the holy Melchizedek Priesthood which we hold, we anoint your head with this oil which has been consecrated and dedicated for the healing of the sick in the household of faith."

I could hear Granna trying to stifle her sobs in the background, and then Elder Jensen's voice took over — strong, compelling, loving, and firm. I could not have disobeyed him. "Dear Sister Emily Jean Knowles, I command you to return to life and health — to be made well and to live to complete your mission upon the earth, for a special mission was given you at the time of your birth."

I opened my eyes and thought how different the dim light of

the front room was from the light I had just seen. I could feel again too, and I felt incredibly heavy. Breathing was an effort, but I had to keep doing it because Elder Jensen had to be obeyed.

"We bless you that your mind and body will heal and function normally, that all injuries will heal and leave no lasting effect — and we bless you that you will continue to be a force for good in the lives of your loved ones. We further bless you with a disposition to be obedient to those who watch over you and to be obedient to the commandments of the Lord Jesus Christ. These blessings and all others which the Lord may add, we seal upon your head in the worthy name of Jesus Christ, our Savior. Amen."

"Amen," echoed Elder Comstock and Uncle Bob and, quaveringly, Granna.

I turned my head to seek her out. "Granna," I said, my voice hoarse and dry-sounding. "I'm all right, Granna."

They were all around me at once, crying and giving thanks. Even my neighbors, Fred and Mrs. Silver, were there. When did they come? I wondered. There were even a few others from our street, hanging back a little behind Granna, Uncle Bob, and the elders.

"Oh, Lord be praised! Oh, thank you, dear Lord, for this blessing!" Granna cried, gripping my hand. "Thank you," she said stiffly, turning to Elder Jensen. "I don't pretend to understand it, but your prayer was what saved her and brought her back. I saw that."

He shook his head. "The Lord saved her through our combined faith and the power of his priesthood, which we're permitted to hold. We're just his instruments. I felt the power flowing through me — I knew she'd be all right. Welcome back, Sister Emily Jean."

He smiled at me, and I tried to smile back. My face felt as if it was stretching. It was getting easier to breathe though, more normal, and I had feeling all the way to my fingers and toes, which I could wiggle. My head and left shoulder began to ache.

"You gave us quite a scare, E. J.," Uncle Bob said, kneeling beside the sofa. His eyes were red and his voice was shaky.

"I know. I heard you say I wasn't breathing."

"You heard that?"

"Yes, but I knew I was all right. What—what about Cinderella?"

Uncle Bob smiled. "She's okay too. She sprinted out of the way. Roger didn't mean to hit you, you know. He must have put the car into a forward gear instead of reverse because he was upset."

"Where is he?"

"Well, he—left. He was so distraught. Mr. Silver volunteered to go after him."

"Elder Jensen?"

"Right here, honey. You and I will have something to write LaRae about, won't we?"

"Yes, but—" I glanced at Granna, who looked slightly puzzled. "But I have to ask you something important."

"You bet—go ahead."

"When a baby dies, is it still a baby in heaven or is its—um—spirit, or whatever, full-grown?"

He looked a little startled at the question. "Well, as I understand it, it would be full-grown, because we all grew to maturity in our spirit state as children of our Heavenly Father before he sent us to this earthly life as little babies. We used to live with him, and we hope to again after we've learned our lessons here and proved ourselves worthy of returning to him. Does that help?"

"Yep. Because I just saw my twin sister, Ellen Jane, and she was grown up—older than me—but she died right after she was born."

"Now, Emily Jean, that was just a hallucination because of the blow you took," Granna began, but Uncle Bob put his hand on her arm.

"Did you see anything else?" he asked, and I nodded, which made me dizzy. "I saw Grandmother Knowles and my mother and daddy and Grandpa Markham and Grandpa Knowles, and there were some other people kind of behind them. But I didn't have time to find out who they were because I had to come back."

Granna's gasp was audible. "William! Ellie! What—what—did your mother look like?" she whispered.

"She was so pretty, Granna! Her face was kind of heart-shaped, and she had dark, wavy hair and the sweetest smile! She was wearing a light blue dress with a little rosette kind of thing at the neck."

"Oh, my baby!" cried Granna, leaning against Uncle Bob. "That's the dress she was buried in!"

"I'd forgotten it myself," he said softly. "Honey — did any of them say anything to you?"

"Sure. I wanted to go and be with them, but they said I couldn't yet, because I had to come back and live my life and — like what Elder Jensen said — do some kind of mission or something. Only they said it first, and then he said it when he called me back. And that's another thing I have to ask him about," I added, trying to push myself up on one elbow. "Elder Jensen, they said there was something I could do for *them* that they couldn't do for themselves, and they said I should ask you what it was — that you could teach me about it. Do you know anything about that?"

Elder Jensen covered his eyes with his hand for a second, then exchanged a glance with Elder Comstock before he looked at me. "I sure do, Emily Jean. I sure do." Even though his eyes were misty, his smile was broad and confident. "As soon as you're permitted to listen, we'll tell you all about it."

I settled back and sighed, content. There were changes coming, and much I didn't understand, but for the moment that didn't seem to matter. The important thing was the wonderful feeling I had that the pattern and colors of my life were about to arrange themselves into a brilliant and meaningful design after all.